TOMORROW AGAIN

V KNOX

Library and Archives Canada Cataloging in Publication
Knox, Veronica, 1949-
'TOMORROW AGAIN' / V Knox
ISBN 978-1-7750471-5-5

Silent K Publishing
Victoria, British Columbia, Canada

www.veronicaknox.com

for **sarah** and **david**

The Egyptian hieroglyph of back-to-back lions represents the eternal moment between YESTERDAY and TOMORROW

ALSO BY V KNOX

ART HISTORY MYSTERIES

Lisabetta — a stolen glance

*Lisabetta series — books 2-4**

Adoration – Loving Botticelli

Disapp'earring Twice

Woo Woo

The Indigo Pearl

Pearl by Pearl

The Unthinkable Shoes

MAGICAL REALISM TIME-SLIP SERIES

Twinter - the first portal

Time Falls Like Snow

Tomorrow Again

*Snow Behind the Door**

POETRY

I Was There

** works-in-progress*

CONTENTS

THE STORY SO FAR

There are three generations of Stratford-Smyths 'living' in Bede Hall. The fourth is the ghost of a nine-year-old girl, which makes them four generations spanning four dimensions. Venture into the landscape of Bede and welcome. But remember… once through the first portal, you may have to stay!

Book 1 - 'TWINTER – the first portal'

Telepathic twins, Christopher (Kit) and Bathsheba (Bash) Stratford-Smyth who live in a suburb of greater London, are twelve when their Egyptologist father goes missing from his dig in Egypt.

Meanwhile, Bede Hall, a disgruntled stately home in Northumbria belonging to their grandmother, Lady Nan, is in danger and not a little angry, cruelly abandoned in its hour of need, put up for sale while its matriarch, oblivious of her old home in danger of being sold to shady developers, retreats into a fog of distracting memories.

While the Hall faces being turned it into a commercial venture or demolition, Lady Nan dreams on about a previous life she remembers in ancient Egypt.

But the Hall has no intentions of being sold without a fight. In desperation, it summons its considerable powers and orders Lady Nan to wake up and return home.

Lady Nan hears but fails to comply until the voice of her childhood playmate, a ghost child named Snow, joins the Hall's pleas. Snow lingers in a locked room in the Hall's unsettling attic 'cold spot', dubbed the Winter Room from the frosty air emanating from its blue door.

When Lady Nan regains consciousness of her vital eccentric self, she rallies her family's flagging energies in a threefold plan to save the Hall, free her lost friend, and provide a home for her daughter's grieving family.

The twins turn thirteen in chapter 3 and adapt to life in Bede by finding the Hall's resident ghost, but Kit uncovers the village of Bede's darkest secret when he spontaneously stumbles into one of several time portals in and around the Hall. Science-minded Kit denies all things supernatural that delight his sister, and dismisses the strange experiences in Bede, that inexplicably remain invisible to his parents and older brother, as hallucinations caused by the strong botanicals in the Hall's vast gardens. Determined to expose a logical cause for the bizarre local phenomena, Kit refuses to accept a time-sensitive mission until Snow forces his hand. Reluctantly he surrenders to Bede's anomalies, determined to face his destiny.

As the Hall slides towards bankruptcy, Snow hits upon a money-making scheme that leaves its shameless predators out in the cold. But a new revelation thrust upon the twins causes further sibling rivalry when they discover just how old Bede Hall is. Kit and Bash learn they are the twins prophesied in ancient times to resolve a curse lost in time.

While Bash is thrilled to embrace her legacy as holder of the mystical energy grounding the Bede landscape, Kit is horrified to discover that, as his sister's counterpart, he is the designated time traveler assigned to restore the balance of nature from a land dispute begun in Pangea.

When Lady Nan passes away she takes her place as the head ghost of Bede Hall, and in a plan to save her family's future, she recruits her grandchildren and her enchanted childhood toys: a snow globe and a brass hourglass, to help unlock the past.

Determined to prevent a natural disaster that threatens to turn the earth into a ball of blue ice orbiting the sun, the twins, unite with newfound allies from the village of Bede and several ghosts to form a team called the 'Twinters', a name comprised of the words 'twins' and 'winter'.

Book 2 - 'TIME FALLS LIKE SNOW'

It's been three years since the twins arrived to live in Bede Hall. The twins are now sixteen and Kit has had enough of the Hall's games. He has several disturbing secrets to keep and an impossible decision to make.

After the Hall makes a financial recovery from an extraordinary business venture, a new predator arrives, in the form of supernatural origins deep in Pangea's past, infinitely more bloodthirsty than a league of property developers. The twins' unsuspecting parents are taken hostage, and Bede Hall is forced to take drastic measures that require Kit to time travel further than was ever thought possible.

Book 3 - 'TOMORROW AGAIN'

Book three opens with Kit being pulled from a time portal in the Great Sphinx into a hostile Egyptian desert. Disoriented and abandoned but for the ghost of Kha, an ally he bumped into… or rather bumped *through* in the Cairo Museum.

Kit becomes apprenticed to Kha, a master alchemist, and discovers that the ancient science of alchemy is steeped in the magic he once denied. Kit must accept the challenges of becoming a full initiate in the arts of alchemy in order to rescue his parents, prevent a natural disaster, and meet the mother of his daughter, Anna, before she can be born.

While Bede Hall readies for battle on the home front, Kit gathers his dormant magical wits in the ancient land of Khem (Egypt). To accomplish his mission, Kit must visit Pangea and Mars after setting off from Egypt's eighteenth-dynasty, his home away from home, a land dedicated to chiseling facts in stone.

BEDE HALL IS ALIVE BUT ALL IS NOT WELL.

Turning sixteen hadn't been easy. Turning seventeen had been a nightmare. Unbelievably, turning eighteen tops them both.

The PREQUEL 'SNOW BEHIND THE DOOR'

Snow tells the story of her extraordinary past in 'Snow Behind the Door', a work-in-progress scheduled to be published in the spring of 2021.

PART 1

survival

EGYPT

chapter 1
I AM SOMEWHERE

Kit felt as if he'd been wandering down an endless semi-dark corridor for a week but the face of his glow in the dark watch, showed 3a.m. confirming he'd only been inside the Great Sphinx for three hours. The stale air brought back the recent unpleasant mustiness of the Cairo Museum that evoked the same unhappy odor of decaying antiquities.

His escort, Kha, had vanished. Even Kha's ghostly footsteps, that had at least been within earshot, had grown silent. Kit was alone with his thoughts that strayed to false memories of home being the sweetest safest place on earth.

He considered turning around and retracing his steps to the year 2018, if that's how time travel portals worked, which he doubted. Sadly, they didn't operate like the moving sidewalks of an airport where one could rest and glide forward without physical effort. He had to plod one step at a time where time itself was literally out of sight. Perhaps each step was a year.

Kit dismissed this concept immediately. The last thing he wanted to do was count footsteps. Best to focus on his mission to save his parents. First things first, his mentor Dr. Peregrine Brooks had advised. The planet, ticking away like a time bomb, would have to wait.

It was a strange concept to be heading backwards in time by walking forward. How long it would take to travel 3,000 years was something he dared not calculate. And, by all accounts, he was a natural calculator – a kid scientist interested in proven theories rather than adventurous pursuits involving magic and heaven knows what.

And yet, here he was, and wherever he was going, he had to keep moving.

Kit mopped his forehead with his sleeve, resting his shoulder against the Sphinx's dank interior and encountered a patch of foul-smelling mould that stuck to his T-shirt. Pushing back from it dirtied his hands. Wiping them on his shirt only compounded the fusty smell that seemed destined to stay in his nostrils forever, but three things happened in quick succession to increase his speed: an insect buzzed past his face, something tickly slithered over his foot, and the face of his watch went black.

Kha's cheery voice echoed down the passage. "Come along slow coach." His encouraging tone brightened the prospect of an exit. "Times a wasting old chap. We're almost there."

"How much further," Kit called out in a weak voice.

"A few more years," came the reply followed by a chuckle.

And what was with this Egyptian ghost, dressed in white robes who spoke like an English professor? In truth, Kha was already *there,* wherever *there* was. He was calling down the last narrow incline that led to somewhere above ground. And anywhere above ground was appealing.

Kit made a valiant effort to quicken his steps and was rewarded by a chink of sunlight and the brief glimpse of a dazzling blue sky. He reached towards the light that discharged scorching heat as Kha's hand, now adorned with wide cuffs of gold, pulled him to safety – a handshake that welcomed him into the ancient land of Khem, fresh air, and a new life.

The memory arrived again, always the same, sharp and cruel, invading at odd moments to shake Kit's confidence when he was feeling almost comfortable. Ignoring it was literally a waste of time because eventually, it pushed in. So, he let it play, allowing himself to relive the horror of choking in a stifling underground tunnel, and the first joys of freedom to move his arms that rapidly disintegrated into the horrors of blistering heat, overwhelming responsibility, and fears beyond his worst nightmares.

Kit twisted the ring fashioned from Rowan wood on his finger. It warmed immediately and purred like a kitten. Magic from home reached deep inside to comfort him – home being a year, so far in the future, that he was, effectively, living on another planet. His panic subsided enough to remember *when* he was, although arriving here might well have been a week or a year, since. He felt like a frog leaping across lily pads of time that drifted by at odd intervals to alternately confuse and inspire him.

There was no doubt in Kit's mind that time travel disrupted realities into fuzzy probabilities. Without a calendar or a working watch, time ceased to exist. At any rate, the things he once knew as hours were calculated by the position of the sun and the night constellations could no longer be trusted.

His cellphone was dead weight, and his watch had stopped ticking somewhere between Bede and the eighteenth-dynasty. Besides, there had been a glitch. He and Kha hadn't quite landed in the right time. But then, time was erratic – a dangerously unstable 'in-between' space. Not in a land time forgot but a land refusing to fade away, fiercely dedicated to chiseling facts in stone.

Kit had to admit, he was getting used to the sight of smooth white pyramids and wearing the fine linen galabeya of an apprentice alchemist, but it hadn't been easy to accept that journeys were no longer destinations reached in a straight line.

Sand was not yellow. Its subtle shades shifted with the light from silver to pinkish grey and coppery red at sunset. It had surprised him to discover that sand had a smell. It surrounded him now – a sensation of living pulsating minerals, not wholly unpleasant but with oppressive undertones of loneliness and abandonment. But then, all Kit's Egyptian emotions arrived three-dimensional without warning. He lifted his chin to catch an unexpected thrill of freshly mown grass that blew past. It was gone in a heartbeat that left him mourning his childhood, not entirely over at seventeen, such was the last four catastrophic years, too absurd to forget.

Kit reacted instinctively. He closed his eyes and breathed in the stabilizing effects of his ring – aromatherapy from the sacred groves of the Green Lady's forest in Bede, 3,000 years away. Carved from sacred rowan wood, steeped in lavender oil, and accompanied by spells under a full moon, it had been created for this very purpose. 'Use it whenever necessary, to keep a grip," Bash had said. 'We need you on your toes.' She had softened her words with a fake punch to his stomach and the share of a massive bar of chocolate, but it was obvious she had little faith in his ability to carry out a dangerous mission requiring courage and the ability to think on his feet.

Kit concentrated on his sister's face and sent the telepathic distress call that had become his regular piteous plea for help, uttered a dozen times a day. *Bash, please talk to me.'*

A shrill squawk of phantom laughter resonated near enough to make Kit swivel around expecting to see the head of a brightly colored parrot, angled accusingly towards him, eying him with unblinking authority. Words most assuredly delivered by an audible hallucination of his father's testy bird named Pigeon, that used to read his mind at the most inopportune moments according to his perverse sense of humor and his innate ability to spew offense.

"Okay Pidge," Kit said out loud to the sky. "Speak to me. I'm open. Harp away. Anything other than silence would be appreciated." In reply he heard a distinct screech and the echo of Pigeon's favourite word, *'Pooh,'* fading like smoke into the distance.

He smiled. Funny how irritating things could lift the spirit when recalled through the perspective of time travel. Bash called Pigeon irascible, but then her hobby had been pulling people up, correcting them by using fancy words, egged on by their grandmother Lady Nan. Bash's word games, for that's what they were, used to annoy him but the thought of being chastised again for his obsession with science and denial of all things magic made him smile. 'I guess that's what's meant by the good old days,' he thought.

'Bash, I'm thinking of you. If you can hear me, please say hello to the Pidge and Taraq for me. Sometimes, I can almost hear their harping voices on my shoulder. I only wish I could hear yours, and yes,

you DO harp. I didn't exactly arrive here in one piece, not if you consider having addled wits most of the time. I'm getting better. You may remember meeting Kha the last time we dream-shared, whenever that was. He says I'm stabilizing enough to begin my alchemy lessons. Don't laugh. I get how ironic it is that I will have to learn magic in order to resolve the scientific solution of waylaying a few swarms of wasps. Yes, I know, I simplify, and you amplify, which is why we should have made a perfect team. In any case, I wish you were amplifying right now so I could hear what's happening at home. I worry about those wasp swarms and Jack. And I miss you chiding me for… well, anything at the moment. Time travel is complex astrophysics. Temporal glitches are to be expected. Talk soon. Please try to concentrate.'

With a slam, a memory broke his concentration. He was back in day one… again.

Kit dropped from the Sphinx, landing on scorching sand. For an instant he lay curled in a heap like a newborn child. But a few deep breaths sent him crawling instinctively, wriggling on his stomach like a soldier to reach a safe distance from danger. He elbowed his body forward, inching his way through sand that grew increasingly painful until he rolled onto his back for relief. But the unforgiving sun had other plans.

Kit shielded his swollen eyelids from its glare, sending a further shower of the sand particles clinging to his eyelashes into his nostrils. He sneezed and wiped his eyes with a sand encrusted fingertip which made it impossible to see anything beyond his immediate future – a hazy desert horizon materializing between blinks of pain, and a voice urging him to wake-up.

He'd smiled from the realization he'd escaped a bizarre nightmare, turned over in bed to grab a few more zzzzz's, and breathed in… sand!

Thankfully, strong arms lifted him to a sitting position. Fingers pried open his mouth. A fist thumped his back until his lungs jumpstarted and heaved into action. The voice continued to pummel his shoulders. "Come on, breath," it shouted.

After a paroxysm of coughing, Kit tried to say stop, spluttering a sentence even he couldn't understand. "Breath slowly," the voice continued in a bullying tone. "Nice slow breaths. Not through your nose, through your mouth. That's it. Take your time. Shorter breaths. That's much better. Don't try to talk. No worries. You're doing fine. You'll be okay."

A bout of further thumping and instructions ensued until Kit broke free of his rescuer's First-Aid and dropped to all fours, gasping for air. Attempts to stand left him doubled over, head between his knees. From nearby he heard the voice. "Good. That's good. That's very good. Well done. First things first." Someone else had said that recently, but who?

Kit retched into the sand and gasped for breath.

"And there's the second thing out of the way," the voice chuckled. "You're moving right along."

Failing speech, Kit sat back and swiped his mouth with the back of his hand encrusted with sand. Razor sharp grains grazed his skin, grown red and sore from baking in the sun. The fresh scratches stung like insect bites, reminding him of the wasps that had killed Taraq and Anu's parents. But wasn't he Anu's father? Hadn't she reincarnated? But there were two Taraqs. One Taraq was a ghost in Bede Hall whose version of events remained hazy. The second Taraq was very much alive. Kit had named him Tut in jest for convenience sake when his parents adopted him. No, Kit thought, I am *Anna's* father... or at least I will be, someday.

Kha's mouth materialized slowly along with his barked instructions. Kit felt his shoulders being shaken. He squinted at a face only vaguely familiar. Sand coated his swollen tongue, too big for his mouth, refusing to cooperate. He coughed the name "Kha", noting grimly that parts of his body seemed to have time-traveled at different speeds. The sharp realization he was no longer on a familiar patch of planet earth, made him nauseous. The only sound he could make was a dry gurgling in his throat. Clearly, Kit's vocal cords needed to catch up to his brain.

As a science geek, Kit searched desperately to engage his cognitive functions. His brain obliged by telling him to spit out a mouthful of sand.

Kha placed a canteen of water in Kit's hands, covering them with his own to stop Kit's from shaking, and when that failed, he delivered a rough wake-up punch to Kit's shoulder. "Don't swallow," he ordered. "Rinse your mouth and spit. Three mouthfuls. Three spits. *Then* you can drink. Do *not* swallow until your mouth is clear. "When it comes to time travel, the human body isn't as together as you might expect. It's as you say about being online – a series of connections. Sit there and breathe. It will all come back to you."

Kit stared incredulous at his sand-encrusted toes. "I don't *need* it to come back," he said with surprising clarity. "It's all too apparent what happened. I made a huge mistake. Following you was stupid. There will be no more clutching at straws. I wasn't myself, but I am, now."

"You have no idea who you are," Kha muttered to himself.

"I may have even died once or twice in that revolting passage of time. And I remember everything. Being in Cairo, speaking with Madame Sphinx, and crawling through miles of cold stone with hot wind shrieking in my ears. I hate sand. I actually miss sitting on prickly dry grass. Bede grass never invaded every orifice of my body no matter how dry it was in the end."

"And the lavender?" They both knew it was a cheap shot. Kit ignored it, responding with an involuntary admission of the hallucinatory effects of Bede lavender and its invasive need to control him.

"And I remember… sounds." Kit's eyes stung with tears. "I heard my father calling me, my sister chanting from Bede, and Jack barking. I remember you pulling me further away from them." He shrugged off Kha's hands. "You're no friend of mine."

Kit took a moment to reassess Kha as he retreated under a temporary windbreak from blowing sand to check their water supply for the umpteenth time. Kha looked up and sent him a good-natured smile in spite of Kit's sniping at him like a spoiled kid.

Something puzzled Kit. Kha looked strangely familiar until Kit realized with a start that he and his half-brother, Tut, could almost pass as twins. Tut's hair was short and brushed back but Kha's blue-black hair, cut straight to his shoulders in the traditional Egyptian 'page boy' wig, made him look as if he'd stepped out of a tomb painting. Both had exotic golden tanned good looks. Both were tall and moved with the same easy grace that made him feel as clumsy as Bash had always painted him: his head in science and his two left feet mired in logic. She used to rap his forehead which was as irritating as it was painful. *'Hey, you, in there, you're missing the real world.'* – the real world, being the metaphysical bizarreness of Bede Hall that Bash referred to as natural magic. No wonder he'd hidden out, sheltered under the umbrella of science.

Rationality was Kit's stable view of a world gone mad, and always would be. Or so he thought until the reality of the Egyptian desert reduced him to a helplessly dependent child forced to accept his survival by relying on a bossy ghost with the best intentions. Kha was his *only* friend – a tour guide against a hostile environment and a vicious enemy thousands of years old.

Kha's hypnotic chocolate eyes twinkled with humor, no doubt as devastating as Tut's eyes had on the village girls, who followed him everywhere. According to Bash and her friends, Tut's shyness made him more attractive.

Kha was not remotely shy. He was confident. In fact, he exuded confidence as well as the pleasing scent of sandalwood incense and an exotic perfume Kit couldn't quite place that was, thankfully, *not* lavender. Kha had a regal authority, far above the superior attitude of entitlement commonly associated with royalty.

There had been a cat. A talking cat. Following it led to meeting Kha whose initial introduction had been formal, as if Kit had been addressed by an official ambassador of a foreign country rather than the shaman he seemed now. Kha had looked friendly from the start, considering his grim mission, and he certainly acted like a friend after he'd discharged his unhappy duty showing Kit his mummified parents. There was something trustworthy about the way Kha took control, calmly walking Kit through his initial shock. And afterwards, when Kit was forced to accept his role of time traveler that he'd denied for years, Kha handled his fears and objections with great empathy.

Kit's designer running shoes lay beside him upside down next to his lifeless cell phone. Objects that belonged in a museum.

"You are mistaken. I am your *coolest* friend," Kha said, dampening a cloth with water. He grabbed a handful of burning sand and poured it on Kit's swollen bare foot. "As you see," Kha said, "sand is *not.* You're not thinking clearly." He passed the wet cloth to Kit. "Here, pat your face slowly. Use it as a compress. You have quite a sunburn, so don't rub the skin unless you want to be covered in painful scratches." He placed a pair of crude sandals beside Kit's old shoes. "And put these on when you're ready. Your feet need to breath too."

"I've changed my mind. I want to go back. I'm aborting this mission," Kit said from under the cloth, already dry. "I'm going home, right freaking now." He peeked from under the corner of the cloth, lifted by his heavy sigh, preparing to plead his case with the Sphinx for returning home.

A volcanic outcrop of sandstone as big as Bede Hall interrupted a vista of empty sand. It offered a feeble sliver of shade as sunlight traversed its surface, giving it the appearance of an enormous sun dial. The compress fluttered to the ground.

As Kit watched, orange shadows on one side lengthened and licked the surrounding sand with an amber beam. The sun's laser sharp ray continued to sweep the desert floor in a wide arc. For a heartbeat, the hill shone brilliantly – a massive lightbulb glowing incandescent without a hint of shade until a magenta shadow emerged on its far side and embedded itself under the sand.

The sky darkened to navy blue as a million comets streaked across it leaving a puff of white streaks like the faded entrails of fireworks. The stone hill, starkly silhouetted against a starry night, remerged as a new finger of golden light played over its surface, revealing stratifications of colored rock like bands in a giant layer cake. It was awe inspiring. Like watching an eclipse.

"The sun's rays can't move that fast," Kit said. "Why am I seeing things in time-lapse photography. Did I just witness an entire day and night in ten seconds?"

"It was more like a week," Kha stated flatly. "We're catching up."

"To what?"

"To where we're supposed to be."

"Where the hell *are* we? We have to find the Sphinx. If she has any compassion she will listen to reason."

"Going back requires going forward. And *that* takes time. And as for an eclipse, duty eclipses compassion. Reasoning with a sphinx, even the Greatest one of all, is an act of futility."

"I'm not stupid," Kit said. "I will use tact and scientific persuasion."

"What part of futility do you not understand."

Pain exploded behind Kit's eyes like shards of glass. He shielded his eyes from a new enemy, Blinding light seared from above. Sweat streamed from the corners of his eyes only to dry instantly in salt crystals, puckering his skin with white wrinkles.

A fresh compress arrived as a welcome blindfold.

Kha massaged Kit's shoulders, his voice whispering gently. "Cunning and guile will be more effective here than all your charm and scientific arguments, however tactful. You're no longer in the twenty-first century," he said. "Breathe slowly in order to synchronize with the rhythms of the past. You will feel better, for it. But transitions take time."

"So you just said. Why do I have a sinking feeling we aren't on the same page."

Kha spoke as a teacher to a small child. "What I said was, going back requires going forward. Kit, we're not even reading from the same book."

"Explain."

"Observe the landscape, Kit. What do you see? More importantly, what *don't* you see?"

"I don't see the Sphinx. Which means we're somewhere else. We've landed in the wrong place."

"Incorrect. We're some *time* else."

Kit shrugged, indifferent to another lecture. "Stop playing games."

"I'm waiting for you to stabilize. I don't want to upset you while you're feeling the aftereffects of ..." Kha raised his eyebrows. "Well, the only thing to call it, is travel sickness. Except here, it's aggravated by the climate where the sun is unforgiving... and, I don't mean this as an insult, but you are a weak English kid in need of pampering. Your body is not up to harsh climate changes. Egyptian sunstroke is serious if left unchecked."

The sun threatened to fry Kit into a statue. He stretched his neck right and left until it cricked into place, flexed his muscles, completed a set of side bends, rolled his shoulders, and shook out the stiffness in his fingers. "Well, I guess I'm experiencing a truly phenomenal case of jet lag, then."

Kha smiled. "Well said, my brother. Adjustments take time."

"You're evading the bigger question. Just spit it out. I'll find out eventually."

"Eventually, is a measurement of time. I am in charge of your orientation. Translation... your stability. You must remain calm. You need to eat and drink local food and water in order to reset your metabolism. I was informed of your scientific accomplishments. I have no doubts you will eventually find this era... *fascinating*."

"Then stop speaking to me as if I'm a fragile hothouse orchid and..."

"For what I am about to tell you, my hard-headed brother, you will need to be a mighty oak with the flexibility of a date palm. I am all too mindful of your present state of vulnerability."

Kit held out his hand and waved it under Kha's nose. "See this ring, it's from a rowan tree, a sacred rowan from the Isle of Lindisfarne. It's called the portal tree because it has certain qualities related to time travel. It is ultimately stronger than an entire forest of mighty oaks. I am assured it has protective and healing properties attuned specifically to me, which I might add, were invoked with a great deal of careful hocus pocus guaranteed to serve my best interests."

"And how's that working out for you?"

Kit flailed his arms. "Is there *anything* to eat around here!"

Kha stood, legs apart, and crossed his arms. "Sustenance is on its way."

Kit gave the barren landscape a quick scan. "And could you stop acting like a genie out of a bottle. If we're to be friends…"

"We are to be brothers. We are already brothers."

"Okay then, brother Kha, enlighten me, and for goodness sake conjure up some kind of food."

"I thought you didn't want me to be a genie."

"You know perfectly well I was referring to your tendency to bully me as if you were *my* master. I think it's safe to say we're both Jacks of all trades, are we not, and therefore, master of none or each other. And now, I miss my dog, Jack. Dammit."

"Then why is *my* hair solid black and *yours* has a big streak of white in it?"

Kit looked up, slightly cross-eyed at the ever-present forelock falling into his eyes and brushed it aside with his fingers. "It's called a shock which is rather an understatement. It's a leftover reminder of the Winter Room's power after being subjected to some pretty terrible revelations." He ran his fingers through the flop of white hair that remained untamed. "The first time I time travelled, I returned home in severe distress."

"It is *not* a reminder."

Kit stared long and hard, his eyes hooded. "Then what?"

Kha shrugged with his arms open wide, suggesting his answer was a foregone conclusion. "It is a gift. A sign of the power you will need to survive here. It will set you apart in a good way. It's a gift as significant as your ring and your grandmother's hourglass. You will need all three if you are to survive. Consider your 'shock' as a warning that foreshadows the winter snow of your worst nightmares. A presentiment. In a way, it *is* a reminder, but it's much more. Each time you see yourself in a mirror you will remember your mission. Time here has a way of derailing one's train of thought. You won't have that problem."

"I think you mean if I am to save Bede, my parents, and the world.

Not necessarily in that order, you understand." Kit eyed the canteen and licked his lips. "Can I take a proper drink now?"

Kha grinned. "Go for it, my cynical little brother. Crawling through a time portal for 25,000 years is thirsty work."

Kit slurped water and wiped his mouth with the back of his hand. "And now, tell me this drastic news that will no doubt freak me out. TWENTY-FIVE-THOUSAND!"

BEDE

chapter 2
THE BOY BEHIND THE WALL

January 15, 2018

The Bede sun was as equally fierce as Kit's. The same oppressive heat that laid Kit low, bared the trees of Bede and leeched the chlorophyll from the grass. The Hall's once manicured lawns curled brown at the edges before turning the color of straw. Heatwaves shimmered from the drive like ghosts.

The topiaries crouched into a family of skeletal animals. When they stirred inside their dreams their shuffling limbs snapped and rained down broken twigs. Sage, the topiary sphinx, was the leader. A single wasp alighted on Sage's great head, droning through the open webbing of his eyes. Sage woke and shook it loose, showering bits of dried bark and dead leaves on Sable sheltering in his shadow below. Sable wrapped his squirrel tail over his nose and stirred within his happy memory of a countryside wonderland refreshed by snowflakes.

Sticky heat followed Bash all day, through her worries about Anna and Kit and the troubling effects from the lack of rain on her plants, thankfully hardier than most. Anna, frequently seen lately wearing her red snowsuit, meant she was upset. She had been missing for days. Six was on the move somewhere with Parks. Bash hadn't seen him for weeks. Not even a word from one of the field mice had reached her.

Wearily, Bash climbed the stairs to Winter Room for some relief, secretly hoping Anna would be there in her old haunting grounds but the room was empty. She propped the door open for safety and fell asleep resting her head on the soothing 'headache pillow', always refreshingly cool. She hugged her old rabbit doll, Pookie, that Anna kept on her cot when she wasn't lugging it around everywhere. Its presence was an ominous sign.

A sweet comfort filled Bash as she drifted off dreaming of Six and their pledge of a life together, but a tiny piglet chasing wolfhound Jack in her dream made alarming piggy noises. She woke, disturbed by its squeals. The small square of the attic window showed stars. She had missed dinner. And there was an important after dinner meeting. Had she missed that too? This time the squealing pig was outside.

Sage heard Bede Hall's gates squeal from the far end of the drive. He lifted his head with a warning roar, shook off a blanket of magical snow, and ran behind Kit's Saxon tower.

Bash watched him go from the small attic window on Bede Hall's third floor, knowing full well that the actual January night below was a far cry from the illusion, now visible. Had the Winter Room allowed a true representation of the grounds and countryside, it would reflect the latest in a long line of stifling nights of prolonged summer heat inflicted on Bede since July, and that the snowy lawns belied the true grass underneath, already turning into a desert of grey dust.

The plump white treeline to the south, had been scorched into black skeletons. From the ground floor they linked hands with a stark fence of desiccated oak and beech that enclosed the grounds, quite romantic, in a lace silhouetted against the moon sort of way, but a death knell for the birds' exposed nests. So, the birds had flown, and the absence of a morning chorus had become an eerily silent start to each day in Bede.

Only a single rowan tree grew green and supple, protected by the energies of Lindisfarne and the good graces of the Green Goddess. Charlotte's dwindling colony of fairies tried their best to help but with Parks away so often, it was an exhausting task.

Kit was somewhere thousands of years away, dark side of the moon which sounded friendlier than the cold science-speak – 'out of communication range'. Neither she nor Kit had anticipated their telepathic link snapping like a twig from one of Bede's bone-dry trees.

The landscape was too bleak to hold her interest now that Kit was no longer within mental hailing distance. Besides, she was late. A gathering for her benefit was already assembled in the library, awaiting her presence.

The initial wave of cool Winter Room air was always a welcome respite from the Bede heatwave – like opening a freezer door, which in a way, it was, but it never took long to chill her bones clothed in a thin summer dress, and now, a case of the shivers warned her it was time to go.

Real snow would have been a welcome restorative for her tired trees. Instead, what she saw was a lonely Christmas card scene with a crescent moon hanging like a lopsided smile over an optical illusion brought on by a bewitched room with a season of its own. Her breath turned the frosty glass, opaque. She melted a single transparent fingerprint with her index finger that formed a small peephole the size of a fairy's window framed by a spidery network of tiny ice crystals.

Bash turned away from the window and faced the Winter Room, now licked pale blue with moonlight. It had stayed true to form – a white-on-white experience reminiscent of minimalist décor. Only Anna's old cot held a new addition. Pookie, Bash's childhood toy rabbit, once brown, was now tinted ice-blue with fur the texture of cotton batten. It was Anna's now. She had left the doll in a place of honor on the 'headache pillow'. For a heartbeat, Bash thought of confiscating the pillow. Its cooling properties erased sunstroke and emotional stress. She could do with it on her own bed, what with the heat that plagued anyone who wasn't a natural son of Egypt, like her half-brother, Tut. But away from the Winter Room, the pillow's magic would fail.

"Is that you?" a voice called out.

"Anna?" Bash whispered back. "Where are you?"

Silence.

A scratching sound came from a spot above the headboard, behind the wall. Bash called louder. "Hello? I'm here to speak with Anna," she said. "Or Snow, if you prefer her other name. Who's there?"

More silence.

Bash strained to hear with her ear pressed against the wall and heard the sobs of a child. "I'm sorry you're sad. You must be the boy

Anna told me about. I expect you miss her, too. I can't find her. Do you know where she is?"

Silence followed by a deep intake of breath. "Anna is missing!" the boy exclaimed.

"She is, and I need to speak with her. It's important."

The boy's tears stopped. "Anna's missing?" he sniffled. "I must find her."

"Anna told me you were her friend," Bash said. "Look, I didn't mean to frighten you. If you see Anna, please tell her I'm looking for her. Her family is very worried. My name is Bash."

The longest silence of all indicated the boy had gone.

Bash crashed into a chair in a clumsy exit, heading for the door.

"Wait. Please don't go," the boy called out. "I know you."

An even longer pause followed.

The boy hesitated before he spoke in hushed tones. "We haven't met. I know your brother."

Bash responded instantly. "Where are you?"

A familiar voice screeched the words *'Purple Power... Winnie the Pookie... Pooh has the key.'*

"PIGEON… is that you! Crazy, parrot. Lady Nan is going to wring your neck. What are you playing at. We need you. You must come home."

"Pigeon *is* here with me," the boy said. "He has to stay."

The door blew shut with a bang, startling Bash. "And where would that be?" she said, faking a calm she didn't feel. The Winter Room played tricks when the door was closed.

Pigeon's squawk sounded further away. *'Portal Problem... Lady Nan's Plan... Pooh sticks Please Play or Pay the Price of being a Pooh.'*

"I have to go, someone's coming," the boy said. A sudden scramble of feet and wildly flapping wings sounded like the boy was leaving in some haste. Pigeon shrieked *Panic Purple... Winnie the Pooh... blustery day."*

"You're my aunt," the boy called out abruptly, and then there was a loud slam and silence as if a heavy door had closed.

"I have to go, nephew," Bash shouted into the silent wall. "Please send Pigeon home. I have pressing business, but I'll visit again, soon." She crossed back to the window with its frosted coating and scraped the word 'soon' with a fingernail.

The bedsprings creaked when she sat down. Bash ignored the time on her watch, hugged Pookie tight, and sent Kit a message. *"Kit, can you hear me? I tried using the throne and the yellow chair, but Brooks says I'm too keyed up to focus properly. I'm guessing you're a little keyed up yourself. Anyway, in case you can hear me, I'm in the Winter Room. I thought perhaps the vibes in here would make it easier to connect. Pigeon and Anna are still AWOL (no pun intended). Her friend, the mystery boy who lives behind the wall just spoke to me. But more about him later. By the way, AWOL means 'absent without leave'.*

But there's some good news. Pigeon is with him, wherever THAT is. WHENEVER that is. We're about to have a big meeting in the library with the Twice-borns. Tut is off sulking, avoiding me. I wish the two of you had made peace before you headed off. He's still jealous of you and mistrustful of me, no small thanks to Megeara. Lady Nan says he'll come round when he's ready. I hope that's soon.

We're going to need all hands on deck. Speaking of which, Six is away so we're already short one person... the most important person, actually. He and I are becoming close. I know you don't like romantic talk but he's the one. I miss him. I miss you and Mum and Dad. The Hall is restless and with all the dodgy business and emotions running high around here, I miss Tut. He's been playing silly buggers and avoiding me. Mostly, I miss the times we were a happy family together. At this rate, I'll be missing Rupert next.

Jack sends his love every day. Apparently, dogs and cats and a certain ghost pal of yours, communicate freely. Jack talks to Anubis who talks to Taraq who talks to me. Don't do anything daft. I'm running late. Time travel is natural metaphysics. Mystical phenomena are to be expected. Talk soon. Please try to concentrate.'

The expression 'running late' preceded Bash's mad dash down the rickety servants' stairs. She was in no doubt the guests assembled in the red library would wait for her, and equally certain there'd be no escaping Lady Nan's wrath. Her grandmother could never abide anyone being late when she was alive, and now ironically as a ghost, she was technically 'the *late* Beryl Stratford Smyth', and more of a strict matriarch than ever. Lady Nan had stressed the urgency of her granddaughter, the newly designated 'Mistress of the Green', making a good impression, chiding her for being a muddleheaded daydreamer. *'Young love can wait,'* Lady Nan had admonished, and Bash had replied *'But it really shouldn't have to.'* These days of heightened tension meant they stalemated often.

Zooming was no way to make a calm entrance to the most bizarre meeting of the Twinters, dubbed twice-borns for obvious reasons. Besides, emerging without warning from the servants' hidden door behind a bookshelf was startling enough. The non-invited local pack of village gossips, led by Sylvia Fox, would have called the gathering a spiritualist meeting and made disapproving faces. She could imagine them murmuring oohs and aahs in lowered voices at appropriate intervals over their teacups. In any case, they would have been partially right, the meeting *was* a gathering of spirits, hardly conjured up, considering the special guests lived *natural,* if not *normal,* shoulder-to-shoulder lives amongst the ordinary villagers. Their collective eccentricities explained away any peculiar behavior or unusual clothing, confirming Lady Nan's often repeated truism that eccentricity enhanced a multiple of virtues.

Lady Nan had explained the day before. "It's time," she'd said. "We can wait no longer. The Hall is oddly silent on the matter when I ask, and now it's left to me to rally the troops. We're at war, Bathsheba. Well, almost, at any rate. Your brother is missing, Anna may have gone after him, and if she left through the Winter Room portal she could be anywhere. It isn't stable. But then, neither is she."

Bash nodded. "It's terribly wicked of her vanishing without saying goodbye. This is one of the reasons I never want to have children." Fortunately, her grandmother had been too distracted to pick up the particular gauntlet that was an increasingly a sore spot between them.

"I wish Pigeon was here," Lady Nan grumbled. "He was my righthand spy."

Bash, on a private mission of her own and keen to avoid one of her grandmother's icy stares, concentrated on her shoes. "So, how can I help?"

But there were no forthcoming icy stares. Lady Nan was preoccupied. Too befuddled at the time to notice the signs of a dreamy granddaughter with secrets. "Luckily, we have plenty of *left*-hand spies," she said before she issued her orders. "You call Charlotte and Parks. Just say the word 'twice-borns'. Tell Taraq to find Tut. These days he's always with Peregrine. I have to go to the village." She then turned, dismissed her without a glance, and walked through the Hall's main doors, mumbling incoherently into a wall of shimmering heat. "Christopher, for goodness sake call home... Where on *earth* is Anna! Really, Pigeon, this is no time to desert us."

"You might have said please," Bash called after her.

Bash jammed the ceremonial circlet of lavender flowers on her head that Lady Nan had told her to wear and made her way to the library with it falling over her eyes. Taraq met her head-on zooming up the stairs, but there was no bumping into him because, like always, he breezed through her body and swirled around her in a mini tornado for his own amusement, the way Kit had taught him. "There you are," he said. "The natives are restless. Lady Nan sent me to find you."

"Well, here I am, as you see, so float ahead and tell them I'm on my way. I just need to ..."

"Love what you've done with your hair, by the way," Taraq said, reaching a transparent hand to straighten her lavender flowers. "Ooh, they're freezing. Three guesses as to where you've been."

"Pardon?"

"Your hair is purple, by the way. Very regal, if you don't mind me saying. Six will love it."

"What! Bash pulled a strand forward and gazed at it cross-eyed. "Okay, this is *not* good."

"Someone let the Winter Door close," Taraq chided in a singsong voice.

"Tell Lady Nan I'll be there in 'the shake of a lamb's tail'."

Taraq spoke from above, dizzy from making figure eights on the ceiling. "You know, I never *did* understand that phrase."

Bash shouted after him as he whooshed away. "Just say it, nicely. And find Tut. He's probably with Brooks."

Taraq's last words drifted lazily behind him. "You forgot to say please," he said, giggling.

chapter 3
NOTES FROM PLANET EGYPT

Barely an hour had snailed by since Kha leveled Kit with a single sentence. He'd stood behind Kit to steady his charge before pointing to the long outcrop of sandstone looming over the otherwise barren desert. "That rock formation IS the Great Sphinx," he said.

Silence ticked like a time bomb. "I don't understand."

"You're looking at the Sphinx's matrix. It hasn't been carved, yet."

Kit swayed slightly off-balance and fell to his knees. "Are you saying…"

"Yes. That we've travelled *way* back, in order to go *way* forward, later. 25,000 years as the falcon flies. And, to 'cap that little pyramid' of useful information, we have to travel WAY further than that to even come this far." At this, Kha joined Kit on his knees and spoke gently. "Do you see now, why I need to be assured of your fitness to travel?"

"And if I'm not?"

Kha squeezed Kit's shoulder. "We wait. I teach. You learn."

"I can't imagine how anything could possibly go wrong," Kit said, gawping at the mound mocking him. After some minutes, he shouldered his pack and walked over to it. He planted his sandaled feet firmly into the sand and placed both hands on the rockface. His backpack slid noiselessly to the ground as Kit leaned his forehead on the stone's weathered surface, arms outstretched clinging to shallow fingerholds, and kicked it with enough anger to show his displeasure, ever mindful of his exposed toes. A few cleansing breaths calmed him. "Madame Sphinx," he whispered, "please help me. I know you're in there."

A slight disturbance of hissing cats coming from deep within the outcrop's heart, spelled danger. But he heard a faint replay of the conversation he'd had with the Sphinx, barely hours ago, according to the clock in his tower. When he closed his eyes, he could see the blue wall-clock with no hands that Bash had given him for their thirteenth birthday.

A throaty voice corrected him. "Millenniums, dear boy," the Sphinx whispered back. Her sigh rushed through Kit like a dry wind until her words reverberated louder, the rumbling echo of an earthquake in Kit's brain. "Only time can erase misdeeds," she roared. "To find your parents and save the world you must enter another portal from which there is still no guarantee you can return. Time has a mind of its own. I ask you the same question as before. Is this acceptable?"

"Yes, Ma'am."

"You must conquer the 'rule of nine' and learn the meaning of 'time is of the essence'. You are in good hands. Listen to Sibuna. Listen to Kha. Listen to Memory. In time, I will send you an army of advisors. Test them all. Furies are tricky."

Kha rolled over in the sand, leaning on one elbow and scrutinized Kit scribbling in his ever-present logbook. "You seem busy. You must have questions. What are you thinking?"

Kit spoke without looking up from the page. "I'm thinking that I'm extremely glad I packed a couple of spiral notebooks, a box of pencils, and a pencil sharpener. I doubt papyrus and I will be intimate friends for a while, and I need to document everything. I haven't been studying science all my life for my health."

Kha made a derogatory cough in his throat. "It was *precisely* for your health and the health of everyone else."

Kit's hand paused writing and raised his eyebrows. "I take your point."

Kha drew a figure eight in the sand, idly rubbed it out, and paused to squint at the horizon. Seeing nothing, he drew the symbol of infinity again, much larger. "May I ask what you're writing," he said. As always, the unspoken title, 'Master', hovered over Kha's words in a speech bubble only Kit could see.

"It's poetry for… for someone who appreciates creative writing,"

Kit said, his voice catching. He took a deep breath. "So, I'm writing it for Bash. Maybe you can point me to the nearest mailbox."

"Sorry, I asked," Kha said, not looking remotely apologetic. "There's no need to be sarcastic."

Kit faced his friend. "Look, I haven't quite got my desert legs yet," he said, and returned to his notes. "And I *am* writing poetry. I wasn't being rude. This is how my thoughts come when I've been completely gobsmacked by things I shouldn't remotely believe in. I'm afraid serious scientific observations will have to wait until I feel grounded. Right now, my academic senses are severely compromised. This place seems more like an hallucination after walking through Bash's lavender field."

Kha stayed Kit's arm. "Are you experiencing any dizziness? I've been ordered to watch for symptoms. You're flushed and dehydrated."

"It was almost this hot in Bede when I left, but yeah, I did have water on tap, there. My insides are still reeling, so it's probably weird that I'm actually hungry."

"I'd like to hear it," Kha said.

"What?"

"Your poetry. You can read it to me on the way."

Kit checked the expanse of empty desert to the horizon. "On what way? I'm really not up for a long walk."

"We're getting a ride. We got here a little early."

"My dear brother, you do have the gift of understatement." Kit brushed drifting sand from his page, cleared his throat and read aloud: "Some stories are like my grandmother, Lady Nan's, knitted scarves," he began. "Long woolly rainbows with no way to know where they begin or end, but it's the middle sections that keeps one's neck warm. And despite the omnipresent heat of ancient Egypt, my neck feels cold. I get a sudden chill when I can't remember my homeland as clearly as I'd like."

Kha felt Kit's forehead with the back of his hand. "If you're feeling cold, you need water."

Kit clutched his notebook to his chest. "I'm a little off my game," he said. "At least this diary keeps me somewhat centered. I have a killer headache, though, if you have any Aspirin."

Kha kneeled and offered his hand to Kit. "Come on, before you're really ill. You need to take a few steps to limber up. A few callisthenics will help."

Kit ignored Kha's help and continued to address the sky. "How weird is it, that I exist somewhere between two wars with Mars. One is raging, at least it was about to rage when I left home in the year 2017. And what I do here, and I use the term 'here' loosely, will either save or destroy the earth. I remember it was Halloween when I left. How appropriate." Kit shuffled his pages and pointed to his first entry. "Yup, I wrote it down when we were in Cairo. October 31, 2017. That day was twenty-five-thousand-years away."

Kha scooped a handful of pinkish sand and let the grains run slowly through his fingers. He smoothed flat the small mound it made. "I have to tell you that two months have passed since we entered the Sphinx. Which means it's 2018."

"Well, so much for Halloween and a big Happy New Year to me," Kit whispered to himself. He glared at Kha. "I'm still only seventeen, right?"

Kha's eyes creased from his smile. "You are. For three more months… maybe. Give or take."

"I guess spirits really *do* walk the earth on All Hallows Eve. Who would have guessed… well, my sister for one, and Parks, and that witchy friend of hers, Charlotte. And probably, you as well."

Kha grabbed Kit's pencil. "And I'm confiscating this pencil and all the others until you've had a rest. I'm here to support your mission. Missions, I should say. There are a few you don't know about yet. People will die if you don't comply."

"So, no pressure, then."

"Nothing ever changes without pressure."

"You know," Kit said. "It'll probably help me to pretend I was born here in the eighteenth-dynasty during the reign of King Tutankhamen, and let the universe unfold as it should – a line often quoted, by the way, from one of Lady Nan's favorite poems, 'The Desiderata', which is a highly appropriate reference for my present circumstances, as desiderata means desired things. And my serious desire is to go home. Am I making any sense?"

"It's not the eighteenth-dynasty, but we're headed that way."

"No kidding, Sherlock."

"Come, little brother. We both require, I mean *desire*, water right now."

Kit tried to pull himself up on Kha's arm. "You never met my twin sister, Bash. She is…that is, she *will be*, a wordsmith extraordinaire. She's the recently designated 'Mistress of the Green', you know. She's charged with grounding the elemental energies at Bede Hall. It's a big job." He tried to rise and dropped back down. "I don't think I can walk."

"I did meet her," Kha said, more to himself than Kit, "but she won't remember me, Charlotte and Anna were careful to *um*… edit her experience. Please stand and do a few exercises. Nothing strenuous. Maybe move your arms in a circle and bend your knees."

"Well, she would be delighted with my reference because 'desire is a fancy word for wishes, and I wish I would wake up in Livingston to discover moving to Bede had been a silly 'chocolate dream."

"Which is?"

"Troubled dreams of nightmarish proportions that Lady Nan ascribed as the aftereffects of eating too much sugar… in particular, chocolate."

"Egyptian honey is like that… mostly when it's laced with lotus oil. A little lotus oil goes a long way. One must be careful."

"In any case, I've arrived, and to prove it, I'm here," Kit quipped, a snotty remark Rupert used to say whenever he sauntered into Bede Hall after long absences being a prig at college. Kit lay back and scrutinized the sun's position in the sky, determining the hour of the day as its zenith, automatically checking his watch. It had started ticking. "What's for lunch?"

Kha pointed to a sand cloud spiralling behind a fast-approaching chariot, heading towards them. "I'm not sure, but our ride is here. Look."

"One more minute. I need to finish this entry before I lose my mind entirely." A familiar voice brought Kit's head up. It was Bash. "KIT! Where are you? I'm stuck in the dark," Bash said, "but I feel you're close by. Can you hear me? Hello". And in a different female voice, "Please find me. I'm waiting." He listened into the heat for more. Silence… but his ring pulsated, reminding him of his mobile phone vibrating, except the band of rowan wood gave off a strong silent scent of lavender.

"Bash, I'm here," Kit shouted. "I arrived okay. I can hear you fine. But you sound different. I hope you're okay."

The wheels of a gold chariot stopped in a soundless spray of sand, briefly obscuring the fact it lacked a driver. What Kit *did* see was a magnificent blue-black horse tossing a headdress of white ostrich feathers, snorting and pawing the sand.

Kha grabbed the horse's bridle, whispering words Kit couldn't understand.

Kha turned to Kit with a formal bow. "This beautiful creature is Kephura. He brought us lunch. We'll be home by nightfall. It's best to travel after the sun has gone down. I'll be your charioteer for the evening." He reached into the chariot and retrieved a tall basket covered in a cloth of gold that he set in front of Kit. Muffled chirping sounds came from within. "I believe this is a special delivery for you." He checked the tag attached. "Your name's on it, see."

"Let me see that. It's hieroglyphics. What does it say?"

Kha's manicured fingernail traced three symbols. "This is Ki, pronounced kee, Ti pronounced tea, and Kha'at pronounced Cat."

"Then it's for someone else."

"It's the new you. KiTiKha'at. You needed an Egyptian name. And some identification."

Kit sounded out the strange letters and blanched. Who the… who gave me this name!"

A sleek black cat wearing a jeweled collar leapt from the interior of the chariot. "I did," Sibuna yowled, his meow ending in a hiss.

"You let this creature name me Kitty Cat!"

Kha ducked Kit's notebook winging over his head. "It is customary for a new teacher to give a pupil a name," he said, but he was giggling, and if it was possible for a cat to giggle, Sibuna opened his jaws and hissed a smug smile.

Bash's voice called from inside the basket. "Pooh to Pyramid Power," she said.

"Kha," Kit said. "Please tell me you don't have my sister under there. I know alchemists can play some fairly intense mind games. Wait a minute. I know that sound. It's wings flapping against the bars of a cage."

Kha smirked. "In which case, I wonder what could be under there? Some creature, you know, with wings. Maybe a parrot?"

'Pretty Present,' a familiar voice screeched from under the cloth. Kit startled for a second time. "PIGEON! How on earth."

"You say that with such conviction. Yes, Pigeon." Kha whipped off the cloth that revealed a pair of white wings, thrashing, desperate to be free. *'Pooh,'* the wings shrieked. *'Perverse Pathetic and Pitiful Pooh.'*

"I think you mean 'how on Bede', Kha said. "And by present, Pigeon means here and now and not the past."

Kit grinned. "I believe that's a foulmouthed cockatoo, you have there."

Pigeon cackled his best witch's cackle. *'Please pay particular attention to the beak, Science-boy. Tis I, a Proud albino Parrot. A symbolic carrier Pigeon who craves the sky. My native home was lovely, and hot as Egypt.... So... No more English rain or Rayne for me. But Plenty of Snow... if you get my drift, thickhead.' Get it? snow drift... a drifting spirit... a fairy Princess named something cold and white... Perchance, SNOW White.'*

"Anna?"

'Attaboy,' Pigeon squawked. *'Never forget a daughter, I always say, oh wait, you did. Which reminds me, I won't be staying. I have another arrangement, it's a case of deliver and leave you.'*

"Pigeon. What happened? You used to be so..."

'Crimson, lime green, turquoise, yellow, and purple?'

"You're all white."

'Nothing gets by you, Mr. Science. Portal Plumage, THAT'S what

happened. Purple we have in spades. Purple aplenty. It's Perfectly Plain, Science-boy. What happened to your hair?'

"You know perfectly well that the Winter Room happened."

'Bingo. Pick your Prize. A trip to Mars on colored wings or a ticket to Pangea with Kha.'

"White's the best color for Egypt," Kha chimed in handing Kit a folded cloth. "This is better than a baseball cap. I know, I know, you never wore one. I did my research. It's a figure of speech. Kind of like portal plumage. You'll look like a real pharaoh. White linen headdresses are a great leveling device. All men wear these, and you need to blend in. Not that you will with a loud white bird on your shoulder."

Kit stroked Pigeon's feathers. "He's no Horus. He likes words beginning with 'P'."

"Horus would eat this guy for breakfast," Kha said offering Pigeon a crust of bread.

'Pancakes,' Pigeon chortled to himself. *'Plenty of Plump Pancakes for breakfast… and lashings of Egyptian honey… Pooh loves honey.'*

"My brother," Kha said to Kit. "You're going to have to teach your parrot to be less mouthy in public."

Sibuna leaped gracefully onto Kha's shoulder and eyed Kit. "I believe you met Sibuna in Cairo," Kha said.

Kit caught the echo of a feline smile before Sibuna hissed and dismissed him with a flick of his tail. His jeweled collar flashed in the sun as Kha scratched his ears. Sibuna turned his head and winked at Kit. "I can read your mind, little Kitty Cat," he said without moving his mouth.

Kit recoiled. "NEVER CALL ME THAT!"

Pigeon flapped his wings, clearly startled, which triggered a noisy contest of wings against hissing fur. Kha held up his hand. "Easy, Kit. Sibuna had to test you in order to gauge your frame of mind. You simply must not react to Megeara's teasing lest she gains control over you. And be in no doubt that she *will* tease you. Be thankful that Sibuna is another of your teachers."

Sibuna and Kit had a staring match while Kha sorted through the provisions. *"And the winner is Sibuna,'* Pigeon screeched, taking off to settle his nerves.

Kha busied himself poking inside a small trunk inlaid with ivory flowers that issued sounds of clinking jars and bottles, and aromatic odors that entered Kit's nose like a swarm of bees.

"Phew! That smells like a bad chemistry experiment," Kit said.

'It is,' Pigeon cackled.

Kha set aside two gold beakers, a tiny ebony box, and a ceramic jar that contained thick foul- smelling brown liqurid. He filled both beakers to the rim. "Drink this," he said. "And swallow these. A half dozen tablets descended into Kit's hand. "They're salt tablets for dehydration. And drink *all* of that. You have a mild fever." He raised his eyebrows over his own drink in a toast. "It contains a few extra ingredients for your personal entertainment."

Kit's face puckered. "That is truly disgusting."

"It's only beer, but this," Kha said, flourishing a clear quartz crystal from the ebony box, is strong medicine for emergencies, taken only as required. It's called 'The Way of Happiness' for a reason. It's undiluted lotus perfume enhanced with crystal energy, aged for years inside hollowed out quartz shards. He twisted the seamless stopper. You can have one small whiff now to clear your head. Sniff too much, and you'll hallucinate, and there's no guarantee *what* pretty pictures *your* crazy mind will come up with. This crystal vial is for you. Treat it with respect."

"All things considered, I *may* be mildly unhinged," Kit said, downing the last of the beer. He shuddered. "We don't have to drink that every day, do we?"

Pigeon swooped low over Sibuna's head and landed clumsily on the edge of his basket. *'Beaker a day... Putrid and Pungent... Pretty Pictures... Perfumy... Positively enchanting ... Kit smells like Pooh... feeling no Pain are we?'*

One hit of the perfume and Kit dropped to his knees. He lifted his face, grinning and giggling like an idiot. "My headache's gone," he cheered, managing to stand but walking was more like reeling. He zigzagged over to the trunk. "I reckon one more little sniff will be okay. My vision is quite… *ah*… clear."

Kha eyed him through hooded lids. "Yeah, I'm glad you're feeling no pain, but you need to remember one thing about the effects of beer mixed with lotus. It makes you *feel* happy, but it doesn't *make* you happy, which is a very different state. Smiling doesn't necessarily mean you *are* happy. And until you're fully here, which you most certainly are not, and considering your present transitional phase of… *jet lag*, giggling uncontrollably for no reason is as happy as it gets right now."

'Past circumstances… Present condition. Better than nothing,' Pigeon remarked. *'Kitty's drunk.'*

Kit woke wearing a heavy gold armband engraved with several Egyptian hieroglyphs, one of them was unmistakeably a cat. He mumbled quietly to himself, still slightly dazed. "I hadn't known, and who could, that time travel was so *time* consuming. Because my life exists thousands of years in the past. Memories of my twin sister, my ass of an older brother, Rupert, and a moody half-brother who lords it over me without reason, are already fading. Bash and I called Rupert Boss."

"Not to worry. You will remember them in good time. It's early days, yet. Think of that armband as an identification bracelet. By the way, it won't come off."

"You know, I take little comfort from your dismissive references to time. But thanks for the bracelet. The terrifying notion that I have all the time in the world overrules your casual take on my present situation."

"It's no longer the present."

"How very witty. But even with *that* kind of time and your *present* attitude, I must establish my priorities. Do I save my parents, stop a volcano, fight a war, or find a magic chair that will tell me what to do?"

"You drink water, eat food, and sleep a few hours."

Kit read aloud as he wrote. "I've travelled here to remedy a mistake made thousands of years from my present 'past'. Sadly, that's as near to the truth as I can manage."

"You're gaining a distinct grasp of the matter," Kha said.

"In any case, I haven't forgotten where I'm from and what I'm here to do. Hey, where's my parrot? If you've lost my father's parrot!" His expression changed from anger to desolate. "My Dad's here, somewhere. He could be anywhere. And if the universe is unfolding as it should, I reckon I'm in big trouble."

"Not yet," Kha said, but the day's not over."

"Nice." Kit slammmed his diary closed on its latest passage. *The great sphinx disappeared yesterday and with it the time portal that brought me here. Today and tomorrow are meaningless words. Yesterday is today and today faces an endless stretch of sand into the chilliest of baking hot tomorrows.* He squinted up at the shape that was Kha, backlit by the sun. "Would it be okay if... I mean, can I have the desert for a few minutes? I need some privacy. To meditate."

"You want to connect with Bash."

"Same thing."

"I have orders not to let you out of my sight. You do know I can't hear you sending a mental message, right?" he turned away and added softly "Unless of course, I choose to."

"Do *you* know I need to keep my vibes separate from yours to be successful?"

"I didn't, but I don't think that's the reason you two are disconnected."

"I'll tune in. If we don't connect in five minutes, it isn't going to happen."

"Good luck. Just remember. There's a reason things happen, which means there's also a reason they *don't* happen, too."

Kit wriggled a comfortable hollow in the sand. Eyes closed, he imagined himself under the rowan tree the night Bash gave him his ring. The ring warmed at the thought. A good sign, but it heated up at the merest memory of Bede. Without seeing the sand, he could hear its voice. It smelled hot. Long ago this sand had been black soil. The land of Khem. The root of the modern word for chemistry. His father taught him that. Kit pictured his father's face and sent him a message even though they had never been telepathic. It made him feel good to know his father could be nearby. As unlikely as it was, he went with the image of his parents sitting in an empty room. They had food and water. They were holding hands. They even looked happy. His mother was looking at a family snapshot. Kit zoomed in on Bash's loony smile. She was always cutting up for the camera when he was the photographer. He heard himself say cheese. It was time to connect.

"Bash. Are you there? If you can hear me, know that I'm unable to hear you. Since you have the throne and the yellow chair at your disposal, it's odd that even a one-way link between us is broken. I know you're trying. I'm having a rougher time adjusting than I expected. But it's early days. The reality (such as IT is) is too real to believe without seriously believing I've gone insane. I have a guide (such as HE is) I think you may have seen him in a dream we shared in the Cairo museum. But he confessed he erased your memories to spare you suffering, so maybe not. The rowan ring is comforting (such as THAT is). I'll continue to broadcast several times a day in a running commentary of what's going on. Even if you don't hear it, it grounds me to hear my own voice. Strangeness is less strange experienced out loud. It's as if it confirms I'm sane. In that regard, I'll take anything I can get. I write my scientific observations every day, including the supernatural ones. Like there's any other kind, here. I actually felt poetic today because I was thinking of you and your obsession with perfect words. So, goodnight or good morning (whatever TIME it is) talk soon, Kit."

A meal of bread and water helped. The quartz crystal warmed in his pocket.

Kha, a good way off, examined the wheels of his chariot while Kit rested in the sunset, using his backpack as a pillow. Pigeon hopped about scattering sand everywhere, rattling on, chattering nonsense to himself. *'Pillow talk,'* he said. *'Headache pillows for whatever ails you. That's the ticket. A one-way ticket to somewhere cool.'*

"Bash sent me a present with instructions not to open it until I got here, Kit announced to Kha. "I'm guessing it's okay to open it, now. I *am* here, aren't I?"

Pigeon answered *'Dear boy. You're here, alright, and so is your dad.'*

"Where's Mum?" Kit asked. *'With your father of course,"* the parrot replied. *'We were close, so I hear his thoughts every day. Your mother has changed from her old timid self. Your father, as usual, is magnificent.'*

Kit pulled several sealed envelopes and a package wrapped in purple paper from his pack causing Pigeon to shriek *'Pack alert... Purple Paper'.*

Bash's gift was two pairs of Rupert's designer sunglasses with a note that read: *'I thought these might come in handy. The second pair is for a friend Charlotte says you will meet. She also says to go easy on your lavender capsules. It's medicine, not candy.'*

There were several more surprises but nothing from Tut. Lady Nan sent the prize turquoise scarab from his 13th birthday wrapped in a printed copy of her, oft quoted, favorite poem the 'Desiderata'. She'd scrawled 'read this every day!' across the top. Brooks sent his father's old binoculars that had seen better days scanning the very cliffs Kit could see in the distance. He checked out a small flutter of red dust on the horizon which turned out to be heatwaves. Kit read the poem silently to himself, but Pigeon flapped about and screeched the line Kit was searching for. *'No doubt the universe is unfolding as it should!'*

chapter 4
A CALL TO DISORDER

A quick look in her dressing table mirror confirmed Bash was no longer a brunette. She was pleased. Surprised that she was pleased. The purple suited her.

On a whim, she removed the stopper on Lady Nan's empty perfume bottle and inhaled a deep draught of carnation and bergamot. The smelling salts of romantic bliss tripped her brain into the land of happy thoughts. Time travel in a bottle, Lady Nan called it, and it did bring back powerful memories. Bash had joked it was Chanel no.9 because Lady Nan seemed to reside on a cloud of the same number much of the time. As always, she felt deliciously intoxicated – so much so that, in the past, others had commented how she looked lost in blissful thought.

She closed her eyes and visualized the last time she'd seen Six when he'd kissed her goodbye. The thought made her misty-eyed. That had been several yesterdays ago, and he said he would be back in three days. Will Six like my hair? She took a last look in the mirror and refreshed her lip-gloss. "Perfect pink lips complement purple hair," she said out loud to the rose quartz scarab – a gift from her father's collection on her thirteenth birthday. It seemed like a hundred years had passed since she was thirteen.

The words Pink and Purple and Perfect brought back another memory of Pigeon's obsession with 'P' words. And he'd squawked something earlier about Purple Power. As infuriating as Pigeon often was, he was insightful, so his message was likely significant. She would ask Lady Nan. Her grandmother would be pleased to know the family's parrot was nearby even if it *was* behind a wall that went nowhere.

In perverse contrast, the crown of lavender flowers she'd been wearing had turned white. Still, their scent remained strong if not stronger. And maybe, in a room full of a dozen extremely astute people, no-one would notice.

She was wrong. A collective gasp echoed around the room accompanied by smiles of approval as she stepped from behind the servants' door, masquerading as a bookshelf. Mr. Leoni beamed at her. "Caro Bash, so pleasing to see a new colorings. You are looking lost in a thought," he said.

Lady Nan stared and said nothing which meant Bash would be in trouble, later. Never mind, Six would be home soon and there would be more kisses. And he was sure to love her hair. Taraq had said so.

Outside, withered trees rattled their bones in the suffocating heat. Moonlight picked out the forms of several topiaries, coughing and shuffling out of their formal grouping, led by the newest topiary, Memory, an elephant, which was why they marched behind her in single file like pachyderms. Only Sage the topiary sphinx waited, immobile and steadfast, choking on the cloud of disturbed dust that his companion's left in their wake. Memory lifted her trunk and trumpeted to relieve the tension that had been building in Bede for eight months.

Normally triumphant, the call drifted through the open windows of Bede Hall's red library, intensifying the melancholy within where several transparent guests, dressed in distinctive attire, sipped iced tea diluted by melted ice. From their expressions, each was lost in solemn thought.

Candlelight flickered festively from the windows of the red library's darkened façade in a false glow, illuminating the walls of books inside. It was no costume party.

The table globe that traditionally dominated centerstage on the room's red carpet had been shunted to a corner, displaced by the family's treasured Egyptian throne heirloom in place of honor for Lady Nan. An old yellow kitchen chair with a thatched straw seat, faced the throne, levitating from time to time as if lifted by unseen hands. The ghosts and the living gravitated to separate sides of the room, flanking Lady Nan, seated with a magic snow globe on her lap that swirled with red snow.

Mr. S's scarab collection in the glass display case, dehydrated for three-thousand-years, jostled restlessly from lifeless inertia to whirring and unfurling their papery wings.

Tut and Bash, solidly alive, sat side-by-side on a leather sofa with wolfhound Jack draped over them, effectively cutting off the circulation in their legs. The blue tassel from the Winter Room's key protruded from Bash's fist.

The small 'petting zoo', accompanying the guests, found places to crouch under chairs and tables. In addition, a dozen honeybees buzzed the bookshelves searching behind the leatherbound books and checked the folds in the red velvet curtains for uninvited guests. Helen Peterson's pet rabbit, wearing a blue jacket, peeked out the mesh door of his personal travel case, and Beegle, Charlotte Findhorn's Java monkey, left dangerously unattended, eyed the pastry trays with keen interest.

The Hall's housecats: Unicorn, Anubis, Feathers, and Snowdrop, sniffed the perimeters of the room and fireplace for intruding vapors, fairy eavesdroppers, and Furies disguised as lumps of soot.

The family's missing parrot, Pigeon, was represented by his empty birdcage – a fact Lady Nan gravely pointed out, was a classic symbol of mortality, in keeping with the classic still-life paintings known as '*momento mori*' – the moment of death. Tut repeated the words, 'totally gruesome' from time to time, in whispers, loud enough for those nearest him to hear.

Consequently, bowls of rotting fruit had been placed in the maze and at the gates to draw the Furies' minion spies away from the Hall.

Bede Hall nattered inside Lady Nan's head. *"You can do this, Beryl. You must lead them. I need you to focus. Kit is counting on you. Anna and Pigeon may be in danger. I am unable to help you."*

Lady Nan tapped the glass ball for attention. Murmured conversations ceased. Only the bees continued to buzz.

Lady Nan raised the globe above her head and spoke. "This contained red storm is infinitely more dignified than the unleashed Furies about to blow in from the underworld. This state of affairs must be addressed. I open the floor to discussion."

Several hands went up.

"Welcome, my dears," Lady Nan said. "It's going to be a long night, so let's get started."

Dr. Brooks sent her an encouraging smile and blew her a kiss.

"Since my grandchildren need to be brought up to speed, a brief introduction is in order." The word grandchildren threw her. Kit was somewhere in time, sent on a life-threatening mission. He hadn't reported in since October, two months ago, and they were well into the new year. "I believe the tension in this room could do with relieving," she continued. "I know mine could. Vincento, my dear friend, perhaps you would go first."

An elegant old man with long white hair and an even longer beard, rose to his full height, his back as straight as a maypole, sage-like despite his odd costume of modern cargo pants, a squashed blue velvet cap, and a lab coat covered with scribbled writing. A trait the others knew to be the result of an insistent discovery in need of documenting when his notebook was full, as it invariably was. "Dear Lady. Your grandchildren are knowing me well from my chemist shop." He waved to Bash and winked. "Allo, Miss Bash. I ave not been seeing you since all this troublings. I am to say that I'm believing Mr. Pidgeoni may be with Kit. If so, we are having an especial ambassador in a place of the highest strategies. We must find, of course, a way to call him. Nick and I have been working on this *problemo*." He sent Bash a radiant smile. "Your purple hair is a being more lovely, *caro*. I like so much."

Nick Wardencliffe stood up and cleared his throat. "Vincento is correct. We are close to a solution. I hate to say it, but we need more time. And I too, concur, Bash's hair is quite lovely."

Lady Nan sat back and listened to her friends deliver their names and the growing compliments for Bash's hair. Strangely, she felt more nervous as a ghost than all her years of worrying while alive. Some present, including herself, were 'twofold ghosts' alternately solid or ethereal as their mood dictated, whimsically appearing the age they died or the age they loved best. Accordingly, old Lady Nan was often seen holding hands with her child self, Beryl the younger.

Role call included a partial count of living members: Bash, Tut, Dr. Brooks, Hannah Johns, and Sarah Goodman. Six was away on lavender business, and Kit was somewhere undercover in ancient Egypt. Charlotte and her fairies were late although Charlotte's pet monkey, Beegle, had accompanied her assistant, Hannah, much to the disgust of the remaining menagerie.

Noticeably absent were the twins' parents, the family parrot and confidante, Pigeon (and Vincento Leoni's especial friend, *Mr. Pidgeoni*), and Anna, Lady Nan's own dear childhood friend, Snow, no longer an official ghost but her great-grandchild, a comatose time-traveller in Bede Hall's future and past.

Ghosts in attendance included: three Lady Nans, Glynis Findlay (the former Charlotte Findhorn), five Stanley Parks, two Bens, one Taraq, and Unicorn the cat. Parks was there and not there at the same time, hauntingly normal for Bede.

Lady Nan's gaze came to rest briefly on Tut's anxious face, his unfocused eyes, and his fidgety hands. She frowned and returned her attention to the assembled ghosts. For a moment, she closed her eyes in meditation. The room waited. The scarabs folded their wings. The bees alighted and ceased their buzzing. Those who breathed held their breath.

A sudden flash of blue light revealed the fairy glamor of the Egyptian Queen, Ankhesenaten covering Lady Nan whose countenance appeared brighter, her voice more commanding as she sat straighter on the throne.

The Twiceborns leaned forward eagerly. Tut left the room in disgust but slunk back almost immediately, and Bash sat entranced. Her grandmother had never looked more imposing. Brooks gazed lovingly at his queen, his own Egyptian glamor flickering like a lightbulb, but he stayed Peregrine Brooks M.D., Doctor of Psychology, consort-in-waiting to Lady Nan, and mentor to Christopher Carter Stratford-Smyth, the Hall's champion time traveller. Queen Ankhesenaten sent him a signal. He held up a hand for quiet. The room was about to witness a command performance, which truth be told, was what everyone had been secretly hoping for.

EGYPT

chapter 5

LOVE AT SECOND SIGHT

"I was permitted to show you a glimpse of Sakkara in the before time," Kha said, as if that explained everything. "It was too dangerous to stay. Say goodbye, my brother. Look around. Take a picture in your mind and carry it always."

Kit turned obediently to the faceless sandstone outcrop as the sun dipped behind it. A hundred transparent men now clambered over its surface like a swarm of ants, marking the charcoal points for the chisels that would come in time: the corner of an eye, the height of an ear, and the width of an upper lip that would describe the eyes and mouth and nose of the Green God, Osiris.

"Before what?" Kit said.

"Before you persuade Pigeon to get into his basket," Kha replied. "And make sure you lash it firmly to the loops inside the chariot while I load our supplies. By the way, Pigeon has an Egyptian name, now. It's Pa'a – an homage to the letter P. My sister named him."

"They've met?"

"Pa'a has been living in the Temple of Bast for several months. SaRa has grown quite fond of him. He follows her everywhere. Drives the temple cats crazy. He's relentless."

Kit made a face. "Yeah. We've met."

Pigeon's eyes were closed when Kit offered him the open cage door. "Your basket awaits, sire. You awake?"

Pigeon ruffled his feathers with a superior attitude. *It's about time… I rather drifted off.'*

"Pigeon old friend, these days, it's always about time, Kit said."

Pigeon blinked owlishly in Kit's face and walked calmly into his cage without a peep. *'The name's Pa'a,'* he squawked. *'You may call me Papa… as in Father Time. Or not, as you choose.'*

"Well look at you. Egypt has had quite the positive effect on your temperament."

'No Pretences, me', Pigeon railed. *'But I won't be bundled... I Propose we Put our best wings forward... Poste haste.'*

Kit shook his head. "But not, I see, on your cheek threshold."

'Special delivery... handle with Proper care... 'Home Kitty,' Pigeon said.

"Between you and me, I hope that's where we're going," Kit whispered.

Kha knelt and bowed to the setting sun. The sand turned dusky orange. The stars in Orion's belt flashed on and off like a neon sign. The night sky brightened to a royal blue canopy glowing with red stars. "It's time," he said. "Hurry. We have an appointment with... with a serious...*ah*... lady, who doesn't like to be kept waiting."

Kha wrapped the leather reigns around his wrists. His muscles tensed beneath his gold armband, suddenly hot as the sun. "Sit tight. Hang on to something for dear life."

Kit sent him a pitying sidelong glance. "Very droll." He chanced a look at his own armband. No chance of it snapping from bulging muscles, there. The chariot lurched forward without warning. Kit stared at the departing Sphinx Hill until it was no longer visible, or was it Sphinx Hall, he couldn't remember which. The image of a frenzied dog team of huskies pulling a sled flashed behind his eyes. He mouthed the word 'mush'.

Pigeon shouted *'Wheeee'* in Bash's voice.

Kit heard a loud click coming from somewhere behind the moon, and the stars went out. He blacked out for only a heartbeat, rising automatically in a wobbly stance. He found his center of gravity and faced the future at Kha's side.

A freezing wind whipped Kephura to a gallop. It swirled inside the chariot, entered Kit's nostrils, and clawed at his entrails with icy fingers. Jack barked close by as if he'd cornered a rabbit. All the while, Kit's mind replayed relentless snippets – a 'Lady Nan's scarf' of lost conversations. *'Good boy, Jack, what've you got there, boy? a willow-the-wisp?'... 'Merry Christmas, Bash said, it's Tut's first snow...*

Daddy, Anna called out... where are you, Daddy?... wait for me, a girl called... wait for me... wait for me.'

Behind them, Pigeon kept up a running mumble interspersed with paroxysms of hysterical laughter. *'Lamb to the slaughter... lady in waiting... time's a wasting... kitty litter. Pooh gosh.'*

There were times Kit swore the ripples in the sand were liquid. He visualized an expanse of ocean and a school of dolphins leaping from the waves, leading Kephura on.

The desert horizon changed to a familiar winter scene from an English Christmas card sparkling with silver glitter. Pink sand. Blue snow. Pigeon screeched *'Pretty Pink... Plenty of time.'*

A blizzard materialized in Kit's peripheral vision and Kephura changed course towards it.

"Stay calm," Kha ordered. "It's only a sandstorm. Take the reigns. You've done it before, plenty of times. You don't remember, that's all. It's a muscle memory... so think back and into the future and remember."

Kit obeyed without question, steering the chariot into the storm. A vision of Jack barked madly at his side. The snow parted. They slipped through the portal into a wall of midday heat. Eighteenth-dynasty pyramids appeared like a mirage. Kit straightened his shoulders as they raced past the Great Sphinx, its head already too small for its body. "You're not as young as you used to be," he shouted to it.

"Too many facelifts," Kha shouted back. "Too many vain kings. Too much rain. Watch the reigns!"

The reigns fell slack in Kit's hands as Kephura slowed. "I can't believe you made me do that. We could have been..."

"Killed? Really Kit, what part of death do you *not* understand!"

The sandstone temple embraced the cliff behind it, blending seamlessly into its matrix – strangely modern architecture, reminiscent of the British Museum with a ramp as well as stairs.

Kit lifted the basket cage and knocked on the wicker. "Last stop. The Temple of..."

"Bast," Kha finished. "and more importantly, 'The Passage of Time' and the inner sanctum of her majesty, Bast."

"The lady we don't want to upset?"

Kha crossed his fingers behind his back in the age-old sign of protective magic. His raised eyebrows confirmed, a definitive yes. His words held the truth. "One lady at a time," he said with a guilty smile.

Pigeon blasted from his basket like a phoenix headed toward the sun screeching *'Passage... Portal'*. He circled Kit once in a victory flap and flew directly to the outstretched arm of a solitary girl waiting at the top of the ramp. Sibuna, was already sitting to her right, casually licking a paw and washing his face, oddly indifferent to the arresting approach of an overexcited parrot.

Kit inhaled a quick sniff of 'the Way of Happiness' and left Kha's side, swaggering in a stupor from the lotus perfume, appearing like a movie star in sunglasses. His outstretched arms blocked the figure of the stunning girl.

Pigeon swooped down and cackled reprimands in his ear. *'Look sharp, boy. Straighten up. What a to-do. You're acting like your misfit brother. And, speaking of brothers, back in England, 'Tut's been acting like a prune, too. He wanted to come here instead of you.'*

Kit had the cheek to reply. "I wanted that, too."

'Maybe Lady Nan was right that Rupert's sunglasses are tainted rather than tinted', Pigeon shrieked back as he returned, innocent as a dove, to the waiting girl.

An unexpected wave of déjà vu made Kit dizzy. *I know that girl. I've seen her before, but where? I can't place her. Nonsense. This place and everything that's happened is playing with my memories and fantasies. Maybe I need another whiff of happiness. I expect she reminds me of a girl I've seen in a movie.* He quickened his pace in time to catch a private wink that passed from Kha to the girl as Kha grasped both her hands. "At last," he said. "SaRa, meet my new brother, Kit. Kit, this is my sister SaRa."

SaRa sent him a gracious smile as she extended her hand, turning it at the last second as if to receive a kiss. "Any brother of Kha's is a brother of mine," she said. Her eyes misted as she searched Kit's face until, at last, she let out a deep sigh. "You found me," she said. "I've been waiting a long time. A lifetime… yours to be exact."

'Lifeline,' Pigeon shrieked. *'magic words… say Pretty Please… Pooh… special tea… specialty… drink it down… one go… welcome to happiness … day one in dolphin school.'*

"Forgive me," SaRa said. "Pa'a reminds me I have neglected my duties. May I offer you mint tea as a refreshment. It is our special recipe." Her voice changed as she lowered her lashes, "unless, of course, you prefer lotus beer."

Kit grinned sheepishly. "Reminding is Pa'a' specialty. Tea please."

'You wish… dream on… special tea… specialty… especially for me,' Pigeon cackled.

Kha stood abruptly, startling Kit by his sudden urgency. "I must see to Kephura," he said stroking Pigeon's feathers. "Be nice, Pa'a. Kit's in a state of shock." He patted Kit's shoulder and whispered in his ear. "Chin up. SaRa doesn't bite. Well, not all the time. I'll take tea with you later. Go easy on the 'Happiness'. Get a grip."

'Magic words of wisdom,' Pigeon gibbered. *'Wonderstruck… surprise Party… tea Party… it's later than you think… girls bite all the time… all the time in the world.'*

SaRa tapped the coil of Kit's notebook with a bejeweled finger. "I recognize this fence," she said. "It *was* a fence, wasn't it?"

Kit's face turned an even brighter shade of sunstroke red. "You have me at a disadvantage," he stuttered.

'Harumph,' Pigeon mumbled in Lady Nan's voice. *'Fancy that, Mr. Plod… What a surprise… gadzooks or what.'*

A blurry memory of rain on his tower roof that sounded like grains of sand thrown against his window, pushed in. Kit almost caught it, but the girl's sudden movements sent a fresh wave of her perfume wafting over him, confusing his past with her present.

"May I?" she said, opening the notebook. She tapped a blank page. "We stood there. I remember those blue lines and that red one. You called out 'who's there.'

Kit blushed himself dizzy. "It's coming back to me," he said. "You were obscured by snow."

SaRa brushed the white lock of hair from Kit's eyes. "And now you've come back to me."

Pigeon buried his head under a wing. *'I can't look,'* he chirped. *'Seriously, Pooh.'*

The image of blowing snow was unmistakable. It cleared the fog in Kit's brain. Landmarks appeared one-by-one. Faint blue parallel lines covered the ground as far as he could see. A red vertical line appeared to his left and beyond it, in front of a metal fence, ranged a row of miniature potholes, extending to the horizon. The coil binding *had* been a fence – a bright silver coil that marked the uppermost boundary of a paper landscape. The row of post holes were perforation marks. He'd been standing on a blank page of his notebook. Someone breathing close by unnerved him.

After a short walk, he'd turned to see if he'd left footprints. The snow lay pristine, but when he shouted "HELLO" the twin tracks of a toboggan appeared, heading away from him at a fast clip. It gently veered right and left as it bumped over each blue line – a clear path with an invitation to follow.

He broke the silence a second time. "Who's in here?"

The answering voice was female, her reply, simple. "I AM. Find me."

The swirling sand revealed the figure of a girl that shimmered once before it blew away as a small twister. All that remined on the white space at his feet were three hieroglyphs inscribed in black ink, enclosed in a cartouche. There was no inference of please about the message, yet it had been urgent, neither a haughty command nor a benign request, most certainly anguished, lacking any hint of an invitation, definitely a heartfelt plea.

Kit stuttered and made up a pathetic excuse on the spot. "I got the impression you were ill."

"I was. I was heartbroken," SaRa said.

"Paths don't appear unless a dreamer is meant to follow," Kit hedged. "Do they?"

SaRa answered by kissing his cheek. "Never."

· · ·

Pigeon took several agitated steps sideways and flapped his wings to clear the air. *'And didn't THAT go well,'* he screeched. *'You're quite the little heartbreaker.'*

"I think she likes me," Kit mumbled, starstruck.

Pigeon nearly fell of his perch laughing. *'Dream on little Kitty,"* he cackled. *'For goodness sake, dream big... Dream big for the sake of Pooh.'*

Even in life, Taraq appeared without making a sound. He approached Kit, eyes averted to the temple floor with something akin to awe mixed with fear. "Master," he said, placing offerings of bread and beer at Kit's feet. "My Mistress, Princess Ankhesenamun sends me with her greetings. She bids me to be of service to you. Master Kha approves. So, with their permission may my eyes meet your face?"

"Taraq old friend!" Kit shouted. "It's wonderful to see you so... so, full of life."

Taraq's instinctive response to a shout in a language he didn't understand was to back away until his back met the resistance of the nearest wall and await his punishment.

Clearly, open displays of affection unsettled Taraq. Kit remembered how he'd automatically assumed a subservient role after they met. It had taken years to become friends. "I apologize," Kit said bowing. "You don't know me. But we will be friends. That is, I hope you will accept my offer of friendship."

Taraq returned the bow. Kit saw his shoulders relax. Taraq smiled and breathed easier. "Princess Ankhesenamun said you would know me with your magic. She allows affectionate displays for my sister and I but Master Ay would kill me for making eye contact or speaking freely to my masters. Princess Ankhesenamun is like a mother to me. "

'More like a grandmother,' Kit thought. "I know your sister Anna very well. She is well?"

"My sister's name is Anu. She is attending Mistress SaRa with a message to expect a visit from the Princess."

Kit sighed at an old memory of Taraq and Anu as skeletons.

"Forgive me. I am new to your language as you are to mine. We will get along fine."

"Fine?"

"Ra will smile on us. You must trust that I will never harm you, but because of Ay and others like him we will keep our friendship secret for your safety."

"And yours, Master," Taraq said. "Master Ay has spies."

Kit blushed. "Ay is not my master. My teacher Kha informs me that Bast has forces at her command stronger than any spy. No spies will penetrate her temple without being detected. Apparently, her guardian, Babylion, will sniff out any intruders and I'm told 'Baby Lion' is always hungry. We haven't met. There are hundreds of cats with eyes that see in the dark. You won't remember them, but the small woodland animals in Bede, that's my home, were the same. They formed an underground telegraph system. They were friends of yours."

"Ay would never harm a cat," Taraq said. "Even his spies are honor bound to protect them. I have visited Bede?"

"You have. It was quite the adventure. It still is."

"You will explain telegraph to me? What is a woodland?"

"For now, others must see me as your master but in private we will be friends. I am *not* your master. There's much I can't tell you, other than we are the best of friends in the future. And you spend time with Jack, my... *um*... jackal. We call them dogs. And you polish King Tutankhamun's throne chair every day."

Taraq bowed his head at the mention of the throne. "I have seen the King's golden throne but never the King. Ay forbids this. I have only seen the King's sandals and heard his voice. Sometimes I attend him with Ay when his Majesty visits the stables." Taraq grinned, clearly proud of his extra duties as a stable hand. "I am good friends with King Tutankhamun's favorite horse, MeritRa."

Kit's first instinct was to look for Taraq on the ceiling, his default retreat for evading confrontations, but the boy looked relaxed with a dreamy smile on his face at the mention of MeritRa. "How much does Princess Ankhesenamun know about me?"

"Master Kha explained your magic is powerful and that the Aten protects you. The Princess is eager to serve you."

"She's my grandmother. I mean, one day many years from now, she *will* be."

Taraq squinted trying to understand such an impossibility. "She's a princess not much older than you, and although she's naturally willful as all royals are born to be. She will prostrate before you as Master Kha commands. And as a friend of the Aten, she will defer to your wishes."

Princess Ankhesenamun arrived amidst a flurry of feline pomp, as Sibuna led her into the sanctuary of assembled priestesses dressed in pleated white robes. Bast, a diminutive cat the same size as Feathers looked harmless for a goddess. She sat on a dais built of cushions, attended by SaRa. Bast locked fiery green eyes on Kit, opened her mouth, and swore.

Babylion, a lioness cub four times Bast's size, rose and circled Kit licking her chops. *'Careful, boy,'* she growled. *'SaRa and Kha assured us that your visit is a mission approved by the Aten, but her majesty will not allow the insults of a human within her temple walls. Do you understand?'*

Kit bowed towards Bast and knelt in submission. "Yes, Ma'am, I am sorry that I can't control my thoughts."

"Send for Kha," Bast hissed.

Kha winked at Kit and stepped forward. "I am here My Lady."

"You have an apprentice, unable to control his thoughts. Explain!"

Kha stood behind Kit, his hands on Kit's shoulders, and faced Bast as an equal. "KiTiKha'at, comes from a land where humans thoughts are private. They store their secrets in their minds. It is not meant as an insult to you. They are free inside their minds which is why they tend to retreat there for… My Lady, this is a necessary thing for KiTiKha'at's health. He means no disrespect."

"I do not hold with secret thoughts, but I understand. Tell KiTiKha'at not to fear me," Bast said. "He will harm himself with such overwhelming fears of death."

BEDE

chapter 6
THE NAME GAME

Queen Ankhesenaten raised her snow globe, turned it upside down and righted it. The room changed immediately. Light blue snow began to fall inside the library and the walls became curved glass. Anubis grew in stature and stared from outside the new wall, his face distorted by the sphere – a royal cat wearing a jeweled collar of the finest gold. The carpet was soon lost under a rising dune of warm blue sand, delighting the guests who immediately abandoned their shoes.

"Timely is a small word that covers a worldwide conspiracy of Bede secrets put in place centuries ago," Ankhesenaten announced. "The time has come to discuss new business."

Anubis batted the glass and gave it a push with his nose. His old friend, Sarah Goodman, his former owner, as if he could be owned, smiled and beckoned him inside with a pat on her knee. He meowed without making a sound and rubbed his whiskers against the glass.

"The Furies emotional tactics suggest we make a subtle counter PR move," Ankhesenaten said. "With this in mind, I propose we change the family name Stratford-Smyth to plain Smith in order to erase the social boundaries of 'them and us' that have already perpetuated years of petty jealousies. If we are to win a war with jealousy at its heart, 'we and they' must bond as allies."

She nodded to Anubis and fitted the words "come inside dear one" into her speech. "Skirmishes transparent to the rest of Britain," she continued. "Will not remain contained in our little corner of Northumbria for long. The liminal boundaries will not hold forever."

Anubis materialized inside by the fireplace and dignified his odd entrance by washing his face as if nothing out of the ordinary had happened and inspected the dry sparkly snow which made him sneeze. Snowdrop padded over. *'Daddy, can you teach me how to do that for my next lesson,'* she said.

'I didn't do anything,' Anubis replied. *'The Queen did it. Or maybe it was Bash, her magic is growing too fast for my liking. She doesn't even know when she's doing it. And, little one, I cannot recommend growing a hundred times one's size as dignified. Remember your roots. We are royal cats of the House of Bast in the black land of Khem. I lived with Sarah's rescue colony until I worked my way into the Hall. She did not find me. I found her. But I hold the old dear in high regard. She's quite selfless the way she helps our British cousins, and one must humor mere humans while in the line of duty.'*

Discovering no-one was watching, Anubis made a circuit of the room, tail held high, to assure himself he was back in charge and of the correct proportions. Sarah Goodman tugged her old friend's tail playfully as he went by. "How's my old Lucky," she crooned. "Look at you all posh with a gold necklace, eh." Anubis doubled back and licked her hand. He hadn't heard his old name in years.

Being the 'cat royale' in charge and of a suspicious nature, he sniffed each leg of the throne chair one at a time. Not satisfied all was safe, he prowled around it until its power shivered his fur into a crackle of static electricity. *'Good,'* he declared. *'Everything is in order, Ma'am. But may I suggest you have a word with your granddaughter. This sort of thing is highly irregular.'*

Without missing a beat, Ankhesenaten scooped him up and smoothed the invisible corona surrounding her guardian until he relaxed.

"If we, and by we, I mean my grandchildren," she said, absentmindedly stroking Anubis into a purring lapdog, "survive this killing heatwave, our planet is barely a year of heartbeats away from perishing under the freezing snows of a volcanic winter."

Scientist Bertie Stein, with his wild unruly mop of white hair, took the floor. "The underlying causes of dissent and rebellion are very real enemies. We do *not* need more enemies."

Dr. Peregrine Brooks rose and stood behind the throne. "The Furies fan petty resentments into physical outrage. Jealousy and anger are their weapons of choice. Envy incites rebellion and causes dissention that weakens us. Discord will never serve the war we must fight.

Fighting amongst ourselves gives the Furies an advantage." For a moment Brooks' glorious Egyptian glamor as Prince Smenkhare, flashed and vanished. "As of today, we lower our social profile and raise a silent army by erasing all slights, real or imagined. Show of hands, please."

The room was silent but for the squeaking of leather upholstery as bodies squirmed in their chairs.

Brooks surveyed the raised hands. Many held up both arms. "Motion carried," Brooks said.

Helen Peterson rose from her armchair to her full height of 4ft. 3in. "Later, I believe we should open the floor to arguments against. We must give voice to any concerns we've missed. I say we air it all and we air it now. Clean air is anathema to the Furies. We can kill them with kindness."

Professor Appleby gave a rumbly cough and took the floor. He patted his pockets for a pair of spectacles, one of the four he always carried on his person to better remember what he'd written the night before and wanted to say. Clearly, for all to see, one pair of reading glasses swung on a silver chain around his neck and another sat, more or less permanently, atop his head. He fumbled through his pockets again, noticed the dangling pince-nez swinging in front of his eyes, and affixed them to his nose. "Bede must rally," he said, without glancing at his notes, "Village and Hall must unite under the Bede banner. Most of the villagers are our allies. The others could be."

"Bash," Ankhesenaten interrupted. "Some villagers are far more than allies, which is why I've invited them to this special meeting. They've been watching you and Kit. In fact, like the professor here, sorry to interrupt Appleby, they've been charged with watching Bede Hall for a very long time. Hundreds of years in some instances."

Tut pursed his lips and crossed his arms in disgust. "Totally absurd."

The professor smiled at the queen, clearly humbled. "Ah, yes. Quite right, Your Majesty. Well said. Now where was I?"

"You were bumbling, dear," Helen Hare, formerly Peterson said.

Ankhesenaten smiled graciously at her old teacher. "Thank you

Appleby. I'm fairly bumbling myself tonight. So much to sort out. Simply put, hyphenated names are universally perceived as hoity toity. We don't happen to be snobs, but we will continue to be set apart as arrogant, all the same."

"Rupert certainly didn't help," Bash volunteered.

By now the sand reached to their knees and the snow stopped. Jack, seeing the tip of Snowdrop's tail protruding from a blue mound, dived under the warm snow and tunneled his way towards her. Unicorn, not to be left out, floated over the snow after Jack and pounced. Jack surfaced with a sneeze and shook himself in a flurry of blue sparkles. He snuffled through the whirlwind of starflakes and chased both cats as best he could, considering they'd run in different directions.

Clive Lucy stood for order. "It's not entirely their fault. A building like Bede Hall sends the clear statement herein lies wealth and privilege. So, can you blame them."

"Bede Hall was purposely created to impose its influence over the world," the Queen exclaimed. "The dawn of time isn't so far off for some of us. Millions of years ago is nothing compared to eternity. The earth had one great land mass. But Pangea's interior was soft and it yielded under pressure. Things fell apart. It was the end of the beginning time. It was the start of the ending time."

"And here we are, again," an anonymous voice said.

The room relaxed. Glasses of lukewarm iced tea clinked in camaraderie. Glynis floated towards the kitchens to fetch the Hall's silver service and fresh teacakes.

Anubis let out a yowl that indicated it was the queen's desire to speak which caused Jack to cower behind Taraq's transparent legs, whimpering. "That said," Ankhesenaten continued, "the locals insist on pronouncing our family name Smithe, assuming incorrectly, it's an elitist spelling to elicit the art of grovelling.

Hannah Clutterbuck, still wearing her wedding dress, nudged her husband and whispered. "Which they do every chance they get."

Teddy Clutterbuck patted his wife's arm. "Calm yourself, dearest. I meant to tell you that I have a new shipment of... what shall I call them? *delicacies* for Leoni and Nick, and a box of old paintings."

"I call them useless tinkerings," Hannah sniffed. "Mechanical doodads only those two inventors would want. Were there any Van Goghs amongst the paintings? Oh, you can tell me later. Lady Nan is about to perform."

Teddy squeezed his new bride's arm, an arranged signal between them that meant, *'yes, I have something wonderful for your collection.'*

Lady Nan spoke from inside Ankhesenaten, and for a moment, nine-year-old Beryl sat on the throne, her legs unable to reach the floor. Lady Nan replaced her child self in a shimmer of light as quickly as she'd come. "They name-drop to flatter us, no matter how many times we tell them how to pronounce it, and when they do, the key word 'myth' is lost in translation."

Queen Ankhesenaten's gaze swept the assembly and settled on Bill Swann.

"Bill, five-hundred-years ago, you asked 'What's in a name?' A question vital to my suggestion tonight. And then you wrote *'that which we call a rose, by any other name would smell as sweet'*, and you were right. But then, poetry usually is. This is my thinking, and please, everyone, bear with me because it may sound trivial at first airing. But a name is never inconsequential, is it Bill. Do you have anything in your second life to add that may enlighten us and hasten a solution to the extraordinary circumstances in which we find ourselves?"

Bill bowed formally. "I have majesty. I jot down my thoughts all the time. The Bede prophecy inspired me to rewrite 'the bleakest midwinter can be our finest hour'. We must make haste. Tardiness is defeat."

"I'm tired," Ankhesenaten announced. "It's nearing the time for me to pass the crown to Bathsheba." She smiled inwardly. "It's almost time to give up the ghost. And tonight, as presiding matriarch of Bede Hall, I speak from this throne for my granddaughter's benefit.

Dear Vincento, you've told me many times during my last incarnation that you're a firm believer of small beginnings that herald big changes. And we need a big change if Bede is to survive. Let no small gesture go unsaid. Bede's family name was created in layers of code for a reason."

"*Si*," Vincento replied. He stood, flourished a turquoise parrot feather from an inner pocket of his coat and waved it at the crowd. "Master Pidgeoni, he is giving me this especial gift when I am taking pictures of his flying. He tell me always to listening for his squawking. I hear him, other day. He saying is please to wait. He is seeing… please to forgive, he is saying, time, she is resetting but not to wait. Bede clocks, they run fast. In the past, they running too slow… must be same for best things to come, *comprendi?*"

Ankhesenaten clapped her hands once in approval. "It is so noted that Pigeon is your special friend. Pigeon speaks fluently in hieroglyphics, not easily translated at the best of times. Letters and hieroglyphs are pieces of a universal puzzle. Thoughts are rarely sent as the crow flies. Between the lines is always the best place to hide pertinent information. Energetic symbols are alive. Their profound truths rely on shared letters and parallel meanings, communicating in meticulous layers. Layers equal secrets – secrets written in the sacred language of twins.

And it is the nature of twins that lies at the heart of our origins. Ben and I are twins. Christopher and Bathsheba are the twins mentioned in the Bede prophecy. Bede and Cairo were once twin cities in Pangea.

The rule of nine governs reincarnation. Another name for reincarnation is time travel. The royal cats from 'the Passage of Time' within Egypt's Temple of Bast, control the time portals. Are they overseers or seers who see too far? Prophecies proclaim exacting amounts of time. Cats have nine lives. A lifeline is the combination of the words 'life' and 'feline'. Nine is an upside-down six. Six degrees of separation is a magical formula." She winked at Bash. "Parks special son is named Six. Magic is the threshold of the physical and liminal worlds. Bede is a liminal world. Time is the continual thread that binds both worlds together."

Brooks leaned down and whispered. "Are you tiring, sweeting?"

Ankhesenaten took her consort's arm with gratitude. "I can't rest now," she replied. "I must deliver this lesson for Bash." She addressed the room, once more, strengthened by Brooks' attentiveness. "Subconsciously, local villagers have deepened the intrigue by their insistence of Smithe. Smithe rhymes with scythe. Death carries a scythe." She nodded to the twice-borns side of the room. "Some of us have met Death more than once. My dearest friends. You were once alive. Yet here you are, still alive, in a manner of speaking, haunting Bede Village. Bede Hall has an old Egyptian name, does it not, Taraq. Would you please be so kind and remind us what that is."

Taraq, ever the dramatist, swooped low, silent as a barn owl from the bubble of air at the top of the snow globe, circled the library once, and returned to his post. "The house of reincarnations," he called down.

"Reincarnation is the reason our family survives," Ankhesenaten said, staring pointedly at her granddaughter.

"Survival mode doesn't get more life threatening than this," Carlton Childe piped up. "I've had overwhelming reports of nightmares and dire daydreams."

"Smyth is a visual play on the word myth," the queen said. "Accordingly, its correct pronunciation, 'Smith' delivers a corresponding auditory signature. The vibrations of both words are identical. Therefore, 'smith' and myth reflect a powerful double truth. The Smyths grew from solid square roots. Human twins are double energies who mirror the dualities of complete truth."

"If I may be so bold Ma'am," Professor Appleby interrupted. "May I say, as a mathematician, I see Bash and Kit – a magical sister and scientist brother seemingly at odds, when in reality, they embody a perfect mathematical proof – a living paradox of square roots in round holes."

Ankhesenaten opened her arms wide. "And when all is said and done, the spells invoked by white magic are merely plain words evoked with love. Invoked and evoked... do you see their subtle difference and blatant similarities, Bathsheba? Both summon. But, one suggests and the other proclaims. Such power is never a coincidence. Bathsheba, if Bede Hall teaches you anything, it's that there is no such thing as merely."

"Quite right, Ma'am," Clive Lucy shouted out.

"A myth is an historical legend. Am I right, Venerable?" Brooks said.

"I'm only an amateur historian dear Lady," the Venerable Read replied. He remained seated, leaning heavily on his lion-headed cane but nodded in deference to the golden throne, "but after filing and refiling hundreds of local records, I *can* say with certainty that history repeats itself, especially in Bede."

"The most telling part of a name is its history," Clive agreed. "It's layers of a story that never ends. At least, Bede's won't if *we* have anything to say about it."

Ankhesenaten used one of Lady Nan's favorite words which made Bash smile. "Paradoxically, legends can be *remade*. History is being made this very night. From now on, I am Beryl Smith." Lady Nan's form returned looking exhausted. Her body thinned.

A collective murmur of dissent filled the room.

"This is to be going too far," Leoni said. "You are queen. Sorry I complain for this to stay."

In the ensuing silence, colored flames leapt in the cold grate. The bees droned a soothing Gregorian chant, continuing their patrol of the bookcases. Rosie, the team's leader, signalled *'Silence. Please gather immediately'* with her feelers. The room turned eerily silent as an appointed bee zoomed low and alighted on Lady Nan's shoulder.

Lady Nan's form dimmed even more. "Honeysuckle informs me we have an uninvited guest in one of the bookcases. Anubis, we are alerted."

A slim volume slid forward from its snug place and fell in a loud crash, startling Taraq and Unicorn who dematerialized like popped balloons. Jack proceeded to run in frenzied circles, sending the settled sparkles airborne over everyone's heads, barking, until Taraq returned to smooth the hackles down his back.

A black imp emerged in a shriek and made several circuits of the room, leaving a red vapour trail in the shape of a figure eight.

Anubis executed a flying leap, caught it mid-air, and tossed it onto the fire where it let out a squeal in a yellow puff of sulphur.

Vincento Leoni, wasting no time, whipped out his camera and took a close-up of the putrid ash, noting its color and measurements on a blank space of his sleeve with a marker pen. Like a true detective, he moved on to take a series of snapshots of the now empty, previously occupied space.

"Good," Ankhesenaten said weakly, returning briefly but wavering. She nodded to Sarah and winked at Francis Fox. "Sarah's cats will leak this information to your good wife. Sylvie's grapevine is infinitely faster than a front-page headline in the Village Bead. I expect we'll be all shipshape by tomorrow lunchtime."

"Let us put our best minds to work and resolve these issues. "Where is Kit? Where is Anna? And where, on earth, is Pigeon? If, as Vincento says, he's with Kit, what is his plan? If we can be sure of anything, it's that Pigeon always has a plan. Something is missing. I ask all of you to consider every possibility. Is it a what or a who or a when? Is it a where or an awar*eness*?"

Bash raised her hand and stood. "Lady Nan! I may know," she shouted.

Lady Nan snapped back momentarily from queen to matriarch and back again.

"You can do this," Kit said in her head.

Bash swallowed and straightened her back. "That is, I *almost* know," she said in her normal speaking voice.

Anubis hissed. His jeweled collar vanished. Ankhesenaten's glamor slipped from her shoulders like a silk shroud revealing an elderly Lady Nan beaming at her granddaughter. "Well, Sheba *Smith*, it's about time," she said.

Charlotte Findhorn wrestled a stolen teacake from Beegle's monkey paw. "Well that was some meeting, kiddo. Hannah was there to represent me and Nimue gave me the fairy's version of a court transcript. For a start let me say, your grandmother takes fairy glamor to a whole new dimension. Second, I'm never going to call you Sheba. But here is an interesting 'Lady Nan kind of thing'. Sheba breaks down into two words, 'she' and 'ba'. A Ba is an Egyptian bird with a human face. Shades, no doubt, of a pigeon we know that loves to mimic human voices."

"I heard Kit. I did. I know I did," Bash repeated slurring her words. "We're connected again. Too short. Much too short. I know I heard him. A person always recognizes their brother. Especially if they're a twin."

"You're delirious."

Charlotte poured a pearly liquid from a flask and whispered something to Beegle that made him leap onto Bash's shoulder and snuggle into her hair. "It's been a long night," she said. "You seem a little tense. Drink this and listen. Now, look deeply into my eyes."

Bash complied, drowning in Charlotte's spell.

Charlotte crooned softly. "That's a good girl. Now, don't be mad. A little fairy told me you were nervous about standing up to Lady Nan, so, I sent Nimue to whisper a little encouragement in your ear. It was her voice you heard. How's the romance, by the way? I have fairy spies everywhere... in a good way. And Doolittle always has the latest scoop."

It was almost impossible to remove Beegle from Bash's hair. Almost... that was the word that had got her into trouble. "I was almost sure it was Kit," she said dreamily."

"Dear girl," Charlotte said. "Almost is the word that got you *out* of trouble."

chapter 7
MIND GAMES

18th dynasty

Kit's mind wandered to the day of his arrival, as it often did after his morning mediation. Kha said he was still processing the details as part of his training. He was, Kha repeated, to run with it, suppression being the nemesis of the laws of alchemy and visualization being a short cut to his initiation.

In any case, daydreaming of Bede felt pleasant after Kit dutifully re-experienced the first excruciating demands of sand and sun, the day he was pulled from the Great Sphinx, when Kha's orders had been shouted from far away, possibly, by the sound of them, from deep underwater.

And then he was there. Back on the Giza plateau, exhausted and flummoxed beyond reason, with an impending need to unstuff his ears and mouth from cotton wool.

Kit made a list: inside of mouth, fluffy as a cloud, eyes watering crusty tears, lips encrusted with the red salt of dried blood. Perhaps it was just as well that he couldn't see the extent of his appearance. One didn't travel thousands of years through stifling tunnels in the Great Sphinx without arriving disheveled. His mind reeled from incessant ringing or was it the phantom blows of chisels against raw stone.

A hundred fears separated themselves into individual thoughts that collided, recoiled from reality, and cancelled all rational explanations of common sense. How, why, and where, defied his advanced cognitive skills, conveniently sidestepping logic and science, ignoring the more relevant concept of 'when'.

Without the benefit of seeing his own face, Kit knew for sure that his eyes were red-rimmed, atrophied to small sore holes in a face beginning to tighten in a suffocating mask.

His clothing had almost, but not entirely, protected his back.

Kit hated the properties of sand. Cloying, clawing, invasive sand. No wonder mummies had cracked teeth. The bread was painfully gritty. Toothache was a big deal. Lotus oil, a natural anesthetic, was in great demand, almost as vital as water. Fortunately, the population was spared the agony of granulated sugar.

Rogue sand defined his new life, slowly manoeuvring into a precise order of priorities. Soon, he and Kha would be on the move. Kha's twin sister, SaRa, was a seer in the temple of Bast. Cats were everywhere, preening, grooming, watching him, ever mindful to give Pigeon's beak a wide berth. There was some tension due to royal cats *being* regally superior to birds, and parrots *feeling* a great deal more evolved and entitled than cats.

Sibuna, most of all, was constantly in his face with disparaging looks, hissing whenever he felt short in his lessons. It wasn't easy receiving instructions from a cat with a superiority complex. Even Anubis, Bede Hall's strict feline guardian and Sibuna's twin brother, hadn't been so demanding.

Kit peered nose-to-nose with Sibuna, to determine if he was sleeping. Sibuna's left eye opened imperceptibly to a slit from which a torrent of sunlight burst forth in a rainbow of colors flashing like a police siren.

"When are you going to ask me?" Kha said. "And don't give me that innocent face. You have a question for me. You've been holding on to that question ever since we met in Cairo."

"Okay okay. You're a pretty clever guy. I never questioned your communication skills. But how are you so fluent in modern English? You don't have an Egyptian accent."

Kha inclined his head and smiled. "I guess it's safe to tell you, now," he said. "You would figure it out sooner or later. I sound like a person you know well. I'm a mimic but unlike Pigeon, I don't copy voices. I copy dialects. I have borrowed the language skills of your mentor, Dr. Peregrine Brooks to make you feel at home and to better impart the knowledge you require for your mission."

"I thought I recognized him."

"And there's another part of me you may recognize. I walk the earth in Bede at the same time I'm teaching you, here. For now, that identity must remain secret. I will simply say this: subconsciously, one always knows what one doesn't know. Memories, dreams, and instincts are significant. For now, all you need to know is that I am Pharaoh Tutankhamun's appointed guardian. I am an alchemist magician of the Aten, the sun. My Pharaoh's name was and remains Tutankh*aten* in spite of being usurped by Amun powermongers. For the purposes of fitting in, we always use the king's 'amun' name. You are to be my apprentice. As of this moment, your training begins. Your initiation is necessary for the success of your mission."

"Charlotte, Parks, and Dr. Brooks have been mentoring you and Bash from the first day you moved into Bede Hall."

"This timing thing is fairly significant too, isn't it?"

"It's everything."

"I'm having trouble staying focused. My memories bounce back and forth out of sequence."

"For a time, you will experience flashbacks. It's natural. One of the hazards of time travel, I'm afraid."

"There's more than one!"

"No need to panic. But you'll need to hang on to every one of your brain cells. Our next stop will be Pangea, but only briefly. Today, our work is here in dynasty number eighteen."

"Did I volunteer? To be your apprentice? Don't get me wrong, alchemy is a science I've lately come to respect. And what precisely constitutes my initiation?"

"Sibuna will inform you of the details. He's in charge as much as me. Endeavor to become his star pupil. Everyone in the world is counting on you, so no pressure."

Kit smiled and held out his hand for Kha to shake. "For the record, I'd like to say something that bears repeating. You are clearly, no friend of mine, but I'm dead pleased to be your apprentice."

"An unfortunate choice of words, perhaps."

Kit pumped Kha's hand and pulled him close. "I chose them carefully. Tell Sibuna to watch his back. I've dealt with his brother for years. See you in class. Bring on Alchemy 101."

Pigeon batted the back of Kit's head with a wing and landed on his shoulder. *'Excuse me, Prince of pooh,'* he said. *'If you can spare a minute... outgoing message... confidential... pigeon-holed for your personal attention.... stand and deliver.'*

"Deliver please. And you needn't be so bloody cryptic all the time. Complete sentences are a fine way to communicate."

'Well... La di dah.'

"Speak now or forever hold your beak."

'Memory says, your ring knows what to do. Listen... don't argue with rowan logic... classified information.'

"Who's Memory? Or do you mean whose memory?"

Pa'a laughed a parroty laugh. *'How obscure of you. How simply opaque. You're quite ambiguous this fine Egyptian day. I say what I mean and mean what I say. I always say it's best for someone, not mentioning any names, to endeavor to hear what I mean and mean what they say.'*

"Pa'a, old chap. I'm a budding alchemist. I can turn you into a goose. Admittedly, I'm no master so the spell may backfire but that's life as a magic scientist."

'Touché, old bean. At your express command, here is the scoop in several complete sentences. *Six and Parks created an elephant topiary to honor your departure. Six named her Memory because elephants never forget. Over and out. This is a one-way message.'*

"That wasn't so hard was it."

'Paragraphs wear me out.'

"But such a resonate P word, paragraph." Kit shouted "Paragraphs Paragraphs Paragraphs," drawing the attention of Sibuna who trotted over "Do you need something, sir?"

"Please tell this silly goose to mind his manners."

"You wear me out," Sibuna hissed. "And Kha is looking for you."

BEDE

chapter 8
A VOICE OF REASON

"Think back carefully," Dr. Brooks said. "Tell us everything. Start from the beginning."

"The beginning was only an hour ago, so I think I can manage that. I went looking for Anna in the Winter Room."

The twice-borns scraped their chairs closer forward eagerly. Bash found herself the center of attention – a storyteller with a rapt audience. Mr. Leoni took out his notebook and finding the pages full, took off his lab coat and scribble on its back. Anubis jumped on Lady Nan's lap and settled into a listening position, ears perked forward, the pupils of his golden eyes, round. Snowdrop batted the bee ring softly until it buzzed huffily onto her nose where she swatted it until it zoomed away thoroughly disgruntled.

Bash closed her eyes until, in her mind's eye, she was back in the attic. "The Winter Room's blue door was just as cold as I remembered," she began. "As was the cold spot outside it. Its escutcheon plate of Jack Frost's face was just as creepy." She shuddered. "A blast of wintry air seeped from Jack's open keyhole mouth. It gave quite me a turn, no pun intended. I got the impression the room was breathing."

She opened her left hand that still held a silver snowflake-shaped key mottled with rust spots. She dangled it by its blue tassel her index finger, slowly waving it back and forth like a hypnotist.

"The door opened smoothly without so much as a click. The semi-darkness revealed a chilly interior shrouded in white. White furniture, white curtains dimly shone from the hall light. Even the inside of the blue door was white. As you may recall the Winter Room has… *um*… colorful properties. Or I should say color*less* properties. So, I purposely left the door open as a precaution against side-effects. There was a draft and it slammed shut." She touched her purple hair. "And *this* happened."

I made no pretense of stealth to disguise my being there although I am aware that I shouldn't without the Hall's permission. But there's as much of a break in our communications as my brother and I. The Hall has been overly… *um*… quiet, but there's a better word that escapes me." She glanced sideways at her grandmother with her best quizzical eyebrow face – one slightly raised. "Lady Nan?"

Lady Nan graciously inclined her head, acknowledging the game her granddaughter was playing. It had been their private pastime that Kit called snootiness and Lady Nan condoned as elegant one-upmanship. "I believe the word you're looking for is clandestine," she answered.

"Yes, of course, that's the one. My footsteps must have alerted the boy. And then I raked opened the curtains which made a scraping sound that reminded me of fingernails on a blackboard. Kit documented how sounds either intensify in there or are silenced altogether. Anyway, it made me cringe. It creeped me out."

"That's what it's supposed to do," Lady Nan said. "The Winter Door is under Parks' orders to keep people out."

"Whenever I get the chance, I peer out the window knowing full well I'll see a unique view of the grounds. I saw the grounds below as a Christmas card scene with a grouping of topiaries covered in frost like a marble sculpture garden. I looked towards the gates expecting to see a pig. I couldn't make them out through the ice fog but surprisingly I heard their hinges squeal. Sage heard it too. There was no pig. He lifted his head with a warning roar, shook off a blanket of snow, and ran behind Kit's tower. He didn't hear me, so I wrote a note in the frost."

"And that was?"

"I wrote the word 'soon'."

Lady Nan reached over and lovingly stroked her granddaughter's purple hair. "Please put the key back immediately," she said gently. "That imp in the library couldn't be the only spy. There are spies everywhere." She winked. "And not the good ones working for us.

Everyone, we meet back here in two days or sooner if there's something to report. We have to have a plan of attack. I have no intention of retreating. We will meet the Furies head on with Bede's own wrath."

Bash stayed Lady Nan's arm. "Can we talk?"

Lady Nan searched her granddaughter's face. "What's up Sheba?"

Bash's formal name, always a slap in the face out of left field, made her more determined. Lady Nan … "Something's been bothering me,"

"Then I'm glad you came to me."

"It concerns Bede Hall. It's not talking to me anymore."

"Have you considered that Bede Hall is the strong silent type? … Ah, I see you are not amused. You want a real answer."

"That would be nice."

"Right now, the Hall is overwhelmed by its past and present duties and the huge responsibilities to come. The moment that has been building for eons is upon us. He's in a state of meditation."

"HE!"

"Okay, down girl. Forget I said that. For now, 'he' is as good a description as any. But moving on, the Hall has not deserted us. IT depends on our ingenuity and loyalty. We trust we're in good hands. Your quizzicality tells me you're quizzical."

"And?"

"And, the Hall can still hear you if you feel like another one-way conversation."

"Wow! I don't expect cheap shots from you. You know, I *am* trying. We *both* are. Kit is dark side of the planet. It would be great if Bede Hall would, oh, I don't know, grow up and amplify its signal. Maybe then, Kit and I could compare notes and get this victory won."

"Did Parks tell you that?"

"Not as such. Charlotte may be privy to Parks' opinions, but as my teacher she encourages me to read the signs in the stars and leaves. But, there *are no* leaves, and the stars are hiding behind a cloud of dust, so clues are murky at best. And as designated 'Mistress of the Green' I feel I should be in the room, so to speak, privy to arcane knowledge that relates to the survival of my job as well as me. But, left to my instincts, I have to go with what I want. Hoping is too weak a word to fight on."

"How about commiserating," Lady Nan said. "Now that's a word worth shouting."

"Well done. Touché. You win. Indignance dissipated, Ma'am, or should I say your majesty."

"I detect a *trace* of indignance."

Bash broke into a smile. "You're impossible... and still my favourite thesaurus."

Lady Nan smiled back and chucked under her chin. "You're still my favorite commiserator."

Bash consulted her dictionary. Commiserator – an adept who expresses sorrow or pity well.

chapter 9
A FLASH IN THE 'PAN'

Kit preferred the evenings when the desert cooled into mauve colors. It was a time when unresolved issues raised their heads to be aired. "What year is it exactly?" he asked Kha. "I need to place myself on a timeline of some sort. And, by the way, where is the capstone of the great pyramid?"

"Well, we don't have day-planners, as such," Kha said. He pointed to the Great Pyramid, blue in the moonlight. "That's our calendar. If you can figure it out, please let me know. You will be the first. And, for your information, the capstone is in place in its astral form. You will be able to see it when you're ready. Until then, it would be wise to remember, it can see *you*."

"Please explain."

"Consider it an act of respect for the loss of Osiris, banished to the underworld – similar to a flag lowered to half mast to honor a fallen hero. Until Osiris in the guise of the Aten returns, the capstone will remain out of sight of ordinary folk. It is, however, always accessible to a magus, that is, a master alchemist. Goswold Mundi was the last great Magus of Pangea."

Kit stared hard at the top of the Great Pyramid. "Kha, can you see it?"

"I can."

Night flowers released an intoxicating scent that reminded him of Bede. He missed home. He missed Jack. The moon over Giza was the same moon he'd slept under in the good old days. Old being a redundant word for a time that hadn't happened yet. "I think I'm gonna turn in early, tonight."

"It's okay, Kit. You don't need my permission to write in your diary. In fact, it's good for you. You're homesick. Writing unlocks the mind. Unasked questions will arise. I encourage you to make a list."

Kit took a deep breath to stop from blubbing like a girl "You know, I think I may be getting a decent tan," he said. "See you in the morning."

THE DIARY

I feel like a kid who wants his mum. Homesickness is not a good feeling. I can't seem to shake

it. Maybe I'm moonstruck. Evenings are the best time to indulge in memoir. Feeling sorry for myself is a morning thing.

Dad once told me the Inuit have a hundred names for snow. I have a hundred names for sand. No wonder, since I'm suffocating in a vast landscape of scorching hot stone crystals.

Dualities are worshipped here. Light/dark, wet/dry, and mostly hot/cold. Kha says all contradictions are the basis for the chemistry of life, alchemy being the chemistry of magic and the father of modern science. Sometimes he calls me an oxymoron to make me laugh. I don't laugh much.

Neither extreme, molten sand or frigid ice are forgiving. Sand vs snow. Some choice for a planet to die.

Kha's been to Pangea and is about to take me there. He says, Pangea was a time of lush green forests with rainfall twice a day at an hour appointed by a magus, another name for alchemists. Sand was unimaginable to them. He says Pangea's climate was similar to Egypt's before the cursed desert-age came. Shades of the Bede Prophecy are everywhere. Substitute snow for sand and voila – no more habitable planet. The only exceptions are Martian wasps that can withstand below zero and molten lava temperatures. So, there we have it. I am to explore environments of liquid stone in order to prevent one of frigid ice caps.

Bede's inglorious summer of 2017 pushed me here. It's unnerving to think the winter of my family's hardest times is yet to be. It could not, under my present circumstances, be described as fast approaching. It will occur in three-thousand-years as Horus flies… as Kha and I are about to fly. As if a sprint from 2018 to the eighteenth-dynasty was a mere stroll. Kha says there's no such thing as mere when it comes to bending time. For a time traveler, it's more like leaping into a frying pan from the fire. The threat of heat is everywhere. The sun is unrelenting. Life during the day is insufferable but even more so for the stone workers who work in back-to-back shifts digging tombs and cutting stone in the quarries.

My daily ritual begins and ends with guided meditations. Kha and I greet the sunrise on the roof of the temple. Afterwards, my appointed guide, Kha's sister, SaRa, escorts me to the workshop. She leaves me at the door where Sibuna takes control of me with his favorite insult 'Cat still got your tongue, little Kitty?'

Ironically, the temple is a perpetual summer school, as is the climate here, bereft of any cold season remotely akin to the mildest version of an English winter, and I left Bede in the grip of an eternal summer that threatened to blight the landscape as well as our family tree. This school stands between deforesting Bede or saving all the trees of Earth. I was brave enough to ask questions yesterday. No small deal when you consider my questions are reported to the Goddess Bast herself – a house cat the size of a brontosaurus. Intimidating but oddly comforting and approachable. I think she's my substitute mother for the time being.

'For the time being'. Four words so easy to write and so difficult to digest. Tonight, my thoughts are what Bash would describe as maudlin. She always knows the perfect word for any situation. One of the last things she said to me was to 'get a grip'. Some days that's easier said than done. Maudlin extends from real pain and suffering. And tonight, I'm just a kid missing his dog.

The Temple of Bast is a conglomerate of time portals that I'm not allowed to explore without Sibuna, a cat who despises me. SaRa is older than me, which is disconcerting. But here's the weird thing… she makes *me* feel older, and so I feel well-matched. Feeling confident in the daytime falls apart at night when there's just me and this notebook. Happily, the pages soak up a lot of my fears. And so, I steam on in the unbearable heat. I can almost hear my grandmother lecturing me on the parallels of steam vs. the loss of self-esteem – something easy to lose when steamed up over a pretty girl.

I caught a glimpse of myself in a bronze mirror. I'm taller, more filled out. The time portal must have altered me. I have to admit, I like this new me. It comes with a degree of unexpected confidence… something that comes in handy when studying at the feet of a giant cat.

SaRa is fascinated by my forelock of white hair. I catch her looking at it when she thinks I'm daydreaming. I am mesmerized by her catlike eyes and grace.

I rely on the rowan twig bequeathed to me as a talisman. Egypt seems to have energized it. It sings to me, by which, I mean it makes humming noises and coughs from time-to-time to get my attention. When I get myself into a dither, I can hear the soothing sound of the rowan tree's branches gently creaking in the Bede wind. I consider it a lullaby because I'm a baby when it comes to the thought of more time travel.

There are many distractions here, and the rowan twig constantly reminds me to hold the image of Bede Hall in my mind. So far, telepathy with Bash has flopped, so I'm hoping the rowan tree that sacrificed this amulet, can speak for me. Bash always could speak with trees. She is the holder of the green energy although I doubt that she's fully aware of her responsibility which, from this great distance, is now obvious to me. She speaks fluent lavender, rowan, and a few other elemental languages I used to chastise her for, before I began talking with cats.

I must get to Tut's throne to speak with her. It's the same one as mine, in Bede. How it made its way into our family as an heirloom is yet to be determined. Uncle Ben inherited it as I did. I only know that twin chairs are our best chance to communicate.

The temple abounds with hundreds of royal cats. And if I once thought English cats were precocious, they're nothing compared to the feline princes and princesses I have to contend with.

Tomorrow is my second audience with Bast. I've been briefed by

Kha. There are royal guidelines. I am to listen and refrain from chit chat. As if I'm likely to engage in small talk with a cat who could swat me from here to the moon if she has a mind to.

The good news is, my audience will be strictly timed to nine minutes, so I should be able to survive without completely dishonoring myself. It's patently clear that honor among cats is no small matter here.

DESTINY MEETS POWER

Bast's ears twitched once and lay flat. It meant she was about to deliver a no-nonsense rule. Her neck collarette sparkled as she lowered her head. But her voice echoed inside Kit's skull. "Very soon, you will meet some of your ancestors. Do you understand?"

"Yes, Ma'am, your majesty."

"Please remember, some of them have no prior knowledge of you and it's vital they fulfil their lives without changing history."

"The prime directive is familiar to me. I shall be discreet – a stranger passing through time, and no more."

"You must be disciplined. Kha and SaRa know the future… all the temple cats do, but be aware, you are only a guest here. My acknowledgement of you guarantees your safety inside the royal compounds. You will be introduced as my respected guest – a magician from a far distant land."

Kit sat in a meditative pose of contemplation, his mouth leaning on his interlocked fingers. Lady Nan's hourglass rested beside him. He raised his head and nodded. "Better to tell the truth. It's easier to remember."

The temple reverberated with earthquake-like shocks as Bast thumped her tail once for silence. "My priests and priestesses roam freely in all the royal palaces. They can be recognized by their jewelry. The males wear golden collarettes. The females wear golden earrings. Consider them your brothers and sisters." She purred at that – a sound that vibrated the walls of her inner sanctum like a jet engine before take-off. "Mind your back, Kittycat. I believe you know a thing about sibling rivalry."

The hourglass's snow swirled in a tiny red cyclone, sucked up through the narrow opening. Kit's face flushed with embarrassment. "You're laughing at me, majesty."

"You need to laugh more. I don't want SaRa distressed. You may go."

"Yes Ma'am."

Kit backed away as Kha instructed. Head lowered, eyes averted, feeling the stairs with his bare feet lest he take an embarrassing tumble under the scrutiny of power.

Sibuna escorted him to his quarters, yawned, showing a formidable pair of pointed fangs and licked his right paw. "My dear boy," he said casually. "You may be considered a hero, but don't let it go to your head. Only cats get away with true arrogance. You really do need to wear your new sandals. It's protocol to be properly attired at all times. You can no longer wear the coverings you call T-shirts. They must be stored away from prying eyes… and by that, I mean spies. Ay has them watching your every move."

Kha slammed an oversized 'Book of the Dead' on a stone work-table. "It's the time of taboos," he announced. "We can't delay any longer. You must put your life on the line and face the consequences."

"Do I have a choice?"

"The time for choosing is over. It's time to put a face on your fears to face up to the reality of waking up and discovering your nightmare was real. A short term solution facing a long-term reality may be all that's open to us. It's your duty to fight fear."

"Do I need to know this now?"

"If not now, when? We're in a situation known as better late than never. It's more a case of immediately if not sooner before it's too late. Are you familiar with the poetic phrase gird your loins?"

"You're saying I must prepare myself."

"atta boy."

"How bad can it be?"

"Several peak nightmares rolled into one barely scrapes the surface."

"Then let's get it over with."

"No such animal. The life of an apprentice alchemist is not easy. You will need to go *through* it."

"Can you present it to me as a good news/bad news scenario?"

"I can, but not all at once. There must be a period of grace between the two. You'll understand why, later. The bad news is more of a warning. An intervention, if you will. One that's been a long time coming which means it's had time to fester."

"You underestimate me. I'm tougher than I look. Have I not proven this by coming here?"

"One would hope," Kha replied paying special attention to his fingernails. "Kit, a field mouse looks tougher than you. Get a good night's sleep. Take a draught of sleeping potion. You need your wits about you. Tomorrow morning we're taking a slight detour. Be prepared."

Goswold Mundi paced his marble halls noting each fresh crack from the new earthquakes that kept a tight schedule plotted each evening on a chart. He checked the King's chamber for the ninth time in as many hours. Kha was overdue, the planet was overdue, and Pangea was in the final moments of shaking itself free of billions of years shackled by a thin crust of unstable rock.

Megeara, true to her evil word, stirred her primordial energies into a witch's brew – a cauldron of untamed chemicals that seeped from Pangea's pores in plumes of toxic steaming water. Soon the Bedean Pyramid's portal would implode and Kha's mission would take on a more serious timeline. The eruptions were measured in the precision of clock time, Osiris's invention as a solar entity.

Every hour on the hour, a geyser of sulphurous steam hissed upwards of 900 feet. The releases were proving inadequate. Solar time would soon be the only reference to eons of hot dry wasteland.

The red planet winked slyly, pulsing like a plastic wasps' nest. It bulged dangerously in the middle, tapering at its north pole like a red pear. Constantly seen, day and night, it beat in time to the heart of war.

Excited voices entered the courtyard window. Aelfric Fairbrother called out. "The pyramid is active. It is dangerously unstable but Kha and one other have materialized."

"Is it the boy?"

"It's *a* boy. Whether he's the *right* one is yet to be determined. They're in recovery now."

Aelfric's brother, Edwin, observed the visitors. Kha was talkative. Kit lay prone as a slab of meat.

Kha ranted in a state of apologetic distress. "I had to push him too fast," he said. "He wasn't ready. He's still an untried boy."

"We received your telepathic message. We're cutting it fine, Kha. Kit will have to fulfil the prophecy to the best of his present abilities. Time will tell is as true a statement now as it will always be. He held a curl of bergamot peel under Kit's nose and slapped his cheek. Kit's eyelids fluttered. He coughed and inhaled the scent of lavender and lotus that filled the room and slowly levitated from the stone sarcophagus as a transparent copy of his physical body.

Kha's physical form still lay on a stone receiving platform.

"Kit will never accept being a ghost. That's what he'll call his ka state. When he learns he had to die to enter here, he will panic. We have to break the concept of ka death to him using scientific explanations. He must be fully aware of the differences between dream traveling and death. He must accept the art of dying and reviving in order to be a true shaman and face the Furies."

Goswold looked grave. "Kit must be encoded with the powerful state of ka-death. If he does not remember of his own accord, we will fail."

Kit stood incredulous over his body. "Am I dead?"

Goswold never hesitated and almost shouted. "The short answer is, yes."

Kit pinched his body. "It's cold. Hard as rock. I look like one of the ancient coffin lids in the Bede churchyard. Those granite knights in repose, carved in stone with heraldic emblems at their head and a loyal dog at their feet. Are you telling me they're alive?"

"The life-force of a marble knight is weak to be sure, but…"

"Parts of them are eroded or broken away. Whole arms and noses have fallen away over time."

"Not fallen. Hacked away. Enemies treat stone effigies as the main chance. Disfiguring them is as good as combat. The furies have sabotaged Bede's warrior heroes for eons."

"Master Goswold, how can they be defeated?"

"They can't."

"Sorry?"

"If fortune favors the attempt, which of itself is a great and rare feat, the Furies curses may be delayed. But the inherent nature of the universe is to fall apart and recycle fears and dreams into new flesh and bone just as the Furies continually churn their venom into sizzling steam."

"This chamber feels familiar. If I'm right, its counterpart is icy cold."

"Correct. The Winter Room rests on these exact co-ordinates within Bede Hall which is, in essence, an oddly shaped pyramid constructed of chronologically spaced atoms. On a map, Bede's force field lies within Hadrian's Wall, The Green Lady's forest, and Lindisfarne. A 'Bermuda Triangle' in Northumbria. Technically it's not a triangle and its power points are strictly Pangean that link Great Britain, Egypt, and a certain location on Mars."

Kit blanched even in his ethereal state. "You're referring to the face on Mars. Kha said I had to *face* something. That's it, right?"

Goswold's apprentice, Aelfric spoke from the shadows. "The thing is, the face on Mars is Megeara's face. Her body contains the soul of Tisiphone, and the mind of Allecto."

Kit paced backwards and forwards eyeing the alchemists hoping to sell him on dying for the cause. "What happened? Look, if I'm to defeat Megeara I should know what went wrong,"

Goswold motioned to Aelfric to be silent with a finger over his lips. "Our 'Pan Gemini', the elemental twins Pan (you know him as Parks) and Osiris (Egypt's Aten), were torn apart over a meddling queen who loved one twin and was jealous of the other. Megeara was in love with Aten. When he spurned her, Megeara's broken heart split into three furious entities. Tisiphone, her soul, banished Aten to the underworld but instead of suffering he took control and became the powerful sun god of rebirth which made Megeara incandescent with jealousy. Her wasp minions are the pure manifestation of her toxic agitation. Allecto, her mind, plotted to destroy the capstone of the Bedean Pyramid as its source of esoteric power. The 'Group of Nine', our magus community, rendered it invisible and she failed. The defeat triggered more anger and revenge, not on our twins, but our world. As we stand here, Allecto's thoughts magnified into strong vibrations are liquifying the plastic core underneath Pangea. It's only a matter of time before the surface rock splits, and when it does our landmass will become a flotilla of enormous islands floating on a sea of magma."

"So, nothing dangerous then. Anything else I should know?"

"We're living on borrowed time and 'the Megeara triad' is our banker."

Kha and Kit stood in ka form, unaffected as a strong wave of vibrations rocked the Bede Pyramid that left a gash in the earth like the wound from a sword. "It's time to go home," Kha said. "I think I should tell you that your body may be altered after your death experience."

chapter 10
A LAVENDER KIND OF NIGHT

The meeting was constructive but had run overlong and the airless library proved too oppressive for the members. At times, even eye-opening. Tut wandered off in his usual funk in the middle of Mr. Leoni's impassioned speech that had digressed into a lecture about birds, interesting all the same, but off-topic regarding the imminent dangers of battles with killer wasps. Brooks would have to take Tut to task. All hands were needed to make a stand against a supernatural enemy able to infiltrate small spaces, darting and stinging at will.

Outside, was as cool as it would get without a strong night wind, but the moon was more forgiving than the sun, and the trees looked like the forest of thorns in a fairy tale. Bash thought of Six and where they liked to hold hands under the rowan tree they'd planted together. That had been a moonlit night as well. It was their magic-moment spot where they first kissed. It made a good excuse to head in that direction and inspect the gates she'd heard squealing earlier.

There was a rustle of dried leaves as Sable, the topiary squirrel scampered by. "Evening Mistress Bash," he chattered over his shoulder. "Sage said I should check the gates. There was trouble earlier."

He was gone too fast to hear her reply. "Good lad."

The rowan would have to wait for a more private visit. She veered left and made a beeline for the lavender field, her special crop, now a pungent acre of unhappy plants that stretched under the moon like a vast bowl of potpourri. She took some comfort knowing that even the healthiest lavender plants looked black at night, so it was easy to persuade herself they were still growing despite their daytime hue of listless blue-grey.

The scent of lavender wafted on a feeble breeze and along with it came the voices of her plants. *"Mistress, we know where Anna is,"* they called. *"We heard her earlier, over by the big wall. Mistress, she's still there."*

The stones of Hadrian's Wall retained most of the heat of the day but were mercifully cooler under the moon. The conversation of two girls drifted through a gap in the bricks. Bash bent closer and shouted "Anna, is that you?" A fairy she didn't recognize flew out and zoomed away.

"I have to wake up now," Anna said. "My aunt is calling me. I'll visit again. I promise."

"Soon," the other girl said. "You must keep your promise. I have friends who don't."

"That's not me," Anna said. "I've had friends like that too. See you soon."

"Soon," came the girl's tearful reply.

Anna materialized in her red winter snowsuit, seated on the wall, a few yards away. She jumped down and waved. "I'm coming," she called out to Bash, "I promised I'd visit her."

Bash met her halfway. "Yes, I heard. Anna, you can't just run off without telling anyone where you're going. We've been frantic to find you."

"I'll have to visit her," Anna said dreamily. "It was awful when Beryl didn't come."

"Did you use the portal?"

Anna's red snowsuit transformed into a summer dress as she shook her head. "Sleepwalking is easier. The sound of Memory trumpeting, woke me. I walked down to the maze to visit her, but the maze wasn't there. See there, where I'm pointing. All those fields where the maze is, was a camp of tents and shops outside the fort walls. I met a girl selling amulets there. Her name is Vita."

"I heard her. You shouldn't make promises you may not be able to keep. You know how you hated being abandoned when Beryl forgot about you."

Anna lifted a silver coin on a leather string around her neck. "I have this, so I won't forget."

"That doesn't mean you will be able to find her again."

"Vita was wearing it. She gave it to me. It's Hermes the god of trade."

"Indeed."

"Vita says Hermes is a messenger. He also guides and protects travelers. See, he has wings on his feet so he can fly everywhere. I'm going to give it to my fa…, I mean, Kit. I may bump into him in a dream. Vita's father is a smithy who repairs the swords of the builder-soldiers who cut stone for the wall when they're not fighting border skirmishes. But he couldn't see me. He was most upset when Vita spoke to me."

"You could have gotten lost."

"I was careful to keep an eye on Bede Hall. It's built over the old fort. It sort of hangs over it like a see through net curtain, all fluttery, so I was quite safe."

"You've been gone two months."

"Oh. Is that too long? I guess I got used to ignoring how slow time went. It made it easier to wait for Beryl, and then my… "

"I unlocked the Winter Room door against Lady Nan's orders to look for you."

"So, we're *both* in trouble."

"I think that boy in your wall is in trouble, too."

Anna giggled in her sleep. "Did you close the door? Is that why your hair is purple?"

Bash steered Anna towards the Hall. "Let's get you home. Lady Nan always forgives you."

Anna's eyes closed. She complied, docilely "Purple hair suits you because you always wear lavender perfume," she said.

Bash growled in her throat. "You know very well that I don't wear perfume. I don't need to. In a way, the lavender hugs me whenever I tend to it."

"Is Pookie where I left her?"

"She is. On the headache pillow. Are you sleeping in the Winter Room tonight?"

"I always need to hug Pookie after a long trip," Anna said.

chapter 11

THE COMING OF AGE

Kit peeled a long shirt stuck fast to a flat stone. "I should have known better than leaving wet clothes to dry in direct sunlight. "It's shrunk," Kit said to Kha citing the hemline of the galabeya six inches above his knees.

Kha shook his head, smiling. "No, my brother. You have aged."

"How much older could I be? Eighteen?"

"Nine years have flown since you left SaRa."

"I'm twenty-seven!" Kit strode over to the bronze mirror. "I'm twenty-seven," he repeated in a whisper.

"Sorry, Kit. The portals can misbehave, but ka death transforms the healthiest bodies. An alchemist has to die several times during a crisis. I'm sorry, but there's no way around it. Time is strange stuff."

"Can it make me younger too?"

"I've never known that to happen. When you met me, I was dead, so to you, I never age."

"And Bede?"

"It's the same. Bash has not aged. She's still trying desperately to reach you with the yellow chair. We must break into Tutankhamen's tomb for the real throne."

"And SaRa knew of this?"

"I cannot say. Time shifts without shame. My sister will accept your…"

"Little abnormality?"

"Let's go home. SaRa is waiting."

"She'll get a shock. We were just starting to click. I miss her."

"SaRa has always loved you, Kit. She has since she was a little girl. Pestering me when you would come. She became a follower of Bast to find you."

"I may be falling in love with her, too. I tried not to. Romance and marriage are against everything I believe in." He stopped and grabbed Kha's arm. "Maybe she likes older men."

"She likes tall men. So, you're good." Kha hid his face. "There will be surprises, my brother. It's ironic but time has no sense of time passing."

Sa Ra had aged too. She and Kit were already in love. And so Kit greeted his lovely wife, large with child, with a degree of intimacy hitherto unknown to him.

BEDE

chapter 12
THE PLACE OF HOURS

Anubis, head feline security guard, and his daughter Snowdrop were making their rounds when a startling bee-size puffball of red soot, emitting coughs and sneezes, lurched drunkenly through the open window and careened into the mirror over the fireplace. It seemed to rally momentarily before taking flight, but it promptly crashed into a glass lampshade and ricocheted into the mantelpiece where it burst into flame, and finally fell in a clump of black sparks. It gave one last wheeze and blinked out. *Pffit!*

Anubis rushed to its side. *"Damn fairies,"* he hissed, giving it a nudge. *"Careful lass,"* he said to Snowdrop. *"Let me handle this. It smells like one of those willow-the-wisps I've warned you about.* Detecting no movement, the cat sniffed more closely. *"Sulphur,"* he declared. *"Horrible stuff. Why do these things always happen when Parks is away."*

A blackened wing unfolded from the smoldering mass as a fairy-shaped creature, stirred. Anubis poked it with an extended claw as if it were poison. A dazed face emerged from the wreckage. One of its eyes was swollen shut, but the other opened woozily. "Is that you, Anubis? You look all wobbly. Whichever cat you are, keep your rotten claws to yourself."

"Didn't die then," Anubis said. *"You lot are a menace. It's lucky Parks didn't see you."*

The fairy staggered to her feet, spread her wings for balance but fell down when one wing refused to unfurl. "Help," she cried… "Mayday Mayday… I have an urgent message for Mistress Bash… I'm dizzy… can't fly… must see her. I know you're a cat. I can smell Egypt on you."

Anubis yawned in her face. *"Your message has probably burned to a crisp then,"* he said.

87

"Stupid cat. The message is in my head. I have to tell her before I faint, you moronic, arrogant, idiot bumbledome. I'm talking to *you*, Anubis."

"Sticks and stones, little fairy. Sticks and stones," Anubis chuckled.

"I'll stay and watch her, Dad," Snowdrop volunteered. *"Bash is in the kitchen."*

Anubis, the Hall's noble head guardian, warrior superior, infinitely over qualified black cat, pranced tail up to the kitchen where Bash was splashing a large quantity of dishwater onto the floor, wrestling with a large pot refusing to surrender. *"Mistress Bash,"* Anubis preened. *"There's a fairy in the library. I think it's hurt. It might be Nimue. I can't make her out as she's covered in sticky goo. But the little minx has Nimue's temper, right enough."*

"All fairies are short-tempered," Bash replied, "so she can't be too badly injured."

"She said she was feeling faint."

Bash stopped scrubbing and dried her hands. "Ah, well, that's different," she said. "Fairies don't faint." She grabbed a jar of dried lavender flowers, a cotton bud, a saucer, and a bottle marked tincture of lavender from the pantry. "Lead on McNubis. Race you to the library."

"Very funny, I'm sure, Mistress," Anubis said and streaked off.

By the time Bash reached the library, Nimue was recognizable. Snowdrop had licked her half-clean. She lay curled in a limp heap, snuggling into Snowdrop's fur. Her battered wings, stained blood red, trembled with every strained breath.

"Poor kid," Anubis whispered. *"Truth is, I never trusted fairies, but I wouldn't see one suffer."*

Bash crushed a handful of lavender between her palms to release its energy, blew it over Nimue, and held a cotton bud dipped in lavender extract under her nose. The scent of concentrated lavender acted like smelling salts. "I saw the whole thing," Nimue wheezed. "We had no warning."

"Good girl," Anubis said to Snowdrop. *"Bash will take over now. I'm going to lick that nasty goo from your paw, then it's off to bed with you or your mother will have my whiskers."*

A saucer filled with dried lavender made a perfect sick-bed. Bash placed Nimue upon it gently and covered her with more flowers.

"No warning at all," Nimue whispered.

Charlotte stormed into the room breathless and angry, carrying a reluctant Beegle under one arm. "We're well and truly in it now, I'm afraid," she said. "How is she?"

"Lavender is an amazing sedative. She's asleep," Bash said. "I'm no fairy doctor, like you, but Nimue has always been stubborn. I think she'll mend."

"Nimue, my dear one," Charlotte fussed. "You must rest, Nimbus and Fioretti told me what happened. I'll tell Bash the news. You sleep, my dear."

Beegle, completely stirred into a frenzy, shrieked monkey obscenities at Anubis. Anubis, never one to back down, arched his back and swore in his face. Snowdrop, apprenticed to her father, joined in. Charlotte tried to silence them with one of her looks and failed. She opened the door, tossed Beegle into the hallway, and turned on the cats. "Out. Out all of you, this isn't good for Nimue."

Beegle jumped on Anubis' back which somewhat escalated the ruckus and Snowdrop hung onto Beegle's tail, so it was a three-headed creature that bolted up the stairs.

Bash turned on Charlotte. "Here's another idea that's *not* so good… Beegle, let loose in the Hall. You have to catch him. I'll sort out the cats. Now, before they…"

A crash from above had Bash taking two stairs at a time. Anubis and Snowdrop shot past her followed by a stream of bouncing apples. Beegle chattered after them, clutching an apple, sitting inside an upturned bowl.

Lady Nan materialized at the head of the stairs. "BATHSHEBA, I left you in charge. You were only doing the washing up. What on earth is amiss!"

"There's been an accident. Charlotte will explain she's in the…?"

"She's right behind you," Charlotte said. "I'll grab the Beeg. Maybe he can play with Taraq.

Taraq, never far from a kafuffle, and always in earshot of his name, popped in. "Noise fit to wake the dead," he cackled.

"CATERWAULING," Lady Nan shouted. Bathsheba, please note this fabulous word. It's not used nearly enough. Taraq, be a good lad and take the monkey outside. I will sort out Snowdrop. Feathers will sort out Anubis. I want to hear about Nimue's accident."

Bash smoothed her apron. "I was in the kitchen. I don't know the details. All Nimue said was there was no warning, and then she fell asleep."

Charlotte stayed Lady Nan's arm. "I need to tell Bash first, in private, if that's all right," she whispered. "It's dire news. She will need the rest of the family, later."

The hallway emptied. "Oh, look where we are," Charlotte said outside the Winter Room. It's the perfect place."

"It might have been if I had the key and we kept the door open."

"The cold spot will have to do. It's rather refreshing considering what's outside. Nimue won't hear us up here."

Charlotte produced her hip flask and took a sip. "Nimue's been through a terrible ordeal but nothing compared to what you're about to. I don't want to upset her any more than she is already. As she spoke, she poured a few drops of elixir into the flask's stopper. "I have dreadful news," she said. "Drink this and brace yourself."

"Not the most encouraging start to a conversation," Bash said. "I wish I could stop my hands from shaking. I prefer to delay bad news for as long as possible," she said. "If I don't hear it, it never happened."

The beaker of tonic smelled of chocolate and oranges. "Drink it down in one go," Charlotte said. "No arguments. Try and stay calm.

You can scream at the moon later. In fact, I'll join you. The impossible has happened."

For a moment, the potion worked, and Bash was flooded with goodwill.

Charlotte started at the beginning allowing her potion to take full effect. Parks and Six had just filled a wagon with new topsoil from Lindisfarne. Nimue, Jefee, and Fioretti were tending a new rowan seedling, nearby. Several dozen imps attacked, spraying them with a lethal insecticide. Apparently, some of the imps were overcome by the fumes of their own potion and perished on the spot. He didn't have a chance."

"WHO? Who didn't have a chance!"

"Parks ran off, but Six caught the full brunt of the stuff, and Nimue was on his shoulder. He's in a bad way."

"PARKS ABANDONED SIX!"

"No, of course not. He'd never do that. Here, give me your hands and look me in the eyes. My dear, it's quite possible that Six is dead."

Bash steadied herself against the wall, tried to grab the flowers on the wallpaper, and slipped to the floor. "No, he's alive," she said in the smallest voice she'd ever uttered. "I'm telepathic. I would know if… well, I would just *know*. The Furies take live hostages. Why would Parks leave Six?"

Charlotte knelt on the floor, unclasped Bash's hands, and shook them hard. "Dear girl. You're not listening. I know how Parks thinks. We always discussed the possibility of him drawing off attackers in an ambush. It's not as bad as it sounds. It's a necessary strategy. Nonetheless, the spray was too toxic. Six was taken away by one of the Furies. They have him Bash. And the Furies will kill a hostage to make a point."

"Take me to him."

"It's not a physical place. It's a 'when' − a when where unimaginably strong magic seals a dark border around an endless hour. Magic like that is virtually impenetrable."

"But your fairies can find it. Their magic is ancient too. Parks will find it."

"Parks is gone, Bash. I can feel it. He can't return until Kit changes the past. My fairies' magic may be ancient but the Furies magic is primal. There's a significant difference. Fairies can sometimes penetrate the 'place of hours' but they can't always get out. Humans don't have a chance. Six is our first casualty of war. Oh, my dear. I am so deeply sorry."

Even the delicate windchime ringtone of Charlotte's phone sounded ominous. She answered, never taking her eyes off Bash. For a moment the message she heard caused her to double over in anguish. The moaning she heard surrounding her came from within. She had to steady herself, and when she turned to Bash, her eyes were wet.

The world slipped sideways. Bash's mouth went dry as sand. Frantic eyes searched Charlotte's face desperate for a sign. "TELL ME. Tell me the truth. WHAT'S HAPPENED? Is Six…"

"That was Jefee. Little Fioretti is dead. Jefee is fine. There's been no ransom note. The darkest Poisons have perverse rules. They take one and bypass another. Fioretti is our second casualty of war. Six is dead."

PART 2

plan A

EGYPT

*"If you don't know
where you are going,
any road will get you there."*
— LEWIS CARROLL

chapter 13
DADDY DEAREST

Sibuna trotted ahead of Kit, tail up on a mission. "You're in a particularly foul mood this morning," he said. "But it shouldn't prevent you from keeping up. We're on a tight schedule today. Things are about to happen. It's in the air. Can you feel it?"

Kit held back and pursed his lips, immediately suspicious. "What *kind* of things?"

"You'll find out in due course. So, if I were you, little Kitty, and thankfully I'm not, I'd watch my tail."

"Helpful. Thanks." Kit resumed walking. "By the way, watching my back is a perpetual order," he called out as Sibuna disappeared around a corner. When he caught up, Sibuna was sitting waiting, cleaning his whiskers. A garden of tall grass enclosed in a low hedge stood to the cat's right, tantalizingly appointed with a fountain and several stone benches.

"Mind if we take a shortcut through this garden," Sibuna said, and without an answer, he bounded over the hedge and proceeded to roll and twist in the grass, clearly enjoying himself. His purrs echoed from the walls and ceiling that immediately flashed in a wild mural of brightly colored bands of light like an animated rainbow. The walls emitted a melodic hum that pulsated faster and faster until the murals were a blur of wavering stripes.

Kit covered his ears and stood back, determined not to be drawn into the hypnotic display by averting his attention to the drunken form

95

of a cat trying to stand and falling down again. "Van Gogh walls," he commented casually. "Nice. I met him once. A long time ago."

The words *'Perpetual... Paroxysms... Pleasure.'* arrived in a swoop of white wings that brushed the top of Kit's head.

"Oh, hello, Parrot droppings. Can this day *get* any worse!"

'Don't give me any ideas.'

"Just dropped in for a taunt, have we? You might as well join the party. SaRa is in tears, Kha won't speak to me, and Sibuna, who hates my guts on principle, is now in a state of catnip euphoria."

'Principles and Privileged Princesses,' Pigeon chortled in delight. *'I did NOT drop in... Sibuna invited me.'*

"No doubt bringing me glad tidings of ... well, I'm out of suggestions. I'm far too angry."

Kit and Pigeon watched Sibuna wriggle and scamper about in a frenzy of delight. He turned, flashed his claws at them once, and proceeded to roll again.

Pigeon soared in a victory loop around the garden. *'Sibuna appears to be a tad distracted,'* he shrieked as he passed Kit. The rest of his remark trailed after him like the tail of a kite. *'As I recall, catnip will do that. Mind his claws. Sibuna can be a might PERKY after a break in the 'Mindful Field'. Lady Nan used to refer to it as a mine field when she lived here, but I expect you know all about minds and lavender fields.'*

Kit wheeled, attempting to catch Pigeon's talons on a fly-by, and missed. "Why don't you just SHUT... UP!" he hollered. His voice shattered the humming sound and unplugged the light show in a fizzle of bright sparks.

Sibuna startled, twisted to his feet, and collapsed. "Is this you keeping up?" he shouted from his groggy stupor.

"So, lavender has an hallucinatory cousin," Kit declared. "Why am I not surprised that catnip comes from *here*." He sniffed the air. "It smells like... it's minty."

'Cloth ears,' Pigeon chided. *'It IS mint. And it's not a cousin, it's lavender's mother. Did you ever listen to your sister?'*

"Not much. I kept myself to myself."

'That explains a lot.'

"I'm upset. I return from some whirlwind detour to Pangea. No warning, mind. And what do I find? My *almost* girlfriend is my wife. A wife expecting my children. And I'm expected to breeze along as if this sort of time anomaly is normal. The… you know… *chemistry* between us was beginning to heat up and I missed it."

'Well it IS normal. So, you have to roll with it.' Pigeon flapped. *'And now you're an alchemist. Better than a real scientist. The Pangea trip probably did you a favor. Stop feeling sorry for yourself. It could have been far worse. Probably did SaRa a favor, too. Your courtship smarts are not exactly polished. Only numpties misbehave.'*

"Sibuna appears to be misbehaving enough for both of us," Kit snorted.

Sibuna barely cleared the hedge and landed on Kit's toes. His pupils were dilated to thin vertical lines. He shook himself as if exiting a pool and resumed his mission. "Keep on keeping up," he said over his shoulder.

Pigeon shrieked *'something's coming… back soon… Probably.'* And flew off leaving a fair number of white feathers floating in the air in his haste.

A startling new, but not entirely unfamiliar, voice boomed off the empty stone walls. It wasted no time on small talk. "Kit. It's time to grow up!" it shouted in the distinctly parental tone of a stern father admonishing an unruly child. "This is NOT a suggestion."

"And you are?"

"You've spoken with buildings before, Kit. As a new resident of my temple, it's my *obligation* to welcome you and perhaps make you aware of your obligations. Please note I did not use the word *pleasure.*"

"Parks? Is that you?"

'Parks is here… Pleasurable… Perfect… a Picnic in the Park.' Pigeon rattled inside Kit's head.

"Almost," came the temple's reply.

"Your majesty? Mistress Bast?"

"I should think it obvious that Bast is *not* a building. But you will be reminded soon enough."

Kit moved closer to the carvings of hieroglyphs trying to discern the source of the voice, but it immediately boomed louder from all directions.

"Kha advised me I would have to master a certain degree of decorum deference before Bast would see me again. Apparently, I can be misunderstood as insolent."

The temple chuckled rudely. "Unless, it's an emergency."

"And?"

"And, watch your back, Kit. No sudden moves is my best advice."

A low growl behind Kit startled him. He spun around to face with Babylion, a lioness the size of Jack, approaching him with her ears back. She too, wore the lavish gold jewelry reserved for royal cats. Kit looked around for Sibuna. He was alone.

"Your attitude leaves me in no doubt of your extreme youth and by youth, I mean immaturity," the lioness growled. "Are you coming or going? It's hard to tell. You've been formally summoned KiTiKha'at."

"Yes, Ma'am."

"Put on your best decorum hat," the temple whispered.

The lioness blinked slowly, still as a statue. "Follow me," she said, her jaw motionless. And yes, I'm telepathic. I know what you're thinking. So think before you speak. and when you meet the goddess tell the truth. She relies on me to translate."

"Babylon? As in the temple of Babel?"

"As in Babble. As in talking, making speeches, announcing, answering questions, as in sorting out the nonsense humans garble all the time. And you're almost correct, except, my name's Baby…LION. You can call me Babs when I'm in a good mood. Lying makes me angry. Pretending not to remember makes me difficult to deal with." She deferred her head sideways keeping her eyes locked, towards the table. "Your hat is there."

Three long ostrich plumes attached to a ridiculous linen cap that tied under the chin, sat on the table. Kit picked it up and waved it like a feather duster. "Is this some kind of a joke or a punishment of some kind? Surely, it's a woman's bonnet."

'It's disrespectful to wave the feathers of Ma'at about,' Pigeon squawked. *'Feathers are not trifles.'*

Babs sniffed Kit's sandals. "It happens to be an extreme honour to wear the feathers of Ma'at. Really, Sibuna. You're falling short of your duties, unless your charge is an extremely dull boy in which case, I will consider any hat he condescends to wear as a dunce cap."

Pigeon swooped over Babs in a loud squawk of haughty laughter. *'The boy has no respect for wings, and Feathers is the name of his cat, your lioness-ship. I had hopes that Kha and Sibuna, here, would expand his mind. He mopes a great deal and he's self centred. All I can say is that it's early days. There's time for improvement.'*

Kit ducked as Pigeon flew towards him. "Hey, whose side are you on! What happened to family loyalty and all that?"

Babs new expression of pity mixed with disgust, commanded Kit to pay attention and remain silent. "Pa'a is loyal to your father and in deference to him, you," she growled. "But the truth is you are a great disappointment to Bede Hall. And if truth be told, to yourself. You've been insolent and broody. You've chosen to believe logic over magic. This is not a true representation of science, is it Kit? It's the word magic that makes you cringe. But you know deep inside that science requires the magical elements of chemistry and physics as much as investigative thinking. And the fact that you're here is no testament to your great courage but the lack of standing up for your principles. You didn't want to come. You bowed to pressure. Being here is a nuisance to you. You want to go home and hide your head in the sand. Is this not true?"

"Is that all!"

"Be as snippy as you like with me," Babs licked her whiskers and snarled. "But I don't recommend you use this approach with Her Majesty. Humans who fail to make friends are mice to her."

'Persistent... Principles... Passages, alchemy and chemistry,' Pigeon nattered to himself.

Babs padded along in silence and quickened her step as she turned into a dark corner that smelled of freshly mown grass. She stopped in front of a distinctly modern cat flap fashioned in gold. "This is the 'Passage of Time'," she said. "It is not forbidden to you but as you can see its not designed for anything larger than a housecat."

Kit dropped to his hands and knees and peered through the flap. He beheld nothing inside but a clear blue sky with fluffy clouds. "This isn't a tunnel."

"Did I say tunnel? I did not say tunnel. I said passage.'

"So, where does it lead?"

"Directly into Miss Sarah Goodman's kitchen."

The sound of an airplane engine reverberated around the walls emanating from a doorway the size of an airport hangar. "The inner sanctum," Babs announced in a gentler tone. "We've arrived and to prove it we're here. Bast is inside. Try to be good."

Echoes of Kit's older brother Rupert's snide comment flashed through his thoughts.

"Sibuna, he's all yours," Babs called over her shoulder. "Your brother sounds smart."

Sibuna nosed Kit forward. "Thanks for nothing," she hissed to herself. "Come along little mouse," she said. "Mommy's waiting."

Bast sat on an unlikely throne – an eight-foot cube of upholstered black leather, matching the armchairs in Bede's red library, in an inner sanctum as large as a football field. This time her head took the form of a sleek Abyssinian cat, but her body was a shapely woman dressed in a clingy silk shift embroidered with red and gold hieroglyphics. One hand petted Babs, already reclining at her feet. "So, Sibuna, you've brought your little Kitty," she said. "Has he come to play?"

"He's here as you ordered, Ma'am. Kit doesn't know how to play."

"Then we must teach him. He's going to be a father. Human father's play with their children, don't they Kit? You once had a father who played games with you and your sister."

"I still *have* a father, your majesty. But I think you know this."

Sibuna, at his side, fell into the paroxysms of coughing up a timely hairball.

"I do know," Bast said. "Cats tease, Kit, and you should know *that*. Are you alright, Sibuna?"

Sibuna winked and inclined his head towards Kit. "Sorry Ma'am. I don't know what came over me. It's the boy apprentice. He grates on me."

Bast sent Sibuna a stern look. "Ah yes, Prince Kitty of Bede. As his superior I expect you to handle him without a fuss. I almost forgot he was here. Thank you for reminding me, Sibuna."

Bast purred and promptly turned into her giant cat form. She growled, lowered her head and picked Kit up by the scruff of his neck.

"This is how a cat mother behaves towards an unruly kitten," Sibuna said clearly in Kit's head. "I advise you to go limp. There's less chance of an injury that way. Cat fathers are a little more rough, but then father's have to teach their offspring that play also trains the reflexes necessary to fight a war."

Bast trotted around the inner sanctum and dangled Kit over her water bowl the size of a small pond. The lotus flowers floating in her water momentarily offered a wave of contentment which dissipated when Bast dunked him several times, shook him like a drowned rat, and gently licked him dry. When she was done, Bast leaped gracefully to a sitting position on her dais, preening and washing the human vibes from her paws.

Sibuna, quite recovered, spoke in no uncertain terms. "Prince of Bede, you are free to go," he snapped. "I've never been more embarrassed. Kha is waiting."

Kha was waiting, arms crossed at the top of the temple ramp. "So, you've met Babs properly, then. How did it go? She's a feline lie detector, and to make matters worse, a spoiled pet. Very tricky to fathom."

"Never mind Babs! Bast made sport with me. She rattled me. She literally shook me. I've seen Feathers carrying Snowdrop, but this was threatening, and her spoiled pet humiliated me in front of Pigeon, and then Pigeon joined in and scolded me, too. I didn't know if Bast was going to drown me or eat me." Kit took a quick hit of the happiness crystal to stop shaking.

"Yes, I got Sibuna's report. There must be no more venting and dithering. If you can't face up to SaRa or Bast, how are you going to survive meeting Megeara or the face on Mars. That reality IS going to come up. The promise of becoming a father is affecting your alchemy lessons, not to mention upsetting my sister."

"Your sister is familiar with the bizarre anomalies of time around here. I'm not."

"No more excuses. Get a grip."

"Doesn't my harrowing experience count for anything? When was the last time an eighteen-foot tall cat played with you?"

"Yesterday," Kha replied curtly. "Bast and I practice combat moves many times to keep me on my toes and to control her strength when toying with humans. She's a cat after all, and she can forget herself."

Sibuna stopped pacing and stared at Kha. "Just tell him and be done with it," he growled. "Pussyfooting isn't going to put a capstone on the pyramid. He will survive… or not."

Kha witnessed Kit's crestfallen expression. "No worries," he said. "It wasn't life-threatening."

The sand in Kit's hourglass turned black. "Not this time," Kit said. "Tell me what?"

Kha shooed Kit away with his hand. "We're done. You are dismissed."

Sibuna, purred so loudly, Kha looked up from his papers. "Sibuna you're gloating. You look positively gleeful."

"Now go," Kha said to Kit. "SaRa is waiting for you. She's been waiting for you several lifetimes. I suggest you find a way to make her feel you were worth the wait."

BEDE

chapter 14
THE MOURNING AFTER

Lady Nan sent Doolittle with a note for Charlotte marked 'urgent'.

Bash is out of control. She's out of her depth invoking spells beyond her clearance level. And speaking of clearances, she's trying to clear her head by 'slashing and burning' as if she's a pioneer clearing farmland. Sadly, she has the land confused. The trees have had to take measures in order to protect the woodland creatures. It will require magic to stop her. I fear for the safety of our smallest animals. The poor girl needs to sleep. Please come. Bring one of your 'special-tea' sleeping draughts. - Beryl

The lavender deva echoed the same concern.

Mistress Bash ran into the heart of our field. Weeping and carrying on, she was. So, we tried to sooth her with a healing song, but our lullaby enraged her. She turned on us and tore up some plants. Such behaviour from a mistress of the green is unheard of. We've never had such a dressing down. She said some hateful things. Threatened to plow us under for cabbages if we didn't grow faster. Her anger left us wilting in a state of disgrace and now her wrath has weakened our once robust immune system and left us vulnerable to attack. We were known for our resistance and now we're frightened.

The ground creatures scurried every which way in a panic to avoid being squashed by Mistress Bash, tearing through the woods brandishing a rowan branch. The branch, wielded like a weapon against the Green Lady's forest, was upset. It called out to its roots for assistance.

'Send word to Lady Flora that her woods are in an uproar. The Tree Roots Portal to the Temple of Bast is in danger of being exposed to the Furies.'

Bash ran, blinded by tears, into the Green Lady's forest, almost drained of chlorophyll, casting spells mumbled in gibberish, knowing full well she hadn't received permission from the Green Lady to use formal green magic. The claws of thorn bushes scratched her face and arms to protect themselves, helpless to stop her.

She lashed her way through brambles that caught in her hair, thrashing her innocent trees, calling for Parks. She called down the moon, invoking the Green Goddess of Lindisfarne to avenge Six, screaming 'SIX IS NOT A CASUALTY. I WON'T HAVE IT! I WILL NOT!' like a banshee.

Taraq swooped after her, trying to keep up, but even though the branches were unable to penetrate his form they caused him harm. Traces of insecticide clinging to the bark made him dizzy. Taraq zig zagged after Bash like a drunken bee, keeping her in sight, which proved daunting as she plunged forward in a straight line – a warrior on a quest. The words 'I won't have it' echoed from tree to tree, becoming a shriek that materialized into purple streaks ricocheting off brittle tree trunks, displacing clouds of insects. Taraq's shout "Lady Nan wants to see you in the Winter Room immediately" finally reached her and she crumbled.

Bash slowly retraced her path of destruction to a meeting she dreaded.

· · ·

Bash plucked a loose thread in the white chenille bedspread in the Winter Room, pulling it with green-stained fingers. A pair of her older brother's famous sunglasses covered red-rimmed eyes and a bruise from the whip of an angry oak branch. "Why are we meeting up here?" she said. "I *need* to see Charlotte!"

Lady Nan removed the sunglasses and examined her granddaughter's eyes. "You should know by now that Rupert's ridiculous sunglasses were tainted more than tinted. You don't look yourself. You never left twigs in your hair before."

"Hiding behind dark glasses feels good."

"And look at the state of your hands," Lady Nan said. "They're in need of scrubbing. Young lady, I'm aware that personal hygiene lapses somewhat during spells of insanity, which is what grief is, and believe me I should know. When Ben…"

"Ben is in the maze playing with Jack," Bash spat. "So, let's not conjure up the memories of old hurts when mine are brand new."

Lady Nan stroked Pookie's fur and tucked the toy rabbit under her chin. "We're in this room, young madam, because it's out of the way. And by 'out of the way' I mean 'out of this world'. It's one of the few safe places away from the prying ears of spies. An imp would turn into an icicle if it tried to penetrate this space. And a frozen imp can neither hear nor pass on the secrets divulged here, even if it *was* dethawed, which is impossible."

"You said places. There are others? Where!"

Lady Nan pursed her lips in a grim straight line. "Certainly, none to trouble *you* at this juncture. You have enough on your plate."

"Charlotte knows these places?"

Lady Nan waved Pookie in Bash's face. "Of course, Charlotte knows, child. Whatever did you think. She's your mentor for a reason. Just as you're her *pupil* for a reason. Parks is a stickler for upholding the rules."

"Except the one for abandoning his own family."

"Bathsheba, you sadden me more than I can say." Lady Nan paused a long time, forehead to forehead with Pookie as if reading the rabbit's mind. "Parks' wisdom is far beyond our understanding. Please, just meet with Taraq."

"Tell me yourself and save me the trouble of finding Taraq. He's all over the place these days but he no longer answers when I call him. He was loyal to Kit. Apparently, I did not inherit that privilege."

"I cannot always be your benevolent grandmother, my dear. Taraq knows more than he lets on about his past. But I will say this much, listen carefully and LET THE BOY GUIDE YOU."

"It's late," Bash said, getting up.

The old bed springs creaked making Lady Nan wince. "That's the sound my old bones used to make when I was alive." She stared long and hard into her granddaughter's eyes. "There are some advantages to being a ghost. Just remember that you can't clear your head the way a pioneer clears a forest."

Bash left the room first. "I'll phone Charlotte instead," she called over her shoulder. "Thanks for the sensitive chat."

Pookie's button eyes blinked at the sound of the door being slammed shut. A thin howl of cold air swept through the keyhole and whistled in Bash's ear.

Charlotte picked up immediately without saying hello. Her voice was faint, clearly the line was faulty. "Bash," she said. "I've heard the scuttlebutt. Is it true?"

"Can you please speak up. I can't hear you very well. There's a ringing in my ears."

Charlotte raised her voice. "What on earth are you doing. What have you got to say for yourself," she shouted. "Can you hear me now?"

"There's no need to lecture me. Lady Nan's already had a go."

"We will not have 'friendly fire', Bash. We simply won't stand for such a selfish, needless, thing. Some poor defenseless creature is going to be crushed underfoot if you carry on like a maniac. I warn you, the trees are not without their defenses. They will put up a fight. Surely you agree it's better they save their strength to fight a true enemy than the appointed Mistress of the Green, responsible for their well being. They miss Six, too. You have upset them. It's part of their pledge of allegiance to Parks… and to me."

"Hoity toity," Bash sneered. "Who made you queen of everything."

"The forest floor is Bede's underground telegraph. The animals rely on us for protection. Helen protects as many fox, mice, rabbits, squirrels, and insects as she can but with Parks gone, it's a superhuman task. She may be a twice-born but she's not superhuman like Parks."

"Then Parks should be ashamed of himself."

"Parks knows what he's doing," Charlotte said. "And he wouldn't be doing it unless it was the best thing for Bede's plants and animals. Flora and fauna are his priorities. If I'm called away, the fairies will look to you for guidance. Take the advice you gave Kit often enough and get a grip. If you are unable to comply, I will appoint Hannah in my absence."

"Fioretti says…"

Charlotte sounded indignant. "I have had Fioretti's report. She never saw Parks abandon Six. She just saw him vanish. She said you were beside yourself with worry."

"My pep talk to the lavender field backfired. I lost it."

"Nimue tells me the trees shrink from you."

"That's true. I frightened them. I didn't mean to. I don't even remember most of it. The sky went black. They closed ranks like enchanted thorns."

"As mistress of the House of Bede, you hold a position of power. Trees bend to such power out of respect and tradition. They will never question your authority but their allegiance to Parks is strong, and since they've pledged to protect the woodland wildlife, they're confused. You can't rampage through the woods without harming yourself or others."

"An oak tree nearly blinded me."

"The forest is defending itself. Six is gone, and it's a terrible shock, but grief must be set aside in order to defend us from the Furies barrelling their way towards us. The twice-borns are there to support you. Take comfort from Taraq. He has some especially wise things to say on this subject. He will be seeking you out on Queen Ankhesenamun's explicit instructions."

Bash pressed call end without saying goodbye, grabbed a head of lettuce from the kitchen, and drove to Charlotte's florist shop, narrowly missing Jack chasing after Sable.

The Florist shop's door chime announced Bash's arrival into a flower shop empty of natural flowers. Rows of vases displaying silk sunflowers filled the shelves. "Hello," Bash called out. "I come bearing lettuce and an apology."

Hannah appeared with a delicate tinkling sound from behind a curtain of glass beads. "Charlotte isn't here," she said. "Can I be of assistance?"

Bash held the lettuce out for inspection. "So far, the heat has been unable to wilt the greenhouse vegetables. I thought Beegle and Darwin might like a treat. Is Charlotte about?"

"She won't be back for a good long while."

Oversized sunglasses failed to cover a long yellow bruise on Bash's cheekbone. "But I just spoke with her on the phone."

Hannah busied herself straightening her sunflower cards.

The sound of a tinny voice singing Jingle Bells followed by a loud crash from behind the curtain, made Hannah jump, sending her card display to the floor. She tripped over the wire shelf in her haste to reach the back room and fell through the curtain where Bash tried to assess the damage to Hannah and the bookshelf that had overturned its contents in an explosion of ribbons and broken glass.

The singing came from a stuffed dodo bird that Beegle had decorated covered with fake greenery. He'd placed a string of pine cones scented with cinnamon around its neck. Hannah limped into a chair after extricating Darwin from a pile of silk holly and shooed Beegle with her apron. "Leave that poor creature alone. She's not a Christmas tree. Beegle's always into things, the little monkey, and there are a lot of *things* for arranging flowers, not including Miss Charlotte's medicinal paraphernalia. Hannah picked bits of fern and baby's breath from the bird's feathers. You haven't met our Dee Dee. An ignorant museum official tossed her in a dumpster because she was too shabby to display. She was the last of her kind."

A childish voice from inside the bird spoke. "You mean, I haven't met *her*," Dee Dee giggled.

"Don't mind Dee Dee," Hannah said. "She's smarter than she sounds. And don't believe any disparaging remarks you've heard about dodos. They were extremely wise. They played with us by acting emptyheaded. Their silliness is an act. Underneath their nonsense is often something important that needs airing as a song or a rhyme. They love nursery rhymes."

"I brought Beegle and Darwin some lettuce. What does a stuffed dodo bird eat?"

Dee Dee sang to the tune of we wish you a merry Christmas. *'We eat our words, Mistress Bash!'*

Bash tore the lettuce in two pieces and coaxed Darwin out of his shell with the smaller half. Beegle snatched the rest and raced off to eat it in private. "Little piggy," Hannah said. "So, what brings you here? Do you need salve for that bruise?"

"I'm here for my regular magic lesson."

Hannah blanched and coughed awkwardly behind her hand. "In her absence, Charlotte left me to manage the shop, which is another way of saying I am charged, at my discretion, with divulging higher magic, or lower magic, for that matter. There are conditions of course, and due to the severity of our situation and taking your vulnerable state into consideration, I must decline. Bash, dear. Take your cue from the color of that cloud waiting for you outside. You must snap out of your anger and snap into the responsibilities of your birthright. It's that simple. It's that urgent."

"Hannah, you sound different."

"You refer to my French accent. This I have dropped since I married Mr. Clutterbuck. Miss Charlotte says black skies at noon means the Furies are bearing down on us." Hannah pointed to a grey mass the size of a cat, hovering and bumping into the shop window. "You brought one with you. It's trying to find you."

Charlotte has studied the cloud the Furies hold over you. Bertie has tracked it. Nick shadowed it as it shadowed you. It changes colors from grey to acid yellow, muddy pink, and brackish green. When one endures the loss of a loved one, they emit an aura tainted by pain. And when they surrender compassion to thoughts of revenge, they draw down the black arts. Once down, they take root and it's the very devil to send them back."

"But that's why I'm here. Knowing a few singing charms isn't strong enough to fight a war. Chanting nursery rhymes like a dodo is child's magic. Parks wanted me all grown up, and here I am. I'm fighting fit and I need a deadlier weapon than a rowan branch."

Hannah watched Bash's car screech away with the cloud attached to its bumper. She closed her eyes and dispatched a verbal missive via Egyptian scarab to Charlotte.

'Bash needs to be informed of 'The Tree Roots Portal' before it's too late. She came near enough to the 'route' itself and almost tripped a land mine. Her sadness still follows her in the form of a dark cloud. It followed her to the shop, and I believe it was the cause of an upset that sparked Beegle into one of his tantrums. Parks said she'd be vulnerable, but now she needs to know the secret of the trees before she exposes Bede to a swarm of new problems that could rob us of a vital link to our ancestral powers. Bede will be defenceless if 'The Tree Roots Portal' is breached. — H Clutterbuck

EGYPT

chapter 15
FACE TO FACE

Kha was sorting what looked like astronaut suits when Kit arrived from being summoned. "Bee keeping clothes," Kha said lifting up a cloth helmet with a mesh visor. "Compliments of your Mr. Parks. And there's no need to look stunned. He and I go way back, so to speak. It wouldn't be wise to tell you every little thing. At least, not yet. Some things are best kept in the dark. Besides, I promised him and promises to Parks aren't made lightly."

Kit looked peeved. "Sibuna said it was urgent. Couldn't it have waited until after breakfast. I was making SaRa pancakes and telling her about the time the movies descended on Bede Hall."

"Sorry to disturb, mate, but it's best you travel on an empty stomach."

"We're going somewhere? You might have given me fair warning. And why are you becoming more and more English. What is going on!"

Kha grinned without humor. "I thought it best kept as a surprise, all things considered."

The Martian landscape looked like a diorama display in a museum case until the wasps came.

"They can't see us," Kha explained. "We're only here to observe. This is a thousand years to soon for our big arrival." He pointed to a steep incline of long cliffs. "We have to walk around that... *ah...* 'hill'. Follow me and don't dawdle."

The mountainous 'hill', made of red rock, turned out to be the face on Mars in profile. "I thought this was the least likely approach to introduce you," Kha said in his matter of fact, teacher's voice. "Fear being the deciding factor."

The surface's bumpy terrain was laced with wide fissures disclosing the entrances of several foul-smelling caves. At first, the chin of the face looked like a regular boulder. It was only on closer inspection from a different angle that Kit connected the dots of eye sockets, nostrils, and the corners of a screaming mouth, a mile wide, petrified at the moment of death.

Kha's observation was as simple as it was detached "Bigger than you thought?" he said simply. An understatement according to Kit's horrified expression.

Wasps came and went relentlessly, entering through the nose and exiting the mouth. The left eye blinked as the creature raised its head. It craned its neck forward to make eye contact, winked, shook its eroded mane, and roared a hurricane of angry wasps from its mouth.

Kit dropped to his knees and was sick into the red sand. "Okay, I've seen it," he said wiping his mouth on his sleeve. "Can we get home, now? Please tell me there's no danger of being stuck here."

Kha strode around the crumbling sphinx listening intently with his ear against the rock. "That depends on which home," he said casually. "Shush, I hear something. They're coming."

Kit's eyes narrowed with an expression akin to hatred. "Where do you think? Home to SaRa."

Kha grinned. "No worries. There's no danger of being stuck here, *this* time."

Kit's shoulders sagged. His face, drained of all color, managed to glow red in the dim Martian light.

"What's the matter? You look stricken," Kha said. "Don't tell me you're smitten with my sister. Do I detect a whiff of romance?"

"You detect, as you well know, fear mixed with an uneasy measure of romance. Both are equally terrifying."

The outcrop of exposed rock shifted with a loud creak and lifted its shoulders displacing a ton of red sand that lifted eerily in slow motion, on a landscape bereft of wind. Exposed granules of crystal quartz gleamed over its surface as it settled. The beast took its time.

"I think it can hear us. Is it coming out?"

"Goswold said it used to run around but the war damaged its legs which made it grumpier than usual," Kha offered with an even wider grin.

"It has teeth," Kit observed. "I don't think we should go any closer. In fact, I think we should back up all the way to the eighteenth-dynasty."

A dark chuckle emanated behind the Martian sphinx's leering smile – the sound a million wasps would make if they were laughing uproariously or about to attack.

Kha patted Kit on the shoulder. "We have to go inside it."

"Very funny."

"I never joke on a dangerous mission. I hope you remember the invocation I told you to memorize. The one that calls out your ka."

"I don't even remember my own name."

"It's Prince of Bede, my apprentice KiTiKha'at of Egypt, Christopher Stratford Smythe of Great Britain, Kit for short. Sibuna calls you fraidy cat, but we're going to show him you're made of fierce warrior stuff."

"The joke's on me if I'm ninety-years-old when I see SaRa. My children could be ninety."

"Or your grandchildren," Kha added.

The red sky darkened as the wasps came at them nonstop and hard. Kit flinched and instinctively cowered as they divebombed with incredible speed.

Kha shouted above a sound like pigs squealing and grabbed Kit's arm, pulling him into an unbelievably narrow crevice in the stone hill.

There was no time to fully absorb the significance of the scene because the next second master and apprentice materialized inside a pocket of air, sealed in a blast of heat. It was quieter inside the cave and Kha's normal speaking voice resumed. The muffled sound of wasps grunting and snorting came from behind a wall of Kha's magic.

Kit, too dumbstruck numb to speak, retched on Kha'a sandals."

'Cat got your tongue, little Kitty', a feline voice taunted in his head.

"Not now, Sibuna, toy with me when I get home," Kit sent back.

"But you're *not* going home, Sibuna said. "Not for a million years."

"Stop your teasing Cat-weasel," Kha said evaporating the mess on his feet. "Kit has acquitted himself well. Just remind me to wear boots next time."

Sibuna kept his telepathic link with his master but closed out Kit. "Is KiTiKha'at acquitting himself as well as we hoped?"

"Almost," Kha replied.

Kha remained out of sorts for several days, having failed to foresee Kit's limitations, and gave Sibuna the week off. For days now, the workshop was oppressive with unsaid recriminations and simmering anger. Kit was fractious, nearing his breaking point. Things were changing too fast and his apprentice was not in his head. Kit was coping with too many obstacles on the home front and Kha was worried for his sister's health. When Kit moped, SaRa bore the brunt of his moodiness. The 'Way of Happiness' crystal had to be replenished more often and it's effects were less effective. Kha had let the side down. Parks would be angry and yet it was no-one's fault. Ay was strutting his usual obnoxious self and getting to Kit. There were days Kit slept in and wandered in the desert riding one of the temple's horses. Luckily, he was a natural horseman, but emotional stamina was taking its toll.

Kha admonished himself. He'd taken too much for granted that Kit was compliant. He wasn't. Kit was quite rightly resentful of the rules of time that constantly undermined his confidence. His odd growth spurt had changed his physical appearance but bypassed the essential art of growing up slowly. Kit remained the shy clumsy boy who sought refuge in his tower. He was still running away. In short, Kit was homesick.

Bast's little ploy, intending to shame Kit into accepting the joys of fatherhood, had backfired. Tactics that intimidated her followers proved ineffective. Kit was not a follower. Resentment, humiliation, and anger led to depression and bouts of insomnia. And he'd taken to riding in the desert at night.

Sibuna sidled past Kit with a sidelong glance of disgust and headed for a recreational break in the Mindful Field. "Time out for bad behavior," he hissed over his shoulder.

Kha watched him go. Sibuna was being too hard on Kit and would need a dressing down, something cats of his stature were inclined to resent. Apologizing was not a common feline trait.

He unlocked a medicine cabinet with a quick spell and reached for a jar of catnip and camphor ointment – a balm that soothed the worst human anxiety attacks when rubbed on the temples. Today he would have to be Kit's therapist and physician. He would call on Dr. Brooks', Kit's former (but continual) mentor and custodian, to win him over with tried and true compassion, common sense, and his line of expertise as a psychologist.

"This was not the shamanic journey I planned," Kha said handing the jar to Kit. "Use this salve the way I showed you after that unfortunate incident with Bast. Take some deep breaths and listen carefully. I have an apology to make. Something went horribly wrong. I don't understand how your test got away from me. I lost control which means we both have work to do, and that works starts right now. Megeara is raging more than I thought. I'm sorry, my brother. I never meant for this to happen."

The pressure in Kit's head receded and along with it came the memory of his embarrassing performance and his failure to pass a test that was not even the 'big test' whatever and whenever that would be. "As long as it doesn't happen again," Kit said.

"Oh, but it will," Kha said. "And it will be a hundred times worse. This was a test run. The wasps will be bigger and tougher… and next time they will be real."

"At least I didn't get older this time."

"Sibuna told you it was a test."

"I thought he was joking. I never know with him. You might have told me."

"Then it wouldn't have been much of a test. No worries, tests can be taken again. Until you pass."

"Why did you make those wasps earth-sized? They were hardly in keeping with a giant face."

"Quantity makes up for size."

"Did you have to make them squeal like pigs?"

"Yes, I did. Because on Mars, wasps *do* squeal like pigs."

BEDE

chapter 16
THE GRASS IS ALWAYS GREYER ON THE OTHER SIDE

Taraq was there in Kit's old room at the top of the tower stairs, arms crossed, waiting like a genie, floating three feet off the floor. "Brooks," Bash panted out of breath. "I need to see Brooks."

"I'll have to do, Mistress," Taraq said. "You'd better sit and catch your breath. Brooks is locked up with the twice-borns and can't be disturbed. Although, I have to say you're more than a little disturbing these days. But, contrary to your belief about my loyalty, I heard you and answered your call." He spread his arms wide. "No need to thank me."

Bash squinted into his face and spat the words, "You never liked me."

"No. I was *afraid* of you, but now that you're all melodramatic, I find you annoying. I'm not afraid of annoying people. But if I wasn't already dead, that look you just gave me would have killed me for sure."

Tut blundered into the room, tripping over the last step, and addressed Bash. "I saw you running up here as if the bats from hell were after you."

Bash smirked. "Yeah, I saw a ghost."

Taraq spiralled over to the window like a twister and looked out. "No problem. The bats are on their way," he said, with an equally lethal smirk.

For a moment, Bash looked worried. "Are you serious or just spouting off?"

"I'm seriously spouting off," Taraq shouted. "Take a look at the sky. It's acid yellow under a thin wash of blue. Kind of like green scum. Now, who could have created that!"

Bash shook her head, and remembered Tut was present. "Tut, thanks for asking, but I'm *not* fine. What do you want?"

"That's no way to talk to a king, even if you *do* think you're a princess," Taraq said.

"Taraq and I were about to have an argument," Bash said drily.

Tut ducked his head and backed away. "Sorry, I'll go."

"You may as well stay in the corner," Bash said. "So you can throw me under the bus. You will eventually. That seems to be the trend these days. So much for sympathy."

Taraq blocked Tut's exit to the stairs. He grinned and pulled the throne chair to the center of the room. "Please stay, Your Majesty. Try this on for size. No protesting. You're the man of the tower, now. You have as much right to this throne as any member of this family. More in fact."

Tut blanched and turned to go. "But that's the thing. I'm not, am I. You *know* I don't belong here." He looked at Bash. "She knows it. Kit knew it, and so do the twice-borns."

Taraq led Tut to the throne and sat him down. "Nonsense. This throne was made for you," he said. He spun in a blur of molecules to stand before Bash, once again in the stance of a small genie. "I have to say, you're rather scruffy for a Mistress of the Green. Not very royal, are you. And you might think of combing that temper out of your hair, Mistress Bossy Boots, along with half the forest."

Bash lowered her eyelids in contempt. "Anything for you, freak. I'll wait here for Brooks. I won't say a word."

"Excellent. I want you to listen and say absolutely nothing for five minutes. Then you need to apologise to several people, plants, animals, and ghosts, not necessarily in that order. You can apologise to me another day. If I was alive, I wouldn't hold my breath."

Tut seemed calm, enamoured of the chair. He too, closed his eyes, but in a state of delight. His body relaxed into the curved back of enamelled gold, and he gripped the lion heads on the armrests. The tension in his hands relaxed. He'd seen Kit sprawling in it, awkwardly trying to find the best position for his gangly legs, too long to meet the floor without splaying forward. Kit had complained how uncomfortable it was. He, Tut, had never felt so at ease. "I hope

Brooks will show me how to use this," he said aloud. "I had a dream that I could reach Kit if I sat in his chair."

"*Your* chair," Taraq corrected. "Splendid. I'm sure Brooks will be honored. He's been waiting for you to come around." His smile faded as he faced Bash. "It would seem you were well named, bashing about the forest like a jabberwocky with a sore head, creating mayhem. Hardly anyone notices me, so I get about unnoticed. I was there when Sable, too afraid to ask you himself, pleaded with Anna to make his simple request, as you're in charge of general gardening matters. All Sable wanted was a friend. Creating another topiary squirrel would have been no great difficulty for you. Parks 2 would have done the job if you ordered it, but you snapped at Anna and shouted you were too busy for stupid plants. And, last I saw of Anna, she was crying, and headed towards Hadrian's wall. No guesses where *she* was going. At least she *has* a friend. Not to worry, I found Sable a friend. As it turns out, Jack is gloomier than usual and could do with a good squirrel chase. I also met with Helen and Francis and asked them to take a cutting from Sable's roots to use later. Sable may have a brother, yet. No thanks to you."

"Eavesdropper!"

"That's my job. What do you think ghosts do. Do you know yours! An ice chip off the old Rupert," he called after her, before remembering his duty. Taraq turned a beaming smile on Tut. "And as for you, Master Tut, I need a private word with you *before* you see Brooks."

Anna made her way to the wall looking over her shoulder and ignored the whispered warnings of the lavender. They were nosey and told tales. "Bash won't care," Anna shouted back. "She doesn't care about anything these days."

As usual, the stones in Hadrian's Wall were baked too hot to touch from the winter heatwave.

"Vita," she called through a large chink in the wall. "I'm here." With that she merged into the stones and stood on the other side where it was raining. The stones were cool, surprisingly not steaming in the cold drizzle.

Vita was waiting. "I dreamed you'd be here today," she said with a fierce hug. "Look I've brought you something." She was clearly proud of a new amulet threaded on a leather thong bouncing on her neck. It was gold.

Anna looked closely at the fine detail of a man driving a chariot pulled by three horses.

"It's Mars," Vita said. "It's the hardest one I've ever made. I found a damaged gold brooch and melted it down when my father was away. I'll give it to you later. But we must hurry if we're to see the turtle."

Anna, caught up in her friend's excitement, ignored the word turtle.

The clash of metal against metal greeted the girls long before they arrived at the practice field where a hundred soldiers stood shoulder-to-shoulder in the sodden thatch grass. – a legion dressed for war on ground that horses had churned into a sea of liquid mud. The army paraded, in a noisy clatter, in formation, legs splashed to the knees with grey sludge, their sandals caked with clay.

A hundred solemn expressions fixed on a commander who fared no better in the grey drizzle. His eyes flickered once as the girls passed his line of vision, but his head never moved. His unexpectedly barked orders made Anna jump. "Does he always shout?"

"Always. And don't think he hasn't noticed we're here. My father says he can see out the back of his head. He's noticed us all right. Any moment now he'll shout at us. I come here all the time and it's always the same. Children have orders too. And it's to stay clear of the training grounds." She waved in the vague direction of another metallic sound. "That's the smithy where my father works. There's always repairs to be made even after a mock battle."

A pile of abandoned shields stacked high outside the door streamed with water. A man emerged, threw a shield on another heap and took the next broken one inside. "That's my father," Vita said. "He knows I'm here, too. I will be in trouble, later, but it's easy to distract him.

He's exhausted when he gets home and there are nine of us, so he either forgets or gives up. In any case, he will lecture all of us for my crime, gobble down his food and head to the tavern."

A dozen soldiers stepped forward from the ranks and formed a loose circle.

"They're going to make the 'turtle'," Vita said. "Watch, it's my favorite."

"The turtle?"

"Wait and see. They're going to form a group underneath their shields held close together like the shell of a turtle."

"And then what?"

"Watch." The turtle shuffled forward and advanced slowly as one creature. "Nothing can harm them. Shields placed together like that are like a suit of armour." The huddle moved surprisingly quickly, mired as it was in ankle deep mud. The commander shouted orders to stop and the turtle turned to march left then right.

"How can they see?"

"There's always tiny gaps between the round shields and a leader on each side gives the orders. In the field of battle there is no commander near enough to issue orders. Swords sprang from the shell that swivelled to engage an imagined enemy. Once stopped, the shell exploded like the opening of an umbrella and each soldier took the stance of attack, brandishing the former piece of shell that had been their wall or ceiling. They lunged and shrieked terrifying noises. At a word from the commander, they backed into each other forming a new circle, and the turtle reappeared in a crash of shields, looking like an overturned bowl.

A team of soldiers rained blows upon it, but no swords penetrated. Vita explained. "Shields nearest the ground prevent attacks on their feet which would bring the whole enterprise to a heap of sprawling men vulnerable to the enemy. The shields are made of leather circles laid to overlap like slate tiles in a roof, strapped together with wire so if, in the siege of a castle or great hall, burning oil was poured from above, it fails to penetrate. Metal shields would burn them. Most of their armour is leather, anyway. My father makes the studs and straps and repairs the ones that break. It takes him every day from dawn til' sundown. And he has several apprentices."

"Are they going to war?"

"Hardly ever. I've never seen them on the march other than a small party sent to settle a skirmish. But they practise for war, and the war stories told around the hearth keep everyone terrified. This fort is still being built and there's the wall to finish. Trenches to dig. I doubt they'll finish in my lifetime. I'll be an old lady of twenty before they're done."

"Old!"

"My mother died at nineteen. My new stepmother is already fifteen. Men live much longer. My father is almost thirty."

"In my time, Bede is preparing for war. We don't have shields or swords."

"Make some. Shields are easy. She waved her hand at a shanty of huts mired in the mud. The children of the camp collect scraps from the leather works, trim them into squares and soak them in vats filled with foul ingredients. I won't tell you what's in it. Three layers are pressed together in a vice until they dry like roof tiles. We punch holes in the edges with an awl while they're wet. My father taught me how to cast amulets in the fire. I'll show you…"

"Clear off, Vita. I see you," the commander bellowed. "You've been warned."

Vita's father appeared at the sound of his daughter's name. He plodded towards Vita in a straight line, through the field, slipping sideways through squelching mud. He was waving a stick and shouting angry words. "Off with you girl," he shouted. "Go help your mother." He winked with his back to the commander and pulled a small leather pouch from his shirt. "Here. These came out of the molds but an hour ago. They need polishing." He cuffed her ear for the commander's benefit and smiled. He raised his voice. "And I'll polish your backside if you keep disobeying my orders."

The commander's leather gauntlet studded with iron nails waved Vita's father away. "No children allowed on the field," he barked at Vita.

. . .

As the girls beat a hasty retreat across an expanse of muddy turf, Anna tripped and fell to her knees. Her hands, swallowed by mud, emerged squeaky clean.

"Come on," Vita said. "There's something… I mean, some*one* I want to show you in the garrison's hospital tent." She glanced at Anna's clean hands. "How is it your hands and shoes stay clean? And why can't my father see you?"

"I told you. I'm not here in body, Vita. I'm sleeping hundreds of years away. I expect that's too far for your father to see. You're special…" she gave Vita's arm a squeeze. "*We're* special."

Vita towed Anna forward in the direction of a several long tents that looked like a street of flimsy row houses. Their sides flapped in the wind making sounds like distant thunder as the girls picked their way forward.

Embarrassed now that she was impervious to the weather after seeing her friend's feet, blue with cold under their coating of dried mud. Mud was deliberately piled on shaped into brick clogs, and when dried, formed a scanty barrier against the cold but mud didn't stay dry for long in the rainy north of Britain. She'd wanted to bring Vita a pair of boots, but they'd discussed the impossibility of her explaining them and that they'd be taken away to be burned. And worse, Vita would be shunned as a demon child and her family driven off.

There was no activity in the middle tent, apart from the flicker of a lantern above one of the beds. Several rows of empty cots made of wood and leather twine held straw mattresses. The smell of nearby horses was hardly sanitary in a hospital that a shared wall with a stable. Pigs grunted in the next tent.

Vita pointed to the dimly lit corner. "He's over there by the little butterfly," she whispered.

Anna edged closer keeping her eye on the butterfly, obviously agitated by their presence. A flustered voice silenced her fears. "Oh, it's you, Mistress Anna," it said. "Miss Charlotte said you would come." Fioretti flew around Anna's head and returned to hover over her patient. The form of a young man shrouded in a threadbare horse blanket, looked like one of the carved knights she'd seen in Bede's churchyard. "He's over here," she whispered. "Please, keep your voices down."

"That's Fioretti," Anna said to Vita. "She's a fairy."

"The ghost of a fairy," Fioretti corrected, continuing to weave a protective canopy of light around the cot. But there were gaps in her creation like the burn holes of an old cloth.

A table on the other side of the room held a red apple, from which a single bite had been taken, marred by a bruise, three wormholes, and a set of black fingerprints.

The pallid face of Six, was revealed stark and statue-like against a straw pillow. His bier, for that's what it looked like, rested on a floor of black ash that smelled of sulphur, an odor Anna recognized as the Furies signature. Anna held her nose and grimaced.

"That's the pigs," Vita said.

Anna stood next to the bed and gasped. "Six!"

"Is he a friend of yours?" Vita exclaimed.

"He's my uncle. And he's missing in battle. But I see that he's not dead as we feared."

Fioretti flew closer to Anna and curtsied in mid-air to Vita. "I've orders to guard him, but you mustn't tell Mistress Bash you've seen him or the creature may come and move him. You must go quickly. She hears everything."

Anna turned a stricken expression to Vita. "I promise to return tomorrow." Her eyes widened at the empty string around Vita's neck. "Oh, Vita. Your beautiful gold amulet. It's gone!"

"It was *your* beautiful amulet," Vita said in tears. "I have no gold to make another."

Anna flew to the florist shop with Jack at her heels. "Miss Hannah, Bash said to report my findings to you. I tried to tell her but she was angry. She shouted 'Don't tell me, tell Hannah. She's in charge, now'. She didn't want to hear my news. Mrs. Clutterbuck, I know where Six is."

"Oh, dear girl, you didn't tell her about Six, did you?"

"No, Aunt Bash told me to get lost, which was a strange thing, considering she was so happy to find me only a day ago."

Hanna flustered about in a tizzy, turning left and thinking better of it turning right, "Thank goodness," she said. "Anna, you're not to worry your head about Six. He'll return or not. All in good time, little one. Although there's nothing good in it I can see. We must remain hopeful and," she held a finger to her lips, "silent for the time being."

Anna made Jack sit and gave him a treat. "I need to report something else that's important ... we should order soldiers' shields. Parks 2 or 3 can fashion them. The Rowan tree has already agreed to shed the branches we'll need. They promised to fall, already thatched, if we ask. All that's needed are the frames and we can use old bicycle tire rims. I can make Mr. Leoni a drawing."

"Mr. Clutterbuck has a pile of tire rims rusting in the yard."

Jack sniffed Dee Dee and sneezed. Anna sniffed the air. "I smell fire. Is something burning in the kitchen?"

Hannah fussed around Dee Dee with a feather duster. "No. I'm afraid Dee Dee was in a bad accident. She was a prize exhibit in the Ashmolean Museum, the last dodo in existence, and some clod of a lad threw her on a bonfire during a massive clean up. Serious mistake. Heads rolled. Sometimes that smell of a ghost fire surrounds her.

Pigeon heard her cry for help, and as you can see, she was more or less, saved. Teddy found her in a dumpster and brought her to me." Hannah crooned soothing words to the bird. "There there... be a love and ignore Jackie. Sometimes dogs can be impolite, but they don't mean to be. They're not like cats who pride themselves on being superior."

Hannah listened carefully to someone who wasn't there and made a few sketches on paper. "Did it look like this? Or this?" she asked the air. "I've seen pictures of the Roman soldiers in an old book. I'll look it up and order Parks 3 to make nine shields poste haste from the brambles of the rowan fallings. I will inform the Rowan trees. Magic is much stronger than leather."

Dee Dee's wings moved almost imperceptibly, dislodging a few pink tail feathers that fell on Jack's nose. Jack shook his head and growled at them, but Hannah picked them up and placed them in a shoe box. "I'll glue them back on later," she said to the bird. Dee Dee chuckled. *'Birds of a feather stick together. Wheeeee,'* she said. *'the spring is sprung the grass is riz I wonder where the birdies is. The birdies, they is on the wing. Now ain't that absurd, I thought the wing was on the bird.'*

It was midnight when Anna stole into Bash's bower. She snipped a lock of her aunt's purple hair and placed it in an envelope borrowed from Lady Nan's writing desk. Aunt Bash's face was troubled even in sleep, which made Anna wonder if that was how she must have looked in her own winter bed, barely three years in her past.

Feathers made her evening rounds looking for Snowdrop. "I can't find my daughter anywhere," she asked Lady Nan who suggested Sarah's kitchen. "Her father forbade her to leave the estate."

Taraq followed Feathers to Bede and waited in Sarah's larder to deliver Snowdrop's message. "I saw her with Sage, asleep in her old spot. I'm going back there myself. Shall I escort you?"

"I doubt you can fly as fast as I can run, but thank you," Feathers answered, distractedly before streaking off into the trees through the Green Lady's shortcut.

Sage was far from apologetic. "Mistress Feathers," he said with great dignity considering he was a shadow of his former lush self. "Snowdrop is in Egypt, meeting her destiny."

chapter 17
THE BOY KING

The Temple of Bast glowed white in the unforgiving heat of afternoon. It was the 'hour of rest'. The unbroken rhythm of pounding stone from the nearby quarries sounded like a ticking clock. Thin slivers of lilac-scented shade moved over the roof like a sundial. The temple cats sleeping there, stretched towards the heat like sunflowers.

Deep inside the temple precincts, a shaft of reflected sunlight quickened the pyramid of sand in Lady Nan's hourglass giving it the illusion it had melted to red glass. Pigeon saw it in his dream.

Near the inner sanctum where the worst of the heat was unable to penetrate, the priestesses rested. Babs padded silently on her rounds while Bast slept. The gentle flap of the 'right of passage portal' opening and closing announced the occasional departure of a dreaming cat or the arrival of a returning one. Babs inspected the portal sniffing it the way a housecat sniffs for mice. The comings and goings of each cat were approved before sending them on their way with a playful cuff.

As was the custom, the 'hour of rest' conserved the essential feline energies required to oversee the natural flow of time.

SaRa, heavy with child, resting on a pallet, had drifted off to play with her unborn children. She smiled, safe inside her own dream.

Pigeon dozed fitfully across the room perched beside Lady Nan's hourglass, cackling to himself, his head under a wing. *'It has begun,'* he screeched in his head. *'Kit... stir your stumps, boy... Panic attack... alert the Passage Police. Where is Parks! Watch out for Jackals... it has begun!'*

Babs streaked through the curtained door. "Who dares to disturb Bast during the sacred hour of rest," she growled. "Oh, it's you, Master Pa'a. Shame on you. You know the rules. Screeching inside the temple, even to oneself, is not permitted unless it's an emergency. Piercing thoughts shatter the restorative energy of deep sleep. Is there an emergency?"

'Well, something has certainly EMERGED,' Pigeon replied coolly. *'I must find Kit. Kha needs be notified.'*

Babs flicked her tail like a whip as she slunk away. "Master KiTiKha'at is regrettably predictable," she telegraphed. "You can find him in his regular afternoon place. Kha may be summoned in the usual ways. I don't want to remind you again. Screeching is forbidden unless something dire has taken place."

'Condition Purple.' Pigeon chattered quietly to himself. *'Red glass at noon – an alchemist's doom.'* Kit was away again, off to visit a dog who wasn't there – another hallucination of wolfhound Jack.

There were two things Kit had discovered about Egypt. The consistent frequency of heatwaves formed images of wished for people. He saw Jack most mornings after meditation, waiting for him a few yards off, even before the baked sands had settled into a glaring white carpet. Kit always ran towards Jack holding his breath, hoping his magic had created a miracle, but it always ended in disappointment with him collapsing onto his knees to embrace the phantom dog he knew in his heart could not be there.

The second thing was that the temple cats were serious actors.

Sibuna continued to watch Master KiTiKha'at's daily ritual with half-closed eyes. How could a human be so slow. And so completely doolally over a smelly Jackal that didn't even exist. There was no accounting for the Bede creatures. How his brother Anubis could put up living in green wetlands run by such weak humans, seemed a waste of time. But the temple spoke of great deeds to come and Sibuna's instructions were to comply with Kha's orders with as much dignity as possible, considering subservience to an untried boy was quite beneath his rank. But Bast was wise. And if SHE welcomed the boy with removable black eyes, then he would do likewise in a way that honored his position without dishonoring his line. The prospect of failure gave him a wobbly tummy in need of the 'Mindful Field's' therapeutic effects.

Kit easily located the disturbance that caught his eye, with Cornelius's battered binoculars. He silently thanked Brooks' foresight, or was it hindsight, at least a dozen times a day, for slipping them into his backpack. Today's object of enquiry was lodged behind the Sphinx's ear – a miniscule white blob of fluff that stretched into an unmistakable fully-grown Snowdrop.

For a moment Kit thought he might have sleep-traveled back to Bede and looked about him for a familiar landmark or his form sleeping in the shade of a date palm. He often napped in the afternoons, wandering outside his body after conjuring an image of Jack which was common enough after one of Kha's remote viewing classes.

Jack hadn't materialized. But something else had. And that something was Snowdrop.

The white blob of fluff had already caused a stir inside the temple as the feline inhabitants swarmed from it excitedly and collected at the base of the Sphinx's rump. A hundred gold necklaces and earrings glinted in the sun as they waited for what was possibly another foreign goddess joining them from a distant land. She or he, had to be of great importance to be so familiar with the great stone lion.

To his surprise, Kit had traveled no further than a few steps from the temple precincts. He made his way through the mob of expectant cats, looking for all the world like a fan club awaiting a celebrity, but eager to follow advanced feline protocol by assuming an air of indifference and respect at the same time.

Sibuna pushed in ahead of him, sleek and important, tail high, and took his place of honor in the front row of fifty or so cats of every color and stripe. ArTuRa, Kit's cat attendant, materialized at his heels. He stared at Snowdrop in astonishment. His fur crackled with electricity. He had dreamed of her for weeks and here she was.

Kit parted the cats with small purposeful strides, pocketing his binoculars, which for some reason the temple cats found as objectionable as his sunglasses. The binoculars swung around his neck as he lowered the sunglasses perched on top of his head to his nose. He tiptoed respectfully past Sibuna who gave his removeable eyes a disparaging hiss. The boy was hiding again.

"Snowdrop. It's me," Kit called out. "Well, aren't *you* a sight for sunblind eyes, all grown up. Are you here to fetch me or are you a mirage?"

"A marriage," she replied, her eyes locked on ArTuRa's. "Definitely *not* a mirage."

Kit's best British sandals easily out-sandaled the local makeshift coverings of papyrus leaves and rope. ArTuRa, guarded them as attentively as all his magical amulets, or himself for that matter, as a badge of honor: Kit's camouflage backpack that opened and closed with bewitched teeth, two separate pairs of removable black eyes (sunglasses and binoculars), an ebony box that hummed tunes once-in-a-while (cellphone), an assortment of enchanted paintbrushes he called magic markers, and the tall 'Glass of Hours', were safe. Every item was laid out in a careful pattern according to the English boy's wishes, formally, KiTiKha'at Prince of Bede, Master Physician and Magician, initiate of his majesty Lord Kha, and wife of Lady SaRa, their appointed priestess.

The only thing Bast's royal cats accepted without question was Kit's turquoise scarab. Such noble scarabs were given as much deference as the great goddess herself. Even Bast deferred to royal scarabs. But confrontations with the Prince's 'White Horus' with its disagreeable ear-splitting shriek and flapping wings, were avoided as much as possible.

"Careful master," Sibuna hissed drily. "It could be a trick of the light, again. I wouldn't want you to be disappointed."

Snowdrop leapt gracefully into Kit's arms and snuggled into his neck, much to the shock of the gathering. A shiver of power rippled the fur on their necks. An unheard of, public display of affection. Such a strange language. Such dainty toes… and not the right number, either. Collectively, the temple cats bowed their heads respectfully to give Kit and his Bede cat a semblance of privacy, exposed as they were.

Snowdrop followed the mob's protocol. She bowed formally, first to Sibuna and then to Kit. "Uncle Sibuna, my father sends his regards," she said. "Kit, Bede Hall is on high alert. Especially for a message from you."

"I'm too far away. There's too much interference of rays and vibrations. Communication is garbled static," Kit answered. "It's not for want of trying. How is Jack?"

"Jack is full of beans, but your sister is unwell. She's not herself, at least we all hope her old self will return soon. If I *am* able to get home, I shall tell her you enquired about her health."

Kit shrugged. "I'm not ashamed to admit, that as much as I love Bash, I miss my dog, fiercely. You should understand that given your relationship with Lady Nan."

"Lady Nan is a queen, Kit. No less than the goddess Bast and the Pharaoh Tutankhamun."

"I haven't forgotten. How could I. It's not every day that your grandmother can turn into a queen or a child in the space of a few seconds. So, if it's not letting the proverbial 'cat out of the bag', how dire *is* this news of yours?"

Snowdrop shook her head. "There's no need to be flippant, Kit. Six has been killed by an exploratory swarm of Megeara's wasps. Parks is undercover, literally, in the forest. Charlotte is on edge, Pigeon is missing, and Bash has crashed into the persona of a bully with a sore head. Not coping would be an understatement."

"I know her badgering nature more than anyone," Kit said. "She'll snap out of it." He gestured to the landscape. The Great Sphinx's tail twitched once. Snowdrop read it as the sign Sage had told her to expect. "Pigeon is here and there, doing what he does best in parrot secrecy."

"Snapping is exactly what Bash is doing. As for me, I have a mission. How can I help end this war? I'm here to serve you, Bede, and the planet in that order."

ArTuRa, staring equally hard at Snowdrop, addressed Kit without moving his head. "May I be of further assistance, Sir?"

Kit's blue scarab shuffled on the sand and faced the sun. The assembly watched as it unfurled its papery wings, took to the air, and landed on Snowdrop's head. It was a sign. The scarab had chosen, and by choosing, bestowed honorary favor upon the cat stranger from Bede.

Kit held Snowdrop higher. "This is Snowdrop. She is a beloved friend from home. Please welcome her. If you don't like the idea of another visitor from Bede, I know you can act as if you do."

Back in the temple, ArTuRa ran ahead of Kit and stood waiting by the 'Glass of Hours' for his instructions.

Please give Snowdrop the grand tour," Kit said. "And at your earliest convenience request an audience for her with her Majesty. Inform Babs that Snowdrop is a distinguished guest from Bede." He stroked ArTuRa's fur. "Snowdrop, I'd like to introduce my special companion, ArTuRa."

ArTuRa preened at the compliment. He was a god's companion, not his slave.

Snowdrop's green eyes scanned the handsome black cat before her. She pronounced his Egyptian name slowly, savouring each syllable: "AR... TUR... A." She sneezed which meant she had hit upon a great truth. "Arthur, it is then. You remind me of a legendary British king. Not entirely sure why, but there it is. A thought comes and stays when it's supposed to. King Arthur had great powers of leadership. I am happy to meet you and follow you into the Temple and its ways. As you see, I did not follow the usual passage protocol to get here. But I assure you time traveling between two enchanted sphinxes is highly in order. Please lead on."

Arthur listened respectfully to Snowdrop and attentively to a message only he could hear. "Master KaTiKha'at, Lord Kha commands that you meet him by Her Majesty the Sphinx, immediately," Arthur said. "The matter is urgent."

Snowdrop turned to Kit, shook out her fur, and placed a paw on Kit's arm. "Run along. I have work to do. Arthur here, will deliver me back to you as you require." She lifted her head to listen and slowly turned a sad gaze upon Kit. "Something has begun," she said. "There's no time to waste. Bede Hall is under attack."

Kha pointed to the daily pilgrimage winding its way to the Great Pyramid. "Take a peek, my brother. Behold, the wonderous boy king and his entourage."

Kit, winded from running, exhaled, in awe. "Wow, is that really him?"

Kha faced the procession, staring blankly like a statue. "A celebrity teenager with the confidence of a spoiled child. Not unlike another teenager I could name."

"I am *not* spoiled," Kit countered testily.

The conversation continued with Master and apprentice, of equal height, shoulder-to-shoulder, staring ahead like soldiers in a sentry box.

"Says you," Kha muttered from the corner of his mouth.

"I was never carried about in a basket chair, shaded by servants in white kilts waving ostrich fans or surrounded by half-naked security guards and standard bearers in full regalia."

"Well, King Tutankhamun is a *god* and you, my brother, are only a budding alchemist."

"I can't tell from this distance, but he doesn't seem to exude the power of his famous golden mask. It's odd to think he's the dehydrated broken body with the grimacing death skull, that I know from Howard Carter's famous photographs."

"Being dead for three-thousand-years takes its toll."

Kit shivered. "I remember seeing my parents as mummies. "No doubt Tutankhamun's ghost fared better. Taraq's ghost takes the form of a healthy kid but I saw his skeleton in-situ once, and I can assure you, it was not pretty. When bottom jaws fall away it looks like a skull is screaming. He paused "You know, I think I may have seen too many photographs from digs and museums than was good for me. But right now, it's amazing that I, a teenager from the twenty-first century, am witnessing the most famous Egyptian pharaoh in the world. I could go up and touch him. He's a movie star."

Kha stayed Kit's arm. "A movie star who doesn't give autographs. Look, Kit, that boy is considered a god. He is out of bounds… untouchable."

"No kidding, do you think I'm completely stupid?"

Kha grinned momentarily before sobering. "I have to tell you something. Not to be repeated, you understand. The truth is, the King is *unable* to walk properly. He presents best when seated on a throne or a horse. That crown he's wearing covers an abnormally elongated skull. Ay explained it all away as the gift of the god Amun. In any case, the people will only believe so much and they need to see him as reasonably healthy. I'll explain more later. Also, for now, the King's name is Tutankhamun. His 'Aten' birth name is never uttered unless you want to die a grisly death. Wait here and for goodness sake stay still. Remember your profile is anonymous for a reason. You can take this as a 'no sudden moves or emotional outbursts' command. You are, for our purposes, in an everyday situation that elicits no overt reactions. I will be right back."

Kit opened his mouth to speak but it was too late. Kha sprang to life, brushed past him, and approached the king. After a brief exchange, the king glanced in Kit's direction and nodded. Kit remained motionless. His arm itched to wave back. It felt rude not to wave.

Out the corner of his eye, Kit saw Kha back away from the king before turning to face him. His expression was one of exasperation. "I can see that you have a question for me," he said.

"A whole pyramid of questions. For one, how is it you don't avert your eyes like everyone else?"

"I am a magician and physician. It is my privilege to act unflinchingly equal. Eye contact may be permitted for you *after* I arrange it, but any other kind of contact is forbidden. For you, touching the king would be a death sentence."

"When do I get to meet him? Today? When? I promise to behave. No waving or shouting hurray. I had no idea you were so high up the social ladder."

"It's not social. Nothing here is remotely social. It's ancestral through and through. NEVER forget that. By the way, that summons? Tutankh*amun* wanted to know who you were."

It was Kit's turn to grin. "What did you tell him? The king acted as if you were his friend."

"I was Tut's companion during his childhood and as his Master of Horse I enjoyed the unique honor of saving his life. King Tutankhamun is no champion charioteer. He still has a limp from a broken foot carelessly caught in a makeshift stirrup. Circumstances determine he's more scholarly now, content to discuss his interests with the philosopher I appear to be. Discussion relaxes him. He's almost eighteen, like you used to be a thousand or so years ago. His birthday is in a few days. There will be a celebration – a pageant where Tut will showcase his new chariot. That's dangerous at the best of times."

"Has the king time-traveled?"

"Alchemists can produce miraculous things but other than the Temple of Bast there is no concept of time as anything more than the passage of the sun every day. But that grey-haired geezer leading the procession, striding like a peacock… he knows all about time travel. His name is Ay. He's Tutankhamun's vizier. The big cheese, as you would say, behind the throne. And by the way, that little *parade* is more accurately, a *charade*."

"You'd think he was wearing a wristwatch and listening to check if it was ticking. And now he's talking to it like a walkie talky."

"Correct on two counts. He is listening *and* talking, but to his bracelet. Now why do you suppose that is?"

Kit shrugged. "Is he insane?"

"Ay has not only infiltrated the rival Amun priesthood, he runs it, which means the Temple of Horus his stomping grounds and that man can stomp harder than most. And yes, he's quite insane. Too much power will do that."

"I *am* a little familiar with the eighteenth-dynasty. You pick up a lot when your father is an Egyptologist. I know the vizier Ay from the scribes' records."

Kha grabbed Kit by the shoulders and shouted. "Listen up, Kit. Scribes write the propaganda they're ordered to write on pain of death. History is always biased towards the guy left standing able to proclaim victory after a battle. If nothing else gets through your thick skull, I want you to fully appreciate that you are *living* in the true unedited version Egypt's history. We are *not* rewriting it. You *will* meet Ay face-to-face, and if you want to survive long enough to save your family, you will follow every single rule I give you, without question. Please say you understand."

"I understand, but…"

"There are *no* buts. You've not mastered enough to ask questions. And very soon, you will have to supply answers to impossible questions. If you've ever heard of the expression time is of the essence, it is time to heed it now. Ay stands in front of the Furies but he's no less a pawn than the rest of us. Luckily for us, he thinks he's a player. Take him down and the battle with Megeara is half won."

"Okay, okay, I comply, master."

"Never look the vizier in the eye unless commanded to do so, and if that happens you will have either done something incredibly good or incredibly bad. When you do cross him, and you will, it's better to have given him reason to admire your guts. Even false bravado is big here if you choose the right moment. Otherwise silence is expected. Silence is smart. Let this be the time you study Ay's moves. When you 'walky and talky', anywhere, you have one thing to remember. Ay is your enemy. Repeat that back to me."

"Ay is my enemy."

For all his swagger, he is Megeara's mouthpiece. Allecto's plaything and Tisiphone's flunky. For what he is about to do may you be truly terrified."

"I feel like I know him."

"Kit, he was your grandfather, Hilton Cadwick in the flesh, the man who made you call him Captain. So yes, he's more than aware of time travel. And now you have an inkling of how Tut's throne came to be his son Ben's chair, and subsequently yours."

"So, I'm already in big trouble."

"The biggest and it will get bigger."

Kit's mood deflated to a look of fear. "My grandfather hated me. He despised Brooks."

"Your mentor Peregrine Brooks is fully aware in Bede, but here as Smenkhare, Tutankhamun's brother, he is sadly uninformed. Reincarnation is a funny business. It's what you would call an inexact science. Selective memories are rarely remembered in a straight line. Sometimes it takes a ton of years to fall on your head to wise up. Brooks still protects your grandmother who, by all rights, is beyond protecting in her present state. But that's love and duty. You must learn these things for yourself."

"Is that going to be part of your teachings?"

"It most certainly is *not*. Although human chemistry is most certainly a powerful ruling force that informs decision making and breaking in equal measure. Oh, and your Uncle Ben's hero, Howard Carter, is here too. He lives in a settlement of tomb diggers in the Valley of the Kings' as a foreman of works. Three guesses which tomb he's working on."

Kha grabbed a fistful of Kit's shirt as the procession swerved closer. He prodded Kit's chest and whispered. "Stay calm. I need you to pay closer attention to the king's courtiers. I think you may know the man…"

Kit lurched forward, stayed by his shirt collar. "Dad!"

"Keep your voice down. Or all our work will count for nothing!"

"But that's…"

"Your father, yes I know. You can see by his glazed expression he's not fully conscious. So, let's rescue him very soon, shall we. And we won't be able to do that if you panic. Cunning and staying calm is our best chance. Your father is in no immediate danger. Just keep a cool head."

Kit swallowed hard and choked out the words "I'll do my best. Is my Mum?… Where is my Mum?"

"Quite safe, sequestered away. As a female, she rarely ventures out. As Ay's daughter, she is somewhat protected by the future, but not indefinitely. Ay has little regard for sentiment. In this time, your father is still Ay's future Egyptologist son-in-law who, by poking around the Valley of the Kings in the 21st century, is messing with his legacy. There are secret historical papyruses with crimes and dates and ancient bad press releases that go missing. Ay is big on power. Megeara is shrewd, she bequeaths jealousies equally to her enemies *and* allies for her own amusement, and supreme power fanned by unparalleled jealousy is a double force to reckon with."

"Okaaaay?"

"Ay's ego makes him vulnerable, which is good for us, but only if we remain as shrewd as he is. Arrogance eclipses street smarts. Use yours well. You must think on your feet. I hope your brother, Tut of Bede, imparted some of that. Why do you think Megeara pitted the two of you against each other?"

Kit groaned. "And I was the one who nicknamed him Tut in an inspired moment."

"Yeah, who says there's no such thing as a coincidence. A friendly ghost who happens to have the same name as your 'soon to be adopted' brother, who is about to rescue your missing father, arrives at an opportune moment after a perfectly timed business venture manifests in the nick of time. Who knew."

"Are you saying we can be more than one person?"

"Twice-borns can. Kit, the young man you are now *is* another person, so far above the science geek I met in Cairo as to be laughable. Except there is nothing funny about elemental battles of power. Elementals can be a special pain. Controlling your outbursts is going to be your true initiation."

But Kit wasn't listening. He was mumbling to himself with a smile on his face. "I saw my Dad. I saw him. He's not dead. He's not a mummy. He's alive. My parents are alive, and I can save them."

Kha snapped his fingers in Kit's face. "Listen to me. An alchemist can live multiple lifetimes simultaneously. The reason I look so familiar to you is because we met a few years ago in a lucid dream. I was the street kid, Taraq, who saved your father's life. I was the stepbrother you renamed, Tut. From today, Tut's suppressed memories will slowly resurface in Bede. The old score between you must heal for your mission to succeed." He snapped his fingers a second time. "We've only scratched the surface of your mind-blowing apprenticeship."

Kit blinked at Kha, grinning madly. "I wasn't listening. What did you say? I saw my dad. I saw my dad!"

chapter 18
TIME MARCHES BLACK-WARDS

Lady Nan tapped her foot as she scanned the blue sky. Her arms were crossed but she listened to Anna, with her senses wide open.

"My dearest oldest friend and granddaughter," she said. "You were right to come to me. Friends are more important than ever during a crisis. And we're deep inside a doozy, aren't we. But this, I *can* tell you, you are helping Vita every bit as much as she helps you. It's a twice-born pact you made long ago."

"What? When?"

Lady Nan waived Anna's protest away with a jangle of Egyptian bracelets. "The details are not relevant for this conversation. Perhaps one day..." she trailed off, misty-eyed. "What *is* relevant is this: Your friend's name is Latin for 'life' and with one little 's' it becomes vista – a perspective where a landscape may be seen in its entirety. In your case, a panoramic view of Hadrian's fort in the past. Vista and vast are linked, too. Take of this what you will, but Vita is playing a part in our present time. Her amulets contained power of which she was unaware. Love will do that. Friendships are *that* powerful. You and I should know. A 'vista' of our history shows life (vita) as a (vast) bigger picture (a vista).

"She helps our war?"

"Unmistakably, yes."

"I don't understand. How?"

"Multifold ways. Ways that unfold like a paper puzzle. Hence the word multiply. All you need to remember, is that one day, when the time is right, you will know. And at that exact same moment, Vita will know too. You enter each other's worlds in dreams."

"It seems real."

"Lucid dreams *are* real. Friends and fiends are real, too. And while we are at war with fiends, it's important to determine if strangers are friends or foes.

Anna brightened after a puzzled moment. "I see the word 'fiend' inside 'friend'

"Bravo. You're another wordsmith like your Aunt Bathsheba. The removal of a letter can make a world of difference, but remember this, if it's completely true, the hidden meaning must remain the same."

"Aunt Bash is acting like a…"

"A fiend? Yes, we all have that in our nature. She has to snap out of it. All we can do is watch her unfold in *her* 'many layers' and love her even when she bites."

"I would still love Jack if he bit me. I wonder what the 'r' in friend, means?"

"I have no doubt you will know if or when you need to know." Lady Nan drew Anna into a hug. "I want to tell you about surprises. We call some of them shocks, but essentially, they're the same thing. If only your Aunt Bash would remember that grief is a necessary surprise, and medicine can take its time when healing a broken heart."

Anna took her grandmother's hand and curtsied. For a moment Queen Ankhesenaten shimmered through Lady Nan's face. And then, her childhood companion, the young Beryl stood before her. Two nine-year-old girls held hands in a room as cold as winter. "Thank you, Rain," Anna said.

"You're welcome, Snow," Lady Nan replied. She kissed Snow's cold cheek. "Now, go make history."

Katydid had done her job. When Bash reached the lavender field, the plants rippled like a flag in the wind at the sound of her voice. The lavender parted in the middle, opening up a path to their centre. Bash's grey cloud followed as low as it dared. For a moment it dipped too low, trying to listen to the lavender's conversation, but it turned a lovely mauve color and beat a hasty retreat hovering at treetop level to wait. The cloud trembled as if it contained a small earthquake, released a mauve vapor, and its greyness returned a shade darker than before.

'We hope you're feeling better,' The lavender soothed.

"I need a place to think."

'You're befuddled.'

"I feel… at odds with myself. It's as if I'm two people. I can see the me outside of me. So, I suppose that means I'm only half-me most of the time."

"You're in shock. That thing following you is clouding your judgement. We will clear your head if you open your mind.'

A strange rendition of Gregorian chant wafted over the rippling flowers which caused several things to happen in close succession: Bash burst into tears, the cloud went dark, and Bash literally, blacked out.

The rain was falling harder inside Hadrian's Wall on Anna's third visit – the day prearranged on a tenuous yesterday, but Vita wasn't there. Anna was pleased she'd thought to bring an umbrella. It would surprise Vita, make her laugh, and the visit would be more dry, at least from the top down.

An old woman sat huddled under a leather shield a short distance away. Anna approached her with her umbrella open and held it over her. The woman was dozing and woke when the rain stopped hitting her shield.

"I'm looking for a friend," Anna said. "Her name is Vita. Perhaps you know her?"

The crinkled face grinned. "I thought you'd never come," she said.

"Vita!"

"You haven't changed," Vita said trying to stand. She grabbed Anna's arm and heaved herself up. "You never showed the next day. I've come here every day since, just in case. I even expected you to show up in the camp. I never stopped hoping and looking. These days, most folks consider me crazy. My family is gone. All anyone knows of me is that I rant about a girl who lives in the wall."

"Well, no wonder they think you're crazy."

"I live in the hospital tent we visited. I'm a kind of oracle, now. It's strange how things turn out. "Your uncle is still there with the butterfly. Once or twice a few people report seeing her light when they seek answers from me. After that, the true seekers believe anything I say… except for the girl in the wall, story. To be honest, I think they're afraid of me."

Anna scanned the landscape. A straggle of Vita's followers stood a way off in a silent group drenched in the downpour. "I see them."

"They're watching me right now. Watching me talk to no-one they can see. I wait for you, rain or snow, at the same time each day. Whatever the weather they can be sure of where I am in the afternoons." She laughed and patted the shield. "As you see, I have my own shield. I guess that makes me a turtle."

"I am so sorry. I told Fioretti I would come. She was supposed to tell you."

"She did. But after a while, I didn't believe her when she said you'd be here tomorrow."

"Vita, I've only been gone one day. It *is* tomorrow, for me."

"Walk with me, Anna," Vita whispered. "The hour approaches when I give prophecies. I've told them about your shiny boots that would melt in a fire and a white cat than disappears when startled."

"Have I made your life difficult?"

"Goodness, no. I thank you every day for waking me up. I met my husband because of you. My children were raised on stories about the invisible Hall that lives in the sky over the fort. I have the most wonderful memories, all because of you."

The tent flap was tied back so the chickens could come and go. Their constant clucking made a nice change to the stench of pigs.

Fioretti zoomed and spun a cocoon of light around Anna. "You see, Vita. I told you she would come."

Six's cot looked more like a bier covered in fresh flowers. "Everyone must leave me a flower if they want a question answered," Vita said. "They can't see your uncle of course, but they do see a cot covered in blossoms. Fioretti told me her name meant little flowers, so I changed my name to Fioretta. My people came from the city of

Firenze in Italy, a long time ago. Did you know Firenze means the city of flowers?"

For the longest time, a transparent girl and an old woman dreamed side-by-side as the rain turned stormy. If Vita's followers had been closer, they would have seen the rain parting in an arc over Vita's head. "Flora is the name of the green goddess, too," Anna said. "She's had to go away until our war is over. I told a friend about you and the turtle, and she's ordered a few shields to be made. So, you're helping us defend Bede. There's another story for you to tell your followers. We call them fans in my time. I think you must be the Lady of the Green Shrine in the Place of Hours that Nimue talks about. She'll be chuffed when I tell her. Funny how things turn out. I only came here three times."

"Third time lucky," Vita said.

Anna placed the lock of Bash's purple hair in Six's hand, still warm to the touch. "Third time lucky," she whispered in his ear.

"Purple is the color of Roman emperors," Vita said. "Your aunt must be an empress."

Anna smiled. "Let's just say she's impressive which is the next best thing."

Anna and Vita trod back to the wall as the rain stopped. "I wish I could leave this umbrella with you," Anna said. "But I don't want it to cause a problem."

Vita was delighted. "I'd love to have it. It's a bit of magic that proves you were here. It will raise my status and I will remember you whenever it rains, which is a great deal."

Anna never said goodbye. She held Vita's hand as she slowly evaporated into Hadrian's Wall. Vita's ghost hand remained for a while, floating in mid-air. Eventually, it waved goodbye and popped like a soap bubble.

Bash blundered into the flower shop. "I may have lost my mind, she blurted. "I remember lying in the lavender field and running here.

There was something I was supposed to remember but I've gone blank."

"Hello to you, too," Hannah said. "I would think forgetting anything would be a mercy. I was about to send for you. Charlotte wants you to know something important. Maybe it will jog your memory. In any case, it's urgent and therefore I *urge* you to pay attention." She looked out the store window. "I see your cloud is still with you, darker and bigger. No guesses why. Your moods affect that disgusting thing. You've been wallowing, my girl."

"I've had a cry."

"That's the very definition of wallowing."

"I'm grieving. Why don't any of you understand."

"That spy cloud absorbs you the same way you absorb it. You're twins. And if you don't turn your thoughts to happier times, I assure you that something is going to happen that none of us will like."

"I can't be happy. Six is dead."

"You are Mistress of the Green, and you can grieve in a positive way with the rest of us meditating alongside you. We have tried to hold your hand, but you shut us out. And not only that, you let Bede fall. You've created a void. The very place where Furies thrive. Six would not have wanted this."

Bash returned to the Hall, grumpy and out of sorts after Hannah's lecture. Sooty fingerprints and deep scratches marred the Hall's front doors and led to the open window of the red library. Anna had reported seeing similar marks on Hadrian's stones. Her bedroom had been ransacked. Clothes littered the floor. Drawers were pulled out and overturned. Perfume bottles smashed. Handprints marred her white curtains, and red ash littered her dressing table covering her rose quartz scarab. The word hello, written on the mirror with pale pink lipstick, was the same eery greeting Snow had written long ago in the frost of the Winter Room for her and Kit. It echoed the message 'soon' she'd left for the lost boy. The remainder of the pink lipstick was crushed to a paste on the carpet. Two bottles of perfume failed to mask the stench of sulphur, but strangely, the goddess bed was untouched, as if protected by a spell. And then Bash remembered when Nimue had visited the day of its delivery, she had muttered several invocations over it, to wish it well, she'd said.

Bash's wellington boots made a crunching sound on the gravel drive as she marched towards the tower which reminded her of the term walking on eggshells. Black patches that looked like old bloodstains blotched its walls.

Tut's voice hailed her. "Hey, wait up. What's the hurry? I think we might be headed in the same direction."

Bash walked faster. A mission to reach Brooks first meant nothing would stop her. Let alone her stepbrother who'd been acting like a jerk for months. "I want to be alone, shove off," she shouted without turning around. Tut balked and turned to see Brooks coming up the drive. He would get to see him first, after all.

The black stains continued up the spiral staircase but the open room at the top was worse, Kit's caldera poster was streaked with soot. His gyroscope and Newton's cradle lay overturned on the floor, half covered in ashes. The blue clock with no hands that she'd given Kit on their thirteenth Birthday had hands drawn on its face with charcoal that pointed to twelve o'clock. The Egyptian throne was nowhere to be seen.

Bash descended the stairs in a fog and met Brooks and Tut at the bottom. She gestured her head upwards. "The Furies have left their calling card," she said. "The throne is gone."

"Let's take a look together, shall we," Brooks said, his face ashen. "Maybe Megeara left a message."

But once in the room, there was no soot damage, no messy ashes, and the blue clock was on the wall. If it had had a real face, it would have been smirking.

"Tricksters," Brooks said. "Are you sure of what you saw? Furies can be dashed cunning."

"I saw what I saw," Bash hedged. "I didn't come here to waste anyone's time."

Brooks rubbed his hands together briskly, washing his hands of further discussion. "All right, you two. State your business. It seems like I must teach two birds with one lecture. Ladies first. Bash, I am very sorry for your loss, but now there are greater stakes. Time is of the essence, as we say. Childhood is over. If we are victorious, you may be fortunate to experience a second childhood later, after this fiasco is over. You can grieve for Six then. That is, if we're still here."

Bash sank to the floor in a swoon, holding her head, swaying and moaning.

"What's the matter," Brooks said. "Are you in pain?"

"In pain. Yes. Emotional pain," Bash whimpered. "I just remembered the last words Megeara shrieked at me, *'it's better to fight while angry… now rather than later. It was my anger that brought Megeara forward. It' all my fault.'*

Sarah Goodman was washing the last saucepan when the cat flap startled her. A black cat wearing a gold necklace strutted forward, tail up on urgent business. "Young lady," it said. "My name is Sibuna, twin brother to Anubis, older by nine seconds. Please direct me to the flower shop of Miss Charlotte. I have news."

Before the cat flap could stop swinging, the transparent form of Anubis burst through the closed front door. The twin cats stood whisker to whisker. Sibuna's wide paws from his extra toe looked almost comical beside Anubis's trim paws. Anubis lowered his head in deference to Sibuna and solidified. "Brother. It is good to see you, but I fear your visit brings bad news."

Sarah still smiling from being called young, dried her hands on her apron and opened the door. Her cottage, being the last in the main street, bordered on open country which made it part of and apart from, the village proper, just as her cat flap was the gateway to and from feline power. She proudly referred to the stone wall in her garden as Hadrian's baby brother, saying it marked the border of liminal and earthly space. She pointed towards the town. "It's the first shop on the left. There's always a fairy on duty lighting the window even if Hannah isn't there."

"I will be right behind you," Anubis said. "I have to speak privately with Sarah."

Sarah and Anubis watched Sibuna streak away, leaving a trail of blue lightning behind him. It hung a few inches above the road, snapping with sparks, and suddenly went out as if it had been switched off.

"*Hmph*," Anubis commented. "Looks remarkably like willow-the-wisp footprints if you ask me. Not that the nasty things have feet. Nicer colour, though. And it doesn't smell." He shook out his fur like a wet cat. "Miss Sarah, can you see through me? I'm not used to using my ka form."

"You're as solid as always. So, that's the twin brother you hardly ever mention."

"It is."

"What are my instructions?" The phone behind her shrilled with its special *urgent* ring.

"You're to wait by the phone," Anubis sniffed peevishly at the phone. "Well, that's my duty done, then."

It was Ben. "Come to the Hall," he said. "Bring all your chocolate biscuits. It's going to be a long night. I love you, Valentine."

The day before Valentines Day had arrived without flower power. The next day, romances would have to bloom without blossoms.

The flower shop door jangled like a windchime as it blew open. Hannah looked up from arranging a vase of silk roses with Anna, and blanched. "It's far too soon," she said. "Oh dear! Has it begun?"

Sibuna made his formal bow. "Miss Charlotte… and… I'm sorry, I wasn't expecting anyone else. Yes. I'm afraid the war has escalated."

Hannah stepped forward and curtsied. "My name is Hannah Clutterbuck, Hannah Johns that was. Charlotte is away. But whatever you say to me, she will hear. And this is Anna, Kit's … *um…*" she raised her eyebrows a touch, "daughter."

"I am Sibuna." He tilted his head studying Anna. "Miss Ani and I are about to meet in a few weeks," he said. "I am the unfortunate messenger bearing bad news. Something enraged the Furies and they're attacking early to surprise Bash. She should not have provoked Megeara."

Hannah pushed aside her flower shears angrily and flumped into a chair. "I warned Bash this could happen. That girl needs a good slap."

Dee Dee giggled from the corner. Sibuna turned and acknowledged her with a bow. "You must be Dee Dee. Pa'a sends his greetings my lady, dodo." He shook his head. "I meant to say, your good friend *Pigeon* sends his greetings."

'I am two two Dee Dees,' Dee Dee chortled. *'Dum dee dee dee… diddly dum. Not so dumb. Slap me silly.'*

Anubis sauntered through the open door of the shop. Within minutes, Hannah gathered up her coat and called out to Anna. "I have to go out dear, please watch Beegle and see that he doesn't eat all the snapdragons, will you. They're his favorite."

While Anna rooted in the cooler for Darwin's lettuce and a sprig of baby's breath for Beegle, Dee Dee began to hum and sing. *'It's clouds illusions we recall… we really don't know clouds at all.'*

chapter 19
TIME PUSHES FORWARD

Kit had been dispatched at dawn, on several errands for Bast herself, with explicit instructions as translated by Babs. "You're not to return home," Babs growled, "until you receive direct permission from Her Majesty. Compliance is expected. Kha has been made aware. Now, go about your assigned tasks."

"How will Her Majesty contact me?"

Babs glared at Kit and whipped her tail like a lasso. "Are you simple? Direct means you will KNOW." She slunk away and snarled over her shoulder. "Believe me, Bast will leave you in no doubt of her wishes."

SaRa's laying-in took place on month nine within a dimly lit anteroom off Bast's inner sanctum surrounded by the nurturing energy of the temple's female cats. The scent of fresh catnip wafted in from the cloistered garden.

As each mother cat joined the circle, their purrs amplified into a sacred chant that filled the birth chamber, easing SaRa into a meditative state of calm expectation. And as her time grew near, the intensity of their singing acted as a sedative until SaRa's ka levitated to oversee the birth of her twins. It floated high above her physical form – a meditating woman, seated in a birthing chair.

Ani arrived first, her violet eyes and glowing transparent skin causing a murmur of delight from the priestesses. "Your daughter is a dream traveler," one of them whispered excitedly to SaRa. Within seconds of being whisked away to a ritual bathing with water infused with lotus petals, Ani's skin resumed a natural golden tan and her dark hair turned white.

Word spread to the male cats outside that a dreamer had been born of the house of Pan, and set off a celebrative yowling, causing Peri to turn in SaRa's womb. Two priestess midwives called for quiet as Peri followed his sister into the 18th dynasty and was pronounced healthy. A small silver streak in his dark forelock decreed he would follow his father's footsteps. A second festive yowl broke the usual quiet of the temple.

SaRa's ghost's smile matched the one on her face below. Her ka circled the newborns, turned and lay floating on its back, and serenely drifted down to settle into SaRa's body.

A cloud of microscopic lotus fairies swirled together forming a fragrant mist that hung over the pair of cradles bestowing various spells for health and happiness. After a time, a procession of feline nursemaids, led SaRa and the babies past the animated wall where they paused to be cleansed by the aura of flashing colors before being presented to the goddess.

Bast received them in her human form. "A dreamer *and* a traveler," she marvelled. "A New Age of Gemini is begun. Goswold's prophecy has come to pass with Christopher and his sister Bathsheba, and now doubly confirmed with Bede's next generation and Egypt's legacy through the offspring of our newly-adopted son, KaTiKha'at, and our beloved daughter SaRa." Bast paused to wink at ArTuRa, "and another line, if I'm not mistaken, and I never am. Our SaRa is a mother, safely delivered of the Pan Gemini. Remember and celebrate this day." She transformed into her rarest matriarchal form – a sleek translucent white tigress with silver stripes. "A banquet of fish and beer is in order," she declared.

The sun was in its zenith when Kit was summoned by a visitation from Her Majesty on the Giza plateau. Bast in Tigress form, cuffed Kit playfully, and when he was barely conscious, she dismissed him by washing her whiskers as if he wasn't there. When her paws were immaculate, Bast licked Kit's face to restore his wits sufficiently enough to regain his bearings. "Now, go home reluctant father," she purred. "Your children are born. One, and mark this word carefully, is in *peril*. The other is a dream traveler. This means she will disappear from time-to-time. But, have no worries on that score. She will have many happy returns."

Kit walked dazedly through the marketplace, escorted by Pigeon crowing *'the Pan Gemini are born. One Perfect Prince Plus one Precious Princess,'* in a royal proclamation. The temple steps, lit by dozens of glowing jars, quickened Kit's pace. Kha stood halfway to the top of the stairs like a waiting sentinel beaming like the proud uncle he was, with arms open wide. "All went well," he called out. "Mother and offspring are in perfect health." Pigeon flashed off in a white blur and reached Kha first where he lit on his proffered arm.

By the time Kit reached them, Kha had seated himself and was feeding Pigeon precious dates and nuts. He stood, dislodging Pigeon who flew to the bowl of delicacies and helped himself. Kha pulled Kit into a bear hug and thumped him on the back. "Congratulations. I need you to sit."

'Your brother-in-law is in shock,' Pigeon cackled. *'Bast gave him a bit of a rude awakening. But I do believe it's had a Positive effect. He may have even grown up a little.'*

The semi-conscious scientist side of Kit's brain wanted to know how alabaster jars could give off such bright light. Kit's alchemist-self guessed it was a secret of magic that Kha would explain sooner if he didn't ask. A shadow of worry crossed his face. "I need to catch my breath, but I want to see SaRa and the…" he smiled, incredulously. "I have children."

'Happy Birthday,' Pigeon said under his wing. *'Time marches on.'*

"SaRa is well," Kha repeated patting the stone beside him. "Hello? Kit? Did you hear me? I need you to sit. You need to catch up with what's happened. The children are healthy. Your family awaits but …"

"No no no. You can't get away with but, anything. Not this time. I won't have it. Look, if something is wrong, don't soften it. Isn't part of my training toughening up by accepting the unacceptable. Well it worked. Here I am and I need to see my wife."

"SaRa wants me to impart something… and don't look terrified. It's something she and I thought may happen. Something completely normal in both our ancestral lineages, where atypical presentiments are expected and welcomed as gifts. Twins born through our bloodlines arrive with preordained extrasensory abilities."

Kit tapped his sandals impatiently. "Gifts that go on giving. Yes, I'm all too aware."

'He's got the key to the door,' Pigeon sang. *'Never been twenty-seven before.'*

You were an astrophysics geek ahead of your time – a science-minded student, academic, single-minded, and ultimately logical. Bash is a natural botanist with a pretentious open mind that embraced the metaphysical world. Your destinies were written in Pangea. Your children's future is written here in hieroglyphics – a dual language that imparts messages in surface pictures as well as in deep esoteric thought. This way the uneducated masses understand a level of instant communication and the house of scribes can share a world of arcane knowledge only possible to digest through years of study. Translation, your daughter is a dream traveler."

As Kit stood to leave, Pigeon swooped, divebombing his head squawking *'Destination Pangea!'* Kit gathered his cloak about him and sat down. "Tell me something I don't know. Anna transported me to the future when I was sleeping. I guess dream travelers can do that. Everyone thought Anna was a summer ghost who haunted the Hall during hot spells which, ironically, manifested in the cold spot in the attic."

"Anna didn't create that spot cold. It was cold long before she arrived," Kha said. "Contrary to the classic rules of paranormal appearances, a cold spot isn't the result of a human ka absorbing local heat in order to manifest."

Kit waved pigeon's continual bombing passes away. "There are several ghosts in Bede Hall, not the least of whom is my grandmother who, I can assure you, can be seriously chilling in many ways, but her appearance is never preceded by a blast of cold air."

Kha assumed the formal pose with his arms crossed that he kept for serious lectures. "The laws of 'ghostly physics' are mathematical proofs refuting that excesses of expelled human ether (souls of the dead) soak up unsuspecting victims wandering in the afterlife. Cold spots are rare pockets of inner-space – time voids where no heat exists, formed by powerful past-life connections. Anna was left alone in an entire world grown cold from a volcanic winter. That's as cold as it gets before life is extinguished."

Kit blinked at Kha. "Anna has a rare gift… and?"

"And she will have a tendency to physically disappear when she travels. Which can be unnerving to parents unfamiliar with the metaphysical world. You may not see Ani when you meet your son. Ani has been dream traveling for the best part of the afternoon. She's quite safe but, well, she's not here and we have no way of knowing where in time she is or are able to call her back."

"But Ani's a helpless baby. Where could an infant possibly go?"

"Ani is never helpless when she travels. Ani can be any age from any one of her past or future lives. She can be an animal or a chair. She can also be dreaming normally like any other baby. If you see her, that's what's happening. Dreams where Ani travels are special. There may be years when she doesn't travel. It's a 'take it as it comes' thing, I'm afraid."

"I have to go. SaRa must be worried sick."

"My sister has been schooled in the magic of alchemy since she could walk, and she has long accepted this might happen. So, no, she's not even a little upset, other than worried how you will react."

Kit grinned. "Ani takes after me."

"Close but not quite."

"I was born a time traveler."

"Time travel and dream travel are worlds apart. Time travel is physical. Dream travel is astral. Your ka left the maze with Anna but not independent of her. Your body remained in the maze in your present time. When you time travel your molecules dissemble and reassemble. Anna had to hold your hand all the way to the future, didn't she?"

"It was like Peter Pan and Wendy, with arms spread like wings, on a fingertip-to-fingertip flight."

"Pan has a lot to do with it. It bodes well that your intuition is dead on. I'm mentioning this as a vital cog in your training wheels. Take it in. Process the weirdness and move on. We need to, as you like to say, 'advance to Go' and collect our reward for playing the game."

"Winning is sweet. I came here to win back my world."

"Winning is an empty reward that lasts a few days. The true reward is destroying the enemy so it has no ugly head left to rear in the foreseeable future. Megeara has three heads and all the accompanying limbs as well. Annihilation is the key – ANI-ihilation. Ani is the one to watch. She is a natural alchemist. She's been waiting a long time to save you."

Ani and Peri lay swaddled on a bed of lotus blossoms, foot-to-foot, heads facing north and south in the same stone sarcophagus. Kit was appalled. "This is one custom I will never agree with. I'm beginning to see why my father called Egypt a death culture. A sarcophagus is a bed of death."

"It is also the bed of life. It's the dual energy of coming and going. A sarcophagus is a landing pad for incoming time travelers, newborn kas, and a launch pad for a ka when it departs the earth. Why else would it be placed so reverently in the King's chamber of the greatest pyramid on earth. The King's chamber is a time portal leading directly to the Winter Room in Bede Hall. Ay treats it like his personal limousine. One day he will enrage Osiris enough to be sorry. So let's bring Osiris home as soon as it's earthly possible."

Cornelius lifted his drinking cup in a toast. "Here's to a fairly bizarre birthday party. It's not everyday one visits their first grandchildren in the presence of a cat as tall as a two-storey building.

"So, you've been updated on Egyptian mythology as it relates to Bede Hall, then."

"Pigeon and Babs were most accommodating."

"You wouldn't have believed Bash or I if we'd said anything," Kit said. "I didn't believe her either, not for our entire first year at the Hall."

"I wasn't completely oblivious to the vibes," Mrs. S said. "The gift of second sight was obviously in my DNA but I deliberately ignored it to upset your grandmother. Our relationship was never on an even keel. I saw fairies in the flower beds, but they looked an awful lot like butterflies. And on occasion I thought I saw movement in the topiaries."

Bast gave out a bloodcurdling roar at the full moon from the roof of her temple echoed by roars from the Great Sphinx and Sekhmet. Three great tails flapped hard enough to rock the foundations of the temple, cats squirmed in the beds of catnip planted for the occasion nine-months earlier. And as the temple cats lapped up saucers of beer, Ani, disappeared for nine seconds without causing a fuss. It was a test dream.

BEDE

chapter 20
FIRST STRIKE

February 14 – 2019

The blue clock lacking its mechanical innards chimed midnight as three storm clouds brewed in the stratosphere over Bede Hall. Without being summoned, the Twinters drifted outside to stand under the stars still twinkling behind three blobs of black ectoplasm beating like diseased hearts. All seemed calm until the stars sucked themselves into a single mass of red light, turned into iridescent wasps, and began to buzz in acid yellow swarms.

The sounds of hammers and power tools continued to make music from inside the stables. Leoni and Nick heard the wasps and rushed outside just as Brooks called out "AIR RAID TAKE SHELTER", code for 'gather in the underground kitchens, immediately'. Since most of the Twinters had settled in the Hall for several months, each Twinter had staked out their spot. The kettles boiled almost before the first twice-borns arrived.

Brooks' voice broke through the din of wasps once more. "Who's got Jack?"

"He's with me," Helen shouted. Jack barked to confirm his safety.

"That includes you, Leoni," Bertie shouted. "And don't forget to bring Nick with you. Five minutes. No dawdling."

"We are being there now," Leoni called back. "Six minutes, immediately, pronto."

A swarm of heatseeking wasps dive-bombed the garden.

"Parks should be here," Bash said under her breath.

Hannah heard and answered "He's somewhere nearby, never fear. We can't understand everything he does."

"TUT, BASH, ANNA where are you?" Brooks shouted.

"Here," Tut yelled. "Anna is inside with Feathers."

"Here," Bash echoed.

"Well, you two should be in the kitchens by now! ANUBIS... get the family inside."

Bertie stood at Brooks' shoulder. "Unicorn and Snowdrop are with Lady Nan," he said. "It looks like wasps only, this time. We have to help Vincento and Nick. We need their machines to counteract the bigger fish. Wasps in quantity are annoying but they aren't Furies. I thought we had more time. To tell you the truth, I thought the imps would attack first."

"We did have time," Brooks said, "but there were... *ah*... a few mixed signals."

"Signals that needn't have been sent," Hannah said. "Mistress of the Green be damned, that girl needs taken in hand."

Brooks shook a stray wasp from his hair. "That was my job but now I need backup, Hannah. We read Bash the riot act and keep her under wraps. That cloud of hers or any wisp of it must never be allowed inside. The chimneys are especially vulnerable. Each one must be constantly monitored for intruders."

Appleby released a flare into the triple cloud and dispersed it with a puff of flame. "Too bad those Fury hags like fire," he pointed out. "We may have just tickled their fancy."

"Present and accounted for," Bash said in a stage whisper for Hannah's benefit. "Like that'll save us."

Hannah peeled Beegle from around her neck. "Bash, dear. Be a good girl and take this fellow inside for me. Darwin and Dee Dee are already in the boot room. And can you please lock the Beeg in the aviary. We can thank your mother for building it for Pigeon, and for goodness sake hide the key where the little monkey can't reach it and close the door."

Cocoa steamed on the stove making the rooms a network of saunas. Brooks stood and counted heads.

"Nick are you here?"

"I'm just headed out to turn on my new fans," he said. "Hang on to something. They're going to blast freezing air in here if all goes well. There was no time to test them until now."

"Now would be a great time for cooling off," Brooks said. "We have every faith in you, maestro."

Moments later, a refreshing wind gushed through the warren, stirring papers and ruffling hair.

A cheer went up for Nick who appeared in the doorway wearing a victorious grin. "We have lift off," he said. "Now that's what I call serious air-conditioning."

"I've got the small-ones underground," Helen said. "The rabbits have opened their warrens to one and all. The trees can freak out the wasps by swaying. It seems to unnerve them. The tree nymphs can be fairly aggressive when push comes to shove. The imps will be more trouble. We have to have something in place to surprise them."

"Nick's working on an electronic grid and a canopy. He said he would give us an update on his progress, tonight."

"I am still here," Nick said. "damage control is under control," he added mysteriously.

"Venerable has first watch in the tower. We're connected by cell phones, so all we can do is keep watch, take turns, and play cards."

"Or Scrabble," Clive said.

"Or chess," Bertie added. "One thing we do know, is the Furies can't keep their alternate manifestations for long. And wasps need something to sting or they get bored."

"Bored wasps tend to buzz off, no pun intended," Appleby said.

The wall phone flashed a blue light from the number nine on the dial – another of Nick's inventions.

Bertie picked up. "Venerable says the clouds have changed colour and are pushing off," he said.

"Everyone, listen up," Brooks shouted. "For the past few hours, we've made a party of our confinement. I believe the wasp cloud was affected by our cheerful mood, so, please think more happy thoughts. Be extra vigilant of your negative emotions. Be mindful of any fleeting mental disturbances, especially feelings of jealousy and malice. None of us are immune to the emotional blackmail of elementals with tricks up their sleeves, or whatever passes for sleeves. Nothing is beyond their cunning. The Furies will throw every conceivable trick at us. We must monitor each other and find ways to amuse ourselves. Remember, TO AMUSE IS TO CONFUSE, and, as unlikely as it seems right now, deep down our enemies fear us. Happiness hurts them."

Morning broke on a bustle of rallyings. Helen consoled the ground troops of the wildwood with their rations of nuts and seeds. Her pony express of mice, rabbits, hedgehogs, and squirrels were back in action. "Spread the word that Nick will be giving a short tutorial in the maze at sunrise," she instructed the scarabs. "There are safety precautions – a map showing where to avoid the shocks from live wires. Nick's device is designed to stop imps in their tracks, not to injure mice and rabbits. There will be no grazing in the Hall's gardens. Keep close to the tree roots. But watch out, they have ways of tripping one up without intending to. And don't, for goodness sake, loiter around the entrance of the route portal. This means the lawns are off limits whenever we're under siege or when the parameter's blue fairy lights are on. They will be on permanently at night to discourage imps, so, scampering to the Hall is forbidden. The dragonflies, scarabs, and moths will convey messages until further notice."

The foxes prowled the treelines of the Green Lady's forest. The barren treetops attracted a legion of fearless intimidating, and more importantly, immortal, tree nymphs.

Charlotte's sprites and fairies kept their own precious links with Parks a secret.

Sarah was back in her cottage with Sibuna overseeing the comings and goings of the 'passage of time' cat flap. Sibuna, overdue for his duties with Kit, snuck out when Anubis arrived to relieve him. "I wish I was going with you," Anubis said. "I miss Egypt."

Engineers Leoni and Nick, commandeered Bertie, Brooks, Bill, and Ben to war machine duty while the two inventors tinkered with the final adjustments. Teddy Clutterbuck supplied them with strange looking spare parts from his garage. Vincento Leoni's ornithopter was nearing its first flight test. His other, more secretive project locked away in a horse stall, was nearing completion. Ben bragged that it had freaked out Taraq – which promised an intriguing development not to be missed. Leoni assured everyone it would be *'pleased to entertainment'* and, of course, *'helpingly' to the war effort.*

Teddy Clutterbuck took Clive and Tut to load a truck with old bicycles, gears, springs, and tire rims for the goings-on in the stables. Lady Nan and Glynnis baked bread and pies and put up pots of stew and soup, muttering incantations about the virtues and disadvantages of being stable and unstable, as it related to horse sense vs chaos.

Hannah and a teenage Beryl kept the tea, coffee, and sandwiches coming. Anna and Taraq took Jack for a walk and watched him chase Sable – a playful 'wicker' squirrel and a lively grey dog. The Parks family were finished making their quota of shields. Anna demonstrated the Roman's turtle formation with grapes and walnut shells on the kitchen table while Leoni expressed his admiration for his countrymen's ingenuity.

The rest of the leafless topiaries, under the leadership of Sage, guarded the trees, plants, ivy, greenhouse, and the lavender crop, since Bash, their usual champion, was confined to the Hall until further notice. The only thing *she* would be monitoring was herself. Nine-year-old Beryl wandered the maze scattering dried catnip in search of Unicorn.

All the while, 'the Venerable Read' manned the tower, scanning the sky for ominous cloud formations and rated their densities. Bash sulked and was charged with reading Winnie the Pooh to make her smile. Fat chance. Her cloud hovered outside her French doors waxing and waning as the wisdom of Piglet and Owl amused the child within a teenager fighting the urge to chuckle. Now and then Anubis and Feathers slunk past, patrolling the doors, windows, and gates.

The enemies, even the imps, came from the air. Taraq was put in charge of all winged creatures, apart from Charlotte's fairies under Hannah's authority, in a flying squadron of bumblebees, dragonflies. But they were out of their depth facing down thousands of wasps and were on high alert inside, checking out every corner of the Hall and outside, checking keyholes, roof tiles, and the chimneys. Mr. S's collection of scarabs were more formidable with their hard shells and metallic-like wings. Valuable as they were, they were also trained in Egyptian combat against the Furies and were as invaluable as they were indestructible.

Nick emerged with several strange looking contraptions and began assembling his power grid, designed to hinder the surge of imps, on the exposed areas of lawns and drive. At intervals, it would be shut down so the housecats could shake the life out of the imps stunned bodies. After which, Parks 2 and 3 would rake them into piles and dump them in the pit they'd dug behind Kit's Saxon tower.

Francis Fox set up a veterinary clinic in one of the vast pantries and Clutterbuck upped his deliveries of medical paraphernalia. Helen and Glynnis rolled miles of bandages.

Meanwhile, Bede Hall said nothing.

At the end of the second night, the Twinters gathered to watch inspiring movies. Some read their favorite children's books. Some shared stories of their own long-ago adventures. Bash ceased to shiver in her sleep, and for an hour her cloud dissipated into a creamy mist.

Sarah played her collection of Gregorian chant recordings to serenade the sleepers and soothe the worriers.

From inside the boot room, Dee Dee sung Beegle and Darwin a lullaby. *'lavender grey dilly dilly, lavender black. I'll guard the roof dilly dilly, you watch your back.'*

EGYPT

chapter 21
RANDOM ACTS OF SERVITUDE

Pigeon complained of bawling infants, day and night to which Kit replied, 'what goes around comes around'. When Bast heard this statement, she chose to ignore Babs' interpretation that Kit was cracking-wise. Instead, she acknowledged Kit's wisdom and praised him for his insight. Kha shook his head at the matter, exclaiming cats were unpredictably perverse.

"Perverse *and* disgusting," Kit added when Pigeon told him Babs had severed the twins umbilical cords with her teeth and lapped up the afterbirth. And when Pigeon remarked there had been no complications in the births, Babs had replied that 'complications begin long *after* human children were born. Especially when a *certain* overseer wants leverage over a *certain* up and coming pharaoh who wants to marry another *particular* King's intended wife, not mentioning any names.'

The sound of a dozen chisels from the depths below greeted Kit at the entrance to Tut's tomb. Soon he would see his father. The secret meeting had been arranged with Sibuna under Bast's watchful eyes.

Descending into the subterranean world of the Valley of the Kings was less daunting than Kit expected. Even without the electric lights he'd experienced on the family's Egyptian trip in 2018, the deepest interior spaces were resplendent with dazzling light.

Reflective bronze panels strategically spaced every few feet down the tomb shaft redirected sunlight into the darkest corners. But regardless of the light, the mustiness of air choked with stone dust and the odors of natron, camphor, and embalming fluid made him dangerously lightheaded.

The slave boy ahead of him had silenced the workers, who by the time of his arrival, were on their knees with bowed heads.

Slavery was embarrassing but Kit had a reputation to maintain as a visiting magus. Everything got back to Ay. The workers and slaves who seemed subservient on face value were, almost to a man, representatives of Ay's network of spies.

Cornelius Smyth was already on site, giving orders, but he too, kept a low profile and offered no overt show of eye contact. He greeted Kit with the deference his title demanded as an elite stranger by kneeling until Kit gave him permission to stand and maintained a distance from his son until all but two of the workers were dismissed. The two workers allowed to remain were Senta'aten, known as Sent and Ta'aten called Tee. Cornelius introduced them as true friends who retreated respectfully to the deepest antechamber to eat their rations in privacy.

"We can speak safely," Cornelius said. "Even when Sent and Tee are in the same room. As my appointed assistant, Kha wanted you to see this place as soon as possible." He scanned the chamber's murals – paintings in the making of familiar gods and goddesses in a parade that marched in single file around the first room. "It's a glorious sight is it not. Living history. A tomb in the making. Art in the making. For an Egyptologist it's a dream come true."

"Kha tells me there's more."

"I have a genius painter on my staff. He must be a magician, too, because the figures in his paintings step down from the walls and dance around. You could have knocked me over when Kha told me that not only were you here but apprenticed to become an alchemist. Even so, it is not safe for you to be seen with me outside the tomb. It would hardly be fitting with your station. I don't flatter myself to be anything other than a jumped-up servant, here. Ay has it in for me. But he was obviously aware you would come and now I realize why I was groomed to have this job."

"Apart from being abducted and ripped from your home?"

"I have no recollection of the event. But Kha did tell us an extraordinary story about Furies and fairies and what not. If your mother and I hadn't witnessed the pyramids under construction, we would never have even given him the time of day. But there it is. Some things must be processed a long time. What you have to understand, is that my true home was always here, when I was away on a dig. And now, your mother and I are experiencing a remarkable second chance. We've never been more in tune. I doubt we could have maintained such closeness living in Bede Hall. Lady Nan's energy keeps her the matriarch of Bede Hall even in death. We always said we could feel her presence and disapproval. It didn't bode well for a private life."

"So, Kha hasn't explained the reincarnation aspect of the times, then?"

"He hedged around that subject, but we weren't ready. So many astonishing sights had already been difficult to accept. We finally had to acknowledge magic as a constant reality. Kha worked with us to adjust. He's a natural therapist and so are the medicinal remedies he concocts. He said believing the unbelievable was a necessary first step that would lead to further revelations in time. He references time a great deal. And time travel explains so much."

"As an accepted servant of the royal family you are no doubt within close proximity to Smenkhare and Ankhesenamun."

"They're a tad distant, but then they should be, and it is better for your mother and I that they are."

"No bothersome matriarchal vibes, then?"

"None to worry about. Naturally, there's a pecking order. Why do you have that tortured look on your face?"

"Dad… there's no easy way to say this. But Ankhesenamun IS Lady Nan. Smenkhare is Dr. Brooks. Perhaps they aren't as aware of their future as I am, but I hope Mum isn't intimidated."

Mr. S paced as best he could, navigating the spaces between the trunks of afterlife paraphernalia. "Quite the opposite, your mother is in her element. Completely at ease. She's even eager to put down roots here."

Kit shuffled through the thick dust, stone chips, and stacked boxes, and sat beside his father. "There's more," he said gently. "The vibes you felt from Lady Nan were right on the money. Bede Hall is ripe with ghosts. Lady Nan never left when she died. She remained the boss although now the reigns are passing to Bash. I have no idea how that's working out. They were having a bit of a clash when I left. And since Bash and I are no longer telepathically connected, I have no news on that front. What I *do* know is she will be giving Lady Nan a good fight. And speaking of fighting. Bede Hall is either at war or expecting an imminent attack from a supernatural enemy."

Cornelius sat down heavily on an unfinished sarcophagus lid to take it all in. "It's true that twins have an extra connection. Why didn't you tell us it was more?"

"We liked having something special that was just ours. Neither you nor Mum were open to such things. And after a time, it became normal to hide."

"I think I've had enough surprises for one day. I meant this day to be a simple meeting for us and an introduction to the two artist chaps who are the true masters of this tomb. You will be working with them through Kha's instructions. Sent and Tee are brothers – a painter and an architect."

Cornelius called out in Egyptian. Sent and Tee, returned, refreshingly at ease, smiling as equals. Mr. S had showed them how to shake hands. The odor of onions preceded them. They had kept back a portion of royal onions – the missing hybrid between long-stemmed green onions, leeks, and modern bulbous spheres with purple skin, and offered them to Kit.

Sent wiped his hands down his tunic stained with turquoise and crimson paint. Colors had also migrated from his hands to his face making him appear to be wearing war paint. He grinned a mouthful of bad teeth and pulled Kit by the arm to his painting in progress, explaining excitedly in a language translated by Cornelius. "This rectangle is a door. I showed Sent how to make a drop shadow to make it seem 3-dimensional. It represents the door of a temple for King Tutankhamun's ka. A small temple barnacled outside this tomb where offerings of food and flowers are left for the deceased. I taught you about those. I suppose I forced a great deal of Egyptian history on you when you were growing up."

"No worries, we got our fair share of fairy tales from Lady Nan."

"And now, I suppose, you're going to tell me that Bede fairies are real."

Kit looked away. "As well as her magic snow globe and enchanted hourglass."

Cornelius frowned. "I remember her lugging those toys about. I thought they were harmless and that she was a bit of a kook."

"They're magical touchstones. Bizarre, but ultimately their visions are true. And Lady Nan is definitely eccentric."

The tomb quickened with a muggy charge reminiscent of the static in the air before a thunderstorm. The painted door opened slowly with the sound of rusty hinges.

Cornelius grabbed Kit's arm and pulled him back. "Let's be cautious," he whispered. "We don't know what to expect."

"I don't think anything is harmless anymore," Kit said. "But I think we can expect a surprise."

chapter 22
HAPI BIRTHDAY

April 6 – 2018

It was still dark when the vigil of Twinters formed a circle around Bash's goddess bed at 6 a.m. "Wake up Mistress," Nimue said. "You're only nine twice."

Appleby, cleared his throat… *ahem*… more than twice, actually."

The Twinters grinned. Each one carried a blueberry muffin sporting a lit birthday candle.

Bash opened her eyes, half awake, with a sheepish, but none-the-less, considering her woeful outlook, impressive smile. "I'm eighteen, Nimue, I think you're confusing me with Anna who's always nine."

Appleby, wrote an equation on the portable slate he now carried for unexpected calculations, and held it up to approving nods. $18 = 1 + 8 = 9$. "One plus eight equals nine," he said. "Technically, you'll also be nine when you're twenty-seven, thirty-six, forty-five… and so on."

"It's Kit's birthday as well. I wonder how he is and 'when' he is, and if he has new friends to celebrate with. I hate to think of him sad and alone."

"Not to dwell, Mistress," Hannah jumped in. "I'm sure he's well. Sibuna is sworn to secrecy but he knows where Kit is and, although he doesn't seem well disposed towards him, Kit's alive. What Sibuna *was* able to say, well he chuckled actually, was that Kit was not alone."

"Cats don't chuckle all that often," Anna said. "So, my fa… I mean, Kit must be well."

Bash grabbed her hand. "It's all right to call Kit your father," she said. "Yes, it's strange to wrap my head around such a thing, but nothing's stranger than time travel."

Nimue fluttered in Bash's ear. "I have some news to cheer you, later," she whispered. "When you're alone." She raised her voice so everyone could hear. "Word has it, Taraq has a few surprises in store for you. Although surprise isn't quite the right word. He can be a tad abrasive with his surprises."

Bash's smile waivered slightly. "So, it's a punishment then."

"I *am* here… and I *can* hear you," Taraq said, rising above the gathering. "I assure you it's nothing severe. Well, not after the first few minutes, anyway. Sorry, but that's my style, and in this case, it's utterly vital."

Bash muttered a despondent, "I can hardly wait."

Jack, wearing a purple ribbon around his neck, jumped on the bed. An attached tag read: *Lady Nan has made your favorite potato pancakes for breakfast. Get em while they're hot.*

Bash's face, suddenly crestfallen, sent a murmur of alarm through the gathering.

"Six loved potato pancakes," Lady Nan said. "I wasn't thinking."

"Yes, he did," Hannah concurred. And it would make Six happy to know Bash would enjoy them on this special day – a Mistress of the Green celebrating a 'nine year'."

"Please to make way," Leoni shouted. "for my happy returnings for Miss Bash."

The Twinters parted as a miniature hot-air balloon floated towards Bash with a fairy in its straw basket scattering purple confetti sprayed with lavender perfume over her head.

Nick hollering "YES, YES, THAT'S IT!" caused a stir followed by shocked silence.

Nick slapped Leoni on the back and lifted him off the ground with a bear hug. "It's utter genius. A fleet of balloons releasing a spray of insect repellent would make a huge dent in the wasp swarms."

Immediately, the Twinters broke ranks, blew out candles and deposited their muffins on Bash's dressing table.

Leoni issued instructions. "I can be having a quantity of the balloons from Messr. Clutterbuck, and we are not to be needing the baskets."

"That's right," Nick said. "As long as the balloons are sprayed with wasp poison, they will do the job. And I can make timers that release a pin to burst the balloons which will scatter the repellant with better effect. We will need a team to make them."

"Can we make small devices on wheels to stop the imps on the ground?" Sarah asked.

Clutterbuck joined in excitedly. "I have boxes of wind-up toy cars."

"Too slow and awkward, but I know how to make a good slingshot," nine-year-old Ben added, his mouth stuffed with an entire blueberry Muffin.

"All right, birthday girl, I'm putting you in charge of air balloon production," Brooks said. "We can formulate a plan while eating pancakes. Last one to the kitchen is a rotten boiled egg."

Bash caught Taraq's eye. He beckoned her over with a hooked finger. "For this day to go well, I ask that you get dressed and meet me in the tower right away. And please don't give me that look." He called out over the dispersed Twinters and singled out Anna. "Anna, please set aside a plate of pancakes for Bash. She will be detained for half an hour."

Bash entered the tower a little piqued. "Hello," she called out. "I'm here for my punishment."

Fioretti greeted her at the top of the stairs. "Right on time, Mistress Nine," she said. "The grand 'poohbah' is waiting." And, as an aside, "Afterwards, I'll tell you what I hinted at earlier."

The tower felt wrong without Kit. Even the blue clock hung crooked. The place was a time capsule of Kit's energy, so powerful Bash imagined she could hear him thinking.

Taraq sat on the throne chair, which was unheard of as he idolized it as a sacred relic, always hovering over it protectively in a constant state of servitude. "You look like the caterpillar in 'Alice in Wonderland' on that thing," Bash said. "It's a little too big for you, but then it *is* out of your league is it not?"

Taraq bristled, annoyed that Bash had delivered the first insult. "It is *not* a thing."

"Well, *you* are."

"Nice way to say thank you."

"Thank you for being a freak of nature."

"You know, for a nine-year, you're not all that wise. In fact, I'd say you were an idiot, but that's just me."

"Thank you again."

"I say this as an astute observer. Brooks taught me well. How you've failed to process the obvious anomalies surrounding you, escapes me. I have one question to ask you."

"Proceed."

"Am I dead?"

Bash eyed Taraq suspiciously. "I believe so."

"And yet, here I am. You talk to me everyday." Taraq extended his hand. "Touch my arm. Is it solid?"

Bash locked her arms behind her back. "Sometimes."

"What a revelation! Can you tell me what you just learned?"

"You're inconsistent."

"I can be as solid or as transparent as I choose."

"Which means?"

"If the worst has happened and Six *is* dead, so can he."

"I don't understand."

"It means, you and Six can still be together. Just as the ghost of Ben is with Sarah, and Brooks is with the deceased Lady Nan. The same way Anna still plays with Beryl. And since you've declared far and wide that you don't want to have children…" he winked. "There's no need for a physical husband. Is there…. Well?"

The only sound in the room was the tips of Fioretti's wings painting the circumference of the room with a ring of white stars.

Taraq shimmered into his ethereal form and hovered cross-legged nine inches above the throne. "More like a caterpillar?"

"Why has this never occurred to me?"

"You're an idiot, springs to mind."

"One way or another, Six will come home. I can wait for him. I can wait forever if need be."

"Throw that birthday girl a fish," Taraq shouted.

"I could kiss you."

Taraq popped out. His voice came from the ceiling. "I'm good, thanks."

Bash moved towards the stairs and looked back over her shoulder. "It's a shame I can't punch you when you're smug like that."

This time, Fioretti met Bash at the bottom of the stairs. "Please sit down and listen," she said.

Bash grinned like the Cheshire Cat. "Go ahead," she said, plopping down on a stair. "I can take anything, now."

"Six is sleeping the sleep of death," Fioretti said. "The same way Anna dreams in the Winter Room, which means they can meet on a mutual plane of life and death. You, not being in a similar state, must wait on the sidelines. But as a coma is not strictly death, there's a chance Six will survive. In fairy time, only a moment has passed since the attack. In your time, Six is lost to you in 40 A.D. in Hadrian's fort – a building now sleeping beneath the dreams of Bede Hall.

Fioretti pointed out the window. "Bash, my dear. Six is right over there, under the maze. I can take you to the exact spot. You can the place anytime. And dream travel may be learned if you really want it."

Lady Nan's words played back in Bash's memory. *If you want something enough, a little thing like dying won't stop you.'* she'd said.

"Brooks can teach you," Fioretti added in a stage whisper.

Bash returned to the kitchen and ate a pancake in a state of bliss after her cloud zapped itself inside out in a sputter of angry red sparks. Hannah was astounded and called the other Twinters to look. "Maybe a flock of bluebirds will appear in it's place," she said.

In the end, someone had to show Bash the folded note left under her teacup.

"I wrote it," Sarah said. "Considering Pigeon has no hands. But it was dictated to Sibuna and from Sibuna to me."

The note read… *There's a surprise waiting for you in the Winter Room. Go alone. Go now – love Pa'a.*

"Pa'a? Pa'a who?" Bash pronounced the letter P as if stuttering. "PaPaPaPigeon… Pa Ah… the hyphen between two vowels reminds me of… oh… Ma'at. A double 'a'- two syllables separated by a hyphen. It's an Egyptian lexicon, awkward to pronounce in English. Pigeon loves P words!" Bash scraped back her chair and raced out the room. "Pigeon's in Egypt!" she shouted. "He's with Kit. He's behind the Winter Room wall!"

Hannah nudged Anna's elbow. "You can give those pancakes to Jack and Beegle, now. I doubt our fearless leader will have an appetite for a while."

The sound of giggling and soft thumping followed by silence met Bash outside the Winter Room door. For a moment she rested her forehead on the wood and slowed her breathing. Once composed, she lowered her mouth to the keyhole and felt a familiar breeze on her lips like a frozen kiss. "PIGEON ARE YOU IN THERE?"

The key shook in her hand and refused to fit. She tried several times and had to repeat the forehead therapy again. By the time the key slid effortlessly, and the door had swung open, the gentle thumping had started again. This time it came from inside the closet portal.

A once around the room confirmed no large parrot was present unless it was invisible. But the closet, half-sized to accommodate the slope of the eaves could house anything. Opening it alone was irresponsible but what if it was Six. "State your business" she shouted foolishly to the door. Laughter ensued. "My business," something said. "Is that I want to get out." It was spoken in a decidedly amused voice. It was not Pigeon, that much was plain.

"My name is Hapi. I am here to see Mistress Bathsheba Carter Stratford-Smyth. I have a special delivery birthday message and a lotus seed for luck. Are you she?"

Bash warmed her hands under her arms, grabbed a candlestick, and opened the portal door. For a moment nothing moved on either side of the threshold. Bash stopped breathing and whatever it was stopped laughing.

"I'm coming out now. Ready or not," it giggled. "There's something really wrong with you."

Bash wielded the candlestick like a baseball bat. "Yes, I'm Bathsheba, and I'm not in the mood for stupid tricks. So, if you're an imp, I'm armed. I swear I will knock you senseless."

A tiny beak materialized in the darkness closely followed by the head of a bird the size of a bumble bee.

"Come out of there," Bash blurted. "Give me the message and be on your way. Are you a parrot? A baby parrot?"

Whatever it was, flapped around in merriment. "I'm almost a parrot," it snickered. "Make a perch for me. Be a branch. Hold out your arm. Pretty please."

Seconds later, Bash stared into the round eyes of an extremely tiny white sparrow with a parrot's face – an Egyptian Ba.

"Pigeon what happened to you? Are you under a spell of some kind?"

My name is HAPI spelled with an 'i' not a 'why'… sorry I can't help making jokes. I'm a Ba bird and your friend Pigeon says *ahem…* many happy returns of the day! It's sort of a pun."

"I don't see how that's a pun."

"My name is Hapi and I can't return to Egypt. I belong to you, now. I am your birthday gift. And there's more." Hapi lifted one spindly leg and rattled the miniature papyrus scroll attached to it.

Bash dropped the candlestick. "My father was an Egyptologist. I *know* what a Ba is. A Ba bird takes the face of someone who has recently died. It's a spirit bird. Is Pigeon dead?"

"Goodness no! I would never do that. I absolutely do NOT do that. It's far too gloomy. But I *do* take the face of whoever I'm talking to or the person you want to see most or the person sending you a message. My only purpose is to make you happy. Pigeon thought I would be good for you after receiving reports of your gloomy attitude."

Hapi's face changed to Bash's likeness and flew to the window. Startled by the frost, the white sparrow with purple hair flapped around the room and perched on the footboard of the cot. "I don't much care for your windows here," it said.

"Hapi is the name of the Nile god," Bash said unrolling the scroll. A small purple seed fell out into her hand. She scrunched her eyes to read the impossibly small scrap of papyrus. "Can you read this for me."

"Certainly," Hapi said. "I would be happy to." She giggled. "I am Hapi too. It says, and I quote, *Bash make an appointment with Carlton. He knows all about dreams. Tell him I sent you. More positive thinking wouldn't go amiss which is why I'm sending you little Miss Hapi pants. It's her job to cheer people up. Kit wanted to swat her like a fly. She tends to grate on one.*"

"Now *that's* a pun on great," Bash said.

"Your brother is *not* easy to please. I tried and tried, but Pigeon saved me. The rest of the message says, and again, I quote, *Happiness can be annoying. At least you know what the date is. To Kit, it's a birthdate of quite a different color. He can barely keep up with the millennium. I send you love from the eighteenth-dynasty to your 18th birthday.*"

Bash smiled. "Welcome to Bede. Hop onto my finger. I'm late for a meeting. You'll have to come with me. There are several cats around here, and they're nervous of strangers at the moment. Especially ones with wings and beaks."

"I also have a message for a Mr. Vincento Leoni," Hapi said. "Perhaps he will be at your party. And Pigeon said you're not to lose that seed. It contains magic."

Bertie Stein called the impromptu meeting of the Twinters to order. "It has been brought to my attention that our Tut has been troubled over a matter of some consequence. We're here today, to assure him of his rights and to ease his anxiety. As a master physicist, I will preside over these matters, but if any twice-borns have something to add, please raise your hand. If Bash or Tut have any questions they may ask them at the end, but if I've done my job, I may have addressed and shed light on those questions." He nodded to Tut in the front row. "Are you ready, son?"

"Yes, sir."

"Tut, your anxiety has been palpable for months. You must try to settle down. It's all good, Tut. It's all very very good, as I hope to show you."

Bash sat with Hapi on her shoulder, once again wearing a parrot mask. "I'm ready too, sir," she said.

Bertie peered over his spectacles lodged halfway down his nose and smiled. Did anyone ever tell you look like a pretty, but rather bizarre pirate, with purple hair?"

"I am too Hapi to care, sir," Bash said to laughter and thunderous applause.

Bertie motioned for quiet.

"First, allow me to make something crystal clear from the off. The universe is not *ruled* by math, it IS math! Time is math, space is math, science is math, and magic is math. That said, time travel is considerably out of the box. It's *weird* super math."

Tut let out a sigh.

Bertie heard and sent him a wink. "Believing that meeting oneself in time negates their previous existence and alters history both personal and universal is a misnomer. Once-borns cannot time travel more than once. Past lives remain separate from present lives. Time portals lock one's age… and sometimes they don't."

"It doesn't sound like math," Venerable interrupted. "But that's higher math for you."

"Nothing changes," Bertie continued. "People clone and parallel seamlessly into the nature of what is. The Tut of today and the Tuts of yesterday and tomorrow are perfectly compatible. As for the curved space theory. "Tut, my boy, I'm not giving too much away when I tell you that you've already lived a life in ancient Egypt and offered history an amazing legacy. You hid a tomb so it could be discovered by a man you used to know. Cornelius helped you do that. And the world has been captivated by the time capsule of a life that may have been lost. You saved a boy king. And the boy king as a twice-born will pass that on."

Tut shivered uncontrollably. When Bash took his hand, the snow globe rocked slightly.

Professor Appleby finally found his reading glasses and promptly dropped them. "Many unsung heroes must wait until a time traveler revives them," he added.

The library seemed to expand. Books floated from the shelves and rearranged themselves. "That history repeats itself is partly true," Bertie continued. "It does *not* recreate itself. It restores itself over time. The term overtime has a far greater meaning than working late, which is why you can stop overthinking (worrying and obsessing) how you've failed. I invite you to consider your gifts. An average person has fleeting thoughts and fuzzy memories whereas you remember names and faces of everyone you've met over several lifetimes. You were born in the country you love most, and saved an archaeologist dedicated to preserving and celebrating your culture. Going back for you is going forward for history's sake. You are part of a great mystery. Doesn't that make you proud? Doesn't it inspire you to return to the past?"

Brooks stood gazing proudly at his new student. "Your destiny is through one of Bede's portals. The loves of your life await you there," he said. "Taraq will tell you more about dream travel. The three of us will discuss unlimited travel passes, one-way tickets, parallel reincarnation, doppelgangers, clones, the nine-year-gap, age jumps, parallel timelines, and rare incubus personas, later." He nodded his thanks to Bertie who beamed with pleasure that Tut was smiling. "And in the meantime," Brooks said, "until you go, you can live here as the 'true and worthy son of the house of Bede that you are', in perfect timing. For all intents, the 'Rule of Nine' of the space/time continuum recognizes 6 as an upside down 9. We can address their subtleties in depth another… well, *time!*"

Bertie bowed to Brooks. "And as for the mathematical analysis of today's date, April 6, 2018, contains the 18th year of a millennium year in addition to a 'nine year' for the Mistress of the Green. You might say it is a rare age of twins."

There were no questions.

· · ·

After dinner, Hannah brought Dee Dee and Beegle into the gathering. Most of the Twinters split off into small groups. Leoni and Nick had their head's together, deep into discussions of war machines, mechanical animals, and electricity. Anna and Lady Nan discussed Pigeon's many virtues with Sarah Goodman. "Pigeon is a true messenger," Anna said. "I'm going to call him Hermes when he comes home."

Leoni heard and called out "He is my especial friend who is letting me to study his feathers."

Lady Nan, countered. "He's a private eye, a spy, and a tape recorder, all in one."

"You said he was your Nike messenger," Sarah said. "Who will deliver word of a victory."

"I did, which reminds me Pigeon is also a memory bank, a map reader, a hypnotist, a scold, and a schoolteacher. And Vincento is right. He's also a dear friend."

"Parroting is his job," Anna said. "Or is it pigeonholing?"

Dee Dee laughed uproariously, and her dropped feathers were duly collected. And then the room quieted as she sang. *'Happy Bird Day to us. Happy Bird Day to we. Happy Bird Day mere mortals. Happy Bird Day to Dee.'*

When the evening movie, started, Tut pulled Bash into a corner. He looked stricken and excited at the same time. "As soon as I can use the time portals at will," he whispered. "I have a plan, best kept under wraps until the last possible moment. But I need you to pull it off. And you can't tell anyone. I need to know if you're in. I promise it won't harm," he winked, "a soul." Tut kissed Bash's cheek. "I'm late," he said. "A dynasty has been waiting for me a long time."

Bash drew Tut into a tearful hug. "Well, I guess I'll be seeing you very soon, then," she whispered in his ear. "I'm in."

PART 3

sacrifices and martyrs

EGYPT

chapter 23
TIME AND TIME AGAIN

Tut's form materialized as a corona, temporarily backlit by what appeared to be the sun. "Mr. Cornelius? Dad? Is that you?" He shielded his eyes while they adjusted to the dimly-lit tomb. Fear changed to incredulous joy at his first glimpse of the eighteenth-dynasty.

"Well, I was right," Kit managed to say. "It *is* a surprise."

The portal behind Tut turned from day to a night sky and sealed with the grating sound of stone against stone as he stepped forward. The painted door appeared as before. Nothing to suggest three-dimensions other than the innovative use of an illustrated drop-shadow.

Cornelius crossed the space between them, arms outstretched. "Welcome son," Cornelius muttered into Tut's shoulder within a warm hug. I'm over the moon to see you, my boy." He held Tut at arm's length. "You're taller. How long has it been? Yes, yes, I know, time is no longer a way to measure height or anything else anymore."

Tut grinned. "I prefer to call you Cornelius if that's okay with you. And I'm happy to be anywhere, but especially here."

"I'm happy with Dad or Cornelius."

Kit stood rooted to the spot. Tut's perfect white teeth and dark eyes set him on edge, but it was the obvious exclusive happiness of his father and brother that clenched his stomach. His words echoed back, distinctly hollow. "And me," he said, his voice cracking. "I'm here as well."

Cornelius pushed Tut towards Kit with a pat on the back.

"Kit!" Tut exclaimed. "I'm actually here, can you believe it."

Kit stood back awkwardly. "I'm a little surprised," he said coldly, punching Tut's arm. "I have to say, you really know how to make an entrance."

"Thank you, Master KiTiKha'at," Sent said from the shadows,

accepting praise for his painted door. "Master Kha taught me the art of perspective."

"And, I have to say, I'm a little rattled," Kit continued, facing Tut. "Why are you here? Has something happened at home? Shouldn't you be helping Bash."

"I belong here. Taraq and Brooks sent me, but mostly it was the throne's doing."

"You *are* full of surprises. My best friend and mentor *and* my throne chair. Is nothing sacred to you. You've been a busy bee."

"Make that a wasp watcher. They continue to darken the Bede sky in waves, and the weather has taken an even worse toll of the land since you left. Bede is practically a desert."

"So, the perfect climate for you."

"Here and now is perfect for me, thank you very much," Tut said frowning. He turned to Cornelius. "Wait until I tell you what's happened."

Cornelius stopped Tut with the palm of his hand. "And I want to hear everything, believe me. But we're not on holiday here, and I want to get your mother home, so while Kit plays a game with portals, I play a game with Ay and his flunkies. He assumes I'm drugged because I act like a robot. You must do the same. Sad as it is, slaves here are invisible and taught to be automatons but we use that to our advantage. I was only reunited with Kit a week ago and he's been here over a year. Time isn't exactly finite."

"Exactly why it's you who should be briefed," Kit said to Tut. "A lot is happening here. Before you step outside this tomb, you need to know, that we're technically undercover all the time. We don't converse or make eye contact with each other. It's best to pretend you have no friends here. Do you understand?"

"Yes Sir." Tut saluted. "I'm not an idiot. I know you're on a mission. Fill me in. I'm dying to go outside."

Kit raised his eyes. "Death is out there looking for you, so don't go acting like a tourist."

"Now now, Kit. There's no need for fear tactics," Cornelius said.

"Now is such a loaded word, Dad. And there's fear around every corner."

Cornelius gave a forced laugh. "Yes, I suppose it is."

Tut faced Kit head on and stood to attention. "Understood, Sir. Reporting for duty, Sir."

"That's right, soldier, this is *my* territory and you're a visitor. How long did you plan to stay?"

Tut's arms flapped at his sides. "I'm home, Kit. This is it for me."

Kit squared his shoulders, equally perplexed. "You look so... so Egyptian," he finally said.

Tut crossed his arms and shrugged. "Surprise!"

Cornelius spoke quickly, sensing trouble. "Well, this is quite a day. Both my sons in the eighteenth-dynasty." He pointed to the painted door suddenly ajar with light. "Is Bash in there too?"

Tut took a deep breath and followed Cornelius's lead. "Bash is fighting the good fight back home. That is, my *old* home." He shot Kit a dirty look. "This is where I belong from now on."

Kit felt a twinge of anger and dug his fingernail into his hand to prevent him from slapping Tut's face. "Here today, gone tomorrow", he said, "Or is tomorrow still yesterday? I'm never really sure."

Tut made a point of examining the wall frieze that was still wet. "I thought I knew all about Egyptian art," he commented. "But I've never seen a painting of sunflowers in a tomb before."

Sent stepped forward "That is my vision," he said. "I dream about them all the time, and so, here they are. I paint what I see."

Cornelius emerged from the tomb first, wearing a mask-like expression, his lips tight below a blank stare. "To the palace," he said to his slave in the monotone of a drugged man. A modern distracted man giving instructions to a bored taxi driver.

From the bottom of the steps, the boys heard Cornelius's chariot leave. "We will leave together," Kit announced with formal authority. "My chariot driver will drop us at the marketplace. Dad will be there doing an errand. After we spot him, I will go my own way. It's known that I prefer to walk the last leg to the Temple of Bast where I live and work. You can follow *Cornelius* on foot. Pretend you're a street kid in Cairo and you'll have no problem."

Tut ogled the square of bright blue sky above them and nodded. "Just get me out there," he said. It was a command not a request.

Kit steeled himself for an argument and chose diplomacy over tact. "Whatever you do, do it slowly with your eyes averted. Mom and Dad are in danger. So, no swaggering. Act like a worker bee and fit in. From this point on you are anonymous. Megeara and Ay must not become suspicious, but as there are thousands of men who look like you, you might pull it off. My teacher, Kha is more or less in charge until we, that's Kha, my parents, me, Pigeon, and now you, meet in secret to formulate a plan. Plans are in a constant state of flux."

Tut smirked. "So, you're not in charge?"

Kit ignored the sarcasm. "Officially, Ay is in charge. You may know his name from your history books. He's a wee bit tyrannical is all I'm saying, and I haven't worked my butt off to mess up now."

Tut forced a chuckle to deliberately mock Kit. "So, *Pigeon* is in charge, then."

"Pigeon has diplomatic immunity for now but like most things around here, his position is tentative. He's playing his part by being as obnoxious as ever. Somehow, he gets away with it."

"And so it seems, do you," Tut said testily."

"Ay knows Pigeon from the old days… that is, the new days. Don't look at me like that. Just go with it for now. But take note that Ay was once my grandfather and my grandfather was the king of bullies."

A gleam of wonder returned to Tut's face. He shook his head. "I can't believe I'm going to meet King Tutankhamun," he said beaming. "Taraq said I was to meet the King as soon as possible."

"It's actually, King Tutankh*aten* but we oblige Ay by using Tutankh*amun*. It's true that Taraq *is* here. I've seen him with his sister. Who, by the way, is also my newborn daughter, or she *will* be in a few thousand years, and yes, I hear the insanity in that remark and most historic references that I make. One gets used to the strangeness of seeing people in multiple incarnations. It will only make sense when this nightmare is over. But I assure you that Taraq is in no position to dictate terms to anyone. He's lower than a scarab, here. He is a slave boy with no memories of Bede. I am briefing him slowly."

Tut and Kit strolled through the market, heading for the temple. "As usual, your timing stinks," Kit said, tension dripping from his words. "Dad and I were having a moment when you barged in. And then, off you two go to meet Mum before I've had a chance to say hello."

Tut stayed Kit's arm, his expression exasperated. "Look, in case you hadn't noticed, I don't have a watch or a calendar. The portals send us *where* we're supposed to go and *when* we're supposed to be."

"Have you considered you may have breached that?"

"Have you considered the rules breached themselves to save you?"

At that moment, the crowd parted in deference, and not a little awe, to a pure white cat strolling through the stalls of the street vendors. Tut followed their eyes. "That looks an awful lot like... it *is* Snowdrop. The portals must be working overtime."

"Portals always work over time. That's their function. How can you be so offhand about being here? It nearly toppled me. We're not in England anymore and, as you see, neither is Snowdrop."

Tut stopped short and shocked Kit with a nasty sneer. "One: this is my natural environment. Two: these people are my ancestors. And three: blood is thicker than water."

Kit focused on his new sandals during Tut's answer. "Snowdrop shouldn't be in the market," he said after a time. "She's supposed to stay in the temple." He paused again and shifted his weight. "You left Bede because you felt diluted?"

"I left Bede because I WAS diluted. But please, don't misunderstand me, I was happy to be so, until you and Bash found your destinies with titles and extraordinary powers. I was not part of your history. But here... here, I'm *making* history. It was an easy decision to make after Taraq gave me the royal tour of my family tree."

Kit picked up Snowdrop and held her out as if she was a treasure presented on a pillow. The crowd backed further away and bowed their heads. "Royal? Taraq is a lowly slave."

Tut raised his voice in disgust. "Do you hear yourself! There's no better credible tour guide than Taraq. And he ought to be considering this dynasty was his hometown. He'd have come with me, but he won't leave the throne chair. His loyalty to that chair is intense."

"I know," Kit said sheepishly. "We've met. But where are my manners. I should introduce you to... oh, wait, it may not be allowed. I have to check the rule book. There's a strict pecking order here. I'm apprenticed to a master alchemist, now. And I have to check in with protocol details. It's too easy to screw up. And I want to get home to my wife."

Tut grinned at the word wife. "So, you got your wish. You're becoming a scientist. Way to freak out Bash, and you've apparently gotten over your fear of girls."

"Egyptian science is a much wider picture. Bash would approve. It's the original science of magic. Did you know that the word chemistry comes from the land of Khem?"

Tut nodded indifferently. "Yes, I knew. Is it my turn to show and tell, now? Because Bash has been through some unsettling changes. Six died. After that, she became quite the dictator. In the end, it was Taraq *the slave* who turned her around. I think she's on the mend but its always dodgy with her mood swings. In any case, she and Taraq are pals for the time being. And speaking of pecking order, I have to meet your *master*, Kha. Brooks said it was important and Taraq agreed. Can we go to him now? I feel as if I know him somehow."

"Taraq agreed? He must be insufferable with power."

"No. You're quite wrong. He suffers greatly. I worry about him."

"Rules again, brother. There's only a few thousand serious ones. Dad is in bigtime with the in-crowd here as assistant to King Tut's overseer. Mom's status sky-rocketed along with his and she's changed. If she had a choice, I think she would stay here."

"Did you say you have a daughter?"

"I have a son, too. Twins. I was as shocked as you. Surprises are relatively normal here until someone you thought you knew arrives through a painted door."

Kit arrived at the temple and headed for Kha, bursting into the workshop in a dither of bitterness. "I come all the way here, to save the world," Kit ranted. "And what happens? I lose my father, *twice*. Tut is far better suited to being my father's assistant. And now I hear that my sister lost her cool in Bede, and god knows what damage was done."

Kha lurched suddenly and overturned the table laden with papyrus scrolls and jars. "You and only YOU are the one who must save the earth. I don't call *that* redundant. And in case you've completely lost your sense of destiny, be a stand-up scientist and observe with fresh eyes. Cool off! Can't you see that Megeara is fanning the flames of your jealousy. It's Christmas morning for her, so get a grip! Drop the petty childhood rivalry and take the wind out of the Furies' sails. And do it now, before it's too late!"

Kit laughed hysterically. "Perfect. You're advice is to let things drop and my sister's last instructions were to get a grip, which was cruel, even for her. Are you sure you don't know her?"

Kha's expression of disgust tempered Kit's tantrum. "Sit! And listen. As sure as you and I are standing here, the three of us are working out some incredibly complex karma. Tut has taken on a difficult task to save a truly precarious situation. It's not always about you."

"Tut brought back all the old resentments about sharing my father. How am I supposed to process such a thing? I was jealous." He paused as a memory surfaced. "And how is it even possible that you and my perfect brother can share the same physical space?"

"Bury your jealousy before it burns you to the ground, Kit. Tut and I are separate entities who happen to share a common experience. It's no small thing, and it can be used to our advantage if we keep our heads. I had no foreknowledge of what Tut intended to do, which means it was a spontaneous decision that impacts your mission. One day you will thank him. Be glad Tut is here. It's part of a greater plan even I don't fully understand. Let go of this petty competition that's festering in your brain because Megeara will not. Your brain is her battleground. Sibling rivalry plays into her hands, and I assure you, she plays to win."

"What has Tut done!"

"He has grown up. What are YOU going to do!"

Kit crammed his sunglasses on his head, knowing it was dark outside. "I need some air," he shouted, stomping out, upset there was no way to slam a beaded curtain to show his anger.

Out on the Giza Plateau, Kit scanned the smooth casing stones of the Great Pyramid willing the capstone to appear until a sharp pain at the base of his skull made him dizzy. His eyes found the spot where a few 'twenty-first-century years before, his missing father had waved to him from a spot halfway up its north face. Back then, the casing stones had long been robbed out, making the surface appear like a giant's three-dimensional puzzle with multiple hazardous routes to the flat platform at the top.

It had been when he first met Tut, then Taraq the street kid. For certain, they had been dream traveling. He and his new friend were on a mission to save Cornelius then, too. And back in England after Taraq had been adopted by his parents, he'd given Taraq the stupid nickname, Tut, that occurred to him as a joke. Megeara was stirring up his old feelings of resentment. Kha was right, as always, and it was on Kit to step up and 'get a grip'.

There was nothing remotely funny about the present situation. Now, everyone required saving. He had resented being volunteered, vaguely proud to be nominated even though there had been no choice in the matter. The Bede Prophecy made sure of that. It was Goswold and his brotherhood who had sealed his present fate.

He and Tut had ridden here on horseback on a cool desert evening like this one. It had been a magical day. They were friends. The future before them as kindred brothers shone bright and clear. All was well. Cornelius would come home, the Hall was financially secure, and he and Bash delighted in celebrating Tut/Taraq's first Christmas with snow and a tree decorated with colored lights. Even then, Kit had pretended not to see the fairies in the pine branches polishing the glass bulbs. Jealousy was nowhere in sight.

Miles away, underground in the Valley of the Kings, a stone ceiling moved with the painted star constellations of the night sky. The figures of animal headed gods painted by Sent, stretched their legs and dropped to the floor where they walked, still two-dimensional, and embraced each other. They shared a meal of bread and onions and rifled through the treasures in the many unsealed boxes. Osiris, the green god, tried on the dead pharaoh's bracelets, and King Tutankhamun himself, restored to the perfect body denied him in life, admired his new chariot, a thoughtful gift from his friend Kha.

The steep red cliffs turned purple in the early evening. Workers trooped single file up a narrow path worn into the rock from years of footsteps, heading home, passing another shift making their way down. Somewhere in one of the shifts Howard Carter marched towards his destiny.

BEDE

chapter 24
RANDOM ACTS OF SCIENCE

Nick Wardencliffe burst into the kitchens grinning madly. "Gather ye one and all," he crowed. "I have a ground-breaking announcement to make. Please, everyone, drop what you're doing and gather round." He picked up a large ladle and rapped it on the table. "I call an emergency meeting of the Twinters to order. Bash is excused as she's with Leoni in the stables still working on her experiment."

A collective moan spread quickly. Helen Peterson, in the process of giving mouse Katydid her daily schedule, changed her instructions. "Summon the other Twinters, dear. Check the tower. Apparently, there's no need to look in the stables. If you see Anubis tell him to search the grounds and upstairs."

Katydid visibly recoiled. "Begging your pardon Miss Helen, but if it's all the same to you, if I cross paths with Anubis, I'm going to hide. We mice were told he wouldn't catch us, but my father told me when I was old enough to squeak, that cats can't help themselves from hunting us and to only reason with them as a last resort. And by, the way, Cyril sends his regards."

"Cyril?"

"The tree nymph. He came back with a message from Parks which he can't remember, so neither can I."

Everyone present, exchanged anxious looks. "Nick, be a good fellow and tell us your news before the others arrive."

"Look at Nick's smile," Ben said. "It can't be bad news. It isn't, is it Nick?"

Clive Lucy closed his book and leaned back in his kitchen chair with his arms behind his head. "Nick may have snapped and gone doolally," he mused. "Intense thinkers often do that."

Newton Appleby replenished his coffee with six spoons of sugar.

190

"In which case, I reckon there's at least ten high-achievers who have trouble tying their shoes in this extremely cramped command centre."

"Speak for yourself, Appleby."

"I was. I am. I always do," Appleby replied.

Clive Lucy nudged Appleby's elbow. "Nick," he remarked stifling a yawn, you've always been a tad highly strung. It's no stretch to state you live on the eccentric side of the street. Have you lost your mar…?"

Nick cut Clive's question short by performing a happy-dance, which for him, was nothing short of bizarre. "There's absolutely no need for stricken faces," he said. "I have great news, and no, I haven't lost my marbles. You know as well as anyone that part of being a twice-born is being quirky."

"I have to say, you look like that cartoon canary who outsmarted the cat that's forever stalking him," Clive remarked.

"Tweety and Sylvester," Sarah piped up.

'Thuffering thuckertash,' Dee Dee chortled. *'I tink I thaw a puddy cat a creepin up on Katydid.'*

"I've done one better," Nick said. "I have outsmarted the imps."

"Next time, while you're inventing," Appleby said. "Would you throw some sort of bat signal type beacon together, so we can assemble without an army of mice having to chase us down."

"Piece of pie," Nick said. "I can do that in my sleep if someone reminds me."

"It's piece of *cake*," Sarah corrected. "Sorry to interrupt. Please proceed."

The commotion of three people trying to enter the same narrow door simultaneously indicated that the full card-carrying membership of Twinters were present.

The Venerable, clearly winded from the descending the tower stairs, limped in on Tut's tail, close enough to overhear Nick's announcement. "Before you begin," he panted, "and before I'm overcome by your newsflash, I also have something to report." He rapped the floor with his jackal-headed cane. "Please, someone jolt my memory when Nick's finished. Many thanks."

Nick held up both thumbs in triumph. "Marvellous, a segue at last. May I jump in?"

A collective murmur of *please get on with it* echoed from person to person.

"Anyway, speaking of jolts and electric shocks in general, I have modified the power grid to create a more efficient method of disposing imps. It eliminates the threat of accidental shocks to one of us or our four-legged friends. And as for our intended target of two-legged *fiends*, it's a highly effective deterrent."

Helen leaned over, grabbed Nick's ladle, and hit the table. "Approved by unanimous vote," she announced. "Any new business? I'm late for a meeting in the Root Portal."

Brooks waved her towards the door. "If you have to go, we'll fill you in on the details later. Judging by Nick's expression his head is about to explode."

"I must report Bash's scientific discovery which rather inspired me," Nick said, holding the top of his head as if it might float off his shoulders.

"Goodness," Lady Nan declared. My granddaughter's a busy girl. She abandoned her budding tyrant phase and entered her Joan of Arc chapter only a week ago, and now you tell me she's a scientist."

"I was tinkering with sound waves," Nick explained. "And it occurred to me that electricity hums a bit like a purring cat. It's a beneficial sound that works on the same principle as Appleby's white sound machine that helps him sleep. You know how his teeming brain keeps him awake. His creative gift is relentless and that takes a toll on the powers of recuperation. White sound gives him a break, so I got to thinking about the pros and cons of sound. The art of lulling hence lullaby-ing, demonstrated by Sarah's Gregorian chant recordings."

Sounds can hypnotize by smoothing out spiky brainwaves as in Appleby's case, but they can also irritate to the point of madness. Case in point, madness is one of the Furies' weapons. They use it against humans and it's about time we turned it back on them and their vermin. Intensely negative audible frequencies beyond Jack's super extrasensory hearing disrupt lowlife entities, in our case, imps. I've recorded the screeches of attacking imps and how it unsettles our nervous system and turned the tables. Why not use sounds that ultimately soothe us to irritate the imps."

"And where do the cats come in?"

"Anubis caught an imp the other night and Leoni caged the thing. It put up such a fuss he had to put it into his isolation tank for fear of its shrieking giving him a headache. It's the sound of, well, not to put too fine a point on it, evil. Prolonged exposure to such negative frequency decibels virtually enslaves us to the Furies. Result? Petty jealousies evolve into truly harmful thoughts, and in turn, potentially physical dangers. Torturous sounds irritate the human collective subconscious in a 'fingernails on a blackboard' way. Place a human in a listening booth with that and watch them curl into a ball screaming for mercy. And of course, that is only a mild example. Humans can withstand much, but not insistent audible torture."

Francis Fox offered his professional opinion. "I know for a scientific fact that purring cats calm human anxiety."

Nick slapped his hands together. "Well, Leoni and I have discovered that the sound of a purring cat or a calm human heartbeat causes imps to cringe in pain. They're not built to withstand happiness. Soothing sounds break their spirits. In short, they implode. Our captured fellow, actually burst into dust. And we tested the dust in case there were residue impurities. It was benign. All this changes my power grids. We don't have to shock imps into submission. We can literally lullaby them to death."

"Tinkering pays off," Carlton said. "Dreamed solutions often work."

"Don't wasps and bees buzz in irritating ways?" Venerable asked.

"Not exactly," Francis said. "The droning of bees is a lazy relaxing summer sound, the buzzing of angry wasps is a warning of being stung. No-one's partial to being stung."

"The wasps will still need to be dispersed with the hot-air balloons," Nick said. "But we don't want to pollute the air with insecticides. And this is where Bash's mood therapy discovery comes in. That day when she was crying in the lavender, her malevolent cloud soaked up her grief and increased in size and darkness. But as soon as the lavender chanted to her, something extraordinary happened. The cloud withdrew and turned from grey to lavender-blue. It flickered like a dying light bulb. I honestly believe if Bash's depression hadn't resurfaced, her stalking cloud may have exploded like the imp."

"Leoni and Charlotte have used lavender for years," Hannah said. "Leoni, in his cough medicine and Charlotte, in her honey and soaps. Tinctures of lavender are well-known antiseptics."

"Bash has been busy with the plants working out a long-term solution. But the breakthrough came from Egypt. Apparently, Hapi brought more than birthday wishes from Egypt. That Pigeon is one smart bird. Lotus flowers are powerful hallucinogens where Hapi comes from – many times stronger than our lavender. Pigeon sent Bash a magic lotus seed."

Lady Nan leaned forward. "There's history to back this up. The ancestors of our Bede fairies sprang from a crop of Egyptian lotus flowers. Taraq and I were there!"

"Anna often spends whole days in the woods with Nimue's colony," Hannah added. "She loves fairies to the point whereby some of us have to beg her to stop extolling their virtues. This is another example, by the way, mild as it is, of auditory torture. It's how shrewd children get their way by wearing parents down until they give in. Nothing sinister, but you see how constant bickering can trigger outbursts of serious anger."

"It's true," Helen said. "Nimue loves to recite stories of the ancient lotus fairies who came to Bede through the time portals and settled in Lindisfarne. Anna loves to listen. Hapi brought a lotus seed with her. A few days ago, Bash planted that seed in the heart of her lavender field. Nimue set up an around the clock fairy guard to chant magic incantations, and a small plant grew. And since lotus flowers thrive in water, Bash took a rose bowl of lavender water into the field and transplanted the seedling. It looked like an upside-down snow globe. The flower blossomed and now it has reproduced in a large aquarium. We can move the experiment to the lake, now."

"We scientists call growing plants in water, hydroponics," Nick said.

"Leoni always says that the student must surpass the teacher," Brooks said. "By the same token, sometimes the science must surpass the magic."

Lady Nan was intrigued. "With the fairies on board, I predict Bash's experiment will succeed within 42 hours. A potent lotus seed direct from ancient Egypt nurtured by a band of dedicated fairy nursemaids in partnership with Bede's mermaids is a formidable combination. I fully expect that the surface of the lake will be covered in a flotilla of fragrant lotus flowers in no time at all. Nimue is over-the-moon with delight. The fairies are inspired."

"Somewhere Mistress Charlotte is dancing and singing," Hannah said. "And it's all due to Bash putting 2 and 2 together."

Lady Nan stood taller than usual. "Venerable had something to say."

The Venerable appeared flustered and patted his pockets. I must have put it…"

"In your mind," Lady Nan prompted. "You've put it in your mind."

"Quite right, Milady, Your Majesty, Ma'am. I went for an early stroll this morning and wandered down the track of the Roman Wall and came upon a young girl. A stranger. She was holding up a length of string with something shiny threaded on it. It wasn't the first time I'd seen her. I just forgot to mention her."

Anna perked up.

"And when I got closer, she vanished into the stones. She wasn't there. She simply dissolved. At first, I thought I might need stronger eyeglasses, but now I think we may have a new ghost. And I was wondering if she was friend or foe, so to speak. I've lived in Bede a long time and never seen her. And now that I'm using Kit's telescope in the tower, I see her quite often. She sits on the wall and walks across the lawn into the maze. Sometimes her path is reversed."

"Was she wearing sandals?" Anna asked.

The Venerable looked up and to the right where his memories were stored. "She was carrying an umbrella."

Anna headed out the door. "Stay Jack. Your four legs aren't safe where I'm going. At least not yet." She kissed his nose. "I won't be long, and then we can find Sable for a game."

Anna called Vita long before she reached her own spot for entering the Wall. She was so intent on seeing her friend that she failed to notice Lady Nan following her.

"Whoever she is, she has to be formally welcomed for her to stay," Lady Nan said behind her. "Ghosts rarely know the rules of haunting without someone to help them. I'm here because sometimes it takes another ghost to communicate them effectively. And in my authority as matriarch – I'm a welcome committee, if you will."

"It's my turn to visit," a shy voice said from somewhere in front of them."

"I can see your muddy sandals," Anna said. I'd know them anywhere."

Vita's face swam in next. "I don't materialize all at once," she said. It looked odd without a middle to connect them. "You've been here before? The Venerable said he'd seen you walking out of the maze, wandering towards the treeline."

"I don't remember. Every now and then I find myself in the maze. I walk around a bit and wake up at home. I found the Unicorn statue you told me about."

"You're dream-walking like me."

Vita shook her head. "Now don't get all sad, Anna. I couldn't help dying a year or so after you left that last time, and I think I just wanted to follow you, but I could never stay long enough to find you. I'm a ghost, Anna."

"This is my grandmother, Lady Nan. She's here to help you."

Lady Nan embraced Vita. "Dear child. There's no need to be afraid. What's happening to you is natural. Bede Hall is your home or you wouldn't be here." That said, she promptly transformed into the nine-year-old Beryl.

Vita pointed to the dip in the land between the lake and the maze. I lived there. It was a settlement that supplied the Roman soldiers with food and trinkets, cooking pots and blankets."

Beryl hugged Vita more tightly. "Yes," she exclaimed. "I can see it."

Three nine-year-old girls, one of them holding a transparent cat, headed to the Twinters' kitchen headquarters.

From the corner of her eye, Anna glimpsed the hazy outlines of the army barracks and the camp followers' shanty town as if drawn in pencil on tracing paper over Bede Hall's landscape. The fort faded in and out but the hospital tent she knew to be Six's resting place solidified enough to block out the ravaged topiary grove behind it.

Hannah and Lady Nan met over tea in Hannah's deserted kitchen. "Super twins share their finest qualities in subtle ways even when they appear so at odds," Lady Nan said. "I have no doubt that somewhere in Egypt, Kit is delving into the magic he once denounced so fervently."

Hannah set her teacup in its saucer deliberately without making a sound. "Some days, the prophecy is not as cloudy as it once seemed."

'Unclouding', Dee Dee said in a loud voice. *Dee-clouding. Poof, no more cloud.* And then she sang out strong and clear. *'Oops there goes another rubber tree cloud.'*

"So now, we needn't use insecticide," Lady Nan, said. "We use Bash's new perfume."

'Smyth no. 9' Dee Dee chirped up and sang eerily: *'Humpty Dumpty sat on a wall, Humpty Dumpty had a great fall. All the king's horses and all the king's men couldn't put Humpty together again.'*

chapter 25
ALL THE KING'S HORSES

"I believe Ay has been meddling with alchemy and produced an incubus or two," Kha said searching through a pile of scrolls. "He is not a true adept, so, if he *has* conjured these creatures, it could only have been through the combined efforts of the Amun priesthood's black arts and the Furies." He paused and mumbled "I had it a moment ago" to himself. "It must never fall into the wrong hands."

"That's encouraging," Kit said helping rake through the clutter on Kha's workbench.

"Look, Kit. We have magic powerful enough to counter incubi, but they have the advantage of surprise. Alchemy cannot reach into the future minds of psychopaths and know what devious plans are afoot because infamous plans change from moment to moment, and even more so, from bad to worse. We know psychopaths are consistently up to no good. All we can do is keep vigilant and remain flexible. We must be ready to react and adapt. Lady Nan would say adept and adapt are connected in curious ways. I would have to agree. I planted that thought in her mind when she was Ankhesenamun."

"Are you sure that Ay has these incubusses?"

"Incubi," Kha corrected. "Yes, absolutely. I've overheard Ay speaking with invisible creatures but never seen the form they take. I heard him call them by name: Dismal, Smudge, and one other I couldn't make out. But I do know this: An invisible incubus following his master's orders is perhaps one of the most dangerous opponents we, and by we, I mean *you,* could ever face."

"That word 'face' haunts me waking and sleeping. Could you, perhaps, use another."

"I could but it does no good to soften the truths you must confront."

"Thanks," Kit said sarcastically. "Confronting is so much easier to deal with."

"What you are *dealing with* is the absolute antithesis of easy. But that said. May I suggest you spend the next few days meditating on your childhood. And in the meantime, please help me find that scroll I handed you marked INCUBI."

Kit found it easily. "You need a filing system," he said. "I can help you with that. A good scientist has to keep track of data."

Kha looked up, smiling. Distracted, he ignored Kit's offer. "I want you to remember the days at your grandmother's knee."

"Ah, yes. The good old days where imps and monsters were things in fairy tales. Life was so much easier when there were no actual fairies."

"That is precisely what I want you to remember. And Kit, this is not a request. It is the most important lesson of all. Consider it your final exam."

"At least tell me why."

"I am not permitted to say more. I must attend the King's birthday celebration tomorrow. He's going to show off his new chariot. Your task is to stand out of sight and scan the crowd. I don't feel good about tomorrow. But stopping Tutankhamun from taking the spotlight is as unwise as it's impossible. That boy loves an audience."

Kit withdrew, sullen. "How am I supposed to fight black magic!"

Kha resumed shuffling papers. "You've no time to sulk, my brother. There's work ahead that will not only hearten you, but I believe you will find the science of the experiment, fascinating. Today I must prepare the king for his pageant. When it's over, I will introduce you to one of the least understood secrets of alchemy. One that also loves an audience."

The next day proved to be a challenge. The sky was too blue. The gold too bright, and the horses too skittish. More significantly, there were too many wasps. Several extra slaves had to be employed to brush the offending insects away from a field of antsy horseflesh and disgruntled charioteers. The impatient horses, ready to bolt, turned their heads into the wind and shied away from the buzzing of wasps.

Charioteers' attendants made last minute adjustments to their owners elaborate paraphernalia while the charioteers quenched their thirst with beer.

The king's favorite horse, MeritRa, strained from his handlers, tossing his head until the slave assigned to him became alarmed for the precious white ostrich feathers on the horse's headdress. MeritRa protested his confinement by pawing the sand with his gold painted hooves and whinnying impatiently. He kicked out, narrowly missing the ankles of a slave offering him a handful of oats.

A flurry of soldiers and slaves and tinny music announced the arrival of the king, resplendent in formal ceremonial dress, amidst a procession of courtiers. Ay, among them, strutted tall and imposing, uncharacteristically calm behind Tut in his portable chair. He checked the sky and nodded to an unseen companion named Perilus, confident in contrast to the teenage king, as yet an undeveloped boy not overly fond of chariot driving.

Tutankhamun, as he was then called, had been born with complications, explained away as gifts from the Aten to set him apart from ordinary men. He resembled his father Akhenaten's sleight build, elongated skull, and characteristic hunchback posture. His mother, Nefertiti, pampered him more than her daughters, who also took after their father. Tut's younger brother, Smenkhare, mercifully inherited his mother's noble bone structure and beauty.

Prince Tutankhamun rarely walked. He was carried on chairs to accommodate his unstable gait. His sloped shoulders and wide hips were hardly noticeable when seated and his elaborate clothes and dazzling jewelry made him look regal, in spite of people coached into averting their eyes lest they notice an abnormality.

Tut's muscles were further atrophied from years of a sedentary lifestyle, unsuited for controlling a powerful horse. But knowing himself to be a god, Tut presumed horses and wasps would obey his commands.

King Tutankhamun was lifted from his portable chair and installed in a special cradle of straps in his chariot that held him upright. "The wasps are gathering, majesty," Ay said. "The horses are unhappy. I suggest we begin. It's vital we allow the wind to disperse the wasps before there's a stampede.

King Tutankhamun, had, at Kha's insistence, caused his chair to circumvent MeritRa, in order that servants could scan horse and chariot for signs of sabotage. Other than a single overly large wasp crawling on the horse's muzzle causing it to twitch, nothing was noted. The king ordered a slave to brush it away. Shivers rippled the animal's flanks as another wasp buzzed an inch from his hide.

MeritRa flinched as it landed. He reared, jostling the chariot. Alarmed, Tut ordered MeritRa to remain calm. The horse continued to toss his mane and snorted to be let free but the slave boy, Taraq, more terrified of his king than MeritRa was of a wasp, braced his feet apart, gripped the reigns and held the horse's head low while another boy fastened his headdress tighter.

Ay bowed his head as he approached the king. A slave bearing a gold box materialized at his side. "A gift from Kha and I, your majesty," he said. "To mark your eighteenth birthday."

Ay fastened a gold bracelet emblazoned with winged scarabs, prancing horses, and a connecting circle of slyly inverted ankhs to the king's wrist with a snap. Immediately the creatures quickened, jostling each other as they shuffled to attention.

"Do not be alarmed, your majesty," Ay simpered. "You will feel a pleasant vibration from Kha's magic."

Ay adjusted the double crown on Tut's head so the gods Wadjet and Nekhbet – the royal cobra and vulture of upper and lower Egypt, faced forward, perfectly aligned to the center of Tut's forehead.

"There," he said, handing Tut his reigns. "Give MeritRa his head when you pass the standard bearer of Horus, and remember, this is a parade not a race. Keep a steady pace as I taught you and let MeritRa show off. Remember," he winked knowingly. "Ankhesenamun and Smenkhare will be watching." Ay opened his hand and blew three seeds into the insignia of Tut's crown, patted MeritRa's neck, and stood back. "It is time, majesty."

Perilus's feelers found a miniscule opening in the bracelet's clasp. His wings fluttered once as he deflated into a harmless black seed that lodged between Tut's skin and the heavy layer of jewel encrusted gold. Wadjet, the fat cobra on Tut's crown, uncoiled and thinned into a slithering viper of beige death, writhing its way downward.

Once animated, the scarabs inflated into wasps. The tails of the horses lengthened into enchanted snakes that slithered down Tut's arms to wrap around his wrists. The deadly viper from the crown clamped around Tut's ankle, writhing hypnotically before it bit.

The accident was over in seconds before Kit had time to register the events.

The sound of splintering wood, the screams of terrified horses, and the uproar of a hundred attendants sent shockwaves through the honoured guests and common spectators.

The king's alarmed guards dispersed in several directions at once. Kha and Taraq reacted instantly. Kha thrust a roll of linen in Taraq's hands, threw a sack of medical supplies over his shoulder, and ran into the chaos, braving the stampede of panicked horses.

Charioteers waiting to take the field ordered their slaves to unshackle their terrified horses, lest a dozen more unmanned chariots cause more injury.

Clearly the king's chariot had overturned from a sequence of unfortunate mistakes. MeritRa bucked, careened in a wide arc until finally unfettered, he ran free.

Kit searched the crowd for Ay and found him, surrounded by his regular mob of sycophants, looking both apprehensive and smug. He strode briskly, barking orders, managing to appear in charge, accusing the slaves of sabotage. Frightened slaves cowered in his wake as Ay signalled his guards to take them away.

Later, when Kit played the accident back under hypnosis, the scene ran in slow motion. It showed Perilus, ant-sized, crawling from where it had lodged under the king's linen cap that lined the heavy double crown of upper and lower Egypt. It showed Perilous puff up into its abnormal size and sting Tut's right eye repeatedly.

Tut winced in the pain and brushed the wasp from his face, tearing the skin with the sharp metal of his wrist guard but the swelling caused his eyes to water blurring his vision. Kit saw it from Tut's perspective – an inseparable vista of sand and sky spinning out of control. Another wasp blossomed from an innocent looking black seed under Tut's gauntlet and stung his fingers. Two other demonic wasps attacked his wrists already swollen from snakebites.

Disoriented, Tut dropped the reigns which at first seemed to entangle his ankles but it was clear his right leg had been lashed to the carriage floor by a separate leather thong that shouldn't have been there. A leather thong that was a poisonous viper!

MeritRa, feeling the reigns slacken, lurched out of control veering from another wasp attack.

The chariot teetered on one wheel, the axle snapped, and the shattered parts held together by copper hinges and leather cords, jerked along behind.

Tut was dragged along with the splintered remnants of his shattered chariot to be crushed under its wheels. It took several soldiers on horseback to subdue the terrified horse still trailing the chariot's axle. Tut had almost been torn in half. He lay bloodied, thrashing on the ground, a part of his brain exposed from his crushed skull. His flattened crown lay on its side, the golden figures of Nekhbet and Wadjet trampled by hooves, lay broken into common fragments.

The shocked crowd remained eerily mute, stunned that a god had been injured like a mortal.

The king shouted accusations of treachery even has Kha administered an elixir of strong herbs and applied unguents that acted as anesthetics. Other than Tut's broken legs twisted into unnatural angles, his bloodied arms, laid formally across his chest in the pose of a mummy, made Tut look like a composed corpse. Taraq held the king's head while Kha bandaged Tut's shattered skull. The two exchanged looks of resignation as they escorted the king from the field on a stretcher, his torso covered in a gold cloth, his head wrapped in bloodstained linen surrounded by a swarm of blackflies. An exposed ankle showed the swollen twin puncture marks of a cobra's bite.

Mercifully, King Tutankhamun was dead within 24 hours from the venom coursing through his bloodstream long before his injuries killed him.

Wadjet, the royal cobra, uncoiled from the battered crown and burrowed under the bloodied sand. Nekhbet the vulture, silently rose from the chaos, circled the fallen king once and evaporated in a puff of red smoke.

Kit sat in gloomy solitude hunched into himself like a tortoise hiding in a shell. Kha, preparing the experiment, studied his apprentice's body language before he broke the silence. "I can read your fears, Kit," he said gently. "You're dwelling on the possibility of another trip to Mars. It would be a lie of omission if I failed to mention at least one more foray is inevitable. But let me add that if another trip is forthcoming, it's good news. Think of time travel as time slipping. A gentle transition from spaces linked by events that may not happen."

"It feels like body surfing on a tidal wave."

"Think of yourself as skipping like a stone over the surface of a calm lake."

Kha stirred a saucer of blue fire with a drop of distilled poison. The flames reacted like an injured horse, bucking and twisting. When he sprinkled his formula over the white coals of a brazier the chemicals exploded into three acid colors of red, yellow, and blue that spat a sulphurous odor into the room.

It formed shapes of predatorial shapes that chased each other over the walls and ceiling. They floated over the bubbling cauldron that looked enough like the mouth of a volcano to jolt Kit into the memory of a certain poster on his tower wall where a red spot marked the Yellowstone caldera seen from space.

The shapes congealed into a thick sludge of black droplets that squealed like beads of water jumping on a sizzling griddle. Tiny creatures leapt about in a miniature battle, and for a moment Kit was entranced by what appeared to be a lively computer game. "The spark that survives our physical body is our ka," Kha said. "The spark that survives this experiment is the ka of a creature you've never met."

"An incubus?"

"Almost. Let's call it the distant cousin of an incubus. A delicate wiry creature – a tiny male lion with wings, the size of a hummingbird, hovered over the table, slightly stunned. "Welcome little survivor," Kha said.

Kit smiled and held out his finger to pet it. "It looks harmless enough."

Kha rolled his eyes. "It's a Pygmalion," he said. "A positive incubus. Go on. Make friends if you dare. I called him for you. Don't be alarmed if he's a little ruffian. Rough is what we want. Cruelty and spitefulness separate incubi into allies or foes. If everything checks out, we've created a loyal ally that's not averse to biting off your finger but will ultimately be of immense service. Oh, and he will be vain to the point of madness. An incubus has the ego of a giant sphinx."

Kha frowned and chewed his bottom lip. "Ay has three, last count. You saw their destructive power during the *accident*."

"You mean incident. Tutankh-whatever was murdered. Why are we ignoring that?"

Kha busied himself mixing a potion. "And we have to match them in number. Warring factors have to have an even power structure. We're ignoring nothing but there's no-one to report to."

"So, we're in an arms race?"

"It's more a race against a clock but most of all, it's a battle of wits and you have to be ready. A race of incubi is about as tough as it gets. Be warned. It's never a fair fight. Anna is in Bede. Which suggests your newborn daughter is there, too."

"Anna took me to an horrific Winterland when I was thirteen. I'm afraid she will be nine forever."

"Her mission was to help Queen Ankhesenaten, and inadvertently, Beryl."

"Lady Nan?"

"Anna will always stay with Beryl until Lady Nan chooses to move on, to be reborn. Anna is comatose – a form of sleep capable of sustaining a human life form that also heals the depleted energy of longstanding travel sickness. That, in a word, is what your daughter needs. Respite from prolonged travel sickness."

"How can we help her out?"

"Your incubus pygmalion will fight for her. It was grown to support its master to the death. You are this one's master."

"Hello little Pyg," Kit said in a singsong voice. "My little bluebird of happiness in the time of war."

Pyg immediately turned blue, tested out a range of shades before settling on turquoise, and gave a subdued roar. *This colour suits me best, don't you think?'*

BEDE

chapter 26
A STUNNING PERFORMANCE

A low-lying shimmer like heatwaves on a summer sidewalk made Bede Halls front lawn look like a spooky movie set staged with dry ice theatrical effects. In reality it was less whimsical, considering the special effects were the accumulated dust of a thousand imploded imps swirling as low-lying residue.

For the ninth time, Parks 2 sprayed it down with water infused with a single drop of 'Smyth no. 9'. Within the hour the lawns appeared to be sprayed with purple paint and new shoots of grass emerged as lime tendrils reaching for the sun. Later in the day, the same area of grass had grown lush and thick to hearten the mood of the Twinters, inside now, dining off fresh lettuce and hothouse tomatoes because, quite by accident, the newly dubbed 'Mistress of Botanical Science', Bathsheba Carter Stratford Smyth, had made a second discovery. The decontaminated evil extracted from imp DNA was perhaps the purest source of good imaginable.

Bash's concoction triggered a major chemical reaction no less significant than the dynamics of matter meeting anti-matter. When demonic entrails encountered the neutralizing effects of her enriched formula, the expected toxic waste failed to materialize. Instead, although she and Leoni had labeled reconstituted imp slurry as inert fertilizer, it was more of a 'rejuvenizer' – a powerful anti-imp inhibitor with a surprising bonus side-effect. Lavender's enhanced healing properties scrambled communications between wasps and their psychopathic commander-in-chief, Megeara. Smythe no. 9 was a voice disrupter, too. Sadly, imps were able to hold their breath and were immune but on the bright side, electric shock therapy and happy sounds continued to zap them senseless.

Overnight, the squeal of stricken imps drowned out the relentless buzzing of confused wasps.

. . .

Brooks raised his teacup in triumph, "Another imp attack bites the dust," he declared. "Here's to white sound, Leoni's ornithopter, Nick's, literally ground-breaking 'stun gun' grid, and Bash's breakthrough formula. May their continual mission for absolute pest control turn the tide for a Bede victory."

A cheerful Leoni gave his own toast. "The science, she must be always over surpassing the magic," he said.

"What my distinguished colleague is wont to repeat, is that the student must surpass the teacher," Nick said. "Well done, Bash!"

Leoni, mildly put out, managed a retort. "Have I not been repeating this very complimenting honouring thing my whole life, Nicholas?"

A mild smattering of applause made Leoni bow, all smiles.

Brooks' smile froze as he picked up the thoughts of a twice-born he respected above the others.

Newton Appleby showed willing by sipping his tea in a corner, feigning a jubilance he didn't feel. Brooks' eyes met his across the room. What passed between them was the truth once-borns tend to ignore when fighting evil: Immortality breeds an impenetrable shield around a spurned elemental and that humans are marshmallow helpless in the wake of a deity with an axe to grind. 'Our triumphs only fuel Megeara's anger,' Appleby said. 'No good will come of it."

In their heart of hearts, both men knew their recent win was temporary. For all her longevity, Megeara was a spoiled child having the tantrum of all tantrums.

Brooks motioned for Appleby to follow him outside.

Bede's grounds seemed to glow under a welcoming moon. The topiaries basked in the moonlight, rustling their newly sprouted buds. A gentle wind breezed a sense of peace over the two old friends. It seemed like a dawning new world.

"The gravity of our present situation is not lost on me," Newton replied after a time. "When that apple fell on my head… well, all I know is, happy accidents can change the world. Bash's discovery was a windfall… or was it? I detect an alchemist's touch."

Brooks dropped onto the grass. Immediately, a new sense of purpose rushed through him. "Newton, you should feel this grass. It's wonderful. It's… well, there's no other word for it. It's absolutely energizing. And it's given me an idea. What if Kha is teaching Kit as the three of us planned? And what if Kit's doing better than we hoped. Perhaps the twins' telepathic skills are repairing themselves. Bash is headstrong. It's likely she wouldn't be aware of a subtle influence. What do you think, are we just a couple of old worrywarts?"

Appleby stubbornly refused to sit. He stood hands on hips, rivetted by the aerial ballet of several bats picking off stray wasps. "Twins are a force unto themselves," he said rocking on his heels. "Even I don't fully understand it. But we both know fighting fire with fire is as pointless as chemical warfare, even if curative botanicals *are* the main ingredients." His voice trailed off as he observed the topiaries swaying together in a kind of ritualistic dance. "Fascinating," he said. "Sage is stirring the energies of the grass into a lime-green vapour. Can you see it?"

Brooks laughed out loud. "I can hear it," he said. "But not with my ears. Sit. Newton, you have to try this."

"No thank you, sitting on damp grass plays havoc with my rheumatism. But wait. I can hear it through my feet. How invigorating."

Memory drew in the green energy with her trunk and sprayed it over the others. Sable was positively 'over the moon' and scampered about in circles.

Perhaps the sweet smell of victory *was* within reach. But the truth remained that Bede had upped the ante and humiliated the enemy – a ploy that never failed to unleash unimaginable chaos. The gauntlet was down. The stakes were raised. A challenge had been written in blood and Megeara was just the entity to crave its taste.

The sounds of good cheer reached Brooks and Appleby from the open window of the library. Suddenly the laughter ended, replaced by Hannah's recording of Gregorian chant always played as a soothing finale to their meetings.

The topiaries heard it too. They turned as one to face the Hall. An intoxicating pulse drummed the ground serenaded by monks.

The maze grew bright from a light in its center until it glowed in the shape of a fort. Green horses pawed the ground and tossed their manes. The ghosts of Roman soldiers paused in their work to listen.

Just as mysteriously, the spectacle subsided, and the topiaries drifted back into their usual formation. But the sky over Bede remained green with pink stars until it turned golden with the dawn.

The most adept Bede warriors meditated every morning and evening into a state where death, wasp stings, the emotional blackmail of a triplet of putrid hags failed to register. Lady Nan applauded them, citing meditation to contain the same energy as medication. "I know it may seem we're making light of our latest victory, our thoughts remain with Kit, now facing, I suspect, far more sinister attacks alone and apart from his family."

The inside work of manufacturing had been broken down into teams of worker bees into the sweet smell of success. Vats of distilled lavender and a heady odor from the newly named 'Lotus Lake' petals kept up a constant supply for the balloons. Hannah trained a battalion of volunteers who reached their greenhouse shifts under the protection of Anna's turtle formation, pressed into service under rowan-plated armour.

The Twinters gathered for the unveiling of the ornithopter which was lightened by Leoni's mechanical lion revealed like a magic trick when Bash did the honors of removing a sheet covering a shape the size of a small car that purred like an enormous kitten. "Please welcome Galileo to planet Bede," she said. And there he was, a resplendent purple lion that bowed his head regally to his admirers as he moved forward.

Leoni pressed a button behind Galileo's ear and his purring progressed to a pleasant growl as his clockwork 'engine' fired.

Leoni, speechless with pride, stood, his camera at the ready, beaming his infectious smile. To document the launch, he took close ups of the audience's hands as they applauded. Riveted by each shot of a smile and a raised eyebrow, he became distracted from studying the variations of muscles that affected joy and humor.

Bash held Gali-leo's control box and put him through his paces while Leoni polished the ornithopter. When he gave a signal, Bash pressed a red button and Gali-leo threw back his head and gave a roar that startled Anubis into attack mode and sent the stable mice burrowing under the straw.

"And he is a practical warrior attraction," Bash announced to the crowd. "Mr. Leoni based his creation on the Greek myth of the trojan horse loaded with surprise warriors. She pressed a lever that opened a door in Gali-leo's chest and a dozen imp-seeking spheres billowed out like soap bubbles and popped to great effect, each with its surprise payload of concentrated perfume.

Oohs and aahs followed with a rousing version of 'For he's a jolly good Twinter' sung to Leoni who, finished his polishing, was taking pictures of a scarab beetle in Hannah's hair.

Leoni took center stage and wheeled out his adapted ornithopter with Tut and Brooks assistance. "She is as you are saying, a cropping duster, yes." Enormous swan wings with their spines connected to pulleys and guywires flapped noisily.

Like a real swan it was ungainly landing as well as taking to the sky, but once airborne it was a graceful sight, part swan with two large barrels in its talons, and part unicycle with Parks 3 manipulating its flight pattern clearly enjoying his new role as pilot. Nick's remarkable pump sprayed a fragrant mist with each pass over the gardens and delivered a payload of crushed dehydrated lotus petals to Bash's lavender field that revived the plants overnight.

The Ceremony concluded with Dee Dee singing *'Swanny, how I love ya how I love ya, my dear old Swanny. The folks back home will see Kit once more, when time has cleared the Winter Door.'*

Late that night, a confusing telepathic prediction of sabotage arrived from Nimue to Bash: *"beware the arrival of a confused boy ... a wild child close to home ... rebellion is near."*

Bash confronted Lady Nan in the morning. "Nimue warned me about a boy intent on sabotage. Is it Taraq? He's always been a wild card. He's belligerent with me. Shows no respect. So, I don't understand why you suggested he guide me."

Lady Nan raised her eyebrows, shook her head, and sighed the sigh of a bemused grandmother. "What I *said* was, let the *boy* guide you, and we were in the Winter Room at the time. Details, Bash, details. Use your intuition. A Mistress of the Green must be on her magical toes. Respect often comes disguised as wit."

EGYPT

chapter 27
SWITCHAROO

Lady Snowdrop of Bede and her official guide, Arthur, the former ArTuRa, waited in the open to greet Mr. and Mrs. Cornelius on the steps of Bast's temple. There was no pretext. Grandparents visiting their grandchildren, son, and daughter-in-law, was a natural event. The tomb artists, Sent and Tee, walked behind the party carrying food, beer, and gifts.

The temple cats barely looked up from their catnaps other than to respectfully defer to Bast's new favorite, Snowdrop, by opening one eye and falling asleep again. Even Babs paid sincere homage to her, and the besotted Arthur rarely left her side. Some said the cat from Bede was a magician like her master, KiTiKha'at, and that she had ensorcelled him. Others were sure he'd been ensnared. In any case, Arthur's status reached new heights after being summoned by the goddess Bast as a regular attendee to accompany her morning meditations.

Snowdrop made it known she was there to recruit travelers for a mission to save a place called Bede – the land of lush green forests mentioned in the ancient scrolls of Pangea. Tales of water falling from the sky piqued the cats' natural curiosity.

The temple cats had grown soft, cossetted by their privileged status and offerings from the followers of Bast who feared as much as admired them. In any case, the cats took great pleasure in their self-importance. Besides, it was amusing to keep humans on their toes.

Snowdrop's troops, as she called them, would follow her to the future and save Egypt by saving another temple. The twin temples shared a war. Pitted against a common enemy meant humans and cats from both worlds needed to make a concerted effort at friendship. There was no room for petty jealousies. To be fighting fit, the mollycoddled cats needed to train as warrior hunters. For the present, combat practice took precedence. Rank held no power.

And when Bast called for volunteers, it became a competition to prove their loyalty to each other, their mates, and their goddess. Snowdrops's pampered troops soon formed a disciplined army to match the Roman legion locked inside Hadrian's Wall.

Pigeon fluttered ahead of Cornelius screeching his usual 'hello I'm here' screech, but Babs silenced him with a steely look as he entered the temple and licked her chops. He returned her stare, beak in the air, acting smug. Like Arthur, Pa'a had won over Her Majesty Bast in their private meetings. On these occasions, Babs was ordered to wait in an outer chamber, growling in her throat, daring anyone to cross her. And whenever Pa'a emerged she escorted him to the temple steps and watched until he'd flown far enough away to look like a small white cloud and disappear. Only then, did she pad back into the inner sanctum where Bast took her human form and made a fuss of her.

Hosts, SaRa and Kit welcomed the gathering of their kinfolk in silence. Kha arrived through Bast's private time portal with Tut, both dressed in identical plain galabeyas. Tut wore a page-boy wig that made them look remarkably like twins. Arthur and Sibuna prowled the outer halls for unwanted ears, the nine-month-old babies were admired and taken off to bed, and the floor cushions were rearranged in a circle. Kit arranged Lady Nan's hourglass on a mat in the center. Snowdrop curled next to it and appeared to be sleeping.

Small talk and laughter filled the air until Sibuna yowled the all-clear, proclaiming the area safe from spying eyes and ears. The two male cats stationed themselves like miniature sentries either side of the entrance to keep vigil.

Sent, as acting scribe, seated himself outside the circle. Kit supplied him with his own portable desk, a roll of blank papyrus, a writing stick and black paint. Tee refreshed the wine and took his place beside Sent. SaRa brushed Kit's lock of white hair from his eyes with her fingers, kissed his forehead, and whispered that it was time.

Kha paused briefly to scan the party and resumed his casual discussion about Kit's apprenticeship with his proud parents. SaRa knelt between Kit and Tut, beaming confidently at Kha.

"Above all, the student must surpass the teacher," Kha was saying, staring pointedly at Kit.

Tut perked up at that and punched Kit's arm playfully. "Those were Mr. Leoni's last words to me. That man is never wrong."

Kit made a display of rubbing his arm as if it hurt. "He's eccentric," Kit observed, "but entertaining. He was Pigeon's biggest fan."

Pigeon fluffed out his wings. *'Brilliant man, Leoni. Profound scientist. I miss him.'*

Sent dipped his painting stick in the paint preparing to write but Kha motioned for him to stop. "I'm sorry," he said. "I should have mentioned that there's no need to write everything we say. I will indicate *when* you're to write. We only want a simple list of ideas, not a transcript of our small-talk." He winked at Cornelius. "Besides, the small talk is about to get considerably larger."

Sent put down the brush and glanced sidelong at his brother. "Transcript?" Tee leaned over and translated by taking the makeshift brush and drawing the sign for 'list'. Sent's shoulders relaxed, Cornelius smiled his approval, and Pigeon cackled to himself *'Painters... the salt of the earth.'*

Kha lowered his voice to a whisper, riveting everyone's attention. "Something incredible will happen here tonight," he said. And as he spoke his plain galabeya transformed to the multi-colored robes of a magus. "I ask that you close your eyes and welcome the moment. Tomorrow will never be the same." As he spoke, a transparent vision of Anna, nine-years-old, entered the room holding Ani. She smiled and vanished.

Kit's ring hummed out waves of lavender. SaRa covered it with her hand and squeezed. Kit stifled a nervous laugh. "And so ends the small-talk," he said.

Kaleidoscopic colors appeared on the curtain wall like splashed paint, pulsating in bursts of red, turquoise, and lime green and settled on a backdrop of bright purple. Tut put his head between his knees and giggled helplessly. "Oh brother," he said searching for something to anchor him. "I feel kind of giddy."

Kit and pulled Tut into a rough hug. "One of the first lessons Kha taught me was that giddiness is the start of magic. I'm sorry for being such an arse."

"Somewhere, Megeara is having a really bad night," Kha said to SaRa.

Cornelius cuddled his wife. "How are you holding up, my love?" Mrs. S's face was transfixed with happiness. She giggled and kissed his cheek. "You haven't called me that for a thousand years."

The sand in the bottom of the hourglass swirled like a tiny tornado and was sucked into the upper chamber where it hung, exposing a tiny maze below. The oil lamps dimmed and blinked out as the room glowed with white light emanating from a star hovering on the ceiling.

As the light dissipated, the flames of the oil lamps surged brightly, and the mood became sober. "And now to the business at hand," Kha said, back in the garb of a citizen. "We have our work cut out for us, starting now."

Cornelius lifted his beer in a toast. "It's about time," he said which lightened the mood to one of contained excitement. Everyone clicked their glass on the hourglass and the sand's gravity returned, dropping one grain at a time into a perfect pyramid. Snowdrop continued to sleep but her white fur had turned the color of lavender.

The circle closed into an intimate gathering. Kha drank to Cornelius's toast and closed his eyes. The others held their breath. When Kha finally spoke, it was with the unflinching authority of a general commanding an army. "We must act fast while the people are in the first stages of shock. We know Tut is near soul death and that when he succumbs, he will have died the ordinary death of a mortal. The populace will remain ignorant until we say so."

"Not an ordinary death," SaRa said loudly. "It was murder!"

"No-one suspects foul play. Teenage gods do not die. "Only a few people at court know Tutankhaten is comatose but it's only a matter of time before word spreads and panic ensues. And during that chaos, Ay must act dutifully as if Smenkhare will be crowned." He glared at Tut.

"That, as you know, can never happen. Smenkhare would be sacrificed so Ay can become the leader of a new dynasty."

Murmurs of agreement caused Sent to load his brush with paint. Kha nodded for him to proceed. As Sent's eyes gazed unfocused on a distant horizon of sunflowers, the walls reflected what he saw – a frenzied purple sky with racing clouds and waving trees. His hand trembled as nervous hieroglyphic symbols appeared on the papyrus. *Crown Smenkhare*, he wrote.

Pigeon flew into Sent's topsy-turvy sky, circled the animated landscape, and flew back out with a delirious squawk, no longer white but with feathers returned to brilliant lime-green, turquoise, gold, purple, and crimson. Everyone gazed in awe at the new 'old' Pigeon. Tee gazed in awe at his brother.

Kha bid Tut stand. He brushed imaginary dust from the shoulders of Tut's robe and walked around him like a courtier showing off a fine slave. "Now, look at 'Tut of Bede', here, and tell me you don't see what I see. He's in good health. He could pass for Smenkhare's handsome brother and because ceremonial pomp covers a multitude of birth defects and the people have always averted their eyes, our 'Tut of Bede' could pass for the former king. I need a double ruling on this. I say we replace the dying king with our own Tut before the night is out. It's only a matter of time before…"

Cornelius took a long draft of beer. "He's a credible imposter to the masses, but can he fool his courtiers?"

"Courtiers are toadies," Kha continued. "And toadies are terrified of their Pharaoh and each other. Always have been, always will. If anyone knows this it's you, Cornelius. Now that you're no longer being sedated, you survive by pretending to comply. The courtiers accepted Tutankhamun's inherited deformities without question. Some of them didn't even *see* them. Or if they did, they knew to look the other way, keep silent, and play along."

'Pomp Pompous is as Pompous does. Stay Popular… child's Play…Pecking Performance,' Pigeon repeated happily to himself while gnawing on the cuttlebone Tut had brought him from Bede.

Kha pushed Tut down on the pillows and sat beside him. "Ay won't play along. In fact, he'll be apoplectic. Not to mention aggressively vindictive. Tut will be in grave danger until…"

"Until Ay's dead," Kit finished. "I suppose killing him is *my* job."

"It is not," Kha said. "Your *job* is to destroy the Furies. Ay will self-destruct when that happens. Which means? Anyone? Come on Kit, think."

'Please Play along,' Pigeon muttered. *'Mr. PoPlectic. What a great title.'*

Kit slammed down his beer. "Why are we even hesitating. We know Ay orchestrated the king's murder. And soon he will take the throne."

"Literally," Kha said. "After his coronation, the throne will be taken to Bede. Ay's big plan is to run Bede as Lady Nan's husband. Megeara promised him Bede and he's fool enough to believe her. Greed will do that. Greed covers a multitude of deficiencies too."

"We'll have to remove the dead king's body from the house of embalming, tonight. Our Tut will be paraded out in the morning when Ay addresses the gathering crowds.

"There's nothing like a surprise revolution when you're not expecting one. We merely replace one revolution with a better one."

"Merely," Kit said weakly. "Bash would have come up with a better word."

Cornelius warmed to the plan. "The people will believe a god can restore himself. Kha will announce the king is well. Tut will step forward in perfect health without the use of a chair. Ay won't have to fake surprise but he *will* have to appear overjoyed. The people will settle down and the chariot spectacle will be absorbed as a miracle."

"The courtiers will be stunned as usual and cower. A healthy vigorous god as pharaoh is much more intimidating, and superstitions run high. Tutankhamun is already ensconced in the tomb built for Smenkhare. All the people want is a figurehead to fear and serve which is what they will have. The transition must be seamless. A god does not die from accidental injuries. A god is immortal until he's called to the halls of reincarnation. Tut of Bede will bear that out."

"And where will Ay be?"

"Ay will be demoted," Cornelius said. "He will have to bow publicly to the new king for a while. Our Tut will appoint his own vizier. Ay will be out of a job."

Tut crossed his arms defiantly. "And after that?"

Kha smoothed Pigeon's new tail feathers where a single white feather remained. "After that he will make trouble. The likes of which we can barely imagine."

Snowdrop stretched out, nattering in her dreams. Sparkling snowflakes shot from the hourglass as Tut stood. Clearly, he was in a trance. He shook the snow from his hair and announced in a commanding voice. "I'm ready. I've always been ready!"

Kit stared at his mentor and half-brother in awe, no longer jealous of their bond or that between Tut and his father. "Now I understand. I can't believe I didn't put two and two together. I mean, put the two of *you*, together. I have a dim recollection of Kha telling me he was you. I thought it was a dream. But it was real, wasn't it! Tut is your reincarnation." He faced Kha. "When you called us brothers, you meant Tut and I in Bede."

Kha nodded. "I told Kit, not long ago that I had sugar-coated an event with a spell that made him forget something I revealed until he could handle its huge impact." He addressed Tut. "Similarly, as a twenty-first century street kid, you had to be ignorant of your ancient origins. That's what happens in reincarnation. You remember and forget continually until the whole truth is revealed at the right time. Twice-borns are complicated. You are a famous twice-born with an historic past."

It was Tut's turn to face Kit. "I was beginning to remember after you left. I thought I was going crazy."

"And Megeara's influence caused a rift between you and the family," Kha said. "It was always there even when things appeared smooth."

Kit shrugged helplessly. "I'm so sorry, Tut. I hated you for being closer to Dad than I was."

"And I hated you," Tut said, "for being his real son with me an outsider."

Mrs. S was crying softly. Cornelius sat nursing an empty glass. "I feel as if I'm waking up."

Kha nodded to Tee to fill Cornelius's cup. "I hoped this would happen, but I can't control another's memories. Paradoxically, time unfolds in its own time. We are a family of many secrets."

Pigeon flapped around the circle like a crazed rainbow screeching the word paradoxical like a town crier.

"It's the Furies who are complicated. They've had time on their side."

"With Ay on the defensive, I can take on Megeara," Kit said.

Kha stood and paced the room, his worried look returned. Kit sat hunched on the floor and spoke to his mentor in his head. "Tell me the truth. Am I ready?"

"There's more to it than that," Kha replied so everyone heard. "Which means, as I was about to mention earlier, that Ay and the Furies will have to be destroyed in one move. Kit has to be ready for that."

Kit opened his mouth to comment but SaRa squeezed his arm, eyed her brother, and spoke first. "Kit will be ready when it's time."

"All of you are waking up tonight, Kha announced to the room. We're here at this time to formalize the bigger picture. First, we install Tut as pharaoh and immediately step up Kit's showdown with the Furies."

The silence was painful.

Kha's gaze never left Kit's face. "The Bede Prophecy states that Kit must eradicate the Furies. We can help him but not intervene. Also, in accord with Kit's alchemy apprenticeship, I am unable to tell him…" he cleared his throat, "certain things. He must come up with the solution on his own. Tonight's meeting confirms our plan. We install Tut immediately. Kit's training will be more intense which means more intuitive. We act as a family unit. Excuse the pun I am about to say in all seriousness. All in favor say Ay."

. . .

Babs escorted the visitors out: Mr. and Mrs. S, a colorful, strangely silent parrot, and two sleepwalking servants, arm-in-arm. Sibuna led Tut and Kha to Bast's private portal. Snowdrop and Arthur left for their cozy love nest.

SaRa rose to check on the children and returned quickly. "Ani is gone, she said remarkably calm, staring at Kit. "I know where she is. She's with you in Bede and it's cold. White and cold. She's 9 years old." Kit grabbed SaRa's hands. "I remember," he said. "I remember everything. She's safe. She's gone to save us." He hugged SaRa tightly. "That light we saw was Ani, saying goodbye."

"She was saying hello," SaRa said softly.

chapter 28
NIPPED IN THE BUD

Hapi woke Bash at 2 a.m. singing a cheery song. *'Someone's in the kitchen with Sarah. Someone's in the kitchen I know Oh-Oh-Oh. Someone's in the kitchen with Sarahhh, and it's someone you alread-Dee know.'*

Bash reached out to grab her, but Hapi, well versed in evading irritable humans, dodged her grasp and retired to the bedpost to be more helpful if the occasion required.

"He's a lovely lad," Hapi went on. "He reminds me of someone, but I can't place him."

"I should place *you* in a cage," Bash replied. "This better be good."

"It's *all* good," Hapi chirped. "All the time."

"That's what you always say."

"Because it always is. Even when it's in disguise."

The boy sitting in the kitchen made the table look giant sized. He looked terrified but he stared back with courage.

"TUT!" is that you?"

"My name *was* Taraq but Tut gave me a new name. It's Kem."

"How cute is that," Hapi, crowed. "That's Egypt's old name. It means the black land. Isn't Tut clever."

"He's a whiz, alright," Bash said. *Well, he pulled it off,* she reflected. She faced the boy so obviously eager to please. "I expect you're tired, Kem."

"No Miss Bash, but I *am* hungry." He blinked his puppy dog eyes that Bash suspected were far from innocent. Tut, for all his shyness, had been a savvy street kid. A survivor beyond his years. "I'm always hungry. Tut told me to ask you for some crumpets. May I call you Mum? He said that would make you laugh."

Hapi flew a gleeful jig in the air. "Laugh and the world laughs with you," she chanted, flitting around the glass of orange juice Bash set before Kem.

Tut downed his juice in one go and wiped his mouth with his sleeve. "Tut brought me to the edge of something called the maze, but he couldn't stay."

Hapi giggled so hard she sneezed. "AMAZE-ing, but true."

Bash leaned forward on her elbows examining the juice stain on Kem's sleeve rather than face being read by a shrewd boy looking for an angle. "Do you like hamburgers? It's ground beef… meat."

"I had meat once," Kem said. "I liked it."

"Then you shall have it twice because hamburgers were one of Tut's favorite things and we're all stocked up on frozen patties and buns. You're in luck. Crumpets are afternoon treats if you like jam."

Hapi sensed Kem was close to tears and summersaulted over the salt and pepper shakers to amuse him.

Kem timidly placed his hand in Bash's. "I saw someone eating jam once," he said.

"He's a little small for eighteen," Hapi said. "But bright as a silver button."

"I'm nine," Kem said trying to catch her out.

"What a surprise," Bash said. "Sometimes I think the entire world is nine."

"I'm nine-hundred," Hapi announced.

Bash faked swatting Hapi. "Thank you for making my point."

Hapi flew to the window. "Oh, you are very *very* welcome. Anything to please you. Hey Kem, want to hear something funny." She opened her miniature lion mouth and meowed.

But Kem was watching a sphinx made of sticks talking to a small twiggy creature with a sizeable tail. "Sadly, the brief revival of green magic didn't last, and the drought returned," Bash said. "You can't play outside unless one of us is with you."

Tut stared back, blinking. "I never play."

"Hapi and Jack will teach you. Playing means having fun. It's chasing a ball it's…" she paused, searching for another example and drew a blank. "Jack loves to chase a ball, in fact he loves chasing anything. That twig creature you just saw is a squirrel named Sable. Sable is Jack's friend. He and Jack would chase each other all day if they could, but Jack only goes outside when the coast is clear. Fetching a stick is another game Jack loves, but I warn you, once you throw a ball, Jack will never want to stop. Dogs make great friends." Her eyes sought a distant time when Kit and Jack swam in the lake. Kit hadn't seen the mermaids because he refused to believe in such things. "Jack misses my brother."

"The market dogs and I scrapped for food."

Bash was still lost in her memories, watching the mermaids in the lake and missing Kit. "You can be Jack's new friend."

Kem covered the orange juice stain on his sleeve with his hand and spoke in a whisper. "I've never had a friend."

Sage roared a parental roar that brought Sable running. He almost saluted. "Yes, Sir?"

"I must ask you not to overexcite Jack. I can't reason with a dog, but I *can* reason with you. Doolittle brought me a message from Cyril that a wasp swarm has been heard buzzing this way. Tree nymphs have exceptional hearing so it's a warning worth heeding. Do you understand? Wasps can't hurt you, but I don't want Jack to be stung."

Jack bounded past. Sage cuffed Sable's ear but he hared off giggling. "We'll be careful," he shouted, already thirty feet away.

"Boys," Sage grouched to himself. "You can't tell them anything."

The early shift of gardeners had already returned to headquarters under their turtle shell, alerted by Nimue to take precautionary measures even if the sky looked clear.

Doolittle and Katydid scampered behind them. "Who's in charge of Jack this morning?" Nimue asked. "I saw him running loose a few moments ago."

"Bash let him out. She was busy with the boy who turned up."

"Boys don't just turn up," Nimue said.

Doolittle piped up. "This one did. Hapi says it's a secret boy and I'm not to discuss it, but that's all I know, so there's nothing I can say, other than I doubt Bash heard Cyril's warning. Her mind wanders these days."

Nimue made a 'listen to me or else', face, her hands on her hips. "Please inform Bash that Jack needs to be inside until the all-clear and ask one of the ghosts to fetch him."

"Yes Ma'am."

Nimue confronted Hapi humming over the bread and jam that Kem abandoned in the kitchen. "Tell me what you know about this boy," she said. "I'm in a hurry. There's a tornado of wasps on the way. Stay inside."

"Jam's too sweet for boys unused to it," Hapi replied.

Nimue's wings beat faster. "What boy? I'm in no mood for games."

Hapi perched on the lip of Kem's juice glass. "Two surprise boys in one day," she announced merrily. "Perhaps you know a fairy named Griffin who presented himself to Nick Wardencliffe."

"I know all the fairies. I've heard of a Gruffin but never a Griffin. Continue."

"It was luck, really. Griffin just appeared in the stables, out of the blue, at Nick's elbow. Nick said he'd been lost in thought staring at a diagram of his grid, wondering how he could examine its inside clockworks, and Griffin, with his tiny fairy body, seemed like a gift. Griffin said Lady Charlotte had sent him to help Nick tweak something." Hapi convulsed in laughter. "And then he asked what tweaking was. I think he was serious, but it was funny. It made Nick laugh, too. They're both in his workshop if you want to…"

But Nimue was gone – a speck of magic in the distance. Hapi giggled and batted the fairy footprints Nimue left hanging on the wind in a trail behind her like tiny blue stars.

. . .

"Beggers can't be choosers," Nick said. "War machines are tricky. They require tweaking."

"And fairies are tricksters," Nimue countered. "Even me, which is why Parks told all of you to always check with Charlotte before you followed our advice or ate or drank something we offered. Sometimes we don't play nice."

Nick absorbed Nimue's truth using logic. "Well, Charlotte wasn't here, nor is she likely to be anytime soon. There wasn't a full moon, and I was on a tight schedule."

"Did you even think of consulting Hannah?"

"Look, the little fellow was rather useful," Nick replied apologetically. "And talk about timing, I thanked my lucky stars when he showed up. Griffin's size was perfect for adjusting the connectors in the grid's control box. Anyway, he's gone, the work's finished, and no harm done."

The wasps attacked in a steep swift dive from behind a normal cloud. There were only nine of them, but they were enormous. Jack panicked and ran in a circle. His frenzied barking made them more eager. He snapped at a few and missed.

Sage ran towards the scuffle shouting to Sable to run into the maze but instead Sable faced the skirmish and tried dispersing the wasps with his tail. It was over in a second. Sable had no tail leaves to swat them with. His brittle branches snapped into a pile of broken twigs. Jack made it to the greenhouse where Sarah, hearing his frantic barking, opened the door.

The gardeners brought Jack home undercover of their Roman 'turtle', failing to recognize the heap of powdered grey twigs that was once a lively young squirrel.

Bash was contrite but Sage was heartbroken. "Wretched selfish girl," he shouted to Memory. "If Bash hadn't let Jack loose, Sable would be safe."

. . .

Kem snuck out at as the full moon shone pale grey in a darkening sky. With Ben's help, he raked Sable's bones into a tiny grave dug by Parks 3. A solitary wasp, dislodged in the rubble, flew out into Kem's face, slamming into his cheek, stinging several times in one spot until a trickle of blood flowed into his mouth. Ben reported back that Kem hadn't uttered a sound but had shed tears over the sad mound of earth, so tiny and alone, and marked it with the rare scarab he had in his pocket.

Sable's death was a terrible event to mark Kem's first day, but he savored his painful injuries as a badge of honor. He relished being a true warrior wounded in battle and kept looking in the mirror with pride. It was Kem who consoled Bash, later.

Bash chided herself trying to rationalize her oversight under a thin veil of logic. It had been a poor lack of judgement. A terrible mistake. Regret and guilt came in waves, but nothing could change the fact that the Mistress of the Green had failed her calling and an innocent young topiary had bravely sacrificed himself for a friend.

Bash formally introduced Kem at the midnight vigil for Sable. "This is Kem," she said simply. "He was stung helping a fallen comrade. If he looks familiar, it's because he's my brother, Tut, who left a short time ago for the eighteenth-dynasty. Tut asked me to help him meet his destiny and stay in Bede at the same time. He hit upon a creative solution after Brooks explained the finer points of time travel law. They met several times to assure Tut that by leaving he would not negate his rescue of my father. Most of all, Tut wanted to feel like a genuine child of the Bede family. This I understand only too well. His intent was to save the abandoned child he once was from starvation, poverty, and crime.

Kem stood proudly during Taraq's speech. His cheek burned red after blossoming into a large welt. Bash dabbed the sting with lavender oil but with no noticeable effect other than the stinger fell out like a needle and disintegrated in a puff of soot. Cold compresses reduced the inflammation and pain but left a small scar that Brooks said was a positive sign but declined to explain further. "Time will tell," he said, his eyes misting over. "Rest assured, this event will be documented in a way none of you could possibly imagine."

Hapi visited Nick and flew into Griffin, leaving. "We didn't get a chance to talk," she said.

"I tweaked the doodad in the grid control box," Griffin said. "It was faulty because it had been cursed but I fixed it. My work is done. I must report back to Lady Charlotte that my mission was accomplished. It was lucky she sensed a problem."

"Shades of 'Snow White'," Hapi said. "Talk about a good fairy's spell counterbalancing a bad fairy's curse although I believe *that* story was 'Sleeping Beauty'. Don't you just love happy endings."

Griffin smirked. "Well, Bede Hall *does* have seven dwarves heigh-ho-ing off to work in the greenhouses every morning. And if you report I said that to Nick, I'll tell him you swanned off to drink poppy juice."

Hapi made herself dizzy by imitating a tornado to impress Griffin. "Wouldn't that get *you* in trouble?"

Griffin, the same size as Hapi, met her eye-to-eye. "I haven't quite thought it through, yet but rest assured I will figure it out. Now skedaddle, you little ray of sunshine. I have other work to do. I have to let a cat out of a bag," he said. "Or is it *put* all the cats in a bag."

Hapi flew distractedly about the gathering until everyone stopped talking and paid her attention.

"Anna asked me to tell you that she was called away," she announced. "I was with her when she watched Kem burying Sable's remains."

"Did she say where she was going?" Bash asked.

"All she said was 'that's my cue. I have to leave'. I did my best to cheer her up. Afterwards she seemed happy, so all is well."

Sassia, Nimue's young apprentice, nudged her mistress's wing. "Tell them, Ma'am. It's the right thing to do. Or so you've been teaching me. Your fairies were not to blame."

Nimue looked at Sassia with new respect. "Excuse me, everyone," she shouted above the buzzing theories about Anna. "All is *not* well. I believe Nick has something to say."

A sea of perplexed faces turned questioningly to Nick.

Nick's voice faltered. "I have to report a severe problem," he stuttered. "The grid has been compromised. It's literally *unsound* which means we are presently at the mercy of the imps."

"Nick means sabotaged," Nimue said. "By a fairy, no less. I am mortified!"

"I take full blame," Nick said. "I was distracted. I wanted to fix something that didn't need fixing. And now the imps will arrive in hoards with no sound check to stop them. We're going to need hundreds of cats to kill them the old-fashioned way."

Gossip over the coffee cups was strained. Nick and Leoni fielded questions of a new plan of defense. "Lady Charlotte is completely out of communication," Hannah remarked to Helen. "She has been ever since Six's death. Even Nick knew that. He wasn't paying attention."

"Scientists are absentminded," Helen agreed. "They're on a different wavelength to the rest of us."

Hapi overheard and joined them. "But Griffin was friendly and nice."

Helen shook her finger at Hapi. "You think everyone is nice."

"Griffin was telling porky pies," Hannah said. "He could *not* have spoken with Charlotte. Even my discussions with her are one-way messages in code."

"I just spoke with Fioretti," Helen said. "She wasn't taken in. She said she saw right through Griffin. Which, as a ghost, she can do. She said Griffin was a bad crab apple with a grey core."

Grief pushed the memory of Sable and sympathy for Kem to the shadows. Bash drifted outside and wandered the grounds holding Kem's hand, looking lost. Every few minutes Bash checked Kem's sting until he begged her to please stop.

Kem guided Bash to Sable's gravesite. As they stood beside the tiny mound of earth, a blue flutter emerged from the soil as Kem's turquoise scarab flew back into his pocket. In its place was a blue beacon shining like a miniature searchlight that covered the patch of turquoise earth where Sable rested.

chapter 29
THE STING OF TRUTH

Ay was easy to spot, dressed as a beggar in a crowd of citizens wearing their best clothes. Kit shadowed him, resisting an insistent urge to strangle his scrawny sunburned neck. A strong odor of death issued from his robes whenever he moved. Kit recognized the stink of Megeara that he could never forget.

Ay was clearly under Megeara's watchful eyes because from time-to-time the greasy strands of his wig wriggled into maggots. Putrid hallucinations were enough to deter Kit from acting out his revenge, and in any case, he was on a sensitive assignment after he'd sworn allegiance to the family. His agenda was to scan and note any untoward behavior – to blend into the onlookers without making a ripple which worked fine until his phone jumpstarted into a rousing blare of 'Rule Britannia' that lasted what felt like a minute but was only nine seconds. He made a note to tell Arthur to remind him to leave his phone at home and to tell Snowdrop if it rang. And as they were surely together, she would be able to translate its coded message. Now, he mused. What precisely was the significance of a rousing call to arms song? He recalled the words: *'Rule Britannia. Britannia rules the waves. Britons never never never will be slaves'* – a poignant reminder of what ghastly things would happen if the Furies were allowed to rule Britain.

He summoned his diplomatic training and thought of the time Ay had been his grumpy grandfather, the day he'd bullied him over reading too many books. Visions of his father's assistant, Digger, flashed repeatedly. The resemblance was uncanny. Yes, he could see it now by comparing their eyes. Both men's eyes glittered with barefaced hostility. Both were shamelessly callous and bereft of human warmth.

.   .   .

The 'populace' gathered at a respectful distance for the 'new-old' king's first public appearance since the accident. The pharaoh, a resplendently enthroned vision wearing the double crown, was decked out in gold and jewels. He clutched his symbols of office, the crook and flail, remaining far enough away to be seen as an iconic figure of state, and no questions asked.

None noticed the king suddenly flinch and recoil in pain or see Cornelius react by reaching into his sleeve for a 'Way of Happiness' crystal, deftly waving it under Tut's nose.

The twin fan bearers, well trained to stare ahead with a fixed gaze on an imaginary horizon, noticed nothing and kept fanning Tut like a pair of automatons.

Tut's hand twitched involuntarily and his fingers opened. Cornelius managed to catch his flail before it fell. He deftly moved a fan bearer's arm to momentarily shield the king's face, and motioned Kha for help.

The wasp, still embedded in Tut's cheek, had turned to stone. Cornelius reached over casually and plucked it from the king's skin which immediately poured forth a clear viscous liquid.

And then the king did something as remarkable as it was unusual. He stood, held out a hand for the cheering to cease, and spoke.

Tut's English words washed over the startled crowd as a god speaking his special magic. It had the effect Tut wanted. All but the beggar, averted their eyes in fear.

"Beryl sends her regards, Ay," he said loudly. "The fairies of Bede have hidden the golden throne where none can find it. At her command they will burn it."

Taraq arrived silently and whispered in Cornelius's ear. "King Tutankhamen's ka died an hour ago."

Cornelius raised his arm and sent Pigeon soaring a low flyby over the crowds, screeching maniacal parrot laughter. The spectators cowered and dropped to their knees. Ay, standing tall in their midst, was a clear target for the bird droppings that landed so precisely on his wig, now squealing like a Martian wasp.

Tut's performance was brief. Another wave of his hand sent his people grovelling on their knees, terrified from looking at the god and hearing the voice. They touched their foreheads to the earth, begging forgiveness.

Cornelius sharply turned the procession and noiselessly whisked Tut away. Kha sent Taraq for a quantity of 'magical cold stones' – ice blocks packed in straw, stored deep in his private underground cave. Cornelius," he said, we've rehearsed this. Kit will be waiting for me in the temple. You know what to do. I will meet you in the palace with strong painkillers. Anna brought me some antibiotics from Bede."

"Who's Anna?"

"I'll explain later. I will use Bast's personal portal and be there before you. Stay calm." He dissolved before Cornelius's eyes.

Taraq was in shock. He followed Kha's instructions, too stunned to be terrified. Having a specific task gave him courage. He crushed the ice with a stonecutter's chisel, filled a cotton sack with ice chips, and doubled back to intercept the king halfway.

Cornelius made sure the crowd's and the courtiers' eyes were averted by Pharaoh's order.

At first, the King's clothes rattled Taraq, in spite of knowing he was not the true pharaoh, but the grim determination on Cornelius's face spurred him to perform his duty. The future 'Taraq of Bede', discreetly applied pressure to Tut's injury – a steadfast accomplice of a group later referred to as the 'Tutankhamun conspiracy'.

Tut, well versed in street savvy, suffered his pain in silence until he was safely inside his inner sanctum. A noise in the antechamber announced Tut's arrival. A flurry of activity heralded in Tut, with Taraq still holding a compress of ice to his cheek.

Kha inhaled a deeply troubled breath and scanned the throne room. "Welcome home, your majesty." He adjusted Tut's slightly askew headdress and smiled. "The King is dead. Long live the King," he said.

A week of lavender oil compresses subdued the pain in Tut's cheek but not his anger. The crushed body of the boy king slowly disintegrated in his tomb under too many layers of natron and powerful unguents. The new boy king, same age, same name, had technically ascended the golden throne at the moment of Tutankhaten's last breath.

It was immediately apparent the golden throne was as lifeless as the old king. For a moment, Tut of Bede assumed the throne had self destructed in sympathy with its former master. But Kha set him straight. "The true throne is in Bede. Kit's grandfather stole it many years ago after he discovered the portal in the Winter Room. As you may imagine, Lady Nan was outraged."

Tut shut his eyes remembering. "When I sat on the throne in Kit's tower, it felt alive. I believed it chose me."

Kha bustled about checking Tut's bandages. "The Bede throne *is* alive and *yes*, it did choose you. Tell me, when you met Ay, did you recognize him?"

"Sorry, no," Tut said. "But Kit explained he was Lady Nan's estranged husband. Lady Nan once said her husband was stranger than estranged. More than separated and I gathered from her sad expression they were less than amicably married. But she's happy with Brooks. So, all's well that ends well, right."

"Wrong. You're sure there was nothing familiar about him because he knows who you are."

"Refresh my memory."

"Mind your back. Ay is a powermonger. His schemes expand with every mistake Kit or you make. And he has an army of eyes watching your every move. A few of the wasps are incubi."

"Now that you mention it. I didn't like his eyes."

"They were the eyes of Digger. Cornelius's assistant. You probably ran into him on the street in Cairo. He was in league with the tomb robbers you worked for. He was the one who left Cornelius in an empty tomb after a convenient rockslide sealed the entrance, and even more conveniently, he decided to forget where it was. So far, your father hasn't recognized Digger because Ay plied him with regular doses of lotus oil to insure he walked in a perpetual state of twilight."

"Digger is now in league with Megeara?"

"Ay's sights are set on Kit. Megeara's plan for your parents is complete. They were bait. All she wanted was to get Kit here. And now they are dispensable hostages, only useful as pawns. They live while you live. After that… look, Kit can't kill Megeara or her sisters, but he *can* stop them. And when he does, your parents will be free. The caldera in Yellowstone will sleep under a new curse – a fairy tale of life returning to the land. But there are caveats. I will explain later. Kit is under my protection and soon, with our help, he will be ready to fight the Furies with a fury of his own. But my energies are restricted by the rules of magical engagement. I can only help him so far."

"How can I help?"

"You don't know it, but you are already walking the path to greatness."

"Are you psychic? Because you keep answering my unasked questions."

"I receive fragmented visions of the future delivered to me in pictures. Most are too blurry to see, but I piece together what I can, and although the Furies are ferocious and vindictive, they're insanely complacent – so sure of their absolute power they overlook things they shouldn't."

Megeara placed a clawed hand on Ay's forehead. "Forget," she said. "It is tomorrow again. You are a young man once more, smitten with a beautiful girl who is the princess of her mother's heart, captivated by your rival, Peregrine Brooks. If you follow my orders, she will accept you as her duty even if she despises you, and she does. The land of Bede is a powerful asset. You must claim the woman, Beryl, who is heir to it if you want to be master over the Green Man.

Beryl's father despises her and will go far to make her life a living hell. He is tired with the matriarchal traditions of Bede based on the Egyptian ideal and is ready to break the rules. He knows Beryl is in love with Brooks and that you covet her. It's a perfect love triangle for ruining three lives. He will enjoy executing such a plan. Except, you will be installed in Bede as vizier to the great Pan and the land will be under your control."

"And I will be under yours."

"You will be immortal, Ay. You will be in control of many things if you are loyal to my cause and accept me as your mentor. Kha's apprentice is your biggest challenge. He is the prophesied obstacle blocking your path. You must kill him twice. The first time here in mortal combat and secondly, three-thousand-years from now as your grandson. A twin death renders him a permanent resident of the underworld with Osiris." She spat his name as if it was poison in her mouth.

The red and white double crown of upper and lower Egypt, kept on a special stand, cast a malevolent shadow. Ay reached for it but Megeara snatched it and held it out of reach. This is your carrot, Ay. If you want it you must destroy the usurper, and Kha, as well as his feeble apprentice. Then, and only then, I will sanction Pan's territory in Bede to you. You will marry your Ankhesenamun, Beryl, the wilful daughter of Bede Hall and its future matriarch, but you must take her name to win a victory over Pan."

Ay did a doubletake. "You're saying you can send me back to the years when Brooks was courting Beryl and she will choose me?"

Megeara sneered. "It isn't always about choosing someone, Ay. It's letting someone else go and defaulting to a father who demands obedience from a precocious little upstart. You will do well to win him over, first. The two of you have a lot in common.

Beryl's broken spirit will succumb if you destroy someone she loves, first. There are no sacrifices without pain. You will have to kill Peregrine Brooks even though you will fail to destroy his body. Peregrine will survive, and Ben will die in his place. Ben will thrive as a ghost, but the loss of her physical twin will break Beryl. And although Brooks will have a near-death-experience while attempting to save her brother, he will recover. And with his new lease on life, he will remember his former incarnation in foggy dreams of being Smenkhare, and his ka will be able to leave his body at will. Regression will be seen as a positive form of therapy within his profession of psychologist counsellor. No matter. It will appear Brooks failed to save Ben, and Beryl could never condone such a failure.

She will default to being a weak heartsick, and more importantly, subservient, daughter who will comply with her father's wishes to punish herself and you. She won't put up a fight. The portals in the Hall are managed by an immortal gardener who fancies himself a god. His family is dedicated to the landscape of Bede, working the land in secret. Only the matriarch will know of his elemental powers. He will sacrifice his mission in order to fulfil the prophecy Kit hopes to break.

Nothing happens in order. Time is always the same time. Everything happens simultaneously because I twisted time. I dispatched the Pan Gemini through jealousy. I sent a pair of untried twin green gods underground. It was me who the broke the back of this planet. I melted the core of rock that made it unstable.

Your mission is to prevent is Beryl meeting the ghost of a nine-year-old girl – KiTiKha'at's newborn daughter and your granddaughter. Their friendship will ruin you. I will fulfil the destructive forces of fire and ice I decreed. A caldera will erupt in fire and freeze from lack of sunlight. Winter will follow until the earth is inhabited by my legions. It will be a new Egypt. I offer you immortality and when the earth is ours, we will reign in the past alongside the Magus's of Pangea – the new pyramid builders and await the future."

Megeara reached out a sooty claw and marked Ay's forehead with the symbol for the Aten.

Cornelius led Kit into the throne room where Tut sat with the right side of his face hidden by a colorful fan that looked surprisingly like parrot feathers. "Is it any better?"

Tut lowered the fan to disclose a red bloated cheek oozing pus. "You tell me," he said.

"Behold, the kiss of death," Kit quipped. "Sorry, that wasn't funny. It must be painful, but I couldn't resist."

"Anna is here," Kha said softly. "She materialized from the painted door in the tomb wearing a strange red coat and seemed thrilled to see me."

Kit was hesitant to enlarge on his parallel memory. "I saw her too.

She appeared during my meditation. I thought she was a mirage. But she followed me back to the temple, as solid as you please. "She's replacing Ani?"

"No, she IS Ani. Ani aged nine. And before you freak out, Peri is now nine in order to counterbalance his sister. It's all dreary Egyptian physics."

Cornelius settled back in his chair and folded his arms, ready for a story. "Go on, then. You were going to tell me about my granddaughter and a shipment of modern medicines. Now is as good a time as any."

"By the way," Cornelius said. "I have news as well. Tutankhaten's innermost sarcophagus is still open because it requires a death mask. I've commissioned Sent to create one, but it's impossible to make a mold from the old king's crushed face. When our Tut's swelling subsides, Sent will take an impression from him in keeping with the dead king's father's, Akhenaten, and his famous romance with artistic realism. I've ordered Sent to model a new mask in the Roman 'warts and all' fashion. Which means the scar that will inevitably form on Tut's cheek will be part of the design."

"I've seen that mask many times. But now I can appreciate what I assumed to be a careless accident by a clumsy museum curator."

"You're referring to the dent in the golden mask?"

"I am – a dent precisely in the same place as Tut's scar from the wasp sting."

"Be sure and document the truth," Tut shouted over his shoulder. "History deserves a few mysteries."

Pigeon made a dramatic entrance in his new colors, swooping silently as an owl over the crowds and landed on Cornelius's arm. The people gasped at the spectacle of a new 'Horus bird' bowing to their pharaoh.

A voice in the crowed shouted "it's Pa'a. The magus!"

'We must away,' Pigeon chattered frantically. *'Ay has made his annual rounds, recruiting nine-year-old boys for the priesthood. He's taken Peri. Peri is gone!'*

EGYPT

chapter 30
MASTER OF MAGIC

As always, Arthur was careful to follow the Egyptian tradition of cats being heard but not seen in keeping with the Egyptian translation of leaving the master alone to his English requirement of being 'seen and not heard'.

Kit rummaged through several linen boxes for his hourglass and came up empty. "Arthur, he called out, even though the cat was nowhere to be seen. "Do you happen to know where my hourglass is?"

Arthur appeared at his feet, not dissimilar to the Cheshire Cat's materializing technique from 'Alice in Wonderland' – a story Kit had come to view as parallel science-fiction comparable to the hallucinatory madness of Bede Hall.

"I stored it in the box under your bed, Master. It wasn't happy being ignored."

"And is it happier under the bed?"

"I believe so, Master, such is my reasoning of the matter. It has been noted by Bast herself that I am often exceptional at reasoning. I've been keeping it polished with my tail. There's nothing like fur to buff the shine on a brass hourglass."

"Please bring me a filled oil lamp as well, and a length of string."

Arthur trotted after Kit as a shadow might, morphing into distorted shapes against the furnishings. "Would you like me to conjure a fire, then? In order to light the taper?"

"I don't know how I managed without you," Kit said, scratching Arthur under his necklace.

Arthur looked away. "That's what Snowdrop said too. But now she won't have to. We were married this morning. This means that as soon as she's called back to Bede, I will go with her. This may be the last time I serve you."

"Married!"

"Mated for life, Master. Bast must approve of any cat couples who wish to mate. The temple cats are special. He preened. "And special cats equal special kittens. Rather like your parrot."

"Pigeon is special but he's hardly obedient. Never around when you need him."

"He shouldn't be, Master. He is a god."

"He told you that! He's got some nerve."

"Exactly, Master. Pa'a has special nerves."

Kit placed his hand on Arthur's head. "In case you're not here when I return, I thank you most sincerely for your service. Perhaps we will meet again in Bede. I wish you and Snowdrop every happiness. Now, please light the string and blow out the flame until all that's left is a red glow. I have work to do."

Sand stung Kit's bare legs as he walked the short distance to the Sphinx. He spread the blanket and set a jar of lotus wine and the oil lamp upon it. He teased the end of the lit string into glowing red-tipped fire with his breath, and lit the lamp. In the lamp's glow the rowan ring quickened and spun sparks around his left hand that grew into a bubble that enveloped Kit in a meditation room situated in the sacred space between the paws of the Great Sphinx on pink sand as fine as talcum powder.

He prompted his mind to review his childhood memories, folded his legs into the lotus position, huddled under a fine linen shawl, and sipped an entire cup of lotus brew. After a short stare, the sand in the hourglass blew into a miniature tempest.

When it settled, Kit witnessed a familiar domestic scene, taking form when he and Bash were younger, during the age they approached Lady Nan's story hour as a major life-sustaining event like Christmas or a birthday.

Heavy rain shook the latticed windows of the red library, sluicing down the glass. The water jumped and jiggled into rivulets with each crash of thunder. The frequency of the incoming thunder revealed the storm was no longer approaching but overhead. The electrics behaved accordingly and flickered on and off until eventually it was pitch dark and candles were called upon to light the story hour before bedtime.

Lady Nan had the candles at the ready as if she'd ordered the storm. She filled a single elegant tall candlestick and placed it center stage on the table. There was never an actual book in evidence, other than the occasional times when 'Winnie the Pooh' was read for Pigeon's benefit when he was ruffled about some goings on no-one else bothered about. The word Pooh calmed him and as a result all words beginning with the letter p were especially savored. Sometimes it was exhausting to think of a P word at the drop of a hat. Which is why, Pooh, was always a default word, as was Piglet.

The twins, up late during school holidays, had made themselves cozy under a shared blanket by nine o'clock. Each of them hugged a large sofa cushion as if it were a teddy bear which made them look as if they were wide-eyed infants in anticipation of a story that would render them too excited to sleep, rather than brave nine-years-olds capable of sleep at any hour.

Kit and Bash had their nine-year-old feet drawn up into the best position to receive a story. And since Lady Nan's stories were always compelling, the stormy atmosphere boded well for a night of hot cocoa and well-intentioned delightful dread.

Jack, was not yet on the scene, but Feathers curled up on Lady Nan's lap and kept one eye open to catch out the lightning bolts rattling the entire Hall on its foundations. As Queen of the Hall, it was safest to be in Lady Nan's company. Lightning would never dare to strike her.

The clock always ticked louder during story-time and this night was no exception. In fact, it had to tick abnormally loud to be heard over the weather crashing and blowing against the house.

Lady Nan's storytelling voice filled Kit's head. "Please turn off the lights, Christopher. Greek myths are best told by candlelight, so let's not have electricity spoil the mood, shall we. My next story requires ambiance. I know that you like those, Christopher, so I thought, since the last story was about fairies, not your thing, I would tell this one, especially for you."

Bash stared pointedly into Kit's face. "Ambiance just means moodiness, by the way."

Kit stuck out his tongue at Bash. "Everyone knows electricity is harmless when its harnessed," he chided.

"On the other hand," Lady Nan said darkly. "Horses *may* be harmful when harnessed. Pegasus was set free to fly after a terrifying battle of swords and wits."

Kit squiggled into his chair with a smile on his face. This story was going to be good. It was especially for him, and he must remember every word to savor it later.

Lady Nan waited until the twins' attention was on her eyes. "This next tale is the story of Perseus and the birth of his horse, Pegasus – a magical myth of birth and death where evil and light are linked by the heart of a true warrior. Like the jackals in Egypt who survive from eating lifeless matter, Perseus is a survivor who defeats the hideous gorgon, Medusa." Lady Nan paused to waggle her finger at her grandchildren. "Never, ever, forget that human cunning pitted against the ego of an immortal will even every playing field. When faced with adversity always call on the gold of alchemy to overcome the lead of an evil heart."

Bash sulked. "Honestly, Lady Nan, it sounds as if you're going to test us afterwards. We're on summer holidays. No more classrooms no more books, well, except fairy stories. Just tell us stories, please."

Lady Nan stared hard at each child in turn. "Scary stories test your mettle."

Bash nearly edged Kit off the couch. Kit punched Bash's arm and squashed smaller in a ball. "Our metal?"

"In a way, yes, your inner strength steels you against all manner of tests. But mettle is your staying power during a crisis. You might even say it is your spiritual form."

"But not a ghost," Bash added, punching back.

Kit made a grimace at his grandmother for support "There's no such thing as ghosts. Is there Gran?" Kit said.

"Lady Nan, please, Christopher. You know how I despise being called Gran. Words are extremely powerful. This is why I call you Christopher. A spirit may be the nebulous copy of an individual. In Egypt it's called a ka. It's also the core of any thought or deed."

"Is too," Bash taunted in Kit's ear. "I see ghosts all the time."

"Indeed," Lady Nan winked. 'It is the epitome of cool. One might say a 'sub-zero freezing winter' kind of cool. It's staying cool in the heat of battle. But not so cool as to freeze in a cosmic winter. It's outwitting a genie who has tricks up his sleeve."

Kit felt his eyes burn when Lady Nan uttered the word "Cool." His expression looked angry more than puzzled. "What's an epitorme?"

Bash raised her hand. "I know this one. I've been studying the thesaurus you gave me."

Kit pulled Bash's arm down. "Now who looks as if they're in school."

"It's the most important level one can reach," Bash said. "It's the essence of everything."

"Time is of the essence," Lady Nan said.

"What's a thesaurus? Kit asked, and the globe went dark.

It was dawn when Kit awoke, still seated. It was already hot, the cool night sands had drifted over his knees in the night forming a comforting blanket. Immediately he opened his eyes, the ringtone of his phone sprang to life, played a rousing marching band for nine seconds and abruptly went silent. His rowan ring was silent, too, likely exhausted from performing an energy dance on his finger to keep him focused. For once, prolonged meditation bestowed a sense of urgency. His actions were clear, but he wanted to map them out before showing Kha.

In any case, Kha refused to look. All he would say was "I'm sure they're more than adequate."

"How do you know something as crucial as that?"

Kha patted his shoulder. "Because, my brother, you have a shining golden aura around your head which tells me my student is now the teacher."

The time portals of Egypt called out to Kit: the painted door in King Tutankhamun's tomb, the flanks of the Great Sphinx, the Right of Passage portal in the Temple of Bast, Bast's inner sanctum, the king's chamber in the Great Pyramid of Giza, the Bedean Pyramid of Pangea, and one other of which he was unaware – the Yellowstone caldera that linked directly to the screaming mouth of the face on Mars. Victory lay behind one or all of them, and now Bede Hall lingered there too, out of time but within reach.

Entering a portal and emerging from it were parts of a single dream. Lady Nan called it the art of ingress and egress – liminal entrances and exits to the past and future, and back.

BEDE

chapter 31
INSIDE OUT

For an uneventful day and night, the fields and lawns of Bede Hall lay perfectly serene. But underneath the calm, tension brewed in the Hall over disputed counter plans of defense and attack. The woodland and garden fairies were on high alert, never mind their shame that one of their kind had betrayed Parks and Charlotte. The traitor, Griffin had come before the fairy tribunal, held without their goddess, Charlotte, to guide their concerns. Griffin had unanimously been declared guilty and awaited punishment.

Inside the Hall, the expectant mood was offset by feelings of unease. Imps were known to be cagey. They were no doubt playing a waiting game designed to undermine the Twinter's morale. But flustering didn't come easy to the twice-borns who had experienced everything untoward at least twice, and died at least once and some several times, under a variety of trying circumstances.

During the days of dormant imp war, Lady Nan nearly appeared always in her royal Egyptian form, citing it made her thoughts clearer. She assembled the twice-borns and called on Anubis.

"Anubis, my friend, please send word to Snowdrop that it's time. We will require backup in the days to come," she said. "And be quick about it."

"There's no need for that, my brother," a new voice purred. Sibuna parted the gathering, shook out his fur, and held his tail high. "My niece is already aware. The first of her troops is awaiting transport here as we speak. We shall meet them in Bede Village. For now, let me assure you that the royal cats of Egypt are hungry, fighting fit, and in the mood for battle."

Sibuna's tail whipped the air with impatience when Anubis looked him in the eye and announced, "only time will tell."

. . .

Monday morning, Sarah Goodman's kitchen cat flap, decorated with a festive silk holly wreath entwined with Christmas bells, began to revolve in a relentless flapping noise. It jingled festively as a stream of Gingers, Calicos, Tuxedos, Tabbies, Blacks, and Greys, entered Bede. Each, extra-toed cat, wore a sparkly quartz crystal around its neck, that at first glance, appeared to be a fancy I.D. tag, but was in fact a secret weapon.

Snowdrop, arrived at the 'tail end' of her legion. Her husband, Arthur, wearing his gold collar, followed discreetly behind the recently proclaimed 'Princess Snowdrop' out of respect for Bast making Snowdrop an honorary member of her royal family and he her besotted consort.

Feathers streaked in the regular door and skidded into her daughter. "Your father said you were here," she hissed. "Let me look at you. Why on *earth* did you leave without a word." Snowdrop's foot caught her eye. "And how have you come by an extra toe!"

Arthur sidled into Snowdrop and licked her ear. "Bast is so fond of your daughter, she bequeathed her the extra toe bred into all her chosen temple cats."

"And who is this?" Feathers hissed more emphatically, her ears laid back in attack mode.

"Mama, this is my husband, ArTuRa. I call him Arthur. It's easier to pronounce."

"Are you mad? Bede is your true home. Your father will never let you go to… that dry hot place. Sage will be devastated."

"You mean dry and hot like it is here?"

"Don't be impertinent, young lady. You know perfectly well what I meant. Bede's wonderfully wet climate will return in all it's glorious greenness."

"No worries, Mummy," Arthur said. "My true home is with your daughter, and we plan to stay if you'll have us. I've been won over by stories of rain and cool green grass. Not that I see much of either. And because the Goddess Bast said it was my duty to seed a sturdy royal line in her name." He bowed his head gracefully. "We are family."

There was nothing left to say but a polite exchange of feline small talk. Feathers asked if there were any cats left in Egypt, considering the army forming ranks in Sarah's garden. Arthur assured her the troops under his wife's command were a small elite portion of the feline population once bred to reduce the rodent population rampant in the granaries and fields. "Bast's followers, in fact, all humans protect temple cats by law on pain of death," he said, "so, we live a long time. We are treated as superior to humans," he said. "Because we are."

"British mice in general are fair game," Sarah cut in. "But Bede mice are strictly off-limits as are all woodland creatures under Parks' care. In return, no fox or badger or Jack the dog, who wouldn't harm a fly by the way, will harm you."

"That won't be a problem, Mummy," Arthur said. "We have no interest in killing mice, let alone eating the things, or any other," he sniffed the air disdainfully, "rodents. We are vegetarian. A supply of fresh organic vegetables and the occasional fish is all we ask for nourishment."

A loud beating of fifty-four mummified wings battered the windows. "Ah," Sarah said, relieved. "Here are Mr. Cornelius's scarabs to welcome you."

Led by Anubis, the newly-dubbed 'Pied Piper of Bede' by the Venerable, the Egyptian cats prowled and prodded the withered undergrowth and nosed the shrivelled hedgerows. Stairwells and cupboards were duly inspected.

Snowdrop's proud parents, Feathers and Anubis, joined the ghost of Unicorn and Sarah's regular cat colony when she addressed the assembled Twinters. A hundred temple cats crouched into orderly rows up the main staircase as if watching a movie in a theatre.

The Twinters seated themselves on meditation mats on the entrance hall floor below, at a comfortable eye-level for Snowdrop to deliver her lecture.

Much to Snowdrop's embarrassment, Anubis introduced his daughter as the High Priestess Snowball of the Temple of Bast. She forgave him with an incline of her head, took centerstage, and tossed her head so the quartz amulet she wore sent sparks leaping from her amulet to activate every amulet on the stairs.

"The quartz amulets we wear are more than decorative," she said. "They contain heady medications of concentrated lotus essence dried into capsules. We call its scent 'The Way of Happiness'. It was originally as strong as your no. 9 formula, but our alchemists discovered that sealing quantities of it inside quartz crystals enlivened it tenfold. We honor the crystals' power by embedding them in discs made of pure Nubian gold engraved with the motif of a winged scarab embracing the sun. The sun, the Aten, is the source of life. The scarab rolls its eggs toward the sun to quicken its young. Similarly, sunflowers regenerate themselves by turning their faces and their seeds, towards the sun. Humans bask in it to feel well."

Tree nymphs, known for their ornery dispositions and total lack of mirth, were the perfect subjects to demonstrate the effects of 'The Egyptian Way of Happiness therapy'. Snowdrop called forward a depressed tree nymph named Murk and his equally dreary friend, Cheerless.

Murk and Cheerless burst into helpless laughter after a being exposed to the faintest whiff of lotus concentrate energised with quartz vitality from a considerable distance. The nymphs hugged, and looking somewhat embarrassed, joined their concerned colleagues Gloomsbury, Miseryguts, Dreary, and Doomsday.

Arthur jumped in to relieve their distress. "The aftereffect is a mild sensation of benevolent well-being that wears off after several hours," he assured the worried looking band of nymphs. Murk and Cheerless's regular duties as guardians will resume with heightened awareness. So, a small sniff of an amulet would actually enhance all your sensibilities. You may even be more aggressive, in a good way. The 'Way of Happiness' is harmless unless you happen to be a creature to which happiness is lethal."

The nymphs grumbled their approval, and with a nod from their leader, Glumbum, each stepped forward to inhale happiness, and bowed smiling as the Twinters, after witnessing an unprecedented display of tree nymph affection, applauded their spirit of adventure.

"Parks would be proud," Lady Nan said tearfully, back in the guise of her teenage years when she was first Mistress of the Green.

Fortunately, the imps stunt played perfectly into the Hall's hands. The longer the imps dallied, the more feline allies from Egypt arrived in readiness for old-fashioned combat. And although it took more energy to follow the meditative practice of happiness therapy, Venerable still scanned the horizon from Kit's tower with determined enthusiasm, and Nick and Leoni put their heads together to repair the grid.

Snowdrop appointed her troops into teams assigned to every room and at every exit to dispatch any escapees. Each hour that passed gave Snowdrop's troops more time to familiarize themselves with the landscape and position themselves inside the hall.

The temple cats were delighted with the plush sofas and chairs and comfortably accustomed to the extreme heat. One or two expressed a desire to remain in England, after the war, of course, and with Bast's permission.

Snowdrop had trained her troops well, teasing them with moving decoys until boredom turned into a serious cat and mouse game with Bast cheering them on. Not only were the cats' bodies prepared, the royal cats had awakened their predatorial hunting instincts and developed an insatiable craving for imp blood.

And then the imps came.

On day six an ominous chirping cloud darkened the skies over Bede Hall. It circled the grounds several times, swooping low over the damaged grids to confirm the ground was safe.

The cloud dived, opened like a gutted fish and rained down a storm of foul-smelling black slime that sprouted hundreds of legs when it landed. Rancid imps, smaller than fieldmice, breached the Hall, scampering over the roof seeking air vents and chimneys, infiltrating every cavity within the walls for electrical wiring and plumbing. They clambered over the parapets and slid down the trellises woven with the wasted ghost vines of the once lush ivy.

Hoards of imps liquified to squeeze through masonry cracks, under doors, and windows opened a hairline crack. Inside, they solidified, clinging to draperies and picture frames, penetrating keyholes, and loose floorboards, pulling plugs as they explored, too busy to detect an army of menacing cats ready to spring.

The scratching of imps claws on mirrors and windows dilated the cat's irises into focused slits but the temple cats held their positions stealthily undercover, their newly engaged instincts, primed for the exquisite sensation of the hunt, stalking prey with patience and the element of surprise.

Several Twinters lingering in the kitchen over the breakfast teapot, startled when a mass of imps burst in. Brooks, thinking quickly, covered his face with a wet tea towel, rolled a newspaper into a torch, thrust it into the coal stove, and smudged the kitchen. The intoxicated imps, naturally drawn to coal dust, floated contentedly, only to be swatted flat with the coal shovel and frying pans, and batted into the oven. Charred imps vaporized and left the Hall through the kitchen chimney as toxic smoke, soon purified by fresh Bede air.

Everyone carried a small spray bottle of no.9 for emergencies. Cornered imps close enough to be misted directly, turned purple and choked, dropping like flies.

And still, the army of cats hung back waiting under, on top of, and behind furniture, quivering with excitement, their legs itching for the chase, jaws drooling from the anticipation of claw to imp combat. Cats blended into the shadows inert as statues, muscles rippled under twitching fur, feline hearts racing in time to their quickened hunting instincts.

The sound of a ticking clock anchored them until Snowdrop gave her telepathic order and the cats hissed as one feline entity and sprang.

The Hall echoed with the chilling sounds of growling and hissing and the dying screams of stricken imps. Cats once disinterested in the art of hunting leapt into battle wondering how they could have ignored such a gratifying sport for so many generations.

When the electricity failed, hundreds of pairs of red eyes showed the location of each unsuspecting imp in the dark, easily swatted to the floor where they were promptly dispatched by the cats, eager to outperform each other to honor Bast. Royal cats snapped scrawny imp necks expertly until all that was left were heaps of bodies that the Twinters shoveled into garbage bags.

A line formed to convey the bags to a central firepit behind the stables. The battle was won by nightfall.

Exhausted Twinters brushed dead imps adhering to their clothing and hair like sticky buds, too tired to celebrate victory. And then another cloud landed.

chapter 32
A GLITCH IN TIME SAVES NINE

Nine-year-old Anna trailed after Kit and cornered him on the roof. "Are you still afraid of me," she asked.

Kit stared at the pyramids in the distance refusing to face her. "I have to say it's strange to see you again when a few days ago you were a newborn. But the truth is, yes, seeing you is painful. You remind me how selfish I was. You were searching for me, but it was me who was lost. Back when we 'met' there were days when I was afraid of pretty much everything, and I wanted to run away from magic… and you. The apparent ghost of a nine-year-old, freaked me out."

"I understood then and I understand now. By the way, Peri will be all right. Pigeon is with him and he's a tough old bird."

Kit chuckled remembering. "Just like your grandmother – a seriously tough old bird. Irascible in a good way, Bash always said."

"Like you, Bash had to grow up fast. It wasn't easy for her after you left. She thought her future was dashed but it was the hour of her reckoning and it had to unfold, as did yours. I'm sure you can attest that unfolding for a human is hard work. Bash wasn't tough, she was feisty. She faked being tough to save face, but she was as scared as you were. Her emerging supernatural instincts scared her. She compensated by teasing you, and even now, when things go wrong, she defaults to being a bully. Magic means nothing during a personal war. When I left Bede it was almost a desert. The Hall's spirit was waning. An English country garden was never meant to be yellow and brown. You are tougher than you think, Dad."

"You know the future. Will we win?"

"Sorry, no. The future is a convergence – a crossroad of shadow journeys. One road leads to loss and winter, another road leads to the rebirth of a green spring. A dozen others lead to parallel destinies."

"So, it's a coin toss, then. Not very profound or encouraging."

"Time may be double-sided, but actions speak louder than dreams. The future is not chiseled in stone, Dad, and you know how that infuriates Egyptians who were imbedded with the command to chisel a universe in stone to warn the future. I know a few outcomes. I know you must defeat the Furies. I know Peri has to come home. And I know I have to wake up. I'm not in the attic of Bede Hall right now. You and I haven't gone there yet."

Kit turned. There were tears in his eyes. "But we will?"

Anna nodded. "But in the meantime, I'm here where I was born, and I miss my brother as much as you and Mum do."

Kit sniffed and wiped his sleeve over his face. The pyramids caught the rays of the sun, glowing white as snow, hurting his eyes. "Everything hangs on linear events," he said. "I can deal with forward and backwards, but time travel doesn't play fair. It jumps in nine-year anomalies and the gaps are left empty. I never saw you or your brother grow up. I missed courting your mother. It made me crazy for a while and even now I get angry. I thought time was supposed to heal but it's cruel."

"Cruelty is a human invention. Things take time and time takes things. It's the way of the world mirage." She touched his elbow shyly. "Daddy, if I promise not to get in the way, may I accompany you to your morning meditation with Kha? But afterwards, I would like to show you something. I have a special gift for you."

The meditation 'room' was a limestone platform at ground level, open to the elements, swept of sand and covered in palm matting. The seated figures of Kit and Kha acted as the human capstone of a hidden pyramid buried deep below them that dwarfed the Great Pyramid of Khephren. Anna sat apart from them with her eyes closed.

Kha's eyes were closed, too. The buzzing of Kit's cell phone startled him, sounding too much like a nearby wasp. It vibrated a snaky trail in the sand. "I'm compelled to show you a last Pangea/Martian scenario," Kha said. "Where you will be given a secret you already know, but it's up to you to rediscover it. It is critical that you note precisely how you feel at all times. The success of your mission depends on it. Left unchecked, a single subterranean volcano – a pyramid turned upside down, will wipe humanity away."

Kit glanced at Anna. She looked asleep. He whispered lest he waken her. "Mars again, really? Kha? I don't want Anna to come."

"She won't. She's visiting a friend. Chant with me," Kha ordered. "Follow my voice as best you can. I will call your name when you're ready."

A perfumed breeze stirred the folds of Kit's robe as he emptied his mind the way Brooks had taught him so many years ago. "Why does everything have to be a wretched test or a secret? It makes no sense."

"Because, Kha said. "There are unfinished people in the world who are terrified of secrets. Rise and follow me, Kit the initiate. You have done well. It's time to open your eyes and experience your latest accomplishment."

Kit was delighted to feel calm even though he floated several feet above his seated body. A flash of sunlight on his hand showed his rowan ring had turned to red gold.

Kha steadied Kit's arm to maintain altitude. "Let go," he intoned gently. "You have mastered the arts of transmutation and levitation. And now, time must fly. Feel the wings on your feet and shoulders. We won't be gone long."

Below them, Megeara's home planet, Mars, basked in volcanic heat. The landscape resembled a furiously bubbling sea of heaving lava.

Kha heard Kit's thoughts. "Yes," he answered. "This is why we call Megeara's race the Furies."

"When? I mean, how far in the past have we come?"

Kha nosedived towards the ground and made a perfect landing on his feet. "It doesn't matter. The essential information you need to defeat Megeara, lies here, hidden in the open. And, no, I wasn't showing off. I'm testing my reflexes. I have to be ready to save you."

"Save me!"

"I apologize. I used my words poorly. I meant to say I'm your guardian during a crucial test to master negative thinking. Fear is only a thought of something that hasn't happened. Something that can't happen today."

"But tomorrow?"

"Tomorrow is in your hands, Kit. This is not news to you. Goswold's brotherhood chose you and Bash for a reason. We must trust their wisdom in these matters. And now what matters most is that you fully recall what you see. The surface of Pangea is compromised. It is liquifying from the inside out. We can only visit such events of destruction in our ka form. Our travelling bodies will appear lifeless because our life-force will be elsewhere. Essentially, we will be dead, but no harm will come to us, this is an illusion. Open your eyes and look at Mars and Pangea. We will observe ourselves together."

The volatile landscape of Mars blew hot and cold as if it couldn't decide if it was molten rock or solid ice. The ensuing steam on its surface continually reshaped the landscape into pointed crags with each spurt of lava. The crumbling Megeara Pyramid loomed eerily on the horizon – a cone shaped mound of rubble, backlit by white hot steam. A tall fence of red cliffs surrounded it in a three-sided stone henge. The fourth blasted out a mountain of scalding hot mud that instantly hardened into a geometric 4-sided pyramid when it hit a wall of ice crystals. The debris of red glass chips rested around its base in a fiery skirt.

It had risen from the center of a volcanic caldera – a perfect geological birth. Ice sculptures of frozen glass encircled it in a ring of statuesque peaks that looked, to Kit, like splashes of water he'd seen in time-lapse photography leaping into crowns when a hefty stone was dropped from a great height into a lake.

Kha broke the silence. "Time lapses," he said.

"I was just thinking that."

"You misunderstand me. Please pay attention. The meanings of words are critical. You were thinking about a slow-motion photographic effect. I was referring to blunders. Time *lapses*," he said, again. *You* must not. One lapse of consciousness is a blunder we can't afford. Consider this trip your final exam."

The Sphinx of Megeara sat on an island of red glass in a sea of toxic magma. Pressurized molten rock spat from the cauldron, hardened instantly into bergs from the freezing temperatures of the ice-age above ground. Kit made out the details of a giant face through dense steam. It was easy to see the details of a female face wearing the headdress and false beard of an Egyptian pharaoh.

"No humans live here," Kha said.

"Yeah, that's a real shocker."

"It's hot enough to melt our socks," Kha said trying to lighten Kit's fear, "but our kas are astral thought forms, which means that no physical harm will befall us here."

Kit covered his ears from what sounded like the squeals of pigs being slaughtered. "Those can't be wasps, surely."

"They are Megeara's imps that fashion her wasps from stone pebbles. Ay coerced a rogue magus from Pangea's past to animate them a year ago. A Pangean king had been courted by Queen Megeara during the days when Mars was a paragon of industry and technology. He made the mistake of spurning her advances. Megeara's ensuing tantrums may be where the expression 'All hell broke loose' came from."

"What about the toll of emotional harm? The memories of this place will haunt me. In fact, the nightmares I had when I was a child were about this giant stone face. And now, thousands of years later, I'm still that cowardly child, terrified of a monstrous capsized statue that looks as if it had a stroke. I used to imagine its empty eye socket watching me during the day."

"And now you can vanquish that monster. That's what lucid dreams are for."

"And dream travelers have to bear the burden of witnessing human terrors."

"They witness the joys as well."

"My poor daughter."

"Anna is most fortunate. She is a powerful child who had the choice to refuse her gift before she was born. Life reserves a special degree of compassion for its selfless guardians. Comatose sleep is Anna's protection. She enters a coma with the awareness that she's fulfilling her destiny as a vital counterbalance for the world."

The scene switched to Pangea's last moments seen from space. The Bedean Pyramid drifting intact, migrated over a blank sphere with no poles – a bizarre image, swirling lazily the way a leaf floats in the eddies of stream.

Pangea's ruling magi, the old ones, Goswold, Pan, and Osiris linked only by telepathy, hovered above it as spirit ghosts. The capstone floated like the tip of an iceberg, slowly energizing islands of molten earth embedded with seeds into new continents.

The skies flickered with the days and nights of a million years and it was Britain's turn to show its history. Crude mud and straw roundhouses morphed into wooden henges and longhouses. Small villages, farming communities, and fishing centers settled along the rivers and coasts. Crude rafts grew into sailing ships, precious metals surfaced from their matrix's – exposed within caves turned inside out.

Across the channel, out of body shamans taught the cave dwellers of Lascaux how to hunt totem animals in the netherworld.

In Northumbria, soft green mosses covered the stone cliffs and exposed hills. Ground stone weathered into soil and the seeds sprang into forests. Wooden structures evolved into grand buildings of stone. Castles sprouted round towers, parapets, and crenellations. Plunderers raided the shores of Britannia stirring their voices into a melting pot of romance languages. Cultures collided to create new rules and art. Barbaric stories inspired classic mythology. Pockets of wisdom and ignorance receded and advanced. The Bedean Pyramid's capstone sunk into the rich Northumbrian soil and sprouted into the first mud hut, a longhouse, a tower, and a stately home.

The forts along Hadrian's Wall were built and occupied by Roman soldiers. Orders of intellectuals bonded together to record history on vellum scrolls and illuminate manuscripts in the monasteries of

Lindesfarne. The elementals, keepers of the landscape, inhabited holy wells and fairy circles. Abbeys and churches expanded into cathedrals. Roman temples grew into libraries and schools, universities and hospitals, museums, and art galleries. Artisans became master artists, goldsmiths, engineers, mathematicians, physicians, and scientists. Crafts escalated and rose to the heights of fine art, and tin and bronze jewelry were eclipsed by Saxon gold.

Flying over Egypt's distant past, Kit recognized his first landing spot — an outcrop of stone swarming with workers using crude copper tools and bifacial axes. They pulverized stone against stone into powder, one grain at a time. Shallow depressions in the stone became deeper hollows and finally holes that connected into the constellation of a face.

Slowly, the Great Sphinx's lion body took shape. Bit by bit, a neck, shoulders, and flanks emerged. Great outstretched paws clawed the ground. Rains flooded the Giza Plain and washed the sharp contours of the sphinx smooth over thousands of geological years.

Natural crevices in the sandstone cliffs surrounding the great lion expanded cracking into faux blocks and eroded like a wall of giant sugar cubes. Their minerals ground into earth colors: siennas and umbers and ochres. Generations of tomb diggers and stonemasons tramped the valley cliffs from morning to night to work on three-dimensional puzzles only divinely inspired architects could have designed, using techniques lost in time.

Scribes were ordered to blindly copy symbols whose deepest secrets still had to be passed on by an elite sect's word of mouth. Endless miles of chiseled symbols, drawn first in liquid soot, had their negative spaces hacked away until the remaining blackened symbols were washed clean and polished with the paste of powdered stone mixed with oils from boiled animal skins.

Stone dust, bone glue, and blood were spread on scraps of leather and dried in the sun with mud bricks to form crude sandpaper.

The spirits of alchemists animated the living stone. Pyramids rose from flat 'mastaba' platforms, of steps piled in decreasing size, into pyramids with experimental degrees of incline and inner chambers.

Magicians lost their telepathic connections to their ancestors until only a handful of magi remained, elevated above the multitudes of workers who had succumbed to servitude. The great masters of alchemy imparted their arcane knowledge, translating memories into vast wall-like pages of geometric stone. A population of slaves, endlessly pounding grinding and dragging building blocks of stone, stripped obelisks from the quarries of exposed stone.

A decided nip in the air descended with the setting sun. A glittering field of blue-black jewels spread to the horizon like newly-mined lumps of coal until each 'gem' spread its metallic wings and rose en-masse as a cloud of clicking scarab beetles.

Kha slapped Kit on the shoulder. "We have to go home, now. The eighteenth-dynasty awaits."

Kit balked. "I dread what I might find. There is no way to describe how I dread time traveling. But returning is far worse."

Kha turned on him, enraged. "Never *ever* dread! Dreading is negative wish fulfilment – a jinx. Dreading brings bad luck through the laws of tempting fate. A master alchemist is schooled in the art of accepting surprises with gratitude. SaRa chose you without knowing the outcome. She was willing to accept what would come. She had a choice, and she chose you. Outcomes are what they are. The best things are often surprise outcomes. But then, so are the worst things."

"I'm afraid to look," Kit said. "Do I have a long white beard?"

Kha stood back to scan his apprentice. "Surprisingly, you haven't aged a day, but your children have."

"Please don't tell me that I missed their formative years."

"Children such as yours never stop forming. Sadly, time-sensitive visits to Mars and Pangea are a compulsory part of your apprenticeship. A few years must be sacrificed now in order to give your children a future. If the caldera is not capped, they will freeze to death, and it may be billions of years before earth is habitable, should there even be humans to inhabit it. Most likely our planet will never recover. Always filter what you see with the perspective of an alchemist!"

Kit's voice faltered. "You said my children had aged? They were nine months old, barely a day ago."

"Peri and Ani are nine-years-old. You are still 27. SaRa is still nineteen and Bede Hall is waiting for you to shine as their champion. If the sun sets on your failure, the earth dies. All I ask, no insist, is that you remember how you were safe as a ka while witnessing a hostile world. Remember that, Kit. It is imperative that you remember. SAFE AS A KA. Say it!"

Kit saluted. "Yes, Sir. Safe as a ka. Safe as a ghost."

Kha's features relaxed into a sheepish expression. "Look, I may sound like Brooks, but I'm *not* him. I was Brooks' first teacher when he was Smenkhare. I know it's difficult keeping events in chronological perspective but please try."

Anna and Kit walked the long way to his thinking spot. Jack was waiting in his usual place.

"You brought me a mirage." Kit said.

"No," Anna replied shaking her head. "I brought you Jack. He's dreaming, and as I'm in his dream, he's as solid as you or I."

Kit slapped his thigh. "Here boy!"

Jack whined through his nose and let out an emotional yelp of recognition before loping towards Kit like a cheetah. Jack reached Kit in seconds, bowling him over – a grey jackal licking the tears from his master's eyes.

chapter 33
UNFLAPPABLE POWERS

The second wave of imps was a feeble attempt to prevent the Egyptian cats from returning home.

Feathers napped with one eye open under the sparse Christmas tree set up in the library. It twinkled constantly with rotating shifts of fairies volunteering as lights to compensate for one of their kind compromising the war effort. "Not exactly 'evergreen' is it," she commented to the library scarabs.

Mr. Cornelius's scarab collection rewarded her with a renewed display of exercising their wings. Their headquarters in the library display case positively rustled with ancient power.

"It's more like, forever brown," Feathers remarked sleepily to the tree.

Anubis, just in from imp eradication duty, caught the tail end of his wife's thought. "Next year the pines could be green again, my love," he said. "Next year a lot of things will be better. Snowdrop is home with her news. And the imps are losing. A few more days and they will be eradicated."

Feathers rose and licked her mate's ears covered in imp blood. "How goes the battle?"

"Our tried and true feline way of pest control is as efficient as ever but there's still new imps arriving. We need more time. The situation is well in hand, but I don't mind telling everyone that without Snowdrop's intervention it could have been catastrophic. No doubt they're sick of hearing me bragging by now."

Feather smiled at Anubis's favorite word, *cat*astrophic, given to him by Lady Nan. "What's to be done with Griffin?"

Anubis's tail thrashed angrily. "The fairy council has passed sentence. He faces banishment. Not harsh enough punishment in my opinion, but fairy's law is nothing to be trifled with." His tail flicked with pleasure. "The little beast will be leaving tomorrow and good riddance, and from the scuttlebutt going around, Nick and Bash are working on a send-off he won't soon forget."

The morning sparkled clear for Griffin's release. His getaway wasp was kept in the dark while Nick released an enormous killer balloon made from a plastic garbage bag of no. 9 perfume that Griffin had unwittingly helped prepare. The Twinters gathered to watch the launch. It rose steadily towards a confused swarm of struggling wasps and imps as they collided, high in the sky, entangled in Nick's newly fortified force-field canopy. Bash's lethal 'no. 9' communication scrambler easily disabled Megeara's minions trying unsuccessfully to regroup for attack.

Griffin, banished from the colony, waved cheekily from the back of a befuddled wasp, that automatically headed for the swarm. Griffin struggled with his wasp's antennae trying to change the collision course but failed. He sailed into the swarm seconds before it detonated.

The council of fairies below, cheered the toadstool-shaped cloud left to mark its place. "Nice touch," Nimue commented. "From a fairy ring of toadstools on the ground to a toadstool in the sky."

The yowling of impressed cats began with Anubis's laughter.

Ben, eating apple pie for breakfast, toasted the spectacle waving a loaded fork at the dissipating toadstool display. "It only takes one bad apple to ruin the pie," he remarked.

The second wave of wasps was defeated in one day. No third wave arrived. The cats relaxed, groomed each other, and celebrated. The sound of their purrs resounded throughout the land. Later, folks in Lindisfarne reported feeling the earth vibrate in delightfully soothing tremors.

Arthur and Snowdrop debated the benefits of England over Egypt in the moonlight. "Let us not trivialize the wonderful pleasure of cool grass underfoot nor digging in moist black earth," Snowdrop said. "And English beaches rarely have sand that gets stuck in one's toes. Cool wet clay is delightful no matter how many toes one has."

"So you say, my sweet," Arthur replied. "But so far I've only been exposed to dry brown grass and pebbled beaches."

"I grant you, walking on pebbles is not a lighthearted stroll, but there are fireplaces and kitchen stoves on cold rainy days and plush velvet armchairs. It's quite splendid. It will be a lifelong holiday for you, and I can't wait to show you around now the battle is over."

"But the war *isn't* over," Arthur reminded her. "The Furies aren't done. The summer climate continues on a downward course."

"Kit will win the war, and when he does, Christmas will be white with snow."

"And then the rain will come?" Arthur asked, washing his spotless whiskers. "Sibuna said Bast ordered a banquet of frog's legs to celebrate her warriors return."

"I like frogs legs too," Snowdrop purred, "but wait until you taste toad-in-the-hole."

Arthur brightened… "Are toad's legs as tasty as frogs legs?"

"Nothing like. Don't even hope. They're sausages, also known as bangers. Then there's mac and cheese, welsh rarebit, chips and egg, brown gravy, and marmite on toast."

"I haven't seen a single drop of rain, and I've been here a week, my love," Arthur purred. He gazed longingly at the cat door as it squeaked one last flap and came to rest. The temple cats were going home. Egypt called Arthur from within its passageway across time and he had done his duty by refusing to listen. "Water falling from the sky is worth waiting for," he said rubbing his face against Snowdrop's ears.

Snowdrop purred back, looking at the moon. "Oh, it's up there all right. Parks will call it down soon enough. Rest assured of that."

"Will I like this Parks of yours," Arthur asked.

"He will love you," Snowdrop replied.

PART 4

heroes and friends

EGYPT

chapter 34

GRADUATING WITH HONOR

Kit, centered inwardly during Kha's guided meditation, was oblivious to the wonderous pre-dawn light. The night had not yet given up its stars and the grey-green sky hesitated on the edge of pale blue. An innocent breeze tickled Kit's face and pushed his silver forelock from his closed eyes. All was serene within the comfort of his newfound inner home. Even though beneath the calm lurked the temporary loss of Peri to Ay's regular recruitment of initiates for the Amun priesthood.

Kha coached Kit to open his heart to the sun as it rose on the horizon – a sacred moment interrupted by the delivery of a sinister papyrus scroll – a foreboding gauntlet carried on a cushion of hovering wasps. It was signed M, and read: *'Little Kitty, I challenge you to a duel of wills. Meet me in front of the Sphinx when the Aten caresses the invisible capstone of the Great Pyramid. Come alone if you want to see your son again. I dare you to defy your master.'*

Master and apprentice hastened back to the sacred environment of the temple where Kha examined the scroll in a controlled setting. After a few moments, Kha's body slumped over the table, and glowed eerily from within. "It has come," Kha said in a shaky voice. He grabbed for Kit's arm as his authoritative power vanished into a seizure of tremors. "Take me to SaRa," he managed to croak before fainting.

Kit held the lotus smelling salts under Kha's nose but Kha waved it away.

The fears Kit thought were under control surfaced into instant panic. "What's happening? Tell me what you need. Kha! Please wake up."

With unashamed relief, Kit witnessed Kha open his eyes and reach for the lotus bottle.

267

Kha inhaled its scent deeply and rested his gaze rested on the distant horizon. Seeing Kit's terrified face shocked him. Kit's fear mirrored his own, and as his master, Kha's first duty was to brief his untried apprentice for the ghastly ordeal to come, a confrontation arriving too soon for both of them. He managed a strained smile and forced his voice to regain some of his old authority, calming Kit into believing the strange fit had passed. "I am preparing myself. This is normal, it looks worse than it is," he said. "Transitions are challenging. Even so, I didn't think it would take me like this. You see, even a master alchemist is forever being tested without due warning. Stay calm. Everything is as it should be."

"So, this is you accepting a surprise with gratitude, then?" Kit commented.

Kha's only reply was a wan smile and a shake of his head before he examined the scroll once more. When Kha looked up, his eyes remained unfocused, reduced to slits of steely determination, impossible to read. At first, Kit interpreted Kha's expression as heightened rage, but when the truth registered, it was far worse. Kha was sad – an unheard of, and never before exposed, emotion. "Keep your head, my brother," he said, squeezing Kit's hand. "Megeara is trying to rattle you by planting a rift between us." He rolled up the papyrus and tapped it playfully on Kit's forehead. "You must meet the old dragon on her terms. Go alone, but I promise I will have your back."

Kit grabbed the scroll and threw it on the table. His dead cell phone issued a feeble ringtone and stopped abruptly after a few seconds of 'god save the queen'. A burning sensation rushed down is arm into his fingers where his rowan ring grew transparent as glass and filled with colored smoke. It advanced through the rainbow until it released a puff of violet energy in the shape of an iridescent Pygmalion.

The creature hovered in Kit's face and evaporated with a gentle lavender-scented pop. "What does it mean if a new pygmalion appears out of nowhere and pops like a soap bubble," he asked? It wasn't Pyg. This one was made of sunshine."

"Hmmn? What?" Kha brushed away a wasp that wasn't there.

Kit snapped his fingers. "Come back. You were saying?"

"Sorry, I was miles away. "Pygmalions are created from extreme love or hate and as such they come from no 'where'. They implode eventually, when their message is delivered, or its task is completed. Sometimes both."

Kit held his hands over his ears. "No more messages. I'll assume it completed a task of little consequence." He straightened his shoulders and inhaled a deep calming breath. "The thought of you having my back is the only thing that will keep me unrattled."

A spasm of coughing reduced Kha to a feeble invalid for an instant before returning to his old confident self. He embraced Kit in a rough farewell hug. "I have to see my sister. I won't be far," he said, his words choked with tears. He held Kit at arms length. "Even if you *can't* see me." He shook Kit gently by the shoulders. "It is vitally important to remember I will be there. Right?"

"Of course. Are you feeling better?"

Kha nodded. "I will recover. Furies' magic has profoundly disturbing side-effects." He smiled nervously, floundering under a pile of scattered papers for the offending scroll. "It's gone," he commented casually. "And good riddance. It was a nasty piece of work."

Kit uncovered the clay water jar and poured a cup. "You look worn out. Take some water."

Kha accepted the water and took a sip to show willing. "Thank you. Now then, I was about to tell you how proud I am of you. It is my honor to inform you that your final task is at hand. You are ready. And now, I must speak with SaRa, alone. She knows what to do. Now, repeat back to me what I just said and finish your meditation. There's quite a day ahead for both of us."

"Even if I *can't* see you, you will be with me. You are *proud* of me. I am *ready*. My initiation is at hand. SaRa *knows* what to do."

"Yes. Now go. Assume that your little pygmalion soap bubble delivered a message of victory. And always, *always*, listen to your memories. Your imagination and cunning are formidable weapons as deadly as swords and poison. Fairy tales are rife with practical wisdom."

A severe painful grip to Kit's shoulders and a long riveting look of Kha's overriding authority implanted a new deep-rooted memory to ponder.

Pyg flew relentless circles around Kit's head until SaRa waved him away. He perched on the empty cradle and awaited his instructions from Kha. *'Kit is with SaRa,'* he whispered. *'I am listening to her thoughts. She has not yet broken the bad news to Kit. She wishes someone else would. Do you want me to tell him? Kit is strong. His thoughts are on his meeting and he's undeniably confident. You gave him that. You would make a good Pygmalion.'*

"I thank you for the compliment. "Word is on its way. Please distract SaRa and wait."

'She banished me to the other side of the room. I was bothering her.'

"Distractions are supposed to be a bother," Kha reprimanded. "Now go."

'Yes, Master. My apologies.' Pyg returned to SaRa and alighted on her shoulder. *'Kha says to wait,'* he whispered in her ear. *'He has sent a messenger.'*

SaRa nodded and continued to smile on autopilot. She held both Kit's hands, searching his face flushed with excitement, for a chance to speak a terrible truth without crushing his confidence."

"I have to tell you… that is… my brother…"

Pigeon interrupted her, squawking through the temple loud enough to wake the dead. *'KIT… where are you? My dear boy, Ay has attacked Kha in the most cowardly fashion. Your master is dead. Kha is dead! His ghost has spoken to me. Kha is confident that SaRa will explain. Listen to her, he says. She knows what you must do. He also was specific about an incident in your childhood. He says to remember your vision of Lady Nan's special story. Does that make any sense?'*

BEDE

chapter 35
SIX TIMES NINE = 54 = MAGIC 9

December 21, 2018 – the Winter Solstice

The time portals of Bede called out to Bash: the maze, the Winter Room, Hadrian's Wall, the Bede post office, the cat flap in Sarah Goodman's kitchen, the underground Root Portal in the Green Lady's forest from under the roots of the Rowan tree, and one other of which she was unaware – the sundial, Parks' grave marker. Kit was behind one of them or all of them, and now Six lingered there too, out of time but within reach.

The echo of a comforting thought reached Bash in the guise of Kit's voice almost too faint to hear: *'entering a portal and emerging from it are parts of a single dream. Lady Nan called it the art of ingress and egress – liminal entrances and exits to the past and future, and back.'*

Bash crept into the Green Lady's forest under a midwinter moon, sending her love to the oak trees. Cyril, the tree nymph slithered from tree to tree observing her mood until he was satisfied the energy of the Mistress of the Green was melancholy but of good cheer.

Bash knelt beside the rowan she was searching for and humbly asked for help. A flash of green light the size of a blade of grass poking through the earth was the answer she hoped for. It was an invitation to commune with the exposed roots that turned silvery white in the moonlight. *"Yes, Mistress."* the rowan said with great compassion, *"We feel the re-energized compassion of your broken heart. It is time for a healing."* Her fingertips tingled pleasantly as she placed both hands on the twitching root. She closed her eyes on the wildwood's root portal that had evaded her tantrums of grief during her time of sorrow, and opened them on a dream tunnel that led directly to a Roman tent in 40A.D. where a cot, not dissimilar to the one in the Winter Room, but excessively different in that it its male occupant lay covered in a thin shroud like a warrior on a bier. It was reminiscent of the carved marble coffin lids of the heraldic knights in Bede Church, in repose without armor. The bier levitated, backlit by the flickering yellow corona encircling Fioretti's head.

Bash had to remind herself, never having been inside a portal, how Kit described the sensation of time traveling. Secretly, she envied his forays into the 'once was' and the 'soon to be'. After all, it was high magic, far above the conventions of planting by the phases of the moon and the laws governing the growing seasons.

There were times her gardening duties felt beneath her. She had to smile. Lady Nan would not only have poohpoohed her attitude but chastised her that if anything *had* meant to be beneath her, it was surely the ground itself.

It seemed trivial that plants blossomed under her faltering 'Midas touch'. During the time of her 'Blighty', she'd almost felt guilty at the simplicity of her tasks when her brother faced life and death in the throes of time itself. And when the lawns withered into straw and the soil baked hard as clay, and innocent plants shriveled under a rogue sun, and most of all when her lavender field stood out like the blackened clearing after a forest fire, she felt guilty.

Her recent betrayal during her dark days she had neglected her power and even reduced herself to a scarecrow shouting obscenities at her innocent plants – a crop, already suffering the humiliation of failing to thrive.

But here she was, walking, if you could call moving while standing still, walking, towards death of a sort. Lucid dreams were not the everyday wanderings of a brain filing a business report. It was why Anna, in either of her densities, often had a faraway look in her eyes. She seemed like an ordinary girl, but she slumbered like a princess under a curse with the legacy of time travel inside her. And while comatose, she'd made it clear that her worlds shifted and shuffled together outside the rules of chronological order.

For Anna, visiting the Romans building Hadrian's Wall and the fort or 'the ice-age to be' was as natural as a bird flying to its nest.

The tunnel walls cycled into a repeating loop of rainbow colors that led her towards sharing Six's near-death experience.

The sleeping warrior, Six, was as cold as marble. Likely, the way Kit had found Anna when she led him to the future winter that caused so many problems. Six looked peaceful, in spite of his furrowed brow. For the longest time, Bash sat on the foot of his bed keeping silent vigil.

Fioretti fussed around Six like a nursemaid in a sick room, weaving her protective spell to seal the patches wearing thin on his shroud. "It's a bit like bailing out a sinking boat," she said. "One must constantly keep in mind that each thimbleful of water is a moment closer to dry land. Six's precious life-force escapes through the smallest hole in his shroud. I can't let him catch a chill."

"He's already stone cold."

"His physical body may be, but his spirit is warm. If that cools, then death is near. This curse is more Tisiphone or Allecto's work. Jealousy contains heat."

Bash's hand edged closer. "I'm afraid to touch him."

Fioretti clucked her tongue. "If you don't mind me saying, Mistress, it's silly fears that are a human's undoing. And, in your case, it's the brave loving gestures you perform that raise your standing in your mentor's eyes. Parks and Charlotte are forever watching."

"Do you ever see them?"

"I feel them which is more significant. As twin Green Gods, they heal each other by healing the land and the sky. Concentration a human could scarcely dream of."

"I believe I'm dreaming right now."

"You are. But how the dream of a kiss can be so terrifying, escapes me. Lady Nan told you fairy tales when you were small. Think, Bash. Are you a princess in a tower or a prince on a white horse?"

"Both."

Fioretti's pink light grew brighter to a shade of shimmering lilac.

"Excellent. Humans should always be both. Look at Six's left hand… the hand of receiving in magic. What do you see?"

"Bash bent closer. "Something purple."

"When Anna was here, she placed a lock of your purple hair in his hand. This means he can feel your presence."

"Six. Can you hear me?" Bash whispered.

The muscles in Six's hand twitched.

"That means yes," Fioretti said. "Bash, he needs you. He's calling you. He's been calling you for ages… literally, ages."

Six's hand trembled as Bash placed her hand over his and squeezed hello. He answered her by sharing a series of vibrations that coursed through her. She shivered involuntarily as a corresponding quiver in her solar plexus responded to him."

"Lovely," Fioretti said. "You're having a heart-to-heart conversation."

Bash kissed Six's lips, lingering slowly as if it was their first kiss, and sat back, waiting. "Isn't that supposed to wake him?" She closed her eyes. "I've failed."

Fioretti's command echoed inside Bash's head. "Open your eyes, Mistress."

Six stood taller than Bash remembered, his arms open wide. For a moment Bash couldn't bear to meet his eyes, so she focused on the pulse in his neck. "I knew you'd come," he said. "I feel as if I've been waiting a hundred years."

The room dissolved, back into the sunny day in the back meadow when she'd dreamed they were handfast."

"It wasn't a dream," Six said into her hair. "Charlotte presided over the ceremony."

Fioretti flew around them chanting. "You were there. Six was there. All of us were there. Keep kissing. Kissing is the silent language of love."

Six held up the lock of purple hair. "This 'purple heart' may honor my sacrifice, but you are my reward. We have to remain apart for a while, but I will fly to you as soon as my cage door is open." Six's form thinned. "You're waking up, sweeting. It's time to daydream… the rest of the day is ours." As the dream floated her backwards down the portal, Bash heard Six's voice echoing from the rainbow walls. "Your lock of hair will help me find my way home."

Fiorretti accompanied her part of the way with words of wisdom. "Think on this, Mistress. Hapi knows all about abandoning birdcages and freedom. Why do you think she's so happy?"

The sound of Kem crying her name in his sleep hastened Bash's arrival. She found him sitting up in bed, half-awake, his legs landlocked by tangled bedclothes preventing his escape. There are far too many leg traps, Bash thought. I am officially fighting this nightmares business. "I'm here, kiddo," she said, freeing his legs. "You've had a bad dream. I promise you there are wonderful dreams just around the corner. I love you, sweetie."

She had two men counting on her. Three when she counted Kem. Four if she added the boy behind the wall, and five considering Taraq was still a child in spite of being thousands of years old. She had failed to see Taraq's showing-off for what it was, his attempt to fit in. He craved their friendship. And as unschooled as he was in the insulting art of sibling teasing, he had confused rudeness for affection and followed their lead. He had matched their bullying, insult for insult. Only it had backfired. Taraq, a lost scared kid thrust into an unfamiliar world, had come across as obnoxious instead.

Bash gave herself a good talking to. I was the obnoxious one, relentlessly torturing a brother who was as introverted as I was self-assured. So superior and confident, lording it over him with my fancy words, half of which I never understood myself. My god. I was worse than Rupert!

Anubis leapt on Kem's bed, offering himself as a teddy bear distraction. "Lady Nan said to tell you she'll be right up with a glass of warm milk for Kem, and you're to spike it with one of Charlotte's concoctions. Nine drops, she said."

. . .

Bash called out to the Hall as she flipped the last pancake. "Taraq. I've made you special pan bread unless you prefer a plate of bread and onions and beer."

His response was immediate. "Morning Purply-locks," he said, floating into the kitchen reclining on his side. "A little Ba Bird told me the porridge is 'just right'. Are you, by any chance, mocking my culture?"

"I'm a new woman. I've decided to turn over a new leaf. I've decided to be your friend."

Taraq righted himself and sat down. "How are they special? Surprise me. Are they full of chopped pine cone goodness?"

Bash set a platter of small pan bread on the table decorated with raised pinches of dough. "They have ears. Like the mummified Egyptian flatbread in the British Museum."

"I just bumped through Appleby coming off his shift," Taraq said. "He told me he saw Six walking cool as you please out of the maze. Six looked up at old Appleby in the tower and waved before he dissipated. I love that word. Dissipated. So, Six is a ghost. Apparently, he has some reason to want to hang around here."

It turned out, most of the Twinters reported sharing Kem's fears in their own dreams that night. Dr. Carlton Young, the dream analyst among them, announced to the assembly at breakfast, that the ones who slept through the night would likely feel the fear more keenly than anyone. Please pass the maple syrup, and who put ears on the… what are they, pancakes?

Taraq observed Bash the entire day, and she didn't disappoint. She was kind and sensitive with Kem. At sunset, Taraq caught her staring wistfully into the maze. "Six is in there," he said. "I can see him. But he's not able to walk the earth. At least, not yet."

Bash turned a tearful face towards him. "I'm truly sorry for the way I've treated you. I think I've actually been jealous of you."

He reached through the teapot and patted her arm. "You know," he said. "When the rowan told you it was time for a healing it was referring to Six. But now, by your confession, it extends to you, and through you, to us. I may be leaving soon but there's a ghost of a chance we could become friends before I go."

chapter 36
A VICIOUS CIRCLE

Kit rubbed his bruised shoulders all the way to the Sphinx, repeating Kha's last directive until it looped in his mind like a mantra. "Words can be the deadliest poison of all." Kit tapped his armband and immediately felt taller, lighter, and surprisingly rested.

He continued on his way, slowly savoring SaRa's blessing. 'You are not alone,' she'd said. 'I love you and my love is as powerful as my brother's magic. We will rescue our son, together. Peri is in no immediate danger. I can feel that.' Her farewell kiss lingered on his cheek. He was invincible – a father out to save his son and the world. A husband of the wisest bravest woman on earth.

Pyg manifested on Kit's left shoulder. *'Off to war we go,'* he purred *'fighting to the death or beyond.'*

"Thanks, Pyg. That's really helpful. But perhaps you could focus on a more inspiring message, like victory will be mine or something along those lines."

Pyg fanned his wings. *'Just doing my job, Master. I am here for you. Nothing is beyond death. Well, except one's next life.'*

"The only weapon I have is words. Poisonous words. What words will shake Megeara? What is her Achilles heel? What words can kill her?"

'Jealousy springs to mind,' Pyg mused to himself. He yawned, tucking his wings close as if about to take a nap. *'It's her passion. Passions are powerful for a reason.'*

Kit shut out Pyg's incessant nagging. Megeara used jealousy as her prime weapon. Why?

Pigeon made a low fly-past from out of nowhere. *'I'm also here to support the day,'* he squawked. *'Cornelius would approve. He would wish you victory if he knew where you were going. It's for the best he won't know until afterwards. Kha sends his regards and bids me to tell you he's on his way.'*

"Great," Kit said aloud. "Now I have two chatterboxes. One on each shoulder. Insensitive and rude."

Pyg yawned again and settled his chin on his front paws. *'Once a human, always a human,'* he purred. *"one can always count on their weakest link.'*

Goswold's lecture from their meeting in Pangea played back slowly. Megeara had been mortal but after she was scorned by a human king, she turned to dark magic that gave her immortality.

Pyg mumbled in his sleep. *'There's nothing more deadly than a dragon woman scorned who turns to cruel magic for revenge.'*

But Kha had made it clear that immortality was bestowed naturally. Megeara obviously survived for eons another way.

'Reincarnation,' Pyg murmured. *'It's only way a human can almost live forever. It's the nearest thing to immortality. Manipulating DNA is quite an achievement.'*

'That's the truth of it,' Pigeon shouted using Kha's voice as he alighted on Kit's other shoulder. *'A little bird told me.'*

'I'm not a bird, I'm a pygmalion,' Pyg babbled. *'Pygmalions can roar. Parrots cannot.'*

Pain shot through Kit's right shoulder. "Ouch. Keep your talons to yourself, Pidge."

'Sore shoulder, have we?' Pigeon nattered, pecking sand from his feet. *'Pooh sticks, to you. Poor little Kitty. A little tender, is it? I wonder what you're supposed to remember.'*

"I have to think. Could both of you *please* be quiet."

'Say Pretty Please,' Pigeon retorted. *'And then I'll help you slay a dragon.'*

"Three dragons," Kit answered.

'No need to be surly,' Pigeon answered.

'One plus two equals one,' Pyg echoed drowsily. *'Believing isn't always what it's cracked up to be.'*

Pigeon showed his solidarity by flapping his wings and getting his talons caught in Kit's hair. *'Depending on whose side they're on, three heads are better than one. And with Kha at your back you have two heads. Any final revelations, Kitty? Any last words. Any thoughts on words that can kill a dragon?'*

Kit stopped suddenly causing both shoulder 'angels' to grip harder and draw blood. His thoughts came through loud and clear. *'I know what I have to do. In order to fight Megeara, I have to die. I have to leave my body. I have to enter the realm of death and hold my ka in a solid form. Kha and Goswold taught me the secret of reviving myself. Megeara must be distracted enough from being on show to realize the truth."*

Pyg roared with laughter. *'She does love to show off. At least I have a face worth showing off.'*

Kit laughed nervously. "She won't be able to kill me. I remember Lady Nan's story about tricking a genie back into his bottle. I know the words that will trap Megeara. She will be as good as dead."

'Oh, far worse,' Pyg commented. *'She will lose face.'*

Pigeon cackled. *'Megeara will truly be beside herself with rage.'*

Kit arrived at the Sphinx elated, but nauseous from the assault of light and heat. The sun dazzled his headache into seeing double. "Kha where are you?"

Kha's voice surrounded Kit. "Behind you as we planned. Don't' look for me. Focus on Megeara's eyes. You will see her fatal flaw there. She's many things but she can't hide her fears. She was once human. Her fears remain in her mind. Inside the entity she created as Allecto."

Kit wiped the sweat dripping down his forehead, threatening to blind him further. "Not as we planned."

"It was *my* plan," Kha said. "Listen to me, Kit. I knew this day would come when we met in Cairo. You knew I was a ghost. Did you suppose I wouldn't remember the hour of my death."

"You might have warned me."

"We can argue later. You may be your own master now, but I am still your guide. Trust me. Keep Megeara's eyes locked on yours. If she believes you're alone, she will show off. Savoring her victories before they happened was always her undoing. She has been defeated before. Never killed permanently, but defeat is worse for her. She loses face. And I mean that literally. Her statue on Mars will be defaced with your great victory. It will self-destruct from Megeara's rage."

"My great victory? Kha, I can barely see."

"Fortunately," Kha said, "a fine spray of lotus tincture is invisible. Kit felt a cool blast in his eyes.

"Can you see, now?"

"Perfectly. 2020 foresight. I don't know which of her heads is uglier."

"Excellent. Keep the image of that date ahead of you like a carrot on a stick. That date is your secret weapon. It's hope. The year 2020 is your shining destiny. You are a master alchemist with an invisible brotherhood behind you. Fight for your children's future, your wife's undying love, and your sister's life."

Pigeon's voice came in clear. *'Lady Nan bids me to tell you that carrots help you see in the dark. This hour is the darkest. Reach for the year 2020. It is your destination. The word destiny rests inside every destination as a secret weapon. Reaching for a destination slightly out of reach is the sign of a true warrior. For it is in the courageous act of reaching against impossible odds that physical goals are won.'* With that, Pigeon brazenly dropped a long white feather at Kit's feet.

Kit drew a perfect circle with Pigeon's feather and strode brazenly into its center, unarmed. There was time enough to inhale deeply, close his eyes, and tap his armband. The instant rush of electricity through his body formed a relaxing halo of white light around him and made him smile uncontrollably. He waved the feather at Megeara. "You are a coward," he said.

Three incubus wasps issued from Megeara's left ear, buzzed close to Kit's face, and halted, waiting for their mistress's instructions.

"I came alone as you requested, Madame," Kit shouted. "But I see you've brought your sisters to protect you. Two heads may be better than one but three is just plain greedy."

Megeara wheeled, her cloak alive with moving wasps. "Impudent child. My sisters are here to be entertained. It is you who requires protection."

Kit flashed his rowan ring. "As you can see. I am well protected by transmuted gold."

Megeara's laughter coughed hundreds of new wasps from her mouth. She blew them over the Sphinx with her poisonous breath, her gaze locked onto Kit. Dead wasps rained down, peppering the Sphinx's face as tiny explosive pellets. She grinned slowly, showing three tiers of red teeth dripping with strings of foul-smelling scum. She addressed her incubuses "Take his eyes," she hissed quietly.

Three wasps backed away, circled Kit for speed, and dive bombed his face.

Tisiphone, and Allecto cackled to themselves anticipating Kit's agonizing scream that never came. Puzzled, Megeara peered closer to inspect Kit. Tisiphone and Allecto kept well back from her wrath, eyeing each other nervously.

Kha's voice whispered in Kit's ear. "Well-played, my brother. You have her on the run."

Kit's expression remained bemused as he answered telepathically. "Pigeon gave me your message. At first, I was mystified, but then I remembered the day we met when you acted like a pompous genie. After that it was easy. Lady Nan's love of word games and her bedtime story of Aladdin, especially for me, filled in the gaps. It was words that tricked Aladdin's genie back into his bottle, that for all its magic, may as well have been a vial of poison. Sometimes a prison is worse than death. Words can kill. Then I relived the time you and Goswold discussed simulated death over my comatose body. I heard every word. Words can heal, too."

Megeara recoiled and twisted to get a closer view of a human able to withstand a deadly attack of killer wasps without flinching.

The shock of hair, fallen into his eyes, had saved him.

The wasps released themselves from Megeara's clothes and turned to swarm. This time, Kit grinned as the insects passed through him. Stunned to see her second wave of wasps fail after her best wasps flew away, Megeara grew larger.

Kit smiled sweetly and pretended to sneeze. "Killing a human is effortless for you. It's gutless. It may appear as high drama, but it lacks ingenuity. Even your sisters think so."

"You promised us a bloodbath," Allecto simpered. "Entertainment worth waiting thousands of years for, you said. But then you lie to Tisiphone and me all the time. Tisiphone always said you were a bully."

Tisiphone rounded on Allecto. "Well, she *is* a bully. You agreed with me."

"Allow me to express my professional opinion," Kit interrupted. "Megeara. You are a vile power-hungry queen, jealous of your own mind and soul, and its eating you alive. You sound like a second Medusa to me."

"I am second to no-one. I am not Medusa. I am the heart of the Furies. Medusa was fallible. I am immortal."

Kit hung his head. "I stand corrected. But mind and soul control the heart which makes you second to both your sisters. That puts your weakened heart in third place. A heart that was broken by a mere mortal human who damaged it beyond repair."

Megeara flashed her boney fingers in the sun. Each of them ended in a long black wasp stinger dripping with poison. She spread her claws in a fan of death slashing Kit with no apparent ill-effects. She flexed her blood-encrusted talons, thirsty for fresh blood, and took another futile swipe.

"What trick is this, mortal? Tell the truth, you may not lie. You promised. Lie and you forfeit the game. Your son will die."

Kit remained immobile and stared her down. "You can't harm me, Megeara. You cannot kill me because one of your sisters…" he paused and eyed Allecto and Tisiphone in turn. "One of your sisters already killed me."

The buzzing of wasps became unbearable as Megeara processed Kit's accusation. A look of pure venom transfigured her eye sockets into holes of white fire. Her prey was dead. She had been betrayed. Enraged, Megeara flew into a hissing cyclone and turned on her sisters. "Which one of you dared to take this boy from me. He was mine to kill. You knew well, he was being saved as a last sacrifice to seal my victory over the contemptible defectiveness of human men. She flew around Kit's circle gathering up her disoriented wasps. The outcome of the Pangean War hinged on my victory over this puny runt. Are you claiming that victory, Tisiphone? Are you, Allecto?"

"I believe I was the puny jewel in your wobbly crown," Kit said. "Or so, Allecto informed me. That was it, wasn't it, Allecto?"

"Allecto, what is this treachery!"

"Mistress Tisiphone, Madame Allecto," Kit called out in a steady voice. "Have you forgotten your list of grievances, ladies?"

"A list!" Megeara spat. "Which of you made a list? Speak!"

"They both did," Kit said. "I have it memorized if you care to hear it."

Tisiphone glared at Allecto. "Allecto made the list because you decreed that she and I would remain in your shadow until the end of time. I tried to stop her."

"You *are* my shadows," Megeara sneered. "I created you. You are jealous of me but how could you not be for I intended that, too."

"That may be so," Kit said, "but you know full well that Tisiphone is the Furies' soul and Allecto is its mind."

Tisiphone, not to be outdone, cried "It's always about you, Megeara. Endless, ruthless, self-centered, you. Lording it over Allecto who befriended the boy. The boy who, by the way, was more afraid of *her* than *you*."

Megeara spun on Allecto. "Liar. I gave you everything and you chose to eclipse me."

"You took all the power and left us wanting," Allecto fumed. "Something had to be done. A little recognition would have mollified me, but Tisiphone required more. She's almost as greedy as you."

Tisiphone seethed at the inference. "You're the liar, Allecto. It's your endless sense of entitlement that caused so many problems. I saw you kill the boy."

"You tried to drive Megeara mad," Allecto accused. "Not that she wasn't already insane with power."

"What do you mean, tried?" Tisiphone frothed at the mouth. "Megeara *is* insane because I *did* drive her mad."

Kit addressed Tisiphone, plunging into the discussion loud enough to silence all three. "Neither of you drove Megeara mad," he shouted. "A little Pangean bird told me that a man with discriminating tastes, did that long ago. It said she was spurned by a king. No wait, I'm wrong, I believe it used the word spawned."

The appalling odor of stirred pig muck from the fracas of hair pulling and eye gouging made Kit gag. Wriggling maggots surfaced on Megeara's skin and exploded with pus. Terrified wasps flew off in all directions. Megeara, seeing them go, vaporized them for their cowardice.

The caterwauling continued until Megeara was primed for Kit's final blow. "Poor sad wretched Megeara," he taunted. "You couldn't stop nagging your sisters even if you wanted to. Allecto, your own creation, won't let you. Your sisters have generated an eternal whirlpool so cunning that it bites your eternal serpent's tail. And you know the image. It's a cycle that can never end. You were on to something when you told my parrot that your sisters slowed you down."

"Oh really, Megeara," Tisiphone jeered. "*We* slow *you* down? Well no more. Allecto was right. Your authority must be checked."

Kit picked up Pigeon's white feather, stepped out of the circle, and waved it in Megeara's face. "Alchemy taught me to be single-minded. I recognize you Megeara. I know your secret. You're a single hateful hag split into three. A diseased heart, mind, and soul constantly fighting for singular authority, feeding off a depraved illusion of power. This tactic weakened you.

Your wasps are the endless thoughts of Allecto's restless greedy mind. Your incubuses are the creation of Tisiphone's tortured soul. As the heart of the Furies, your perverted emotions have turned to stone.

So, kind of like Medusa, actually. And like Perseus' shield, I reflect your hideous truth back onto yourself. Can you see the terror in your own eyes? I can. Kha saw it. Pan and Osiris will always see it, for they are true immortals. Even Ay sees it.

The earth's core is a hellfire of molten power and while you drink from it you are insatiable for more. Only a fool believes their own lies. And even if you manage to reincarnate, you will have no place to go but back to Mars – a sphinx who succumbed to her own riddle. Your legacy is the battered broken face on Mars."

Megeara whipped herself into a frenzy and turned inside out, exposing her writhing snakelike entrails. The rancid wasps clinging to them screamed their piggy screams and imploded. Her ensuing shriek opened the ground in a deep chasm of molten sand. The Furies hardened instantly into a single red glass statue. With his father's and Tut's help it was easy to smash it and throw the shards into the underworld's furnace. Megeara's parting curse 'Your teacher failed you,' dissipated to empty static inside Kit's head.

"Megeara's last words to me were meant to destroy my confidence," he said to the family, but it was an empty curse. She said my teacher failed me," Kit said. "I had many. And each of them taught me a timely lesson.

Cats taught me that chasing time is the relentless pursuit of chasing one's own tail – a game of questionable entertainment but good exercise for remaining flexible and alert.

Sekhmet taught me duality – that healing and destroying are twin sides of the same coin and that it's the subtle ability to discriminate when and where to use either of them which rules the day.

Bast taught me the art of parenting. That fatherhood is selfless nurturing as vital as motherhood.

My grandmother taught me that the monstrous forces in fairy tales are metaphors for the love that underpins humanity's ability to turn leaden emotions into gold. Lady Nan instructed Bash and I to beware of the three times three 'rule of nine': the three-headed monster of greed, jealousy, and fear that warps compassion, the three magic wishes that can ensnare the soul, and the triple faces of the green goddess: the maiden, the wise-woman, and the crone.

My grandfather's failure to persuade me that controlling others was the pinnacle of success, taught me to revisit Darwin's theory of evolution. His constant bullying convinced me to follow my own truth and that the survival of the human spirit relied on compassion.

Kha taught me the science of alchemy. The true meaning of turning lead into gold, wasps into gentle honeybees, logic into magic, and magic into truth.

My beautiful SaRa introduced me to the alchemy of human love. She embodies the steadfast patience of the ages."

Pyg smiled at his reflection, appreciatively *'I'm proud to say that my duties are officially discharged,'* he said, preening his wings in SaRa's bronze mirror. And with a tiny roar he disappeared.

chapter 37
MISTRESS OF MAGIC

New Year's Day, 2019

For a moment, the wasp legion turned as one, regrouping to attack but a freezing wind pushed their cloud cover aside and blew them from the face of the earth to the face on Mars.

It continued to blow until the sky was clean as a new blackboard on the first day of school. In turn, that first day magic was bleached by the midday sun and whitewashed by January snow that fell in thick silent flakes.

Bash taught Kem to catch them on his tongue and how to make snowballs.

Sage's leaves sprouted green shoots and passed into the emerald season of high summer, morphing into the gold and crimsons of autumn before falling from him in heaps of colored leafy gems.

By half past twelve, the seasons had repeated their sequence of cycles an additional six times. By one-o'clock, Sage was dusted with a sixth drift of snow as powdery soft as icing sugar.

The Twinters pulled chairs onto the lawn, happy to experience a fast-paced parade of heat and cold and wet and dry.

At ten past one, when the maze looked like a package wrapped in white tissue paper, rain fell in a silky curtain and washed the winter away. White snowdrops popped up dotting the new lawn in a pattern of stars.

By 2p.m. the seasons merged in a kaleidoscope of colors pulsating through the spectrum in a display reminiscent of a solar eclipse. Flowers grew, bees pollinated, cherries hung heavy on branches and hundreds of windfall apples rolled along the flowerbeds.

"Well, that's new," Brooks said. "You don't see *that* everyday."

A double rainbow swept an arc over the land, linking Bede Hall to

Lindisfarne and the village. "Is this some kind of collective trance? Are we awake?"

Lady Nan smiled to herself, took a deep breath, and embraced the sky with open arms. "It's peacetime," she mused. "The war has given up the ghost. Happy New Year."

With the Furies officially eliminated, Bash speculated to Hannah that soon she and Kit would resume their telepathic connection and he would come home.

Hannah gave her a kind smile. "Don't confuse logic with magic," she said. "It's time for you to open the way for Parks and Charlotte to re-enter Bede."

Bash's smile evaporated. "How? Did Charlotte leave any instructions?"

"She did in a roundabout way. She has her ways."

"Yes, Bash nodded. "I know those ways, only too well."

"Charlotte maintained a link with the shop through its crazy land-line but it was only used for troubleshooting… putting out the small fires, mostly set by you. Not of late, mind, you've shown remarkable restraint. And don't think the pair of them won't have noticed."

Bash covered her face with both hands. "Where on earth do I start?"

Hannah sent Bash a look of disbelief. "With the earth, of course. Speak to the earth and then gather your ingredients: Lady Nan's snow globe, plenty of Smyth no. 9, and sit under the goddess tree. And there are two powerfully obvious elements to consider: one – there's a full moon tonight, and two – it's the start of a new year. So, nothing to sniff at."

Despair was evident in Bash's stricken expression and the fear in her voice. "I have to call them down tonight!"

"And, forgive me, but you have to do it alone. That much Charlotte always made clear about higher magic. That and the rule of 'three times three'."

"You seem to know more than you first let on, Hannah."

"I know something about priming one's instincts. I expect your intuition will quicken any time now."

Bash closed her eyes and opened her mind. "I invoke the trine of three in the pyramid of power as the triple face of the goddess: By earth and wind and water, I invoke the maiden, the wise-woman, and the crone, here under Her tree and Her moon, as Her appointed Mistress of the Green."

Hannah clapped enthusiastically. "There. That wasn't so difficult, was it. And now you must accept the snow globe from Lady Nan as your right."

Lady Nan received her granddaughter beaming with pride. "Well done, my darling. It's time. The globe has been waiting impatiently for you."

The globe tingled in Bash's hands. Lady Nan dipped elegantly into the ghost of a curtsy. "The queen is dead. Long live the queen," she said.

Bash steadied her voice. "Does Bede Hall know where Parks is?"

"Child. Parks IS Bede Hall! He changes his voice to remain anonymous. He's been waiting longer than anyone on earth to be known for all that he is."

"Then he's already back."

"Parks is lodged in the walls of Bede Hall but not yet where he truly belongs, under the bark of his trees as the immortal Pan. Parks is the Green Man."

"And Charlotte?"

"The Charlotte you knew has changed. As the Lady Flora, Charlotte can never leave the forest. She IS the forest, and the trees are her children. Pan is her consort. Charlotte is the Green Woman."

Bash made her way to the sacred Rowan Grove in the moonlight. Woodland animals lined her path. White rabbits, pale lilac and blue in the moonlight, bowed their heads. Mice ceased squeaking, and owls guided her from above, their wingtips touching to form a canopy.

Charlotte walked from an invisible door in the trunk of the goddess tree wearing a robe of green light. I've been watching you vanquish your setbacks which makes me lenient, I forgive you, daughter."

"I miss my mother."

"Your mother is on her own journey. Your road split at the crossroads of duty and responsibility. She is the mother figure for Tut of Bede's people. Be happy for her. She has found her true place after living a half-life here in a matriarchal society that failed to acknowledge her own feminine powers. In Egypt, women carry the matriarchal power of succession. It was and is, the same for Bede Hall which is why your grandmother inherited her title after her brother, Ben, the only male heir, passed over. Your grandfather and your father had to take their wives' name."

"Tut has people?"

"He is a king. Look in your globe and behold the past becoming the future."

Bash stared hard until her eyes watered and the form of her mother swam into view. She was resplendent in the formal robes of royal status, her hair worn loose as a maiden, fell down her back. Mrs. S looked up as if she heard voices, stared into Bash's face, and waved hello and goodbye at the same time.

"Can she see me?"

"She can feel you," Charlotte said. "That's love for you in her eyes."

"There's a photo of her like that from her wedding day."

"She's eighteen again, in spirit," Charlotte said.

"You're not Charlotte anymore. I will miss you as a friend."

"You will befriend me as an equal. The Lady Flora and her apprentice Mistress of the Green."

Lady Flora's energy flowed freely in Bash's mind and spoke from her lips. "I bring you home," she said.

The animals had fallen into a trance, curled in poses of restful sleep all along the pathway she had traveled. Pan walked towards her, now. Parks' eyes were recognizable but living twigs and leaves had replaced his white hair and he wore a crown of antlers in place of his gardener's hat that he now carried aloft like a crown.

"This belongs to Six, now," he said placing the hat at Bash's feet. "May the two of you reign as the appointed guardians of my Hall."

Parks grew into his elemental power until he was tall enough to hold Bede Hall nestled into its grounds, complete with tower and maze and the sundial, in the palm of his hands. He offered it up to the moon, his earthling protégé kneeling in the grass and the twice-borns on the roof. The Winter Room's window was open, surrounded in a halo of summer vines and fragrant white carnations.

The scarabs flew in formation through the window and landed in their glass case. Lady Nan stood in the library and closed its door when their wings were folded. Her snow globe assumed the dimensions of the floor globe and turned a quarter turn until the land of Khem glowed as a gold embossed shape. It turned once more, and Britain emitted a shaft of white light that reached around the spherical map until it planted itself on the great plain of Giza. Hadrian's wall became a bridge that spanned 75 million years as the continents slid together as Pangea.

Dawn light touched the world as Pan replaced the Hall tenderly in the center of the Lady Flora's forest. Fairies formed tiny clouds of light that moved down the treeline like fireflies.

"The ceremony is begun," Pan boomed.

The figure of Six walked his ghostly form from the mouth of the maze, his eyes fixed on his child bride.

The fairies chanted 'kiss her… kiss her' and by the time their lips met, anyone watching would have seen a young man and a maiden, handfast in love, oblivious to the world.

The inhabitants of Bede Hall overslept as if under a spell as the Hall rested under a gauze like covering of frost. Its façade shimmered silvery white in the crisp air of the new year like an enchanted ice castle in a fairy tale. At nine a.m. sharp, the loud ticking of Kit's tower clock reached the lacy treeline and echoed back across the south lawn to mark the beginning of a new era.

Jack, lying by the banked kitchen fire, startled awake. He lifted his head and howled.

Taraq, curled into the throne chair in Kit's tower, responded instantly.

Sage heard Jack, too, and alerted the other topiaries. A shower of icy diamonds fell from Sage's leaves as he nodded to the little ghost speeding towards the Hall. "Kit's clock is awake and there's strange energy emanating from the sundial," he called out. "We will meet you there."

"I have to let Jack out," Taraq replied, not slowing down. "He's upset. He may be in trouble."

Memory lifted her trunk and accompanied Jack's howling with a celebratory trumpet.

"Jack's not upset," Sage mumbled to himself. "He's excited." He nudged the other topiaries awake. "Stir your stumps everyone," he ordered. "We're invited to a new epoch."

Jack was scratching frantically in what would have eventually become a large hole in the kitchen door when Taraq arrived. He ran in a mad circle until, free, he was able to burst from the Hall. He bounded across the lawn racing Taraq to the sundial.

Kit, dressed in Egyptian robes, stood by the sundial, facing Bede Hall. He was there and not there.

The topiaries, gathered into a circle around Kit, parted for the ecstatic dog that, if Kit hadn't been a ka, would have knocked him over. Taraq watched from behind Sage, quietly sobbing.

For a moment, Jack's ka rose above his body and mingled with Kit's molecules. The two tumbled together over the frosty grass.

Kit stood. "I'll be home soon," he said to Jack. "Now sit. I have work to do."

Jack's ka returned to his body and he sat obediently, panting and helplessly wriggling with joy while Kit outstretched his arms and uttered incantations so familiar to Taraq that the little ghost sobbed even harder.

A jet of dazzling green light erupted from the sundial behind Kit, like a small volcano, bathing the Hall and the countryside with mystical fireworks. The lawn covered in January frost reflected a spring shade of pulsating lime green. The birdbath gushed a fountain of emerald water.

chapter 38
FROZEN IN TIME

The sun was still in its zenith when Ay made his getaway. Pigeon flew into his face, talons first, but other than inflicting deep gashes, Ay kept running. Pigeon made a second pass and grabbed Ay's scalp, clinging to it almost all the way to the Great Pyramid, but Ay, equally determined, never faltered. He wiped blood from his eyes and held fast to the image of an infallible sanctuary of the Kings Chamber ahead.

A sleek black cat ran across Ay's path and he tripped. Sand stuck to his bloody hands. Anubis hissed over his shoulder and continued back to the temple compound, happy with his act of protest. Feathers would be impressed. If Ay had been less relentless he could have turned him into a jackal.

The Great Pyramid's limestone skin reflected electrifying white, shining like the beacon of time it was designed to be. Its subterranean entrance, clogged with the comings and goings of priests running from swarms of irate wasps, stepped aside for their high priest and took the brunt of the stings. Kit's ka ran through them unnoticed.

Ay, ahead of Kit by half-an-hour, had the advantage, but his terror left a red vaporous trail of pulsating footprints like fitful heartbeats in the sand. Kit's ghost viewed them in birds-eye perspective.

Once inside, Kit floated a few inches above Ay's trail of fear as he navigated the slope of the grand gallery, floating almost horizontally to accommodate its low degree of incline. Kit progressed slowly towards the sound of Ay chanting. The deep resonant echo told him Ay was in the King's chamber which meant Ay had access to the time portal that meandered its way to the Winter Room.

Kit willed himself to move faster. The last thing Bede Hall needed during a war or even in its aftermath was a bad apple like his grandfather, returning to their barrel. Lady Nan would know how to sort him, but it may not be a quick solution given all the twists and turns of two shades of magic at odds with each other. Kit likened it to a second war and concentrated on moving faster.

Ay's handprints left from scrambling over the walls were easy to see. His palpable fear had taken a turn for the worse, and his fear made his sandals impossibly hot, they dropped from his feet making Ay's barefoot path glow white hot in the dark. Kit's ring shone like a small flashlight casting a purple light ahead of him. His ka skimmed over them and lifted directly to the torchlight above.

Ay grabbed the torch and threw it, aiming for Kit's head, but it passed clean through without injury and clattered down the sloping passage. A few puffs of fire burst for an instant when the flame reached a thin scattering of straw at the bottom.

The straw flared briefly and smoldered into putrid smoke. Voices behind the smokescreen called out to Ay. But the roar of a lion sent them scattering. Sekhmet streaked through the smoke and turned to face anyone who dared follow her. No-one challenged her formidable teeth and claws.

Kit tested the massive granite blocks, pleased his hand found no resistance. He checked his position and threw his body upwards to where he knew the Queens chamber lay and sprang with his arms outstretch like superman. He streaked through the granite as effortlessly as passing through a gauze curtain and encountered a slight tension from the ceiling and its roof topped with slabs of stone, stacked in an interlocking herringbone pattern.

Ay's frantic voice filtered below but the roof became as glass and Kit made a grab for Ay's blistered feet just as they lifted from the floor. He missed.

Kit slipped through the solid granite between the Queen's Chamber and the King's Chamber as if it was tissue paper, in time to watch Ay clambering into the open sarcophagus. He had failed.

Pigeon flew through the granite blocks easily and perched on the lip of the sarcophagus. *'There's no need to fret, Master Kit. Ay was banned from Bede many years ago and the Winter Portal won't let him through. He is trapped in solitary confinement, and when that's done, he will die a frozen failure of a man.'*

By the time Kit reached Ay, he lay in the Sarcophagus of Time, turned to stone, assuming the familiar pose of a Knight Templar from Bede's churchyard clutching the Bede Prophecy scroll.

Ay's mouth gaped opened in a frozen scream like a victim of Pompei's ashes. Seconds later, his decayed mummy disintegrated to dust. The restored scroll was all that remained on a pile of soot. Black flakes rose like a flood from the emptied sarcophagus and spilled into the chamber.

Pigeon screeched from the air vents. *'Kit, fly to me! You can do it if you keep your ka form.'*

"I feel heavier," Kit shouted. "I'm already shifting to the physical plane. I'm waking up. The opening is too narrow. I'm stuck."

Pigeon mimicked Peri's voice. "Dad, help me. I'm up here with Pigeon. Enter the vent and don't look back. I need you. Please do what Pigeon says. I need you, Dad!"

"I hear Jack barking. He's frantic. He needs me."

'It's a trick,' Pigeon hissed. *'The remnants of Tisiphone's thoughts are still inside your head but she's fading. Jack is well. He has become content with his new life without you.'*

"I abandoned him."

'You're actually in the process of saving him, right now. Continue forward. Remember for all intents and purposes you are dead. At this moment, you're in the final stage of saving your children, your wife, your sister, the world, and me. Jack is somewhere in the future, chasing rabbits in his sleep. But right now, you have a few rabbits of your own to chase.'

"The ashes are up to my chin. I can't breathe."

'That's panic talking. PAN-ic, as related to Pan, otherwise known as Parks, the Green Man of Bede.'

"I'm suffocating."

'You can't suffocate, Numpty. Think logically. Pretend you're a scientist. Work it out. As a ghost you are completely safe. You can't die if you're already dead. And when you do regain consciousness, you

will find yourself back in Kha's studio where you left your body. Get a grip, boy!'

In spite of his fear, Pigeon's words made him think of Bash. "I'm an idiot," he said out loud. "No harm can come to me. I'm dead."

Kha's laughter echoed throughout the chamber, trailed up the air shaft and disappeared.

"Pigeon. How soon can we use the portal?"

'Well, there's the rub, as old Bill Swan likes to say. Time is not equal on either side of a portal. You can use it after a day or so, but you would be stuck inside for a year as the portal, Bede side, takes that long to reset.'

"Is there any good news? And why are you being so polite? If you are a god, which I don't believe for a moment, I am most certainly *not* your master."

'First question. There is good news. Your telepathic link with Bash is now open. You can diplomatically inform her of the delay. Call it a flight cancellation and then everyone goes about their time in preparation for a homecoming the likes never before seen since the movie production returned that lean summer of 2018. Again, as Bill likes to call, the summer of our discontent. Or the winter. Either season is appropriate under the circumstances.

Second question. I was being Polite, as an act of curtesy due a conquering hero.

There is no third question. 'I am no less a god than that falcon, Horus. I mean, I ask you, what kind of a name is Horus.'

"I need to speak with someone in authority," Kit moaned. "Not a bloody bird with a smart beak."

'Talk to the King of this Pyramid, then. I believe he has his voice back.'

A powerful male voice boomed "I do."

Kit felt extraordinarily, smug. "To whom am I speaking?"

"My name is Osiris. In a way I am your distant uncle. Parks has been like a father to you, and he is my twin brother."

"I have seen your green portrait many times, but I never connected there were two entities known as the Green Man until Goswold told me."

"I am a green *god!*"

"Yes, Sir."

"The King's Winter Portal has been compromised. And a portal violated by human hate requires fumigating with incantations, powerful herbs, and sacred flowers. I have been informed Bede lavender is an especially beneficial cleanser with exceptional healing properties. Please ask your sister to load the Winter Room portal with a few bales of the stuff and lock the door. Tainted human vibrations are not permitted in spaces dedicated to healing a planet. Your family is aware of a sudden victory, so it would be kind to let them know of the time flux."

"I am keenly aware of the time anomalies, first-hand," Kit said sarcastically. "I am not the correct age and my children aged nine years in the space of time it takes an alchemist to visit Mars – an inhospitable caldera of a planet, capped by a mountainous stone face I hope to never see again."

"But there is one thing left to do," Osiris commanded. "You must go to Mars, one last time. As the conquered party, Megeara must agree to our conditions as befits our victory. You are the only one who can negotiate a truce. More of an extremely long-term contract."

Osiris grew to a godlike stature that dwarfed the pyramid. "Don't *ask* Megeara for the moon, Kit. You must *demand* it. She's ruthless and tricky on her home world, and especially so in her humiliation. Take someone with you to watch your back. Take Pigeon. It seems I have made him a god, or so he informs me. Accept nothing less than the stars. But travel as a ka. Kas unnerve her. She failed to foresee a master alchemist would show up as a puny boy."

Kit stared at his bare feet. "Thanks. Now two of us are humiliated."

Osiris made no apologies. "I used the word puny because it is how you see yourself."

Kit shrugged. "Pretending I'm a hero would be lying."

It was a bizarre moment for his cell phone to ring. The tune to 'Land of hope and Glory', rang out triumphantly.

'Pretense or Pretend,' Pigeon shrieked. *'fighting words for a Proven Puny hero.'*

"Seeing is believing what may be true," Osiris said. "Believing is seeing what you want to be true."

"Which is precisely why a parrot of my acquaintance believes he's a god."

'I am Precise. I am Perfection. I am king of the Winter Portal. As Pyramid Power befits, I shall be lenient with you,' Pigeon squawked.

Deep inside Tutankhamen's tomb, the figure of Taraq appeared in the painted door and flickered out.

BEDE

chapter 39
CLOSING TIME

The mice express post moved outward in concentric circles from a central den hidden in the roots of the route portal tree like an exploding message. The portals were closing. Which ones it was hard to say. Nigel, the tree nymph heard it from the bees, recently given back their skies. Normally, all business, they were zooming for the sake of zooming without stopping to spread the word, assuming that the blue sky had given them permission to play.

Nigel, normally the source of tree gossip was simply left hanging on the tail end of an excited buzz. He had it on the best authority, having heard the latest scoop from his cousin Antwerp who had been eavesdropping on Hannah's magic 'singing box' conversation. A fox overheard them. "By the way," he said. "That 'box' is a cell phone, and the song is a ringtone. Humans match the music to their mood. So, if it's Mozart, it's a safe bet Master Kit is well. And if it's hard rock… well, you get my drift."

"Not in the least little bit," Antwerp had replied. "Trees don't play games."

The green gods were back. That much was clear. And it was almost enough except the changes coming were big. The bigness of it had the mice in a dither of speculation which migrated to the larger animals more capable of creating havoc on the forest floor. The rabbits who had been on the path when Pan arrived had slept through the ceremonies and remembered the whole thing as a wonderful dream. Smiling rabbits were everywhere, bumping into tree trunks and each other.

One by one the tree nymphs materialized. The morning chorus sparrows sang of better days to come. The king was in his leafy castle and the queen's bees were making honey. Fairies polished the new leaves as they unfurled. And the confused mice ran into each other to share the snippets they'd managed to remember into one message.

Katydid was sure the Winter Room was being redecorated. At the very least, colors were reappearing in its white carpet.

Doolittle had seen its furniture piled in the hallway. And strangest of all, the cold spot was now a patch of warm sunlight. Unicorn and the new cat, Arthur, took turns bathing in it. And was Arthur aware of the rules of prey? It was wise not to assume such a senior royal cat would obey the directives of the house of Bede. Snowdrop herself, seemed a tad loftier than the before time. But then, she had saved the day when Griffin betrayed them all.

Lady Nan had been relieved of her snow globe. The scarabs were back under glass. The Mistress and Master were not to be disturbed. The new boy, Kem, hung around the stables and played with Mr. Leoni's toy lion. The twice-borns were putting the Hall to rights in preparation for the great homecoming. Boxes littered the drive and a smallish van was seen to be ferrying boxes and bags and bustling Twinters, hither and dither. The Parks family had emigrated to parts unknown so as not to confuse the natural pecking order of things.

For the moment, the gardens were in charge of themselves and doing very well. Helen would be holding a conference by the newly-flowing Roman spring, and for the immediate future, the route portal would remain open. The cat flap portal was outside the jurisdiction of Pan and the Green Lady Flora. And was it rude to still think of them as Parks and Charlotte?"

"Thinking respectful thoughts is never rude," Fioretti assured them, and she knew more than the other fairies seeing how she was one of the guests of honor at the great ceremony.

As events were beginning to settle, a happy shockwave traveled the length and breadth of the forest.

Mouse Pipkin noted to Fioretti that it was hard hearing what humans said due to the discrepancies of size. "I can't hear them unless I'm on a table or they bend down to my level," he said.

"And that, Francis Fox said. "Explains a great deal inherent in your postal service."

"Oh, that reminds me," Pipkin squeaked. "I heard about a great deal this morning. What was it… *um…*" His nose twitched harder to jumpstart his memory. "The throne has been sold and Taraq along with it," he blurted. "I rather like Taraq, so, it's sad to see him go, but there it is. Changes are afoot, whatever that means."

"You misheard," Fioretti said. "The throne belongs to Kit and he isn't here *to* sell it. Ergo, you got the facts muddled. And Taraq would never let it go unless it was over his dead body..." he paused a moment to hear what he'd said. "Oh, dear. That *does* confuse things."

"But if it were true, and the portals are closing, it would have to be shipped soon."

"It's a ransom," Pipkin said without thinking. "What's a ransom?"

Nigel, eavesdropping more than usual, slunk off muttering, "Mice. What are they like!"

Theodore Clutterbucks' Emporium was in a state of uproar, taking a much needed inventory after Leoni and Nick had depleted his stock. The cheery new window display exhibited his wife's collection of sunflower greeting cards, in sharp contrast to the usual assortment of dusty curiosities.

Hannah's latest acquisition, Vincent Van Gogh's yellow chair, a gift from the Mistress of the Green, was set in pride of place in her workshop where she kept her art collection and printed her line of greeting cards. "Chickens come home to roost," Teddy announced at teatime. "You stored that chair in the back room for years before you gave it to Bash. And now it's yours." He glanced at Darwin in his box and the stuffed dodo bird on its pedestal in the corner. "How is Dee Dee settling in?"

"Ask her yourself," Hannah said," scribbling a list of things that needed doing.

Teddy continued to talk to himself. "The post office portal is closed. That leaves the sun dial, the Winter Room, the root route, and the maze. I reckon the Hall will close the maze first as it poses too great an open invitation, exposed to all and sundry flying by."

Beegle reached a long furry arm to the sideboard groaning with jellies and teacakes and helped himself to a cucumber sandwich.

The yellow chair teetered on one leg and spun like a top. It was good to be a family again.

"The Hall is having a clear out and I have first dibs." Theodore chuckled. "I guess you could say it's having an over-hall."

Hannah looked over her paperwork and smiled. Business is booming here and blooming over at the shop," she said. "We've worked hard the last few years. And the movie crowd might return. Who knows, nothing is settled. Lady Nan once said the movie business would return over her dead body, but she was alive when she said it, so I'm not entirely sure where that leaves things, now."

Events jostled in the village proper and items were redistributed. Hannah took over the flower shop full-time and brought Beegle home each night to save her stock from devastation.

Dee Dee answered Teddy's inquiry an hour after it was aired. *'Thanks for asking, Mr. Teddy bear. I am doing as well as can be expected, considering the fire damage.'*

Hannah's cell phone blared out a familiar rousing tune from the operetta 'Orpheus in the Underworld' better known as the 'CanCan' song. Dee Dee nestled her beak under her best wing. *'We can can. We will will,'* she muttered and sang herself to sleep. *'I love Paris in the Springtime. I love Vincent in the fall. I love Anna in the new Hall and I love the girl in Hadrian's Wall.'*

EGYPT

chapter 40
PA'A RULES THE DAY

Pigeon squawked like a town crier, all the way to the temple of Bast, flying low enough for Peri, running after him, to grab his tail when his feet tired. The ghost of Kha met them on the temple steps and carried the exhausted Peri the rest of the way to SaRa.

An order for mother and children to report to Bast was waiting for them in the shape of Babs who addressed Kha. "Master Kha. We are sad you have been reduced to your present state. You are excused to complete the tasks you have started."

Kha nodded. "Please inform your Mistress that being a ka is an *elevated* state. I am happy to comply."

Peri rode Babs, entering Bast's inner sanctum like a triumphant warrior.

Pigeon alighted on the dais and reported in. *'What's left of the Furies, and it wasn't much, I can tell you, are banished to Mars. Master KiTiK'a'at is there also, negotiating a treaty with the shell of Megeara, and is expected here shortly.'*

Bast yawned, stretched languorously, and laid her head on her paws, listening with her eyes closed.

'Your sister goddess, Sekhmet caused a stir destroying Ay's troops followers and his incubi of mechanical wasps,' Pa'a continued. *'She healed the injured horses and the Aten priests who put themselves in harms way to slow Ay down.'*

Bast's great tail flapped impatiently, thumping like a drum, sending such strong vibrations throughout the temple that every cat stood their ground and hissed, ready to fight.

Babs opened her eyes and rose, pacing around Pa'a. *'As for the state of the Winter Portal in the temple of Bede Hall,'* she growled, *'as we speak, lotus fairies are cleansing the kings chamber and Kha is* *sealing it until the portal has been purified in our time and fumigated by lavender in the 21st century.'*

"We must send our strongest 'Way of Happiness' medicine to purify the Egyptian entrance," Bast said.

'Osiris speaks once more,' Babs purred. *'His voice was heard in the pyramid complex.'* A jealous growl erupted from her throat. *'I believe the parrot Pa'a received a message from him.'*

"Pa'a," Bast commanded. "Convey this message at once."

Pigeon flew to the goddess and, in passing, made a deposit of droppings on Bab's head. *'Osiris was upset, Ma'am. At his wish, the people in an uproar who were initially unable to be healed, are now sedated and under a spell of sleep. Even now, some of them are disoriented, unused to their astral ka forms, wandering the streets with no idea what's happening. He wants Kha to heal them as a priority.'*

"I heard Osiris in a dream," Bast said. "Kha must obey our master, and we must offer the people sustenance."

Pa'a bowed his head and backed away from Bast's tail, possibly out of control, acting of its own accord. *'At your orders,'* he said, *'a feast is being prepared.'*

A cat spat between Sibuna and Anubis threatened to escalate into a tooth and claw brawl in the outer reception chamber. The cats accompanying them stepped back, unsure what to do. Cats were forbidden to air their differences within the temple.

Babs swore. "You dishonor the goddess's sanctuary." She crouched ready to spring, growling with her ears back.

Sibuna ceased his caterwauling immediately and streaked past Babs. Once in the inner sanctum, he bowed to Bast, contrite. "I apologise for my behavior," he said "but my brother contests my right to serve KiTiKha'at's family. Since you assigned me to teach KiTiKha'at, I humbly claim the right to teach his son," Sibuna said. "On other business, these cats seek your permission to live in Bede."

Bast smiled. "Define humble. Do you wish to go to England as well, Sibuna?"

"No Ma'am. I want to teach KiTiKha'at's son if he stays."

"My brother," Anubis hissed "You are forgetting my position as head guardian of Bede Hall which makes 'Master Kit and his offspring *my* responsibility."

"A master alchemist requires no followers," Bast said. "He walks alone." She turned to the group of temple cats. "Come forward, my children. Of course, you may stay in Britannia. Sibuna, you may go if you change your mind. You have earned the right to choose. I am proud of you. All of you, remember our ways. Honor the blood of your ancestors. Relinquish your golden jewelry. Adopt a human in Bede Village. They will give you collars of a different sort. Wear them proudly. Anubis, I grant you an extra toe, to remember the bond between us."

The honorary god, Pa'a, swanned into the emergency meeting in the temple hoping to be the voice of sanity in a world reeling from violence and a reshuffling of power. *'I bring you reasons,'* Pigeon squawked. *'I bring you endings and beginnings. I bring you doors and windows. Pomposity aside, I hold the list of candidates in my brain. To many of you I say welcome. And to some of you, I bid you sad farewell.'*

His eloquent declaration did little to ease the tension. Present were: 'Cornelius and his great wife' (as they were now called), King Tut of Bede, Kha, Kit, SaRa, and the nine-year-old twins Anna and Peri who linked thoughts, seated on the floor in a circle of power.

Cornelius sighed at his haughtier-than-usual parrot and rapped the floor for attention. "Let us begin with the worst," he said. "Reports please. Out with it."

Pigeon chose to adopt the voice of his old friend Parks. *'To overstate the obvious, a time portal, all of them, are sensitive finely-tuned machines, calibrated with the highest time-sensitive gears, cogs, and wheels, set to alpha.'*

"Alpha being the big bang," Cornelius volunteered.

'Correct my son,' Pigeon-Parks said affectionately. *'The arts of*

mathematical formula take solar and lunar eclipses into consideration as well as the dodgy axis alterations from rogue meteors, and,' he coughed, *'Natural ecological disasters that throw the seasons into overload and adversely push Earth's orbit into chaos from time to time.'* Pigeon closed his eyes and nattered quietly in parrot speech... *'such as a volcanic eruption.'*

"Goodness, Pigeon," Kit said. "You're a scientist. You might have mentioned it. I could have used an ally, way back when."

Pigeon's feathers, no longer static, changed colors until it was almost hard to look directly at the aura he projected. He fluffed his wings and bobbed his head before he scrutinized them inquisitively, each in turn, with his head to one side. *'Visualize, if you will,'* he began, switching to Brooks' lecture voice, *'a tube made of air, both narrow yet infinitely wide,"* Pigeon-Brooks said. *'A funnel shaped clock engraved with a timeline accurate to the millisecond – a mechanism with no human operator to guard it. Instead, humans recognized the inborn spiritual fire of domestic cats and elevated them to the status of formidable gods. Protecting them protected chrono-illogical time. It is said a cat has nine lives. What that means is that every cat prevails over the sacred rule of nine. At Osiris's discretion, cats overrule the goings and comings and stayings through sidereal time. There are no exceptions.'*

Pigeon's voice changed back to Parks of Bede Hall. *'Snowdrop of Bede has already returned home with her consort after conceiving a fresh line of royal cats for the new world. And we call the present state of the earth, new, because the old one was clearly flawed from the first moment a blob of mud floated to the surface of a bubbling sea of dissolved salt. It was charitably called an island. How it survived as long as it did after the disastrous continental shifts of Pangea, is a mystery.'*

"Can I call you Pigeon, now," Anna asked. "Since you're not worshipped as a god. Or, perhaps, Hermes?"

Pigeon preened, cackling with parroty arrogance. *'Potato Potahto,*

I am happy you are alive to call me by any name. But honestly, if a housecat may be considered a god, a parrot is surely in the running! Sadly, Hermes doesn't contain the letter 'P'. But I appreciate the honorary title.'

"Being promoted to the rank of scientist is much more impressive," Kit said.

The persona of Parks returned. *'I've met telepathically with Goswold, and even he is unable to posture a theory that explains the tremendous upheavals' psychic effect on humanity's evolution. I had Sent write down his final message to humanity. If you will allow me, I will read it.'* Pigeon closed his parroty eyes, fanned his tail feathers, and began.

[It falls to me, Goswold Mundi of Pangea, to leave you with an account of our final days. Escaping noxious fumes became Pangea's first priority as an evacuation of women, children, and able-bodied males took refuge in the most stable area to the west. Animals surviving the toxic gasses migrated on floating pockets of the earth's crust.

Under my auspices as the magus Goswold, the elite schools of alchemists, architects, astronomers, shamans, mathematicians, and the entire brotherhood of the magi, collected their documents and congregated to the section of Pangea that, when split in two, would become distant twin lands ruled by the Gemini, Pan and Osiris. Those chosen elite to seed them fled through time portals to what became the lands of Khem and Britannia. Later, after nine-hundred generations had passed, their descendants repopulated the flotilla of new continents, cooled enough to offer sanctuary.

For millions of years the skin of the planet was disfigured from an eternity of magma eruptions. Lava's plague boils sealed over with vicious scars, but time sent pulverized minerals and water to form a sticky sludge that dried in the sun and woke the seeds of life within.

And in a series of epochs, the lands blossomed into farmland and gardens and forests and jungles. The elementals returned from their dreaming to nurture the animals, and the seasons rallied enough to form steady growth patterns of cold and heat, light and dark, cultivation and fallow.

May you continue to honor the spiritual legacy of the land, we, your devoted ancestors, kept alive for your generations as our world perished. May the great healing begin. May you thrive.]

Goswold's historical testimony left the adults speechless. Kha, as a master alchemist, privy to Goswold's bequeathed memories, summoned his immortal powers and created an aura of peace around them. Anna brightened and spoke first. "How soon may I visit my friend, Vita, behind Hadrian's wall? I don't like to keep her waiting. She isn't a good waiter."

Encouraged, Peri asked his own question. "Will there be horses in Bede? Pigeon has been teaching me to ride."

"There will be others to carry on your riding lessons," Kha said. "And I will visit you."

Pigeon let out a loud squawk for quiet. *'I, too, am permitted the freedom to fly to and from Bede,'* he said. *'So, be on your best behavior.'* The room waited for more. *'I am compelled to inform you that the next turn of events is decided for us. Osiris's implicit laws as ruler of the underworld state clearly that once-borns may travel one way, only once – a restriction, I'm sad to say, affects Cornelius and Rayne.*

Cornelius moved closer to his wife. "I have the honor of living my dream in the time of Smenkare and Ankhesenamun. And Rayne and I have found happiness here. We have renewed our marriage vows before the Aten. We will come to terms with staying here."

Rayne gazed at Cornelius adoringly during his speech, smiling bravely.

Pigeon narrowed his beady bird eyes on Rayne Stratford Smyth. *'I hope you are not too upset. It is devastating news.'*

Cornelius's wife's, white knuckles relaxed and turned pink. "I'm over the moon to stay," she said. "I finally matter somewhere. I am in love with my husband. And Tut will need a mother. Kit has his loving wife to look after him. I will miss my grandchildren, but I know enough about Bede Hall to accept the twins' rightful place is in Bede." She sent Tut a smile. "And who knows, my son Tut may marry several wives."

Pigeon clicked his beak. *'And one more thing. Ay's negative vibrations contaminated the time portal for an entire sidereal day which means that he has unwittingly given you the gift of time together before anyone headed for Bede is able to leave. However, since a single Egyptian sidereal day is equal to a full solar year in Bede, your family in England will experience a much longer delay. The Winter Room portal diverts to the Maze Portal and was also adversely affected. Both portals require a reset date of an entire year from the date of the damage in the kings' chamber. Therefore, Kit, at the earliest, you may take your family home on New Years Day, 2020. You will arrive in the maze. I will be staying here. Kha, liberated from his body and time restrictions, is free to go anywhere, whenever he chooses.'*

Mr. and Mrs. Cornelius Stratford Smyth sat dreamily, heads together in a state of marital bliss. SaRa nodded her approval to Kit. Tut took a deep breath of contentment, happy to be in two homes at last.

Anubis splayed his feet, admiring his new toes.

chapter 41
A YEAR OF TIME & ROSES

March 19, 2019 — the Vernal Equinox

Spring came early as a great relief. It was confirmation of the natural order of things returning to the countryside. Birds nested, the rabbit population exploded, and the topiaries burst into green leaves. Sable's cutting sprouted and promised to be a fully-grown topiary squirrel by the end of the year. Jack sniffed at the small twig and was often found sleeping beside it, chasing the newborn rabbits in his dreams with the best friend he missed. A few weeks later, a second twig pushed through the earth a few inches from the first. Sable would reincarnate as twins.

The phrase 'one more time around the sun', begun by Hannah, was soon picked up by everyone as a motto for a year in limbo. It was heard several times a day to offset the general aura of impatience that initially settled over Bede. Eventually, it was shortened to *'one more time'* and finally, an index finger pointing to the sun – *'only one.'*

Still, the residents and daily twice-born visitors kept up a fast-paced schedule of cleaning and planting. A general bustling of wheelbarrows and paintbrushes and feather dusters filled the time from rising late in the mornings for a full English mixed grill breakfast to cocoa before bedtime.

Six, more than the others, dug deep holes for a new grove of rowan trees and beat blankets in order to work out his frustration from so much lost time.

Oddly, the sundial cast no shadow. The tree nymphs gave it a wide berth until Nimue chastised them for being slow-witted. "The sundial," she explained, "is outside the normal world. It was Parks grave when he had been human enough to require one. And from this sacred spot, he had materialized as his original immortal self – Pan of Pangea, Bede's very own master of the trees."

After that, the nymphs left daily offerings of seeds and water laid on the sundial's face for the birds. In gratitude, the birds filled the tree branches with nests, and hatchlings learned to fly once more in the fresh Bede air. Birdsong greeted the residents of the Hall in the mornings, and the sundial cast a shadow once more.

On a positive note, telepathic messages between Kit and Bash had started to make it through the static of thousands of years. They were infrequent and difficult to hear, but it was a clear sign that healing had taken place over more than a blighted landscape.

There was one live portal that still delivered surprises. Sarah Goodman telephoned the Hall to say that Snowdrop, decked out in gold jewelry, and her *'husband'* Arthur arrived in her kitchen with a pair of kittens named Pax and Vita – peace and life. They were both black and white but where Pax was black with white markings, his twin sister Vita was white with black markings.

In April, Kit and Bash turned nineteen. A party was held in the rose garden where Bash dedicated a new rose to her friend, Vita. I dub you the Vita Rose, she'd said and given a toast with dandelion wine brewed by Charlotte's original fairy colony.

The twins were toasted with a special birthday concoction sent by Charlotte that put smiles on everyone's faces for an entire week. That night they told stories around a bonfire by Lotus lake.

Bash recalled receiving the family heirloom 'goddess bed' and the May Day when she'd been introduced to Nimue and the Green Lady, ironically, none other than her friend Charlotte Findhorn in disguise as a florist secretly engaged to Parks. They laughed about the Parks family's disguise and how wonderful it was that Six had gained his independence enough to have been reborn.

It seemed like eons since the May when Bash and Kit had found Snow, a transparent dream traveler who had 'haunted' the 'Winter Room' ever since Lady Nan was a girl. The movie people had come and gone. Taraq had joined the family and Rupert was still away in America trying to act his way into stardom.

Lady Nan occasioned the remark, "Well, the boy has enough designer sunglasses for a dozen movie stars. And speaking of stars."

She pointed to the constellation of Leo. "Wherever Kit is, he's seeing those same stars. He and I often looked at them together for the brief time we shared molecules in the eighteenth-dynasty." She winked at Peregrine Brooks. "Now, let us raise our glasses and remember my daughter Rayne, my son-in-law Cornelius, and Tut of Bede."

Bash's voice trembled, "Happy birthday, Kit. Thanks to you the world is now a safe and wonderful place to be. Come home soon."

Helen toyed with a loose thread on her sweater. "The last year was so Déjà vu. I was either here before, or I dreamed all this when I was a child."

"Let me guess," Clive said. "You were nine."

"Even when I took snaps of Parks' cottage and his tree costume with no feet, I knew, and now, here I am," Helen said twisting a strand of blue wool on her finger. "Robert's not a dreamer so he doesn't mind."

"So, you're not really here? Or not *always* here?"

Helen sighed and abandoned the wool loop. "Oh, in this moment, yes, I'm *entirely* here. I daydream too, you know. Where did you think my stories of animals wearing clothes came from?"

Dee Dee was allowed to visit the lake even though she startled the swans whenever she tried unsuccessfully to take flight. Her tiny voice sang nursery rhymes to Bash and Kit and Tut of Bede as the sun turned the lake gold.

For Bash:

> *'Mistress Mary, once contrary,*
> *How does your garden grow?*
> *With silver bells, and cockle shells,*
> *And pretty Vitas all in a row.'*

For Kit:

You're our king of the castle
come home you lovely rascal.

For Tut:

King Tutankhaten sat on a wall,
King Tutankhamun had a great fall.
All the king's horses and all the king's men
Finally put Pharaoh together again.

And sang herself to sleep:

'I love lilacs in the Springtime.
I love Paris in the fall.
I love Vincent in the Summer
and the lovely lively girl in Hadrian's Wall.'

chapter 42
HOME SWEET BEDE

New Year's Day, 2020

The last thing Kit felt as he left Egypt was agitation that Peri had gone wandering at the last minute. Sibuna, there to oversee the family's departure, assured Kit, hiding his own irritation, that the missing Peri would follow momentarily. "Babs informed me that he ran off to say a last goodbye to Pa'a… *Pigeon*. He can't be far. We will see he gets home. Please do not worry." He reached out his paw, fat with its extra toe, and touched Kit's face with tenderness. "It has been an honor to serve you, Master Kit."

Kit's gold armband loosened and fell away as he climbed into the sarcophagus portal in the Kings Chamber. His rowan ring followed suit by rotating wildly, pulsating heat. Bast's gift, a gold ring – the miniature of his armband, complete with its hieroglyphs for cat, the Aten, and the figure eight symbol for infinity, gave a farewell purr Kit felt inside his chest.

The Twinters, lined up in their Sunday best, spread themselves evenly on either side of the Hall's main door, looking for all the world like the bygone days when the staff of a great manor house were presented for inspection to greet their new master.

Bash made a speech like a commander addressing the ranks of the dedicated soldiers they had recently been. "I don't know what to expect," she said. "Only that Sibuna made a brief appearance in Sarah's kitchen a few days ago with a message from Pigeon that my brother and his family would be arriving in the maze. I gather *family* means my brother's wife SaRa and his twins Anna, and Peri." She checked her watch that had no hands. "I expect them any moment now."

A commotion coming from inside the maze indicated voices raised in alarm. "I thought Peri was with you," a man's voice shouted.

A woman's voice replied. "He said he had to say goodbye to Pigeon, and I assumed he would be escorted to the kings chamber portal as instructed. At least, that's what was intended. I expect he will be along shortly. Your mother was in charge and she doesn't get things wrong."

"Assuming and expecting are dangerously imprecise words. I hope you're right. I'm in no mood to make another journey so soon. If indeed, it's even possible."

Taraq swooped over, graciously circling the maze and performed a controlled drop inside its center. Happier voices issued forth as the waiting Twinters heard Kit introduce Taraq, and Anna greeted him with a squeal of recognition.

Taraq led Kit from the mouth of the maze and a rehearsed shout of Hail Caesar! erupted from the troops, now breaking ranks in a rush for hugs and handshakes. Six took Bash's arm and held back for her turn. She registered surprise, her arms frozen in the act of anticipating an embrace. KIT. You've..."

"Aged," Kit said. "I'm thirty-six, as Pangea decreed. At least I was when I left Egypt. Long trips can be tricky. Jet lag is hazardous to your growth. You can still hug me. I'm not fragile or anything."

Bash's arms remained outstretched. "Who are you! And I prefer you fragile."

Kit touched his white forelock. "Look at you. Purple hair. Quite...*ah,* ground-breaking. Clearly, the Winter Room has a sense of humor."

Kit suddenly missed the weight of his armband. He noted with unexpected feelings of loss, the band of pale skin where his armband used to be. It itched to be remembered. "Sibuna reported you've become quite the scientist." He bowed. "Changes all around," he said shaking Six's hand. "I'm a husband and a father. Speaking of which, my son will be along shortly, his *flight* was…*um*, delayed." He twisted suddenly and peered over his shoulder into the maze. "Did anyone hear that?"

"I'll check the Winter Room. Peri used to hang out there. Maybe the portals got their signals crossed," Anna said. "Don't worry Dad, he can't have gone far." The realization of her words made her blush. "Sorry, Dad. The word far doesn't mean what it used to. Not to me. I waited in that room for you to come back and you never did. Now *that* was far."

Six whispered in Bash's ear. "The Winter Room Portal was officially closed yesterday. The Parks family redecorated it as a surprise for Anna before they left."

"Dad's a master alchemist," Anna blurted out, grinning, so you'd better mind your temper, Aunt Bash, he can turn you into things."

Kit tousled Anna's hair. "She's a chip off the old kidder." He pulled SaRa forward. "Everyone, this is my lovely wife. I expect we shall find a British name for her to avoid confusion. We can't have two Sarahs in the family. Two Taraqs was insane, and we've recently had to cope with two Tuts."

Kem crossed the distance between himself and Kit with his hand extended in friendship. "It's good to meet you again for the first time. My name is Kem."

Kit grinned. "My new baby brother, once removed, I presume."

"You're my Uncle Tut," Anna said when it was her turn. "I'd know you anywhere. How long *have* I been gone? I need to get my bearings, she asked."

"Two years, give or take 14 days," several Twinters replied in unison.

Bash burst into tears and stood sobbing helplessly.

"I don't see Parks," Kit said. "I thought he'd be here."

Bash dried her eyes on Six's shirtsleeve. "We don't see him much anymore," she sniffed, "but he's always here in spirit."

Anna examined the red welt on Kem's cheek. "Let me guess. A

wasp sting? And you needn't give me that look. Your father has its twin."

"Your Uncle Tut is not my father," Kem said. "We are one and the same entity." A puzzled expression appeared on his face. "Anna, what's wrong?"

Anna brushed past him, staring up at the window of the Winter Room. "The curtains moved." She shrieked Peri's name all the way to the top of the stairs. The door of the Winter Room was closed and warm to the touch. The icy mouth of the keyhole smiled lopsidedly. Anna grabbed the glass doorknob and turned it. A loud click indicated it was unlocked. The door swung open, pulled out of her hand as if sucked by a wind tunnel. Inside, sunshine bounced off freshly painted plaster. The mauve shadow of a boy waved at her and vanished.

Hannah's cell phone rang out its lively music hall ring tone. For the space of 9 bars the 'Can Can' song filled the room. The Twinters smiled. Hannah was insatiable about Paris. Her expression went from a cheerful hello to a shrill "What! Yes, I'll tell them." She faced Kit and SaRa with a forced smile. "No need to worry. That was Sarah. She's had a visit from Sibuna. He says Peri is with him in the Temple of Bast."

"That's a relief," Kit said.

With all the resounding elation, no-one paid attention to Dee Dee's poignant song. *I Can Can. Will he he? What is a dodo to do do!'* and then she sang a lively warning song. *'How much is that kitty in the window. The one with the waggley deal. How much is that kitty in the mirror. I do hope that deal is for real.'*

Anna caught the whiff of a problem rumbling through Dee Dee's song. She ran inside, up the stairs to the top floor. This time the door to her old room was wide open. Perfume from the open window drew her inside. Her sad memories of it were gone. Pale colors had begun to sprout on the carpet and sunflowers grew on the wallpaper. "Peri," she said quietly. "Please talk to me."

When it was clear no reply was forthcoming, Anna called out to the

Hall. "My brother is in Egypt. We can get there from this room. I know we can." She yanked open the closet door without fear. A parrot squawked from a million miles away. "PIGEON," Anna called out. No other sounds presented themselves, but a flurry of red snowflakes drifted across the threshold and melted on her toes.

Bede Hall spoke gently as a loving mother. "My walls have missed you, daughter. Do you like what I've done with your room?"

"Do you have him! Anna shouted. "Do you have my brother!"

The Hall was quick to answer. "Child, I no longer control the comings and goings of Bede Hall. I am an archive containing the residue memories of what was. Pan is in charge, now. And yes, in a way, I am forever he, but He is not me."

Anna jumped on the cot and pounded Peri's wall with flat of her hands. She pressed her forehead against the wallpaper. "PERI! I can't hear you. Why can't I hear you!"

"If you calm yourself, you'll find I'm still in your head," Peri replied. "I have to go. King Tut's orders. He's a bit bossy these days."

"I only left you an hour ago," Anna whispered.

"You've been gone three thousand years, Ani," he said, and the wall fell silent.

PART 5

the denouement

BEDE

chapter 43
HADRIAN'S BRIDGE

February 14, 2020 — Valentine's Day

Anna trudged through bitter blowing snow towards Hadrian's Wall, a small red figure in winter boots, her white hair tucked into the red hood of her winter coat, carrying a pair of black Wellingtons under her arm. She waved a red-mittened hand at her waiting friend.

Vita was nine-years-old again. She waved back so hard she lost her balance and nearly fell off the wall. There she sat, perfectly comfortable in her thin tunic, and sandals, swinging her bare legs, perched on her favorite part of the wall where it had crumbled making a natural chair-shaped gap. Snowflakes glittered like stars through her transparent form.

"I need this now," Anna shouted, indicating her warm coat. She held up the rainboots. "But I brought you these. I always wanted you to have a pair."

Vita giggled. "And now I'm a ghost who doesn't need them. I waited for you yesterday. But you didn't come."

Anna clambered up the wall using its ragged natural steps, careful of the slippery ice, and sat down. "Yesterday was two-thousand years ago," she said.

"It's been ages since I've seen you," Vita said, which made both girls giggle.

For a while they sat together holding hands in silence, savoring their time together. Anna caught snowflakes on her tongue while Vita tried on the boots. "These would have been perfect for the mud. It was always muddy in the paddock even on dry days."

"I lost my brother," Anna said simply. "But he's safe in another world."

"Never mind," Vita said, squeezing Anna's hand. "People find things. Eventually. It took me a long time to learn that." She pointed to a jutting stone nearby. "There's simply no point moping. Look. Over there."

"Where? I don't see anything."

Vita jumped down and touched the wall where a glint of gold winked from a snow-filled crevice. "Right HERE."

"Your amulet! It's been there all these years. You were devastated."

"And here it is, found by you, more or less. Devastation is a waste of time."

Anna turned it over and made out the figure of Mars driving his chariot. She held it out to Vita. I can find you a new chain for this."

"Silly girl. Ghosts don't wear jewelry unless they were wearing it when they died. That amulet belongs to someone else now. I think we both know who. Hint… it depicts MARS driving his chariot. Know anyone whose been to Mars lately?"

"Thank you. My father will cherish it, eventually, but right now he's mourning the loss of my brother."

"Anna, promise me you will never mourn me. I can't stay, but I *will* visit from time to time if I can. There's a special bridge between us. Just for us." She paused and took the form of a worried old woman. "I think I'm about to be reborn."

"Maybe you can come and live with me up at the Hall."

The air warmed slightly. The wind died into a tickle and stopped. Melting snowflakes fell as big as marshmallows.

Grandmother Vita huddled under a crude shawl. "What *may* be *will* be," she mused wisely. "I don't think we have any control over destiny, do you, dear?"

Anna was quick to answer with grown-up authority. "I dreamed my destiny. We all do. And I will always be able to find you on this bridge." She brightened. "Well, you're here, now. And you're coming home with me for afternoon tea. I want you to meet my father and a few of my other ghost friends, and you can still be home in time to reincarnate."

"Venerable has me quite addicted to tea and your chocolate

biscuits. We've become quite chatty on my visitations. Of course, he's never seen me old."

"I can do the Venerable's biscuits one better. Lady Nan likes to put on an old-fashioned cream tea with sandwiches and cakes and jellies in the red library. Now, please change back into my *old* young friend so I can introduce you properly."

A gentle hurricane of snow swirled around the girls as they walked arm in arm past horses, men hauling stones, and soldiers on parade.

"Ah, there you two are," Lady Nan said she passed them on the library stairs. "Just in time for trifle. And speaking of trifles, I was about to give a pep talk about walls and bridges. They're same thing, really. Haven't seen you for ages, Vita. Lovely to see you again."

The moment Vita entered the library, she spun around, transfixed, listening intently to something only she could hear. She laughed out loud and briefly levitated. When she touched down, her face was radiant with happiness. "Oh, Anna," she said. "I can feel them. My new parents are here."

Vita's form thinned where she stood, spun into a shimmering cone of sparks, and rose as a luminous pink mist. She swirled in a figure eight connecting SaRa and Kit before returning to Anna.

"SaRa is with child. A girl. Do you know what that means?"

Anna let out a whoop of excitement. "We're going to be sisters!"

The tea party had condensed into a human babble in full buzz. Raised voices trying to whisper, failed, treading too carefully to avoid the elephant in the room – a missing nine-year-old boy, named Peri, Peregrine Brooks' namesake.

"It's thin ice," Bill said to Clive. "I have to say, Kit's wife, Cecilia, is holding up."

"Cecilia?" Clive said.

Bill took a bite of fruitcake and spluttered. "That's her new English name. Beryl suggested it. Kit's wife's Egyptian name was confusing since we already have a Sarah. A name by any other name, you know."

Clive joined them, intrigued by Bill's comment. "I have to say, Cecilia is holding up exceedingly well. But according to the history of Egypt translated by Venerable, she's accustomed to Ay's treachery and handles loss better than Kit."

"She's putting on a brave face for Anna," Bill said.

"Not so," Clive said. "I think Anna has come to terms with her brother living with her grandparents in Egypt. She sees them as a happy family. And I can't be sure, but I think she and Peri are telepathic. So, she has *that*. It's sad, but the boy is safe and loved."

"And by our calendar," Bill commented. "He's been dead for thousands of years."

"Really, Bill. That's rather a morbid thought for Valentines Day," Clive said.

Bill washed down his fruitcake with a long slurp of tea. "I'm only stating a truth. Life is tragic. If anything, we twice-borns should understand life and death."

Hannah passed around crumpets and jam much to Arthur's curiosity. "I'm actually in search of marmite," he said to Hannah. "But I don't know what it looks like."

"It's an acquired taste, Hannah said. "But if you enjoy savory things you may like it. It's one of Snowdrop's favorite treats."

"Then I shall grow to love it," Arthur said. "Now, if you would be so kind, please lead me to it immediately."

They passed a group of fairies dithering around the chocolate biscuit crumbs. "I didn't hear anything in the maze," Sassia said. Thistledown's wings bobbed up and down in agreement. "None of us did. Only Fioretti. She's still over there, listening. She refuses to come inside."

"We must speak with her," Blithe said. "Follow me."

. . .

Fioretti hovered, hands on her hips, at the entrance to the maze, her wingtips red from anxiety when her concerned friends arrived. Bash, Vita, and Anna were already there. "I've been hearing galloping hoofbeats for hours," Fioretti said. "I believe a horse is trapped in there, poor beast. It's been cantering around for hours trying to get out, but the portal has closed behind it."

Vita listened intently. "I hear it too. It could be the phantom sound of Roman horses. The field where they were exercised was under this maze. This *is* the right place." She shook her head. "But it sounds like a single horse."

Anna closed her eyes. "Aunt Bash you *have* to do something, whenever that horse is, it's in trouble. Can you please summon Parks?"

"I believe you're referring to Lord Pan, the Green Man."

"Pan, then."

"I'm not sure you grasp the nature of my position. As Mistress of the Green, I *am* able to *speak* with Pan but summon him? No way. It's Pan who summons me."

Parks manifested in his human form much to the delight of the Twinters. All shook his hand with genuine delight. Everyone heard the horse, now.

"Parks," Leoni asked. "Can the maze portal be reopened? I am sad to see a beautiful horse so in troubled."

"Bash must do it," Parks replied. "She's the Mistress of plants and trees. I'm only a lowly custodian, now."

"Tell me how," Bash said.

Parks fanned himself with his battered straw hat and scratched his head. "I haven't the foggiest."

Six faced Bash at arms length and winked his devastating wink. "You can do this, my love. I have every confidence." His pride caused his form to flicker like a moth in a lantern.

Anna sent a thought to Vita. *Turns out that devastating can be rather lovely.*

Kem pulled at Bash's sleeve. "Please try, Mum," he said. "It needs you."

"Goodness, it's cold," Parks said, blowing warmth into his hands. "A bit *parky* for my liking. Wasn't it summer, yesterday?"

The galloping hooves became louder, more urgent as the horse panicked. Pan, keeper of the animals and landscape spoke with gentle authority in Bash's head. "The opening of the ways is powerful magic," he declared. "Time has a dual nature. It moves forwards and backwards 'in time' to the universe breathing in and out. Bede Hall is the living entity of 'time itself' which is why it requires the energy of appointed twins to contain it. Time is subject to rules. It will only obey the invocations of a master alchemist. As holder of the feminine energy that grounds Bede, you must relinquish control to Kit. There isn't much time. A sealed portal may only be released for a moment, and no more. There is no time to waste."

Kit sped from the red library towards the group of people gathered around the maze. He raised his arms to the sky as he approached, his expression confident, no longer the shy boy dazzled by science, but a magician grown into his power.

Kit bowed on bended knee to Bash, who gaped at her brother in awe and not a little embarrassment. "Mistress of the Green," Kit announced. "I request temporary control of the landscape of Bede. Are you in favor?"

Bash's sense of her calling overruled her amusement, but she couldn't resist sending Kit a wink. He returned it instantly. It was plain they were no longer rivals. Nor were they children toying with undeveloped abilities. The time for playing juvenile chess games of one-upmanship was, pointedly, in the past. New challenges lay in their future, but they took the form of happy expectations. For the present, a frightened animal needed compassionate care and she and Kit were best suited for the task.

She lowered her head in deference to her powerful brother as a proud sister as much as a wisewoman in service to Lady Flora. "I so consent," she said. "Hold hands everyone. Form a semi-circle in front of the maze and stand well back. One thing Charlotte *did* instill in me was the 'laws of ingress and egress' – that entrances are trickier than exits."

Helen crossed her fingers, Lady Nan held her breath, and Brooks looked on as proud as a professor on his most promising pupil's graduation day.

Kit grew to nine feet tall and muttered an incantation to the sun. Hot air and sand belched from the maze. "Drop hands," Bash shouted. "Protect your eyes."

Parks stood enraptured with the spectacle, soaking up the heat. "That's more like it," he said embracing the warmth.

A blue-black thoroughbred burst forth in full gallop, scattering sand as high as the tower. It slowed as it encountered grass slick with new frost and skidded to a stop in front of the sundial. It reared, shook its mane, gave an impressive whinny, and trotted back towards the maze, snorting froth from its nostrils.

"There's something on its back," Venerable shouted. "It's a child!"

Kit ran forward and grabbed the bridle. "It's PERI! Kephura has brought Peri home!"

"Sorry to burst your master bubble," Bash said, "but I think it more likely that Tut *sent* them both, home. And I believe I know why. He's a shrewd bargainer, is our brother. I have a package ready to return to sender." She winked at Taraq. "Don't do anything I wouldn't do," she said.

Taraq curtsied as only a floating spectre could. He swayed and bowed his head. "YES Ma'am, NO Ma'am," he said. "Whatever you say, Ma'am."

Taraq and Brooks carried the throne from the tower as everyone watched. "I'm taking it home," Taraq said, bowing to Lady Nan. "It is the honorable thing to do."

"And you have a few important tasks to complete for me, there," she said.

Brooks grabbed Taraq in a bear hug after the others had had their turn. "You will always be welcome here. Never forget us." He stood to attention, saluted, and shook Taraq's hand formally before leading him into the maze.

"I will miss you, crazy boy," Bash shouted after them.

Taraq waved over his shoulder. "Back at you, Mistress BRASH."

A puff of green light shot from the center of the maze and Brooks emerged teary-eyed. "It's gone," he said. "It was the honorable thing to do."

October 31, 2020 — All Hallows Eve

On the day of reckoning when the Yellowstone Caldera had been scheduled to erupt, the morning chorus greeted the Hall's residents with a hauntingly sweet song. The landscape didn't rumble, ashes failed to block the sun, and the unbearable heat of the previous Fall dawned a fine crisp Autumn day.

Anna and Beryl ran from room to room shouting trick or treat, rousing everyone by banging two saucepan lids together.

Ben and Kem stationed themselves outside, either side of the sundial. Ben blasted the dawn with a tin horn from an old Christmas cracker and Kem beat a saucepan with a wooden spoon.

The previous day, parents, houseguests, and the Hall's resident ghosts had arrived at the breakfast table peppered with flyers bearing the heading 'YOU ARE INVITED' and in smaller letters 'to a May day celebration in October' - *a timely non-explosive fete of food and revelry brought to you by the Bede Prophesy in the spirit of perpetual springtime.*

It went on to declare Halloween costumes were optional but suggested that Twice-borns, should 'COME AS YOU WERE or as near to it as possible!

. . .

Kit exercised Kephura over the dew-covered grass, thundering past the maypole hoisted by Ben and Six that Bash had decked out in yellow ribbons as an homage to Six's homecoming ten months earlier.

Bash laid out Six's ghost costume created from a white bedsheet with two eyeholes cut in the center. The classic Jack-of-the-Green costume of a wire tree had been painted orange to blend with the new trees decked out in autumn reds and golds to be passed around to anyone interested in experiencing the joy of invisibility.

Vincento Leoni came as the 'Mona Lisa', Nick Wardencliffe wore his normal black suit that looked identical to his former incarnation as Nicola Tesla, and Bertie Stein, the former Albert Einstein, found a rainbow-colored clown wig in Theodore's emporium. The empresario and his devoted wife, dressed as a pair of sunflowers – a halo of bright yellow petals framed their faces painted with brown polka dots. Hannah had fashioned green wings sewn onto their green sleeves to represent giant leaves.

For once, the faces of the nymphs smiled in the bark of trees that swayed in fancy dress.

Anna, Beryl, and Vita, considerably younger as a nine-year-old, danced around the maypole. Anna wore a headband with cat ears and an orange party dress, and one of SaRa's headdresses that offset her natural black hair. Bash was Rapunzel in a long wig of purple braids. Kit had his own alchemist's robe embroidered with hieroglyphics, looking like a wizard as his hair had turned completely white with a purple shock in his fringe for the occasion to counter Bash's.

Brooks toasted the Hall, crediting Parks as the inspiration for 'Capability Brown' – the father of the English county garden. Pan appeared at that, beaming with pride. Charlotte curtsied daintily to Brooks acknowledging his compassionate gesture. And at the height of the festivities Brooks borrowed Ben's tin horn to blast for attention.

"Everyone. A little quiet please. Anna has a presentation to make." Anna tugged Brooks sleeve and made a coughing sound in her throat, her eyebrows raised in a question mark. "Correction, SNOW has a presentation to make. For a moment, Anna's hair turned white. She stood shyly in her old cotton nightgown that made her look like the ghost Bash and Kit met six years before.

Anna held up Vita's golden amulet swinging on a length of purple ribbon. "This is a double award. It was made by a friend of mine whose name Vita means life." I dub it a purple heart medal on Valentines Day. It was first given to me in friendship and now I pass it on to my father for overcoming so many obstacles to save everything we hold dear." She glanced admiringly at Kit. "Childhood fears seem small from the vantage point of time. Nonetheless they are powerful enough to hold us hostage forever if we let them. This beautiful amulet shows the warrior Mars riding a chariot, which is fitting. My father visited Mars several times, in spite of the nightmares he carried of a face on its surface."

Snow summoned Kit with her outstretched hand – a small queenly figure with the commanding authority of a child ghost. SaRa nudged her husband forward to the thunder of applause. Snow levitated to enable her to place the ribbon around her father's neck. She looked up at the Hall and waved to the dozen fairies perched on the windowsill of the Winter Room, wings folded, swinging their legs. "Without my father's selfless courage, I would be sleeping in that attic room for an eternity and the rest of you would be sleeping in the churchyard of Bede Village under a mountain of ice. <u>Daddy</u>, it is fitting that you receive this 'purple heart' on the happiest of Valentines days."

Six led the crowd in a hip hip hooray and applause with wild hoots of enthusiastic cheers from Ben that went on for several uproarious minutes. When it died down, Brooks spoke again.

"In deference to our newly decorated war hero, I thank my student for surpassing every lesson I ever gave him." The clapping continued. He waved it down. "And in other business," he said. "I have an announcement of my own to make. A presentation, really." He whisked a cloth from a vase with a flourish, exposing a delicate bouquet of white carnations, that only Charlotte could have provided. He took a ring made from a rowan wood from his pocket, and kneeling, presented it to Lady Nan. "Marry me again," he said, "for the first time."

Lady Nan blushed and said yes. "It's been an amazing journey of lives," she said, turning to face the maze where Sage and his fellow topiaries had gathered. "A maze of lives and here we are, standing on solid ground at the calm epicenter of a special day where a caldera slumbers across the sea."

Brooks rose to his full height, held the flowers high, and spoke like an alchemist delivering a spell. "May Bede Hall reign for another million years as the house of rein...*carnations*!"

The onlookers groaned at his lame joke which made Brooks steal a bow.

Helen, in straw bonnet and shawl took a snapshot with her polaroid camera of Six holding a pumpkin under his arm. "I'm the headless gardener," he quipped. "A kingdom for my horse."

Leoni held the picture and watched it develop, after begging Helen for the honor "Please to show me. This is the developing I find best fascinating. May I hold, pleasing to thank you?"

The pumpkin developed first, then the white sheet with vacant eye holes that floated above the ground. The place where Six's shoes should have been was empty.

Later, Vincento was observed taking close-ups of a frost covered toadstool, a swan feather, and the pattern of ice cracks on the sundial, for his collection.

Lady Nan and Brooks descended the main staircase as Egyptian royalty.

But the winner of the costume contest was a pair of newborn topiaries, Sable and his twin sister, Mable, who suddenly scampered through the crowd in their new incarnation as lilac bushes in full bloom. You both smell lovely, Bash said, tying the first-place blue ribbon to Sable's tail which he promptly flapped in Jack's face, chattering 'you're it, Jack.'

Jack, needing no prompting, took chase with one of Lady Nan's colorful striped scarves trailing after him. "I think Jack is supposed to be a kite," Anna remarked. "Or possibly a rainbow."

Mable laughed at their game. "Sable is trying to impress Sage," she said.

. . .

Vita arrived in grandmother mode, and Anna dressed her as a gypsy fortune teller with several of Lady Nan's natty shawls, brass clip-on hoop earrings, and a red polka dot headscarf. Mr. and Mrs. Clutterbuck provided an old striped Punch and Judy tent for a booth, a round table, and Vincent's famous 'Yellow Chair'. Once seated, Vita beamed up at Anna. "Am I reading tea leaves or cards?" she asked.

"Neither," Anna said, opening a square box. "Bash has lent you a serious prop. It belongs to her now." Out came Lady Nan's snow globe, 'de-enchanted', reduced to a harmless toy. "Use your imagination. It's only a game."

Kem reluctantly stepped up to Vita. "My Mum says I have to have a turn," he said his eyes wide at the snow beginning to levitate inside the globe.

Vita smiled reassuringly. "Well, let's see what's in store for you, my lad. You needn't look so frightened. It's only a plain old crystal ball. It won't bite."

But Kem stared as the snow globe showed further signs of life. Very slowly an image formed from the swirling sand. Kem's former self, Tut of Bede, sat on the golden throne as the Egyptian Pharaoh, Tutankhaten. Once formed, the image dissolved and wavered into another.

The gold throne sat in a glass museum case surrounded by curious onlookers. The back of a small boy could be seen with his nose pressed against the glass. "I know that chair," Kem said, "I think I saw it here, in the Hall, but I don't remember when. I may have imagined it."

The boy inside the globe must have heard because he turned and waved.

Kem gasped. "That's me! How did I get in there?"

Kit spoke inside Kem's head. "It's a *magic* snow globe."

"But it died," Kem said out loud. Lady Nan told me it didn't work anymore."

"Maybe it was sleeping," Vita said. "Maybe it was dreaming of the future or remembering the past."

Kem searched Vita's face. "So, what did the pictures mean? What is my fortune?"

Vita weaved her hands over the crystal ball for dramatic effect. "You may ask the globe what you want to know, but the answer lies inside your heart," she said.

Kem closed his eyes and spoke clearly. "Last night I dreamed of Egypt," he said. "Was I him? Was I a king?" He hesitated before lightly touching a fingertip to the glass.

Lady Nan smiled in his mind's eye. "Tomorrow, if you want to, we will do it all again," she said. "And never forget, Kem, if a magic snow globe wants to show you something, a little thing like dying won't stop it."

AN AFTERWORD

A BRIEF HISTORY OF BEDE

History comes and goes. Empires rise and fall, civilizations flourish and cultures collide. The laws of probability converge and stir up trouble. Geological time advances. Volcanoes explode and cool, seas flood and subside and turn to ice. Ice melts. Species evolve and mutate. Land rumbles into hills and valleys, and grass grows over everything. And in spite of the flowering of art and the inevitable clashes of war, science advances and retreats, and Bede's heart continues to animate each new age, according to its true nature.

From first to last, Bede Hall reigns over the ashes of its ancestors: from a sacred henge built of trees to the great hall of a Saxon lord and a succession of fine houses each grown more grand with human progress.

But before all of it… before Bede Hall inhaled its first thought as a stone pyramid, it was a primordial hill emerging from a timeless sea. A mound of muddy memories, sheltering the seed of a dying civilization where the human race could sprout anew.

Each of the Hall's successive constructions grow phoenix-like from the energy of its previous bones. Which means its latest incarnation is both ancient and new – the oldest and the youngest at the same time. But then, figuratively speaking, everything happens at the same time in Bede.

Within its mystical boundaries, the hamlet of Bede forms an island without a sea. Hadrian's Wall defends the Hall's back, the Green Lady's forest safeguards its eastern border, an Iron Age ditch protects it to the west, and a low fence of robbed stone from a medieval monastery defines the southernmost cottage of Bede Village, marking the edge of the old world.

Saltwater breezes from the west and the sweet scent of Lindisfarne's holy isle to the north, sweep through breaks in the ancient wall to play in the Hall's gardens. Lady Nan told her grandchildren, that on the solstices, it's possible to see a candle burning on Lindisfarne if you put your mind to it.

Bede thrives in its isolation, separate from the bustling world of London, three-hundred-miles to the south. From the air, the old Roman road, Dere Street, still cuts a straight grey swath through the forests where Saxons and Normans once traveled as the falcon flies.

Long ago, Vikings had pillaged from the eastern shore and Scots had raided from the north, yet a serene pocket of calm flourished, protected by energies older than the pyramids.

Faint traces of prehistoric circles, lines, and squares lay etched into the fields. Phantoms of early Bronze Age ditches encircle mounds and barrows that shimmer to life after the rains, and the hillocks of Iron Age settlements play hide-and-seek in the long nettles. Saxon gold shuffles deep under the earth with Neolithic flint arrowheads, dagger blades made of iron, and mosaic tesserae from Roman villas. And all the while, the tips of abandoned cairns poke their noses from mossy banks into the sunlight.

For thousands of years, crude dwellings and settlements crumbled into ruins until a maze of grassy banks sectioned the landscape of Bede into a creased map of curious lumps and bumps, covering the secrets of the ancestors.

Long ago, Bede's natural water features, the sources of ancient power, had been stolen by the Romans for their formal spas and new temples. Springs and streams were rededicated, displacing the old guardians, renamed to merge with a pantheon of Roman gods – immortals 'borrowed' from the Greeks without permission. They built forts over the shrines of the green gods and clogged the sacred wells with sacrificial animal bones and amulets, vanquishing the local water spirits to trickle away underground in disgrace.

In time, their abandoned pagan settlements were absorbed by the dark ages and subsided into shallow impressions left in the clay underbelly of the rich topsoil. Stone circles tilted out of kilter in tired fields, straining valiantly to mark the solstices. Hadrian's great wall stood as a gallant reminder of the long-gone glory days, keeping out marauders while Bede remained steadfast under an ancient spell of protection.

Left to themselves, the old nature gods silently returned to Bede from the netherworld. The face of the Green Man, overseer of the growing seasons and lord of the harvest festivals and woodland creatures, began appearing again in the barks of trees. Flora, the Green Woman, consort to Jack-of-the-Green, gathered the scattered fairies into colonies and fanned the waning magic into sacred fire.

The elementals rallied their weakened whorls of energies into vortexes of great power. Comets, falling stars, and solar flares revisited the skies above the rumble-grumbles of the earth as it stretched and cracked its skin. Fresh waters bubbled anew from sacred springs. Bede's Sprites sent forth its water-beetle messengers, the Egyptian scarabs' distant cousins, to rally the twice-borns. Comeuppances long overdue blew hot and cold out of season.

Vengeances lying dormant for eons, slithered from the withered skins of mummified enemies in a fresh colony of eager snakes in the grass. The Green Man retreated, and Bede Hall, savvy to the magnitude of old scores and subtle reprisals, trained its youngest champions and prepared itself for war.

If time stands still anywhere it's in Bede. If ghosts haunt anywhere it's in Bede Hall!

ABOUT THE AUTHOR

Veronica Knox (V Knox) writes surreal mythological novels reconciling historical facts with imaginative fiction. She explores the creative inner worlds of autistic savants, master artists, and sentient paintings, and in one case, a building with a mind of its own. She loves to deliver art history inside a ghost story. To this end, she's written the biographical series *'Lisabetta'* about the 'Mona Lisa'.

A pair of shoes in a museum motivated her to write the story *'The Unthinkable Shoes'* about a barefoot ghost – the unknown child in the Titanic cemetery. The historical diaries of the artist, Emily Carr inspired *'Woo Woo – the posthumous love story of Miss Emily Carr'*.

Knox explores the discrepancies between reality and lucid dreams, fishes the depths of the subconscious, the afterlife, reincarnation, 'the ghostly lover', and the anomalies of parallel lives and dimensions. Her *'Bede Trilogy'* is a middle-grade time-slip mystery written in literary prose for adults aged twelve and up. It connects the mythological histories of Great Britain and Ancient Egypt. Book one *'Twinter – the first portal'*, book two *'Time Falls Like Snow'*, and book three *'Tomorrow Again'*. The series prequel *'Snow Behind the Door'* will be launched in the summer of 2021.

Knox is a professional graphic designer, developmental editor, and writing coach. A list and excerpts of her books, and samples of her cover designs and paintings may be viewed at :

www.veronicaknox.com

So ends the Bede Trilogy… or does it. The ghost child, Snow, has her story to tell in a prequel. 'SNOW BEHIND THE DOOR' will be published in the spring of 2021.
Thank you for taking time to read 'TWINTER',
'TIME FALLS LIKE SNOW', and 'TOMORROW AGAIN'.
If you enjoyed them, please consider telling your friends or posting a short review.
Word of mouth is an author's best friend and much appreciated. Cheers,

Veronica Knox

ABOUT THE AUTHOR

V KNOX WEBSITE & CURIOUS ART HISTORY BLOG
https://veronicaknox.com/

V KNOX SIGN UP NEWSLETTER FORM
https://landing.mailerlite.com/webforms/landing/f7e8a1

V KNOX AMAZON
https://www.amazon.com/V-Knox/e/B0094K0Q7Y

V KNOX FACEBOOK
https://www.facebook.com/V-Knox-Author-307047433438123/

V KNOX LINKEDIN
https://www.linkedin.com/in/veronica-knox-233bb51b/